MURDER IN THE FAMILY

NICE PEOPLE MURDER

MARY HASTINGS BRADLEY

MURDER IN THE FAMILY

NICE PEOPLE MURDER

Mary Hastings Bradley

COACHWHIP PUBLICATIONS
Greenville, Ohio

Murder in the Family / Nice People Murder, by Mary
    Hastings Bradley
© 2022 Coachwhip Publications edition

Murder in the Family published 1951
Nice People Murder published 1952
Mary Hastings Bradley, 1882-1976
CoachwhipBooks.com

ISBN 1-61646-529-8
ISBN-13 978-1-61646-529-2

MURDER
IN THE
FAMILY

Chapter One

The letter had a frightened ring. That was astonishing to him, for Helen had never been a frightened girl—she had been reckless, overconfident. *Something very strange is happening and I need desperately to talk to you. You are a lawyer—you can be detached. I may be imagining things, but it seems, truly, a matter of life and death. Do come to see your aunt but don't tell her I have written.*

Even as astonishing as the words was the fact that she had written him. In all the years since their angry parting there had been no letters between them until two months ago, when her child had been killed. His aunt had written, enclosing clippings of the shocking murder, and he had sent Helen some difficult words of sympathy, and had got back a terse "Thank you, Calvin," signed "Helen Cromer."

Helen Cromer was a stranger to him and that was the way he wanted it. It had been years since he had been in love with Helen Cauldron and all his young heartbreak and anger was water long over the dam. He had meant never to see her again, never to return to Somerset—he could see his aunt and uncle on their trips to New York.

But this letter was signed "Helen." And the appeal in it he could not refuse. Something was wrong, very wrong, or she would never have written him like that. Luckily, he could get away at once. August was a fairly slack time and the senior partners were both back. He'd make this his vacation—a fishing trip in Tennessee.

He began to leaf through the papers on his desk. Today was Monday. Her letter had been mailed Saturday. He'd be on the road tomorrow. He'd write that he'd be there by Wednesday afternoon. He'd call up Aunt Abbie at once. *Don't tell her I have written.* This was a fantastic thing to be happening.

"It is certainly nice to have you here again," said his aunt happily.

Calvin Morse had walked in on them at luncheon, and now he and his aunt were sitting on the veranda, waiting for his uncle to join them, to go to Helen Cromer's for tea. This arrangement, Calvin found, had been made that morning. Helen must have received his letter this morning. He wondered why she was making it a family party. His intention had been to motor directly to her. Perhaps she wanted to make their meeting seem casual.

"Helen wanted us to come early," his aunt was saying. "She said she wanted to consult you about something."

Abbie said that casually and he gave back, as casually, "What sort of something?"

"I don't know—she just said she needed a lawyer's advice. Will Bently is at Mayo's for a checkup. . . . I expect it's something she wants to make over to Burk. For a wedding present."

A wedding present wasn't a matter of life and death. Then the meaning of the present went home to him and he said, "Burk marrying?"

"Didn't I tell you? Yes, he's getting married next Wednesday. A week from today. It was all very sudden. He's been off and on with this girl for months and then on Sunday he told Helen they were getting married."

On Sunday. Helen had written Saturday. But she could have had an idea. . . . *Something very strange is happening.* . . . Well, it would all be revealed presently.

His aunt was running on: "That didn't give Helen much time to plan the wedding. She had to write and phone the invitations. But she didn't give many—it will be very quiet, of course."

"But why is Helen giving the wedding?"

"The girl hasn't a mother to give it. And Helen wants to do all she can for Burk. He wouldn't take any money from her—not after that will."

Their father's will, she meant. The will that had made Helen forever inaccessible.

"She's putting a good face on it," said Abbie, "even to me. But she can't be pleased to have her brother marrying that wild Rand girl."

Calvin didn't remember any Rand girl, wild or otherwise. A younger vintage, probably. Burk was his age. Thirty-seven. A few months older. Helen would be thirty-two.

"Though the stories about her may not be true," said Abbie, conscientiously. "Only there *are* stories."

"Weren't there stories about Burk? I seem to remember—"

"That's different. And it wasn't the girls that did for him with his father—it was his refusal to go into the Pottery Works. Peter Cauldron had built up those works all his life and he couldn't understand how a son of his could loathe them. And Burk wouldn't even try a month of it. That was right after you left—your last summer—"

His last summer. He had been twenty-three then, just graduated from Law School, the youngest of his class. Helen was eighteen. He had come bursting with plans, elate at the prospect of an opening with a good New York law firm, eager to have Helen marry him at once. And

Helen had wanted him to practice here in Somerset, with Will Bently, her father's lawyer—at least for a little time, she said.

She couldn't, she pleaded, she couldn't leave her father now—there was something really wrong with him though he would not admit it. She had to stay near him. She had promised her mother to try to take her place. It would solve everything, she thought, with that eager overconfidence of hers, to have Calvin start in here, to have them all live together.

The young Calvin Morse couldn't see that anything was wrong with Peter Cauldron except his disposition. He couldn't see anything except that his girl was making excuses not to leave her great house and easy life for the New York walkup, which was all that he could offer, and his stung pride told her so.

Hotly Helen had flared back. It wasn't true. If he could think things like that he did not love her. He had hurled back, "It's *you* who don't love *me*. But why should you? What have I to offer?" Out of all their sentences he could still remember that, still feel ashamed that he had said it.

"Yes, why should I?" Helen had given back, her gray eyes blazing.

And before their tempers cooled Lee Cromer came on the scene, blond, handsome and devoted, and jealousy had played hell with him. On his last night they had parted in hot anger, but though they told each other it was forever he hadn't believed it was forever, not until he heard she was to marry Lee Cromer in the fall. Then it had been such agony to keep from rushing to her that it was almost relief to have the wedding follow quickly. And to this day he did not know whether she had preferred Lee Cromer or whether he, himself, had thrown her to him.

His thoughts came back to consciousness of Abbie's voice, still recounting the trouble between Burk and his father. "They had a terrible scene and Burk rushed out of town. And Peter Cauldron sold the Works—he knew Lee Cromer wasn't the type to manage them—and made the will that left everything to Helen. He died that spring. Of cancer."

Vindicating his daughter's fear, Calvin Morse thought. Putting that young, urgent Calvin Morse forever in the wrong.

"That was before Lucy was born. And two months after she was born Lee Cromer died."

"I know. You wrote me."

And he had not come back. He did not even write. For what was there to come back to? Helen Cauldron was gone. There was an unreal Helen Cromer, a rich young widow with a baby.

"He was found dead in the woods. He was out hunting and slipped on some rocks and his gun went off under his chin. He was a pleasant fellow," said Abbie reflectively, "but I always thought his looks were the best part of him."

Calvin Morse did not want to talk about Lee Cromer. He said quickly, "Where was Burk all this time?"

"Roaming." She amplified: "His college friends found openings for him but he never stayed anywhere long. He was in South America when his father died. He wrote Will Bently he'd break the will but he knew he couldn't—he never tried. His father had left everything to Helen. He left her the money outright. And he left the place to her and then to her children—if she died and her children died, even then the place wasn't to go to Burk but to Burk's children. Peter Cauldron had done just what he said he'd do if Burk didn't go into the Works."

"No wonder Burk was sore," said Calvin.

"Helen was upset. She'd known her father was leaving her the place but she hadn't known he was giving her all the money and she sent some to Burk and he sent it back.

Nobody knew where Burk was then till he went into the Army. He came back—he was a captain then—before he went overseas and he and Helen patched things up."

"Where was he overseas?"

"Italy, France, Germany—he was there over four years. He was decorated for something and if his father had lived to know about it, that might have changed things. Two years ago Burk came back and he's doing quite well in insurance. Quite well for Somerset," said Abbie. "He lives at the Omar House."

"Not at the Folly?"

"Helen asked him but he refused. Oh, he has his room there and he stays there from time to time—especially since Lucy died. But I don't think he likes John very well."

"John—? Oh, John Cauldron. The cousin. I'd forgotten about him. Does he still live there?"

"Oh, yes. Peter left him a house in town but Helen bought it from him—so he could have the money, I think. He's stayed right on. He's a great help to Helen. That's a big place to keep up. John sees to everything. And he's working on a history of the place, putting old documents together."

"I never saw much of him."

"He was a little older—"

Niel Nordstrom came out and Abbie got up briskly. One of the things that made her a good wife, her husband liked to say, was that she never kept him waiting. She didn't look like a wife and mother, Calvin reflected, she looked like a New England spinster, neat and straight-backed, but not the vinegar type of spinster. Cheerful, realistic, alert, that was Aunt Abbie. Niel was a quiet, comfortably companionable man, a general practitioner whom all Somerset depended on.

They drove off and Calvin followed in his car. He had forgotten, he thought, how beautiful this Tennessee country was. Somerset was in the foothills, the town and its factories spreading down into the valley, even the smoke of the factories was beautiful at this distance, and all about was green, rolling country with a blur of blue-green mountains against the sky.

There were changes along the road, new houses with bright-flowered gardens, and the Country Club was different, more verandas and an oblong of cobalt-blue pool that hadn't been there in his young days. More tennis courts. He glanced toward one where Helen and he had played. Bobbysoxers were racing about it now. Betty Meade. That was Burk's flame the last summer. Or was it for two summers? That affair had blown up with the Pottery Works, he supposed.

The road was winding up a wooded ridge. There was a fox farm on the left—that was new—and one or two half-hidden places and then came what they called the Turn. The main highway turned sharply to the left, with high-fenced Cauldron land on its right, and a smaller road ran straight on, the Cauldron woods on its left, more open land at the right. The road ended at the Cauldron gates on the left.

There was a filling station at the Turn now and a fat man in a rocking chair. Calvin Morse looked off to the left and thought of the times he had gone along that highway—first on his bicycle, then in his battered little college car—to a certain place where he had parked, climbed the fence and walked the short distance to Cairn's pool, to their Hideaway, as they called it. He could see a succession of Calvin Morses going up that road and he shook his head impatiently, feeling as if he had strayed into a Hall of Mirrors. He drove on after the Nordstrom car to the Cauldron gate. His uncle had opened it and was driving on. Calvin drove through and got out and closed it. He thought, The old routine.

Darkness spread over him, the darkness of deep forest. Great trees, long past their prime, stretched wide branches above a younger growth that twisted, fantastically, to reach the light. It was rocky land—some of the trees had roots like curving talons about big boulders—and it was steep. The road went off to the right, making a wide circle of the climb, then came to a broad reach of level ground. Calvin Morse looked across at Cauldron's Folly and he stopped his car to look again.

It was as beautiful as any building he had ever seen. He'd taken it for granted as a boy and as a young man; then, at the last, he had hated it so much, feeling it was denying him Helen, that he had never felt its beauty.

But now he felt it. He stared at the great stone walls, the high, mullioned windows on which the sun was striking, at the chimneys rising from every part of it, always at the right distance, in the right balance, at the fine, square tower, not too high, and he felt the wonder of it there on the incredibly smooth green turf by the cluster of old oaks in which crows were cawing—it was all so amazingly English that he felt he ought to call them rooks.

I hadn't a chance, he said to himself. Not against this.

For he was determined to believe that the place had separated them—at least, it was the symbol of the thing that had. The dominance of Cauldron feeling. Her feeling for her father. Young Calvin Morse, early orphaned, brought up at schools, vacationing with relatives, had not understood that power of feeling.

He sent his car forward along the straight avenue to the house. The Nordstroms were already out of their car and a girl in white was hurrying toward them. White. He realized now that he had been dreading to see Helen in black.

He parked and went quickly forward, and he and Helen Cromer both spoke at once.

"Calvin Morse! How nice—"

"Helen! This is—"

They broke off, laughing a little. He left the word to her. She said, her voice a little significant, "I was so glad to hear you were coming."

She had changed and she had not changed. There was the same direct glance, the bright gray eyes with their look of candor and pride. There was the same soft dark hair with the lovely sweep back from brow and temples. There was the hint of mischief in her smile, even with its touch of nervousness. But her face had thinned, had lost its rounded, childish look, and there were shadows under the eyes.

She was running on with a vivacity his old knowledge of her told him was assumed. "It was so nice you could come up today, and come early. Burk and Rita are coming for tea—Burk just phoned. And there's always the chance that Mr. Rawley may join us, so—"

"How is he?" Niel interrupted.

"He seems all right again, really all right. But it's so queer, those sudden pains," said Helen, frowning a little. "I wish he'd go and have an examination but he always holes up in his room—"

"Henry has a theory about him," said a voice behind her.

A man had come out of the archway behind them, a thin brown man so much the color of his tweeds that Calvin thought suddenly of the gingerbread men his aunt used to make. John Cauldron. The cousin. "How are you, Morse?" he said as casually as if they had parted the day before, and shook hands with a politeness obviously perfunctory.

He went on, with a note of ironic amusement: "Henry thinks Rawley is poor-white trash and likes to put on airs. Likes to have trays toted up to him."

Henry. That would be the old colored butler. Nothing seemed to have changed. But who was this Rawley?

John was saying, "But I've got a genuine patient for Niel. George has a bad hand. He got bitten some days ago—when the dog was dying. I expect he tried to make him eat. He didn't say anything about it till now, and it's inflamed."

"I'll look at it," said Niel promptly. He got the black bag he always carried in his car and the two men started off.

"I'm sorry about Jude," said Abbie Nordstrom.

"Yes." Helen's voice was like a cold hand, warding off feeling. "Yes. I thought he was getting better but he wasn't." She looked after the men. "I'd better go with them—if you'll excuse me. Just wait on the terrace." She vanished into the archway.

"She doesn't need to go. But she's like that now. Very tense," said Abbie, looking after her.

"Was Jude the dog?" Calvin asked.

"Lucy's dog. He'd been grieving himself to death."

"There used to be some big coach dogs, white with black spots."

"Jude was one of the puppies. He was Lucy's shadow. He went to meet her that night—"

They walked along the front of the house to the terrace at the end. They sat down and Abbie looked about at the chairs and tea table and said, "This is where we were when it happened. We'd been having tea. Burk had brought Rita Rand—that was the first we knew he was serious about her. And Rawley was here—"

"Who is this Rawley?"

"He's a young artist. Someone Helen got from an Art Institute to check on the paintings. He's a queer fellow," said Abbie reflectively. "Helen says he can talk on art all right, but never says a word on anything else. But John likes him—he listens to John's old stories of the place. That day, I remember, he wore an eyeshade—said his eyes hurt—and not a word out of him. He had a chip on his shoulder. It seems he had started taking Lucy for walks and Helen had stopped that."

"Lucy—? I thought she was just a child."

"Thirteen and she looked older. She was a pretty thing. Blonde, like Lee Cromer. And she was getting to the boy-crazy age."

"Cigarette?"

"Not now. Do you always smoke so much, Calvin?"

"It's intermittent." Not that he minded, he told himself, hearing about Lee Cromer and Lucy Cromer—that didn't mean a thing to him now.

Abbie plunged back into her narrative. "Lucy had gone to the Country Club with some youngsters for tennis and after a time John drove off to get her—Helen never liked her motoring about the country with those youngsters. At her age. We sat here, alone with Helen—"

"I thought Burk and his girl—"

"Oh, they went the time John did. And Rawley went off for one of his walks. We were talking about Burk and Rita. It was a lovely day, just like this."

Calvin thought restively of saying, You sent me the clippings, but he did not. She went on, "John came back. I remember he drove through the archway to the garage and walked back to us and at first we thought Lucy had gone into the house. But he said no, that she'd asked to be let out at the gate. She wanted to walk up the path through the woods. You know how the road goes off to the right in that big circle while the path climbs straight up?"

"I remember."

"Helen didn't like her coming through the woods— it was growing dark then—but John said she'd insisted. She was a willful thing. There wasn't any reason to worry, though. It's a steep climb but Lucy knew every foot of it. We thought she'd be there any moment. Then we heard the dog howling."

She was making it uncomfortably real. The little group on the terrace waiting for a girl who never came.

"At first it sounded far away. You know how the trees shut out sound. Niel said it was probably the dog at the filling station but Helen said it was Jude. Jude had slipped away. He always seemed to know whenever Lucy turned in at the gate. Helen was in a panic and started down the path, John after her, but Niel got in his car and drove down—he could get to the gate quicker in his car. I just stood there, listening. There isn't any sound mournfuller than a dog howling, and this was awful, so high and wailing. I knew in my bones that something had happened but I kept hoping the child had only twisted an ankle and that Jude was sitting by her, howling for help."

He thought of Helen Cromer running down that path. He asked, "Who found her?"

"Niel. He got to the gate and the dog was very near there a little way up the path, just off the path. He was there by Lucy. She was under a bush, as if she'd been pushed there. She must have been jumped on the moment she started up the path. She'd been choked to death, they thought, but later they found her neck was broken. Niel said she'd died at once. That was a comfort."

A grim comfort, he thought.

"I expect the man didn't mean to kill and when he found he had he ran. Or else he heard Jude coming and that frightened him off. I'm sure Jude never saw him or Jude would have killed him. I never saw Niel so shaken as when he came back."

"They got the man, didn't they?"

"Hours later. He was dead drunk—utterly unconscious. He was quite near where Lucy had been lying. They think he circled about, then holed up there, under a rock. He'd finished his bottle there evidently—it was right by him. He says he doesn't remember a thing about it."

"Drunks never do," said Calvin. "Not even pentothal brings back a drunk's memory, I understand."

"The trial is going to be hard on her." Abbie gave a deep sigh. "Well—I didn't mean to talk about it."

Helen came back with John, saying that Niel was finishing the bandaging, that the bite wasn't really serious, only George mustn't use his hand. George was her farmer, she threw out to Calvin. She looked at her wrist watch, hesitated a moment, then said to him, "I want to ask you something—to impose on you for some legal advice. But there isn't time now before tea. Perhaps afterward—?"

Afterward would be all right, Calvin said. He had a feeling that that was the way she had planned it.

"And I want to ask you something, Abbie. About those lists. Burk telephoned a lot more names and if I ask them I'll have to ask more of my friends. Would you look through them with me?"

"Of course."

"But Calvin doesn't want to be bored by lists. Perhaps," she said to him, "you'd like to roam about with John. You might like to see what's happening to the gallery. Rawley's supposed to tell us whether we've a collection of fine old originals or fine old copies."

"How's he coming on?" asked Abbie.

"I wouldn't know. He's got half the pictures down, scraping wood and testing canvas thread and pigment—" She said to Calvin, "Those are the pictures father brought back from England, you know."

He didn't know or, if he had, he'd forgotten. He walked off with John Cauldron, who told him, "Helen couldn't get the man she wanted—that was Lambert. He's famous for this sort of work. But he sent this fellow who's studied under him and who can take his time. He's young but he seems sure of himself. He says we've got a Romney. Helen's just written the Institute to ask if we can trust his judgment."

They had entered the house from the terrace and were walking through the long rooms. Calvin said, "I'd forgotten how big this place was."

It was baronial, he thought. Paneled walls and huge stone fireplaces and stags' heads and all the appropriate, heavily carved oak furniture.

"Very vast," said John ironically, as if detached from all the splendor, but on the wide stairs he paused to point out a design in the paneling and his voice warmed to it. He asked, "Are you interested in the pictures?" and Calvin said, "Not particularly. Let's go to the tower." From the second floor at the right of the main stairs a narrow, enclosed stairway led up to the tower. John nodded, and opened the door and they climbed to the top.

It was astounding, Calvin thought, looking down on roofs and chimneys, gardens and fields. Astounding. His eyes rested on the fields stretching from the back of the house to the woods. Not fenced. Separated by old English hedgerows, ditched on both sides. That took some doing.

"Those hedgerows," he said. "Did the first Peter do all that?"

"He started it. The others kept it up."

"How many have there been? How many generations?"

"Three Peter Cauldrons. And then Helen."

"The first Peter do all the building?"

"All of it. He spent a fortune. His wife's fortune," Cauldron said, in a dryly amused voice. "At the end he was selling their high-stepping horses and his wife's jewelry but the building went on."

"I wonder how she felt about it?"

Cauldron smiled. He had a peculiar smile, a smile that sucked in the corners of his mouth to an air of secrecy as if accustomed to savoring things in private.

"She left some rather remarkable poems," he said. "Hidden in a drawer I discovered recently. I'm working on the old records. Letters and diaries and accounts. Putting the history together. An antiquarian s obsession," he said, deprecating the shy enthusiasm that had shown itself.

He went on: "Those poems leave no doubt as to her feelings. They were her only outlet and she poured herself out in them. In one of them she put a curse upon the place, and threatened to haunt it, gloating at disasters."

Calvin smiled a little. "And did she?"

"There is no evidence of it. I dare say old Peter would have been delighted if she had. It would have made the atmosphere more authentically Old World."

"A gloating ghost. Hm. . . . How about the curse?"

John Cauldron seemed to consider quite seriously. "Well, there are disasters in every generation, aren't there? If you live long enough."

"That's right."

"There wasn't money enough left to bury her," John went on. "So her husband and son—that was my grandfather—dug her grave themselves and rolled a boulder to mark it. You can see it down there. At the edge of the rose garden."

Calvin looked down. The stone seemed small from that distance. He saw a sun dial in the garden and wondered if it said, "I mark only happy hours."

"Why did he do it?" he said. "I mean, why did he build it? A place of this size. What was in his mind?"

John Cauldron said slowly, "No one knew for a long time. All my grandfather knew was that his father had come from England, that he'd quarreled with his people there. He was a second son, and he came with little else than letters of introduction and his good looks. He had more than his share of good looks, if his portrait is to be trusted. He brought that portrait with him, by the way."

He shot Calvin a glance that relished the humor of that—young man with a portrait—then added, "And we have more than the portrait's evidence. The poems were constantly railing against his good looks. One of them, I remember, reviled the 'dastard charm, proud, devil-driven eyes!'"

He quoted it with satiric enjoyment, Calvin thought. Calvin said, "I'm on her side. She had a thin time. Did the poems say why he built this place?"

"No. No—she didn't know the reason. That was found out in Uncle Peter's time. Peter the Third, he was. He was interested in the past and encouraged me to go through the old papers. I was a sickly boy," he said, quite objectively, "with a passion for books, so I spent most of my time in the library. As you may remember—"

"I'm afraid I don't. I wasn't very noticing."

"Most people are not noticing. Well, I unearthed old diaries and records and one day I found a worn print of a place I thought was this. Then I noticed a difference of details and of the position of trees. I'm not boring you?"

"No, I'm asking for it."

"It is interesting, rather. The motives that impel us. You see, we found that engraving was of the old Cauldron place in England. Cauldron Hall."

"I'll be damned. The place his older brother had inherited."

"That's it. I expect Peter had lived there as a boy. Perhaps he expected to go on living there after his brother had inherited, and, instead, his brother had booted him out. Blood," said John Cauldron dispassionately, "is not always thicker than water."

"How right you are."

"Or perhaps he had expected to inherit it himself. The heir might have been sickly or given to horses likely to break his neck. Such a hope is understandable," he said, with an offhand laugh.

Then he said, "But this is all conjecture. All we actually know is that there was some quarrel between the brothers and that Peter Cauldron flung himself out of England and came here. And here, stone by stone, he re-created his old home."

There was a magnificence about the achievement that almost made Calvin forgive the man's beggaring the wife under the boulder.

"And I am convinced," said John Cauldron, with quiet enjoyment, "that he let his brother know. At a printing house in Philadelphia he had a pamphlet made, describing the place, and somewhere he had an engraving made. I found copies of them here and I feel positive that he sent them to England, though there is no record there. I expect his brother tore them up."

"Oh, you got in touch—?"

"Uncle Peter did. He went over to England and looked up his cousins and saw the Hall. That was twenty years ago. Twenty-two years. He brought back a number of paintings he'd bought from them—mainly portraits—and some furniture and tapestries. He didn't claim the tapestries were historic but I'm afraid he did a little pretending about the pictures. That's why we—why Helen is having them examined."

"Can't you check? The family at the Hall could tell you whether the originals were sold or not."

John Cauldron did not answer for a moment. Then he said, "The Hall is gone. A direct hit."

And he was pleased as Punch about it, Calvin thought. He was fighting old Peter Cauldron's battle.

"I've talked too much," John Cauldron said. "Burk must be here—a car came in some few minutes ago. We won't have time for the gallery." But as they came out from the enclosed stairway he said, "We might have a look in," and walked across the open space at the head of the main stairs to the door. The gallery was a long room, not well lighted, for the windows that opened toward the back were deeply recessed—it was on those window seats, Calvin remembered, that he and Helen had torn each other's feelings to shreds.

"When Peter built this," said John Cauldron, "there was only his own portrait to hang in it."

It was either magnificent or ludicrous, the idea of the long gallery with one solitary picture on its walls. He remembered the walls as crowded. Now half the pictures were down, some of them stacked along the floor. He crossed to look at the first picture and saw a small, dark canvas out of which looked the face of a willful, handsome boy with bold features, black hair, and brilliant gray eyes that followed one mockingly.

"Burk, when young, could have sat for it," said John.

His voice was too detached, too expressionless. *That's the knife in his back,* Calvin thought. He said quickly and sincerely, looking at the contours of John's monotone face, "You have a Cauldron look to you too. Not the color, but there's something—"

He was startled at the glint—appreciation? irony?—in the other's eyes, as quickly gone as if a shade had been pulled down. "Yes, I suppose there's something," John assented indifferently. He looked about and said, "I see our expert has fled his post. Shall we go down?"

Chapter Two

Tea was in progress on the terrace. Burk Cauldron was there with his girl. She was the sort of girl, thought Calvin, that in blithe moments you address as "Gorgeous" or "Beautiful." Her hair was bright as new-minted copper and there was a lot of it curling about her neck. She was definitely a dazzler, with hazel eyes and a curved mouth done in the same color as her hair. She looked about eighteen.

Burk had hardened, Calvin felt. But he was a handsome fellow, with the willful look of the Peter Cauldron in the portrait, the same mocking brilliance in his gray eyes. He gave Calvin Morse a look in which Calvin felt something hostile, though his words were cordial. "Ah, Calvin, my boyhood pal! Rita, this is Calvin Morse. Calvin, this is Rita."

Rita Rand smiled briefly, then her glance shifted to someone behind Calvin. A young man was coming out of the house, hurrying a little, one shoulder thrust ahead of the other, his head slightly tilted. He had an odd, arresting face. It seemed almost familiar to Calvin, as if he had seen it in some picture, or in some movie. He had the feeling that he ought to remember something about that face but the association eluded him. Inexplicably the words "bare feet" popped into his mind.

This was Rawley, he discovered. When Helen presented them Rawley gave him an unsmiling look, and there was something wary in his eyes, but perhaps, he thought, eyes got that way from searching for painted frauds. "And you know the Nordstroms," Helen was saying to Rawley, "and you've met my brother and Miss Rand."

"I think I saw you one day in the gallery," said Burk. "But you've been laid up so much—"

"We met him once at tea," said Rita Rand.

It was the way she stopped that reminded Calvin that the tea had been the day Lucy was killed, the day of dreadful memory.

"Did we?" said Burk vaguely. He had given Rawley only the minimum of attention and now, as the young man slipped into a seat, he turned to his sister with the air of resuming a discussion. He said lightly, ironically, "So you don't think highly of the idea of our occupying the south wing?"

"No, Burk, I don't." She was saying it pleasantly, trying, Calvin thought, not to show discomfort, but she did show it. She kept her eyes on the tea she was pouring and said, "Let's not—"

"But you once invited me."

She passed a cup to Calvin, filled one for Rawley. She said, "I know. But that's different. No house is large enough for two families."

Burk gave a deliberate, quizzical look at the house.

"Not even the Folly? My dear Helen, give some other reason than size!"

She murmured, "It's still only one house. It has only one kitchen."

"Vast enough for a battalion of cooks."

"That has nothing to do with it, Burk." She was still looking down, pouring a cup for John. She said, sounding hard pressed and defensive, "It's as I said—no two families can live happily in one house."

There was a moment's silence. Then Burk said, "What about our John?" He spoke as if John Cauldron were not there, his cup at his lips. "Isn't our John another family?"

"John isn't married."

"Ah! Then the objection is to—"

"Not to any individual," Helen said quickly. "Rita knows that. Rita knows that no house can be run by two women."

"Rita has no aspiration to run it, my dear Helen."

The girl gave an unexpected laugh. "I'll say I haven't! I don't even want to live here."

For an instant Helen looked astonished. Then she flashed a look of relief and triumph at her brother. His face tightened. He turned toward the girl. "But to please me?" He said it in a light, derisive way in which there was something slyly menacing. "To please me?"

Calvin expected the redhead to flash back but she said instantly, trying to match Burk's lightness but not making a good job of it, "Oh, to please you—of course!"

"It would please me," said Burk decisively. He was saying it to them both. Then, directly to his sister, "It's what I want, Helen."

Helen was on a spot, Calvin thought. She was dead right that there would be all sorts of complications and conflicts, for Burk was domineering, trading on his charm and others' good nature, but there was the Folly, big as a museum, and Helen had got everything and Burk nothing. Against his reasoned judgment he found himself wanting Helen to stop being sensible, to go soft and generous and throw herself wide open. It didn't make sense because, in her place, he would have fought Burk off, but that's the way he felt.

But Helen wasn't giving in. She looked upset but she said stubbornly, "It wouldn't work out. You know that, Burk. This isn't fair of you. You know we wouldn't get along if we tried to live together. There isn't help enough as it is—Henry and Ida are old. And Dolcey can't do more than she does. You've no idea how much I do. It isn't the way it was when father was making money."

"Or if I'd gone into the Pottery to make money! But we'd pay for our crusts of bread."

"You know it wouldn't work out," Helen repeated. "You'd be happier in a place of your own. In fact—"

She glanced about, confused and flushed. She said, "Oh, let's not go into it now."

"We're already in it, my dear little sister. Have you run out of reasons? I assure you I would *not* be happier anywhere else."

"I'm sorry," she said in a low voice. "I thought you'd want a place of your own. And I—I'd meant it for a surprise—but it's that house in town, that father left John. I bought it back. And I thought you'd like it for a wedding present."

Abbie Nordstrom said, in her friendliest tone, "She really is right, you know. It never does work out."

Helen turned to Rita, appealing and faintly hopeful. "Wouldn't you like that?"

The girl looked nervously at Burk as if to ask what she should say. Calvin's gaze roved along the table. Niel Nordstrom was squeezing lemon into his tea, his strong, surgeon's fingers extracting the last drop of juice. John Cauldron sat quiet, expressionless. Rawley was eying Burk, his eyes intent.

Burk was staring at his sister. "You were really thinking of giving me that?" he said, with an exaggeration of skeptical delight. "You were actually going to give me that house in town?"

Like lightning his anger broke its cover. "The Always-Right Helen! Helen the Invincible! Oh, how clever you were, Helen, how very clever to poison my father's mind so completely! To get everything left to you."

Helen grew very white. She said in a strained voice, "I didn't poison his mind, Burk."

"No?"

"No!" she said more vehemently. "You know I didn't. You know I begged you to go into the Works. I begged you to do what he wanted—"

"But afterward— After I was gone?"

"I didn't poison his mind. That's an abominable thing to say. He told you what he'd do if you refused. You had your choice. You were the one who made the choice."

"My choice! What choice? The business was another affair, another affair entirely. I loathed the business. But the Folly— I had a *right* to the Folly!"

"But he told you—he warned—"

"He had no right to crack the whip. To make the two things one. I was his son."

"I was his daughter," said Helen, spirited now. "I'm as much a Cauldron as you are!"

"Are you? Are you a Peter the Fourth? I was. Peter Burk Cauldron. Nor did you produce a Peter. If father had lived to know that—"

Helen's head went higher, her face even whiter, at the reference to Lucy. She struck back. "Oh, give me time!"

John Cauldron got up. "I'd better telephone White," he said across the table to Helen, his sane, sensible voice ignoring the passion in the air. "We'll have to get back that boy he borrowed—George can't use his hand. I'll see to it." He walked into the house.

Burk Cauldron stared after him until the French windows had closed behind him, then his eyes flicked back to his sister. "At home here, isn't he? If he had the Cauldron good looks, one might suppose that was the reason you haven't married again."

Helen said confusedly, "Well, he hasn't the Cauldron good looks." She seemed trying to pull herself together, to speak lightly. "You'd have some trouble, Burk, to get that story believed."

"Oh, I don't know. . . . A hopeless passion. . . . You couldn't marry, because of the talk—living here like brother and sister. It has its possibilities," he said in a laughing voice.

Helen gave up lightness. She said stiffly, "I wouldn't advise you, Burk, to try to injure me."

"No? But I think I shall someday, Helen." He got up and smiled directly at her—a hard, bitter smile. "I think someday I'll bring home to you what it means to be hurt. Really hurt."

He turned to Rita Rand. "We'll be going now."

The girl jumped up, glancing about uncertainly, her lips putting on a formal, embarrassed smile. As her eyes met Calvin's, she gave him a strangely searching look.

Abbie Nordstrom said cheerfully, "We'll hope for good weather next Wednesday."

It seemed fantastic to Calvin Morse that after these fireworks there would be a wedding here at all, but that seemed still the idea. Helen said to the girl, her voice only a little strained, "I'll call up about those names. I'll call tomorrow morning."

Burk and Rita went to their car. Young Rawley got up. "I think I'll go for a walk," he said to no one in particular and disappeared around a corner of the house.

"Well—" said Helen, rather helplessly. She looked about the diminished circle and tried to smile. "That was quite a tea party, wasn't it?"

Abbie Nordstrom said firmly, "You were perfectly right. It wouldn't have worked. Now Niel and I will be running along. You'll want to have your talk with Calvin."

They sat looking at each other across the table. Henry, the white-haired butler, looking no older than Calvin remembered him, had carried off the tea things and brought drinks. "You'll want something stronger than tea after all this," Helen had said, with a faint laugh. Now that they were alone she seemed at a loss how to begin.

He prompted, "What is it, Helen? What is worrying you?"

She looked quickly toward the house to make sure the door was shut. "It's so many things—"

"Well, what's the first?"

She said uncertainly, as she had said in her letter, "You may think I'm imagining things—"

"All right," he said cheerfully, "I may think you're imagining things. But what things? That letter of yours—that sounded serious."

She moved her glass an inch, then another inch, concentrating on it carefully. When she spoke her voice was very low and carefully controlled. "The first thing is I think they've made a mistake in the man they've arrested. I think he didn't do it. I don't think he's the one who killed Lucy."

"You don't?" He looked at her in astonishment. "Why, they found him there, didn't they?"

"Yes, but it was hours afterward—hours. And he says he never came into the woods until later."

"But that's a matter for the law."

"The law might make a terrible mistake," she said, her voice trembling a little now.

He looked at her in perplexity. "It isn't up to you to—"

"Lucy was my child. And it would be the final horror to me to have someone who was innocent suffer for her death. I could not bear that, Calvin! I could not bear that." Then she fought back the feeling that was shaking her. "I didn't mean to talk like this. I'll tell you quietly. They think it's this boy—he's only a boy, really—"

"Is it someone you know?" he asked quickly.

"Oh, no. It isn't because of that. I only knew him to speak to. He'd only been here a few weeks before. He had a job with old Judd—at the filling station at the Turn. He walked off toward our place, old Judd says, after John drove past toward the Country Club to get Lucy. So he could have got to the gate before she did. But he says he wasn't in the woods till later. He says he has an alibi."

"But doesn't he give it?"

She shook her head. "No. . . . But he wrote me this letter." From a bag beside her she drew out a paper, and gave it to him. "You read it."

It was written in a round, almost childish hand. Calvin read: "Dear Mrs. Cromer: I want to tell you right off that I never did such a dreadful thing. I can prove I never did, because I was with a certain young lady at the time and never came into your woods until much later, but I don't want to tell this unless I have to, because it will make things hard for that young lady. But I can't bear to have you thinking I did such a thing so I am telling you the truth. I feel awfully bad for you. Sincerely, Tex Miller."

"It's such an honest-sounding letter," Helen was saying.

Even at eighteen she had never seemed so young to him and he looked at her compassionately. He said gently, "You can't tell a thing by that, Helen. If he has an alibi he'd better produce it."

"She's probably married—"

"Hard luck for her, but it can't be helped. And there may not be anyone at all."

"Oh, but there is! I've had letters from her. Anonymous letters. Two of them. This was the first."

It was typed carefully on plain paper. "Dear Mrs. Cromer, I beg you to read this, I beg you to believe me when I tell you that Tex Miller is innocent. He was with

me that night till long after the dog howled. I will come
forward and tell this if I must at the trial to save him,
but it will ruin everything in my life. He had no right to
be with me. So I have been keeping quiet hoping the real
criminal will be found. It was not Tex. It was someone
else. It could be some boy from the Country Club, someone Lucy was dating without your knowing it. Some of
those boys are wild when they've been drinking. Oh, Mrs.
Cromer, please, please look for some clue among Lucy's
things. Maybe she kept a letter that would show who he
was. Oh, please look."

The second letter was a shorter but even more frantic
appeal for a search for a clue. Calvin looked up, "You've
no idea who sent this?"

"No idea in the world."

"Typewriting can be traced. But the police must know
whom he's been seeing."

"They say there's no one in particular—that he was
friendly to a lot of girls, but only casually. Sutton, that's
the sheriff, said that he was 'sweet bait.'" Helen's inflec-
tion put the words in quotes. "No one seems to know
much about him. He hitchhiked in. But doesn't that letter
sound real to you, Calvin? I thought it did. And I did look
for clues—I looked through everything. But there wasn't
a thing. Just letters from girls at camp and programs of
school parties and old valentines and lists of things to take
to school. She was going away to school this fall."

He said, distressed, "Don't, Helen! Don't tear yourself
to pieces over this. The trial will decide it. The truth will
come out then."

"But don't you see? If he's innocent, that man, the one
who really killed Lucy is still free. And he's somewhere
about here."

"That doesn't follow."

"But he is, Calvin! And he's trying to kill me."

She said it softly but tensely, with a quiet conviction that held him in shocked silence for a long moment. Then he said, "What makes you say that?"

"There are things happening."

"What sort of things?"

Her eyes met his. "They don't sound much—at first," she said. "I'll tell you. The first was the night Lucy died. I'd been sitting by her, Jude and I—I wanted to be alone. Then I went to my room and shut the door between us. Not to shut her out, but to be by myself, to get my courage together. There was some milk on a tray—that was all I'd asked for—and there was a pill Niel had sent up. Niel and Abbie were staying all night—and Burk. But I couldn't see them. I wanted to be alone."

Her tenseness was painful. He said gently, "But what happened?"

"I drank the milk and took the pill. I had a feeling, not so much of going to sleep but of blacking out. Later—it was much later—I woke up choking—smothering. I could hardly wake. But Jude was barking and lunging against the door. He woke up the whole house and everybody came running. I said I'd had a nightmare—I must have cried out in it and Jude heard. That's what I thought it was then. A nightmare. But now—"

"Now?"

"Now—I don't know," she said uncertainly. "I can't be sure—but I had such a feeling of being smothered. As if that man had got in to me."

"But how could he?"

"Anyone could have got in that night and hidden. It would have been the safest place for him to hide. But I only began to think that after the other things. After I was followed."

"Tell me about that."

"There were several times. Oh, but first there was something else. I was riding the new colt—Burk thought it would do me good to get out on him. I was in our own woods. And something, a stone, I think, whizzed out and hit him. He went up in the air and nearly threw me—I wasn't prepared. It all happened so fast I couldn't be sure what hit him, but it was something good sized."

A dream. A stone at a horse. He looked at her doubtfully. He said, "Some boy might have been shying rocks. Not knowing you were there."

"Yes. Yes, it could have been like that. But it all adds up. The attempts—"

"What about being followed?"

"That was when I went out by myself. I was pretty restless and I used to walk it off, in the woods, beyond the fields. At first Jude went with me but he got too weak. And I began to hear sounds, cracking sounds, a stick breaking, as if underfoot—things like that. The first time I was sitting by a stream and it was right behind me. I jumped up and crossed on stepping stones and took another way back. But, after that, on other walks, I heard them again, cautious little sounds. As if someone was following. And I had the feeling of being watched. It made me turn and go back. I never went very far into the woods—until that last time."

She had been talking in a low monotone, her eyes lowered, her dark head bent, but now she looked directly at him and said, "It doesn't sound like much, does it? You'll think I'm silly."

"You tell me what happened."

"This was last week. That's what made me write you. I went quite far that day. I think I wanted to prove I wasn't frightened—I've never been frightened about things before. You know that, Calvin. I wasn't really frightened that day that Bolter ran away. I was too excited."

The day that Bolter ran away. For a moment he could see the black horse tearing about the turn ahead of him, see Helen swaying dangerously, half out of the saddle. The hardest decision he had ever made was to rein in his horse, not to go thudding after, inciting Bolter to fresh speed, but to trust to Helen's nerve and skill. Helen had come back laughing.

The picture faded and he was back at the table on the terrace with this Helen who was saying, her voice taut again, "I didn't hear anything at first—and then—it was just the tiniest sound but it was quite sharp. A stick cracking underfoot. That's what it sounded like. I looked back and there was a branch moving—in a bush beside the path. As if it had sprung back in place. I told myself it was a deer. I made myself go on. But I heard another sound. And I had the feeling—do you know that feeling?—the feeling of being watched. And then I heard someone moving in the bushes."

She looked up again and said absurdly—he remembered that way of hers of tossing in that question—"And do you know what I did? I began talking out loud, as if talking to a dog. I said, 'Toby'—that's the name of our farmer's dog—'why, how did you get here?' The woods were so thick you couldn't see whether there was a dog in the path or not and Toby's short—though he's fierce. I kept saying, 'Why, George will think you're lost—come on back, Toby,' and I whirled around and ran back, talking all the time. And I never heard another sound all the way back. And I hadn't imagined those sounds, Calvin. I know the wood sounds."

Yes, she knew wood sounds. He was silent, considering.

"I went back the next day. I took Carl, one of our hands, telling him I'd lost something and he must help me find it. And I looked in the bush I'd seen waving—I knew the one—and someone *had* been there. You could see where ferns had been pressed down. And once there was a footprint."

Calvin said slowly, "It could have been someone after a rabbit."

"But he *followed*. . . . All those times."

He said bluntly, "It could be nerves. Or it could be fact. I should think the thing to do was to have those woods searched. Haven't you had that done?"

"That would take a lot of men."

"But the sheriff—haven't you been to the police?"

"No-no. You see . . . I went to him about those letters. John didn't want me to—he thinks I'm crazy to believe in them. He said they were an obvious hoax, a play for sympathy. John—and Sutton too, that's the sheriff—are utterly convinced that it's Tex Miller. Sutton just laughed at those letters. . . . So I didn't tell John about being followed. He thinks I'm all worked up, anyway," she said resentfully, "and he wants Niel to give me something for my nerves. My nerves are all right. It's just that John—"

She broke off, then flung out, "John's so afraid that I'll ask Burk to move in with us that he almost *wants* me to break down so he can manage things!" Then she said, "Oh, I don't mean that! Only John is too anxious about me. He's afraid of my being too depressed. He went and took the revolver out of my room—Lee's old thirty-eight. I made him give it back. I'm not going to do anything foolish— I've got a lot to live for."

"You've got everything."

"But if I'd told him about being followed," she swept on, "he'd believe I was imagining it. Perhaps unconsciously. To prove my point about the letters. Because he doesn't believe there's a madman still at large and I do. . . . So that's when I wrote you, Calvin. You've got a legal mind and you'd be detached."

"Not too detached," he said a little wryly. "Anything that touches you, Helen, still touches me. But what can I do? I can't tell you for a fact whether you were followed or not."

"I know. But you can see Tex Miller and tell me whether you think he's guilty or not. If you think he's telling the truth, then I'll go to the sheriff and make him comb those woods. But if you think he's guilty, then I'll know there isn't anybody hiding there. It—it isn't that I am so afraid of being killed, Calvin. But I'm so afraid of some terrible mistake—in justice. You can tell me what to believe."

It was preposterous and it was pitiful. He tried to make her see that no snap judgment he could form would have a shred of value. But he was so sorry for her, so moved by the haunted look in her gray eyes, that he said he would go, that he would try to gain some impression.

In her relief she looked so spent that he said gently, "Go to bed early tonight, Helen. Get some sleep."

"Yes, I will. I haven't been sleeping very well. I asked Niel for a sleeping pill and he said he'd bring me one. You'll let me know as soon as you've seen Tex Miller, won't you? Sutton will arrange it, if he knows I've asked you—or his lawyer. Regan, his name is. You'll let me know right away?"

"I'll let you know. Sleep well."

Chapter Three

Sleep well. Her mind echoed it ironically, then wistfully. Yes, she might sleep now. It was a relief to have told Calvin Morse. She had been sure that he was the one person she could tell who would not laugh at her. She had been going on her nerves for too long, she thought, trying not to show what she was feeling, and now all the tiredness that she had been holding at bay was overpowering her.

Slowly she walked through the long rooms of the house, feeling a bleak disinclination for every hour ahead of her. Dinner with John. He would be worried for fear she would give in to Burk—he knew her abrupt reversals so well!—and he would want to argue, to strengthen her against Burk. She couldn't take that tonight.

And Rawley might come to the table. That young man baffled her. She had the feeling of something pent up in him and she had the feeling that he disliked her. She had felt that before she stopped those walks of his with Lucy. Of course she'd had to stop them. He was a stranger, and Lucy was so young and eager—he ought to have asked her before he took the child out into the woods.

Perhaps he had liked Lucy and it was his resentment and his feeling for Lucy that was making him so stiff. Two months now—he had been in the house for over two months now—and still he was a stranger to her. He had never said one thing about his personal life. Except that he lived alone, that his people were dead. He was easy to be with only when he talked about painting.

No, she couldn't take John or Rawley tonight. She turned up the broad stairway in an impulse to flight, then, her hand on the rail, stopped as Henry spoke below her. He had been answering the telephone, which was on a table in a corner of the big hall. "Mr. Burk rung up," he reported. "He say he coming back to dinner. Not his young lady though. He staying here all night."

That settled it. She couldn't talk any more to Burk. He was either coming to argue again or to say he was sorry—he had been outrageous and he knew it!—but whatever it was she couldn't take that either.

"All right, Henry," she said. "But I'm not coming down to dinner. My head aches. I don't want to see anyone. Ask Ida to bring me up a tray—just a sandwich and some milk and my thermos of coffee. Oh, and Henry—"

"Yes, Miss Helen—?"

"The doctor's bringing me some medicine later. Have Ida bring it up."

She went upstairs. Her room was at the front of the house, not the master bedroom, unused except for guests since her father's death, but a large room that had always been hers, which she and Lee Cromer had shared for a year. Lucy's room was next to it, with a connecting door, and she went into it, as she went every night, and looked about at the smooth, empty bed, the vacant tidiness.

That night, when they had brought Lucy in, there had been a plate of fudge on the table and a French school-book, open, with a smudged page. The *Livre de mon ami*.

She shut the door to Lucy's room; she tried to shut the door of her mind. It was lonely without Jude. He had slept in her room after Lucy died until he grew too feeble, suddenly, to climb the stairs. He had seemed to be growing better but he hadn't been growing better. He had died a little over a week ago.

Slowly she undressed, then went into the big dressing room which her grandfather had made into a bathroom, and ran the water for a hot bath. When she emerged from the bath she found that Ida had left a tray beside the bed, and opened the bed. She got in and lay back against the pillow. She was not hungry; she did not want to eat or drink. There had been all that cake and tea and the drink afterward. She was tired but not sleepy.

She thought about Calvin Morse. He was kind—he had always been kind under that quick temper of his—and he had a good mind. He would find out the truth. He had seemed the only one she could turn to. He—but she was not going to let herself think any more about Calvin. He was there—that was all that mattered. He would find out the truth. It was too bad there had been that scene at tea. Burk—but she was not going to let herself think about Burk either. Burk would be happier after he was married. Only—why were he and that girl so strange together? It had been different, their first time here. Well, that didn't matter either. All that mattered now to her, she told herself, was this dreadful trial. This frightful fear that injustice might be done in the name of justice.

She closed her eyes and tried to empty her mind. After a time there was a knock on her door, then it opened and she looked up to see Niel Nordstrom.

"I brought your pill," he said. "Henry said you didn't want to see anyone, but doctors are exceptions."

"Of course." She smiled up at him.

"I looked in before, but you were in your dressing room."

"Taking a good hot bath."

"It's only tiredness, isn't it? You're not feeling ill?"

"Only tiredness."

"Then I won't keep you from sleep. But I want to tell you again how much I appreciate that ten thousand for the hospital wing."

Niel had always been at her for money for the hospital. He was fanatic about the hospital, about the people who needed it. She had given the ten thousand in Lucy's name.

He was smiling a little teasingly. "Of course it ought to be more."

"It isn't going to be more." She managed a bantering tone. "I can't spare it."

"I need a hundred thousand."

"That's half of what I have. You'll have to wait until I die."

"I don't want to wait. I'd rather see you getting along on half. This place doesn't need it as much as—" He broke off. "Ungrateful, aren't I? Here's your pill. I'll put it on your tray. I'll bring you more, any time, but I'll not leave them around."

"Why not? They're not strong, are they?"

"One isn't. But thirty-five—"

She laughed. "I can't imagine any stupider way to die than solemnly swallowing thirty-five pills, one after the other!"

He laughed too. "It isn't like that. You could pour them all in one dose. So it's just one at a time."

He was gone and she sat up and looked consideringly at the pill. She did not seem to need it now. If she woke up later, she would need it then. Its sleep lasted only about four hours. She poured out a cup of milk and drank it slowly. She filled the cup again, then put down the cup without drinking from it. She did not want more milk. She picked up the thermos of coffee, then reflected that if she opened it now, to pour out any, the rest would be cold by early morning, and she might wake early. She put the thermos down, unopened.

She leaned back and closed her eyes. Suddenly—it seemed quite suddenly—she felt an overpowering heaviness of sleep.

Slowly, slowly, she came back to semiconsciousness. She was dreaming a dreadful dream, a dream of drowning. She was awake enough to feel it was a dream, that she must struggle out of it, but the dream still held her, stifling her under fathoms of water. She was trying to breathe and she could not breathe. She was drowning. . . . No, she was choking. She was still under water, but she wasn't drowning, she was choking.

One of those awful creatures, an octopus, a monster with reaching arms, had a long tentacle about her throat, shutting off air. But this was only a dream. She could feel it was a dream—she could even remember that she had experienced this choking horror in a dream before. But still she could not throw it off. She could realize that the octopus had been a dream but still she felt choking, unable to breathe; she felt that something smothering was over her face, pressed down upon her face, hard, hard, that she was sinking farther and farther back to unconsciousness.

Then, suddenly, the pressure was gone. The down-bearing weight. She made a violent effort—it seemed to her violent but it was no more than a movement of her head—and something heavy slid from her face. The pillow. She was conscious that she was lying awake, panting, conscious that there was a loud ringing in her ears.

No, it was in the air. The telephone. The bell rang in the front hall downstairs and up here beside her bed, on the extension. The telephone had awakened her. She might have been dreaming only for a minute, for seconds—dreams were very brief, she had heard—though it had seemed to last for an eternity.

Steps were running along the hall, down the stairs. Who could be phoning at this hour? But what hour was it? Her windows were pale oblongs, white with moon.

The other time it had been the dog that had waked the household. Now the telephone.

Her breath came more easily now but the feeling of horror had crept into her bones. Only now it was not a dream horror of deep water and a reaching tentacle. . . . It had happened again. . . . Whatever the meaning, it had happened again.

Her door opened softly. Ida's voice said, "I know that waked you, Miss Helen. You want anything?"

"No." Her voice sounded thick and fuzzy. "What was it?"

"Mr. John downstairs taking it. It's Western Union. Pretty time of night for Western Union," said Ida scornfully. "Near midnight. That Dalrymple girl ain't got the sense she born with."

"All right." Her voice really was thick. Ida would think it sleepy sounding.

"Good night, Miss Helen dear."

Why hadn't she said, Run to the doors—see where he went? Look through the house! You lie there, gasping, and you say, "All right," you pretend that nothing horrible had happened. . . . But you were too weak to talk, to explain. And you were afraid of being thought a fool, a hysterical fool.

But she wasn't being hysterical. It had really happened. Her breath had been almost gone. She still felt queer, all over. And her nose was sore. As if it had been squashed. She put up a hand and touched it. This wasn't nerves. But she'd have to think about it carefully. To make sure.

She waited till John had time to hang up, to go back to his room, then she put on her bed lamp. She propped herself up on one elbow, feeling dizzy when she moved. Coffee would clear her head. She felt eager for some coffee.

She lifted the thermos. It was light. Could Ida have forgotten to fill it? No, it had been heavy last night. She was sure it had been heavy. She unscrewed the cup and took out the cork and tilted the bottle over a cup. Not a drop came out. It was empty. She felt so weak, so craving for stimulant that she could have cried.

She put down the thermos. Some milk then—milk would be better than nothing. She had poured out a cup of milk last night and left it on the tray. It wasn't there. Both cups were empty. Queer. She was sure she had not drunk it. Could she have poured it back? She looked into the jug and it was empty. The jug held two cupfuls exactly.

She felt bewildered. And then the meaning rushed through her. Of course. Sleep was not enough. Nor one pill. And she had not taken the pill. But it was gone now. There had been something in the milk.

Terror poured through her, a terror unreasoning, she tried to tell herself, because now she was awake, the household was awake. The telephone had saved her. He had not dared hold down the pillow an instant more.

But where was he? She looked about her room in panic. Those draperies at the side of the window, those draperies in shadow, at any moment something would creep out of them. No, he would wait till she was asleep. But where was he? Behind what door? Lucy's room? The closet? The dressing room? If only she had told Ida to stay.

She got out of bed. She must move unhurriedly, she told herself, not to seem alarmed. She lurched against the post of the bed, and caught it to steady herself. She was drugged. Her head felt clear but her feet were uncertain. But they would carry her. Gingerly she moved to her desk. She pulled open a drawer, picked up quickly the revolver there. She felt better then. She steadied herself and faced the dressing room. The door was ajar. She flung it open, her eyes straining into the dim interior. The moon was white on the fixtures. Her fingers crept to the jamb and turned on the light.

No one was there. There were her towels, the brassiere she had left on the low chair. She went back and put on the lights in her room. She opened the door into the hall so that a cry could be heard and moved slowly, systematically about the hiding places. No one was hidden.

She looked toward Lucy's door. But now she felt exhausted. She dragged a chair against the door and wedged it beneath the knob. She looked about her, her heart still thudding heavily, and felt a terror of the dark house outside her door, and hurried to close and lock the door into the hall. Her own room, lighted, strong walled, searched, seemed now her only safety. She got back into bed, and thrust the pillow on the floor. She would lie there and wait, she thought. And try to arrange her thoughts. But in a few moments the wave of heavy drowsiness drew her back to sleep.

She woke to a sun-flooded room. She felt surprisingly rested as if she had slept a long time. Nine o'clock. Indeed she had slept long. She got up, unlocked her door, put the revolver back. She went to the bathroom and let cold water fill the tub. Then she heard Ida's voice and looked out.

Ida, small and dark, in her bright blue dress and white apron, was a symbol of the normal, reassuring day. Ida was carrying out her tray, asking if she should bring breakfast.

"No, I'll be down," Helen told her.

"Mr. John says he wants to talk to you as soon as he can."

"All right. Oh, Ida! Is there a pill on that tray? A yellow pill?"

There was a moment's wait. "No pill," said Ida.

Downstairs at the little breakfast table by the window, she thought about it, drinking her coffee, and listening

absently to the prosaic hum of the vacuum cleaner. A
frenzy of cleaning was going on in preparation for the
wedding; Ida had impressed Joe and Carl, the field boys,
into nibbing the woodwork and the air crackled with her
brisk directions. "Lively, boy! Go *into* that carving. . . .
What's that? It's a griffin, but never you mind what *that*
is! You get the dust out of his mouth."

John Cauldron came in and sat by her. He asked, "How
are you, Helen? How's the headache?"

"The headache?" She had forgotten the headache. "Oh,
that's gone."

"That's good. But you don't look too well."

"I kept dreaming, I didn't sleep well. Where's Burk?"

"He left early. Before breakfast. He didn't say anything more, except about the wedding," said John. John
always seemed to know the question she wanted to ask, she
thought, relieved by the information. He asked, "Did that
telephone wake you last night?"

"Yes. What was it? Ida said something about a telegram."

He looked cautiously about, and lowered his voice. "It
was from the Institute. About Rawley."

His voice made her look up. He sounded worried.

"Lambert never sent him," he said. "The Institute didn't
know he was here."

"Didn't know?" she repeated blankly. "Why, they
wrote—"

"Some secretary wrote, you remember. On Institute
paper. Saying that Lambert was sending his assistant. The
same day, as I recall it, came a telegram saying Rawley was
on the way."

"Well—who did send him?"

"I fancy he came on his own," said John dryly. "Your
letter about the Romney seems to have startled the Institute. The president wired to say that Rawley was not sent

by Lambert and that the Institute disclaimed any responsi-
bility for him or for his work. It sounded as if Rawley was
known to them, but—well, we'll know more when their
letter comes. The telegram said he was writing."

"That's very queer," said Helen slowly. "Did you talk
to Rawley?"

"Oh, no—not till I talked with you. I thought, too,
it would be better to call up the Institute first and talk
directly to the president or to Lambert."

"I wish you would. I don't want to wait for a letter."

"I thought I'd go down to Somerset to phone. The connection is better and then, too, I wouldn't be overheard."

"You could talk from my room. But the connection is
better in town."

She poured out another cup of coffee. John Cauldron
was looking at her curiously. "You don't seem very concerned about this," he said.

No, she didn't feel concerned. When someone has been
trying to kill you in the night, she thought, you can't worry about much else. She tried to speak normally. "Well—it
will all be explained. He must be some artist at the Institute. He does know the Institute and he knows painting—
that's all he's ever talked about."

"I think he knows painting," said John, "but the question is—how honest is he? Why did he come? We've no
idea what pictures are in the gallery now—he's got half
of them down and stacked. If there was something valu-
able there and he wasn't honest, it's quite thinkable that
he might smuggle it out and cache it somewhere on those
long walks of his."

"Yes, he could."

And what did it matter? A picture less on those walls
that would never now be Lucy's? She had tried to pretend
interest in those pictures, knowing she must snatch at
any straw to buoy herself, but it had been all effort and

pretense. Her only interest now—and it was a feverish interest—was this dreadful trial. To solve this frightening mystery.

"Yes, you telephone," she said. "And then you talk to Rawley. You can get more out of him than I. He doesn't like me."

Should she telephone Calvin? No, she'd wait till he had time to see Tex Miller. That wouldn't take long. She'd make herself wait.

Chapter Four

Twice that morning Calvin Morse tried to get Regan—A. J. Regan, 17 Main Street—on the telephone, and both times his call was unanswered. At the second call the telephone girl volunteered that Regan might be in court. Calvin decided to try once more, a little later, then go to Somerset and hunt him up.

He picked up his box of flies and took it to the big bay window in the dining room. His aunt had left for her Thursday Morning Club lecture and luncheon and Niel was at the hospital. He had been there the night before till early morning. An emergency operation, he had said.

"Niel's a slave to his patients," Abbie told Calvin. "Some doctors are through when they walk out of the operating room—then it's up to the nurses. But not Niel. Niel doesn't leave anyone who might need him. His sick people are his life."

Absently Calvin looked through his flies, meditating on the coming talk. He had asked about Regan that morning and Niel had said he came from somewhere upstate, starting practice alone. Finding it a little hard sledding, for he'd had only small cases. Regan and Miller used to play pool together and he'd taken the case at once, though there wasn't anything in it for him but the notoriety.

"Miller hasn't a thin dime," said Niel. "And he won't need any," he said grimly, "where he's going."

Calvin remembered that it was Niel Nordstrom who had found Lucy. He could understand the hardness in Niel's voice.

The talk with Miller wasn't important. It was absurd, but he had promised Helen. The essential thing was to get at the sheriff and have those woods searched. It was all too possible that a man was hiding there. Calvin didn't believe that he had got into the Folly that first night, as Helen was imagining now—it seemed to him more probable that she had experienced a nightmare. It was exactly the sort of nightmare to be expected after her child's shocking death. But the sounds in the woods, the conviction of being followed—that was something to be looked into without delay.

The bell rang. Clarissa, he could see, was in the garden, in conversation with a neighbor's maid. He put down his flies and went to the door. Rita Rand was there, hatless, her bright hair windblown. She had been bicycling—her wheel was against the steps—and her blue denim pants stopped halfway down her bare legs. Other visible items were socks, sneakers, and a blue-checked shirt.

She came in quickly, saying with a hint of breathlessness, "Your aunt—is she here?"

"No, she's at her—"

"And the doctor's out?" At his assent she looked relieved. "It's you I wanted to see," she said surprisingly. "Let's go in here."

He followed her into the front room; then she stepped back to close the door. "You never know," she said in a guarded tone. She turned directly to him and her intent look reminded him of the way she had looked at him the day before. She said, "This is a—a professional visit. So you will keep secret, won't you, what I tell you?"

"Professional?" For a moment he thought that she took him for a doctor, like Niel.

"Because you're a lawyer. And I need to talk to a lawyer."

"Wait a minute, wait a minute," he said lightly, to head her off before she said too much. "I'm no use to you. I'm not a member of the Tennessee bar. I practice only in New York."

"I don't want you to practice. Only to tell me something. Perhaps you think it's funny, my coming to you like this, but I feel as if I knew you. Burk talked a lot about you yesterday. He was all worked up. But even though he was furious at you, the things he said made me feel I could trust you. I can trust you, can't I?" she asked, her face anxious and questioning.

This was astonishing. Yesterday she had been a beautiful dummy, letting Burk pull the strings, but today she was alive, a very real, troubled girl. And a very beguiling one. The sloppy Joe outfit was somehow enhancing.

"Certainly you can trust me," he said recklessly. "What is it?"

They sat down on a couch facing each other. Rita Rand demanded, "Can a man get a divorce for something that happened before they were married? It didn't really happen," she said quickly, "but if he thinks it did? If it looks as if it could have happened?"

The corners of Calvin's mouth twitched. "You mean the sort of thing he could get a divorce for—even in New York—if it had happened *after* they were married?"

She nodded, her eyes intent on him.

"But it didn't happen?"

"No. No, it didn't."

"Then he couldn't prove it happened?"

"N-no. No, he couldn't *prove* it. But if he thought it?"

"He would have to have proof. Even if it *had* happened, if you follow me. I can say that, offhand. To give you a really professional opinion, as to whether a man can get a divorce—or annulment—for premarital—for anything that happened before they were married I would have to look up the law in the state of domicile. But if the man is without proof—merely harbors untrue suspicion—I think the suspected bride would be quite without fear of legal action."

"I wasn't sure." But she didn't look particularly relieved. After a moment she said somberly, "He'd walk out on me, just the same. He'd make everyone think it *had* happened."

Calvin considered the situation with outward gravity. "Wouldn't it be a good idea to get the explaining done beforehand? Then there'd be no fear of reprisals."

Rita shook her bright head violently. "Then he'd walk out *before* the wedding. He wouldn't believe me. No," she said, as if arguing with herself, "I'm not going to tell until I have to. Maybe I'll never have to."

"Here's hoping," he said cheerfully.

She smiled absently. The subject had come to an end but she seemed preoccupied. She looked past him and said with palpably elaborate casualness, "Tell me—you're a good friend of Helen Cromer's—did she happen to say anything about getting a letter from Tex Miller?"

Calvin's inner laughter fled. "Yes. She mentioned it."

"I thought she would, somehow. Did she say anything about any other letters?"

"You mean—anonymous letters?"

"Yes. About Tex."

"She said she'd received two of them."

"I happen to know," said Rita Rand, with that same elaborate casualness, "that a girl wrote her to look for clues. Among Lucy's things. Because the killer must be someone Lucy knew. And I wondered—I wondered if she'd looked? I'm asking so I can tell the girl."

"Yes, she looked. She told me that she had looked thoroughly but that she had found nothing."

"That's just my luck!" said Rita bitterly. She said, sounding on the verge of tears, "I *never* have any luck!"

The fiction of the other girl was tossed overboard. She blurted, "Oh, I don't know what to do!"

After a long moment he said, "Oh, yes, you do. You know you ought to tell anything you know." She looked at him in sudden panic. He said bluntly, "If Tex Miller was with you, and not in the woods, when Lucy was killed, you know you ought to come straight out with it. Or Tex Miller will hang or go to the chair or whatever they do to convicted murderers in Tennessee."

"Do you think I don't know that?" she said fiercely. "Of course I'll tell before I let them convict him! If it comes to the trial I'll tell everything. But I've kept hoping there never would have to be a trial, that they'd find a clue to someone else. There's got to be some clue. Because someone did it. Someone got into those woods and killed Lucy Cromer. He didn't just vanish in thin air. I've been waiting and waiting for them to find something."

"Why would they be looking," said Calvin gravely, "when the evidence pointed to Tex Miller? You should have told them at once."

She said defensively, "Tex told me not to tell. He wrote me a letter that first morning from the jail. His lawyer brought it. Tex said not to say a word, not to get myself into it. He said they'd find the real one, that they couldn't pin it on him."

"His lawyer brought it to you?"

"That very morning."

"Then his lawyer knows?"

"No, he doesn't. He knows Tex has an alibi, that he was with some girl, but he doesn't know I'm the girl. Tex told him I would get the letter to the right girl."

"Did he believe that?"

"I don't know what he believes. He asked a lot of questions but I wouldn't answer them."

"He'll subpoena you. Wouldn't it be better for you to tell him before you have to?"

"No, it wouldn't," said Miss Rand decisively. "Because if they find the man I won't have to tell anything at all."

Calvin, turning that over, got out cigarettes and lighted one for her and one for him. "Look," he said reasonably, "it isn't such a terrific thing, is it, to have had a date with Tex Miller?"

"Burk will think it was. Burk and I were practically engaged when I met Tex. You haven't seen Tex, have you?"

"No."

"It isn't just his looks," said Rita Rand slowly. "It's something about him. He's all man, if you know what I mean."

"I think I do," said Calvin gravely.

"I was crazy about him," she said frankly. "And he was crazy about me. The minute we met, almost. I was so crazy about him, after our first date, that I'd have run off with him in a minute. Only he couldn't marry me. He was married."

Calvin thought, *that* routine. He asked, "Hadn't you known?"

"No. Nobody here knew. It was one of those war marriages and they'd drifted apart but hadn't got a divorce. Tex felt terrible to have to tell me. He said he'd look her up and try to get a divorce but I could see he wasn't any too sure. He was afraid she still liked him."

"He sounds—" Calvin stopped.

"Oh, I know what Tex is, all right!" she flung out resentfully. "A big, handsome drifter. Sweet bait," she said in a voice that was stabbing at herself, "just sweet bait."

That's what Helen had said. Quoting the sheriff.

"I wasn't so crazy I couldn't see that," said Rita Rand. "And I had sense enough to hang onto Burk. Burk Cauldron is somebody in this town, and I want to be somebody. I'm tired of being that redheaded Rand girl who isn't in the Country Club set. I thought if I married Burk everything would be all right. I'd get over Tex. You do get over things, don't you?"

Calvin looked at her a moment wondering if the question had sprung from Burk's talk about him and Helen. "Yes," he said, "you get over things."

"But Burk was jealous. He found out I'd been seeing Tex and he was off me for a while. Then I told him that Tex didn't mean a thing to me, that I'd never see him again. He calmed down and we got engaged and he took me to his sister's at the Folly. We had tea there. That was the day it happened."

Calvin thought back to his aunt's account of that afternoon. "You drove off with Burk?"

"Yes, but I had a date with Tex. As soon as I got home. I had to see Tex again," she said earnestly, "to make him understand. Tex couldn't believe I would give him up like that. He thought I'd wait. I had to make him understand. And I had a right to say good-bye to him," she said defiantly.

"Where did you meet him?"

"At my house. We live near the fox farm. Between it and the filling station. Tex worked at the filling station and I told him to come by after I'd driven past with Burk, that I wouldn't let Burk stay. That's why Tex walked off from the station. It was just bad luck that John Cauldron drove past the same time we did, going to get Lucy at the club. Tex headed toward the Cauldron place so Judd wouldn't know where he was going, so of course it looked as if he aimed to be in the Cauldron woods when Lucy got there."

"But how was he supposed to know that she would get out inside the gate?"

"They think she had a date with him. You see, Lucy drove to the club with the Herron boys and their sister, and they stopped for gas and Tex talked to Lucy the way he does to everyone—maybe they'd talked before. Lucy was a right pretty girl. Anyway, the whole town's got it worked out that they fixed up a date then."

"How did Tex get to your place?"

"When he was out of Judd's sight he turned up the highway and cut back through the woods. We are back a piece from the road. I'd got rid of Burk—I'd told him dad was bringing home some friends and I had to get busy. Our girl doesn't come on Thursdays. But dad wasn't coming home."

"So nobody saw Tex there?"

"Nobody but me. But I can swear that he was there till long after the dog howled. We didn't start arguing at first—we fixed ourselves some supper. He was there till long after dark, long after we heard the dog. It was dark when he went off. I don't know what time it was, exactly. I was crying so," she said inconsequentially.

She sounded as if telling the truth. Certainly, he thought, about Tex being with her. But she could be lying about the time he left.

"We had an awful time," she said. "Tex couldn't believe I was serious about being engaged to Burk—he didn't see how I could give him up when we felt as we did. He wanted me to run right off with him. He said everyone here would think we were to be married and that we would be married as soon as he could fix things up. But I wasn't going to get into *that* scrape."

"I should hope not."

"Tex isn't a wolf," she said defensively. "But he was crazy about me and that didn't make him too sensible."

She said it with sober detachment. "But I got him to realize I wasn't going to see him again. Not ever. He felt terrible about that. He wasn't angry—he's sweet natured. He just felt terrible. That's why he went off to the woods."

"Why to the Cauldrons'?"

"I don't know. I guess he didn't think where he was going—anywhere to be alone and get tight and forget it all. He had the bottle on him. He went through the woods back of the filling station and crossed the highway and got over the fence into Cauldron land—the fence is high there but Tex had Commando training. That's another thing against him now."

It would be, Calvin thought.

"I didn't know where he'd gone—I didn't know anything that was happening. I didn't know about Lucy until dad came home late and told me. They'd found Tex then. I couldn't sleep all night. I thought, of course, he'd say where he'd been, the moment he came to, and I kept waiting for the police to come to question me. When Burk didn't telephone that morning I thought it was because Tex had told and Burk was through with me. Then when the lawyer drove up—"

"Keep your voice down."

"When I read the letter," she said more softly, "I could have cried. Here I'd just thrown him over and yet he wasn't dragging me in. That's pretty wonderful! And he hasn't given me away, not all these two months. Even though we haven't been seeing each other," she said, realistically.

Calvin said thoughtfully, "I'm surprised his lawyer stays on the case when his client doesn't confide in him."

"Oh, he knows Tex will tell him before the trial."

"I'm going to see Tex Miller," said Calvin. "I'll have to arrange that through Regan and I'm telling you now so when you hear I've seen him you won't think I'm giving you away."

"I wouldn't think that" She looked at Calvin intently. "You've got that—that something which makes people trust you."

"Lots of rascals have," said Calvin, laughing. "It's their stock in trade. But here's some advice I wish you would trust. Go straight to Burk and tell him the story. Then go to the sheriff." As her face grew mutinous, he urged, "I honestly don't see what there is in that date to make Burk walk out on you. It isn't as though it lasted all night."

"You don't know Burk. He's got a mean mind. The things he said going home about his sister! He knows they aren't true but he'd like to tear her apart, he's so mad at her. And he's all worked up about you too."

"Why about me?"

"Oh, he's afraid Helen will marry again. It didn't matter before if she did, because there was Lucy anyway, but now— Oh, I wish he'd forget about that old place! We'd have a better time living in town."

Calvin didn't care what kind of time Burk had. He said soberly, "You two have done a very serious thing. The sheriff ought to know at once."

"But you won't tell him?" Her eyes flashed up at him in alarm. "I told you in confidence—you said I could trust you."

"I won't tell him until I have given you warning," he said guardedly. "But I urge you to tell him and get it over with."

"I'll do something," she said vaguely. She got up and hitched up her blue jeans and tucked in her checked shirt. "Will you tell me about it, after you've seen Tex?"

"That won't solve your problem. The wedding is next Wednesday, isn't it?"

She nodded, without joy in the reminder. "I keep hoping that something will turn up," she said despondently. "That man might have killed himself afterward or been hurt by the dog when he was getting away and be lying dead somewhere. I've looked and looked for him in the fields along the roads. He must be *somewhere*."

"He's somewhere, all right," said Calvin grimly.

"Well—good-bye." She was standing close to him and she held up her face expectantly. It was, he felt, a purely automatic courtesy and he was startled to find that kissing her was so pleasant. To make it more fraternal he gave the checked shirt a little pat as they walked to the door. As she cycled off, the macabre thought crossed his mind that she was probably going down more lonely roads, looking through more lonely fields, to find a long-dead man. An incongruous occupation.

He found that Clarissa the maid was on the top step, gazing appreciatively after the flashing bare legs. She giggled. "She sure don't look like she practicing the wedding march in a train and veil!"

Chapter Five

"I don't get it," said Regan. "Mrs. Cromer is naturally for the prosecution."

A. J. Regan had been discovered at lunch in the Coffee Shoppe of the Omar House. He was alone in his booth, the adjacent ones empty, a radio going full blast, so Calvin had launched into his explanation without fear of being overheard. A. J. Regan was a solid-looking young man, with a crew haircut, a square jaw, and a blunt manner.

"She's not for the prosecution of the wrong man," Calvin told him. "Those letters have her worried. She wants me to see your client, to form some impression. I tried to tell her just how useless that was, but I couldn't refuse her."

Regan said soberly, "We're all sorry for Mrs. Cromer."

"Those anonymous letters have her worried."

"Has she any idea who sent them?"

"No idea at all. Except she feels it must be someone who is married."

Regan gave him a brief look, then took a final bite of pie, wiped his mouth with a paper napkin, and looked up again. "Well, in a few more days she won't be wrong."

That was telling him, Calvin thought. Regan was eying him a trifle sardonically. He asked, "Does that give you any ideas?"

"It points a finger," said Calvin.

"Yeah. That would give some reason for Mrs. Cromer's worry, wouldn't it?"

"Believe me, she has no idea. No suspicion. If she had," said Calvin slowly, "knowing her—and I've known her all her life—I can tell you she'd urge the girl—no matter what the cost—to come out with the truth."

Regan gave him another look, a long look this time. "Well, strange as it may seem, counselor, I'm believing you."

"If you knew so much," said Calvin, after a moment, "do you mind telling me why you didn't get the girl's testimony in the beginning and keep your client out of jeopardy?"

"Fair enough," said Regan. "I'll answer that one. I was a damned fool."

He went on: "I'll tell you—this off the record, counselor?"

"Definitely."

"My client wrote that girl a letter. Sent me with it the first morning. Said she'd know where to take it. I didn't believe him, naturally. Not after I'd got a load of that red hair. But I let it ride. Are you familiar with criminal procedure in Tennessee?"

Calvin shook his head. "I'm not a criminal lawyer. Taxes."

"Well, it's like this. First the case comes before a magistrate—the justice of the peace—at which time the prosecutor and witnesses for the state appear. The defendant is entitled to have subpoenas issued for his witnesses. I wanted to call this girl but my client was dead set against it. Told me she wasn't the girl, said he wouldn't give the real girl away, said he'd refuse to say he had an alibi if I called her. He wasn't going to give his alibi, he said, till it came to a trial, and he was sure it wouldn't come to that, for they'd find the killer before that. He was so damned sure of himself, I thought so too."

He gave Calvin another look and said, "I guess I played it wrong. The J.P. found a crime had been committed, which there had, and that the evidence was against the defendant, which it was, and Tex was held for investigation by the Grand Jury of the Criminal Court of the county. The legal term of the judgment is that the magistrate—that's the J.P.—binds the party charged over to court."

"I see."

"When you're up before the Grand Jury the witnesses for the prosecution can be called but not the witnesses for the defense. So I had to sit back and let the jury concur in the findings of the J.P. that there was 'probable cause' that my client committed the crime. They returned a true bill and he's got to stand trial before the Criminal Court. That's when I can subpoena her. And maybe I did all right," he said tentatively, "not calling her before. Mrs. Burk Cauldron will carry more weight than Miss Rita Rand. Surprise witness."

He went on: "Anyway, that's the way I've got to play it. I'm letting it ride a few days more. But before the trial I'm going to have a little talk with Mrs. Burk Cauldron. She's going to be my star witness and it's nice to know what your witness is going to say before she's on the stand."

"It would be nice," said Calvin slowly, "to get your hands on another suspect."

Regan's eyes sparked and he said softly, "My God, if that girl clams up—after he's kept her in the clear! If she gives him the double-cross—"

"I didn't mean that. I meant that it would solve everybody's problem to find the real criminal."

Regan said ironically, "True, counselor! You got any ideas?"

"As to identity—no," said Calvin slowly. "I suppose they've checked on anyone that was near."

"Check and double check. The two Cauldron hands were at White's miles away. The farmer and Carl, the stable boy, were working over a sick mare, in and out the kitchen fixing up a mash. Nearest neighbor is old Judd at the filling station and he's lame. Next is Mayhews—away in Canada, house closed. Next the Rands, and George Rand was playing cards in town. Next the fox farm—run by an old couple with four kids under eleven. Nothing then till the Country Club and nobody had wandered away from that."

"How about somebody going through—somebody in a car?"

"They stopped all cars, both sides of Somerset. Alerted the towns for miles around and all the farmers. Everybody turned out. And Judd swears no car went past him after the dog howled. Not till the sheriff drove up. The only thing is," said Regan, "that he could have come and gone on foot. But where is he now? The sheriff hasn't turned up a damned thing. But you want to talk to Tex. Let's go."

Calvin talked to Tex Miller through bars in a long corridorlike room. Regan walked away, after he made the explanation, and the guard stepped politely out of earshot. Tex Miller was a big, blond, boyish-looking fellow with a beautiful gladiator's body and a slow, beguiling smile. Calvin told him that Mrs. Cromer wanted him to know she thought his letter was very honest sounding, and Miller smiled—that's when Calvin saw how nice his smile was—and said, "It sure was a hard letter to write. But I wanted her to know I didn't do it." He seemed to think his simple statement was entirely credible.

Then Calvin said, making his voice very low, "And I've some other word for you. Miss Rand came to see me this morning."

Miller's eyes opened. "She did?"

"She wanted advice—and I'm an attorney, though not in criminal law."

"You know," said Miller conversationally, "that word is beginning to get me."

"I can imagine. Well, she talked to me—in confidence. I advised her to speak out. To give your counsel the facts. And I advise you to."

Tex Miller did not answer for some moments. He drew deeply on his cigarette, then took it out and studied it thoughtfully. He said, sounding embarrassed, "Yes, I guess we have to. I hate to get her into it—but it's beginning to get worrying. I certainly thought they'd be on the right track before this. But they can't do anything to me, can they, when I wasn't there?"

"They've got to know you weren't there."

"I guess they've got to," Tex admitted. "I was hoping—"

"You can't expect Regan to get you off when you keep him in the dark."

"He isn't in the dark," said Tex, with his slow smile. "He just pretends he is because I'm playing it that way. But I guess I've got to play it differently now. But they can't do anything to me when I wasn't there," he insisted, but his insistence did not hide the worry in his blue eyes.

"He makes a good impression," Calvin admitted to Regan, coming out. "But you need another suspect."

"You think so?"

"The jury may think they're lying about the time. And no matter how decent he seems now, who knows what he'd do when he's drunk?"

"I've seen him drunk. He goes soft and sleepy."

"You haven't seen him drunk when he's steamed up over a girl he can't have and runs into something sweet."

Regan looked worriedly at him. "I wish you'd believe in that dumb bastard. I do. I didn't take this just to have a case. He and I hit the beaches—though not together—and we got sort of pally when he came to town. But I could cut his throat for the way he held out on me. Fun's fun, and love's love, but this guy is facing a murder charge."

There was only one thing to do, Calvin thought now— Helen must get the police to search those woods. He planned all the way up to the Folly. Men in cars at strategic intervals on the highway outside the land—that would take a lot of cars. And men inside, beating the cover. He could help with that; he knew many a hideout in those woods. For one place, there was the old cave, the Hideaway.

He parked before the Folly and got out just as the main door opened and a young man came out, the young man he had seen at tea yesterday. Rawley, the art expert. He looked, Calvin thought, infernally young to be expert on anything.

He was hatless, the sun full on his face, and again something about that face, something indescribable in the arrangement of the planes, some subtlety of modeling, made Calvin feel, more strongly than ever, that there was something he ought to be remembering—some association. Again the words "bare feet" came to him. That didn't make sense. Nor did the swift change in Rawley make sense. He had been looking very gay and pleased when he came out, but at sight of Calvin his face blanked out except for a wary, almost hostile, intentness in his eyes.

Calvin said cheerfully, "I hear you've found a Romney."

"Yes."

"That's fine."

Rawley made no response. He waited just long enough to make sure that Calvin wasn't going to say more, then swung off across the turf. Calvin looked after him, thinking it no wonder that old Henry didn't like his manners, but admiring, involuntarily, the swift, easy way he moved. Like a wild thing.

A wild thing. *Little wildcat*. Now he remembered. Of course! Bare feet. He remembered bare, thorn-scratched legs with a blue skirt above them and an odd, provocative face, half sullen, half inviting, with wary eyes, bright as a squirrel's, that had looked mistrustfully at him when he had ridden in with Burk.

That was the summer they were fifteen. Burk was nearly sixteen, big for his age. They had ridden back in the mountains on some pretext of Burk's and the girl was sitting on a log by a stream. He'd been surprised to find Burk knew a hillbilly girl. He could tell from the way they talked that it wasn't for the first time.

She sounded intimate with Burk but whenever he came near, as he walked the horses up and down, she was quiet and embarrassed, twisting her bare toes in the grass and waiting for him to walk on. Once he had looked back and she was laughing and he could see that she was pretty.

On the way back Burk had been in high spirits. "Little wildcat," he had said. Her name was Robin Rawley. Her people were dead and she lived with a cousin. "We aren't saying anything about this," Burk cautioned, and Calvin had been both uneasy and secretly admiring.

The next year he heard the name again. It was said that Burk had got the Rawley girl in trouble and she had gone away. Burk wasn't at the Folly that summer but at some camp. Afterward the incident was never mentioned between them and it had dropped out of Calvin's consciousness.

Twenty-two years ago, that ride back into the hills. This young Rawley could be no more than twenty-one, his unsmiling stiffness an attempt to seem older. Of course, Calvin told himself, he could be mistaken. The likeness was startling but that might be coincidence—look at the doubles for Hollywood stars. But—the likeness and the name?

He thought about the way Rawley and Burk had met yesterday. Like strangers. Burk had spoken about seeing him in the gallery one time and Rita Rand had reminded him that they had met at tea. What had Abbie said about that tea? *He wore an eyeshade and not a word out of him.* Helen had spoken of his sudden fits of illness, of his holing up in his room. Had he been hiding from Burk?

But he had come out yesterday without an eyeshade, he had come out with an air of bravado, now Calvin came to think about it. Burk had been too consumed with his anger toward his sister to pay any attention to him. The name Rawley ought to have meant something to Burk, but Calvin had the feeling that Burk's emotional memories were considerably overlaid. Rawley was not an unusual name about here.

It was very curious. But the young man had been sent by Lambert.

He turned—he had been standing still looking off after Rawley—and rang the bell. Ida let him in, with a smile of greeting for him. "Nice to see you again, Mr. Calvin."

She was Henry's wife, his second wife, Calvin seemed to remember. He smiled back. "Nice to be here."

"You haven't been here for a long time."

"New York has kept me busy."

She knew why he hadn't been back. She'd seen him marching out of this house, his head high, his back stiff.

"You look just the same," he told her. "So does Henry."

"Oh, we keep spry. But we've been through a lot of trouble in these years."

"I can imagine."

She said sadly, "Miss Lucy's going was the very worst. But there's no use crying on yesterday's shoulder," she said, brisk again in the concise way that was once more familiar. "Come right in. Miss Helen's here some place."

Helen was coming down the stairs. She was slighter than he had realized, he saw now; a tall, too-thin girl with that look of spirit about her which had always stirred him. She greeted him eagerly. "You'd better come upstairs—this place is a madhouse of cleaning. That wedding!"

At the top of the stairs she paused. "We can't go into the gallery—there's Rawley."

"He just went out."

"He may come in. And John's in the library." The library, like the gallery, was on the second floor. "We'd better go into my bedroom. My papers are there."

Her clear voice was throwing out the implication that their business was with papers. He followed into the big room and took a chair facing her as she sat down on the end of the chaise longue. "Oh, I'm so glad you came," she said tensely. "I called the Nordstroms finally—but you were out."

"It took a little time." He did not mention the time out for Rita Rand, but told her, concisely, of the meeting with Regan and then with Tex Miller. He said then, "As I told you, any impression, even the most favorable impression, has no value. We have to get the facts. Get those woods searched."

She agreed breathlessly. "Yes, we must. He's there, Calvin. And last night he tried again."

"Tried?"

"To kill me."

He looked at her aghast. "You went into the woods?"

"Oh, no, no. Not like that. Here, in this room. In the night. He tried to smother me again."

"Oh, Helen!" Relief and disbelief were in his voice.

"You think I was dreaming again? Let me tell you. I know it's fantastic, but I'm not hysterical. Let me tell you exactly what happened."

She told him with great precision. About the tray with the sandwich, the milk, the thermos of coffee. About the pill Niel had put on it for her. She told how she had touched nothing but one cup of milk and had then poured out the second cup and let it stand. And how suddenly and heavily she had gone to sleep.

She said, "And then— Oh, it was like the time, that first night when Jude made such a row. Only it was more dreadful. At first there was the dream, that dream of drowning, of being underwater, of not being able to breathe, and then I didn't seem drowning but choking—something horrible, an octopus thing, was reaching out and twining around my throat. And then— Did you ever dream and know you were dreaming but couldn't wake out of it? It was like that, Calvin. I knew all this drowning and octopus thing was a dream but still I couldn't wake, couldn't breathe—I felt smothering."

She was breathing quickly as if the terror of it was gripping her again. "I was awake, I was conscious that I was awake, but still I couldn't breathe, couldn't move. There was something over my face, pressing down, smothering. I think I was just blacking out. And then it stopped. The pressing-down stopped. And I got it off."

"Got what off?" he said quietly.

"The pillow. My pillow was over my face. And the telephone was ringing. It rings beside my bed and downstairs in the hall. People were running down to it—John went down and answered it. And Ida stopped at my door to ask if it had waked me, if she could do anything—I'd gone to bed with a headache. I could hardly answer her, my breath was so gone. But I did answer. And then I managed to get up and look around. I had a gun, Lee's old gun. So I locked my door and slept. I could sleep," she said, "because I was so drugged—that milk had drugged me. That's why I couldn't struggle in time."

He looked at her, dismayed. "Oh, Helen!"

She stared back at him. "You don't believe me?"

"Of course I believe that you dreamed this—that you felt as you say. But don't you see, my dear, it was just a dream? You'd got the pillow over your face—"

"But listen! You don't know the rest. Everything was gone from my tray—except the sandwich. The coffee thermos was empty and I hadn't opened it, and the cup of milk I'd left was gone."

He said gently, "And what does that prove?"

"Why, that they were drugged—all the liquids were drugged. And then emptied out, so there would be no trace."

After a moment he said, "And the pill? Was that gone too?"

"Yes, it was gone. And I hadn't taken it."

"Of course you'd taken it. That's why you don't remember about your taking the other cup of milk and the coffee."

"I never opened the coffee. Not till after. And it was empty."

"Perhaps it had never been filled. Mistakes happen."

She looked at him in open dismay. The excitement went out of her face. Then she said abruptly, in a flat voice, "You think I'm imagining things, don't you?"

"Just what were you imagining?" he asked carefully. "That someone had got in?"

"Yes. Yes, of course."

"There were no signs of breaking in, were there?"

"Why no, but anyone could climb up—in some places it's possible."

"Helen, think a minute. Could he have got in early enough to get at your tray there in the kitchen?"

"They put trays on a table in the back hall till Ida or Henry takes them up. It's—accessible."

"But with people all about—Ida and Henry and Dolcey?"

"He could have got at it in my room—it was there quite a while when I was having a bath. My door was unlocked. Niel said he looked in once."

"Granted that's possible. Granted he could get at your tray and drug the liquids. Granted he could get out of the house when the phone rang without being seen. But how would he know that you were going to have a tray last night? Don't you see that you are imagining—"

"Lucy was killed," she said in that same flat, abrupt voice. "I didn't imagine that. And if Tex Miller didn't kill her, someone else did. And that someone is still here. Some madman—"

"Helen, whoever killed Lucy was a madman, as you say. A crazed creature. Not planning. Now such a madman could hardly come in here—twice—first drug your drinks, and then come back and empty out the drugged stuff and start in to choke you, would he? That would take cool planning, premeditation."

"You make it sound fantastic," she said, after a moment. He could feel the doubt behind her resentment.

"It is fantastic," he said. "You had a nightmare. Both times. A pillow over your face. It's no wonder you had—no wonder you dreamed what you did. You were wrought up."

"You sound like John."

"I'm looking at it realistically. I don't say that you were mistaken about the man in the woods—though there may be an explanation for that. But," he said, determined on blunt frankness, "I am less inclined to believe in him now than I was yesterday."

She looked at him intently a moment, then her eyes lowered to the hands gripped on her knee. Very consciously she relaxed them. "You think it's just nightmares, then?"

"Don't you? Now you come to think it over. Nightmares can be pretty realistic. But the notion of someone moving about unseen in this house full of people— Weren't John and Rawley here?"

"Rawley didn't go down to dinner. But Burk was here all night," she admitted.

"And Niel was in and out. No, I don't think there's any real foundation for belief. You had a nightmare—the pillow was over your face."

"It was pressed down on my face." But she said it with less conviction. Then she threw out with a faintly mocking laugh. "Unless I imagined that, too. But my nose is tender," she added, with reviving stubbornness.

"I expect you've been fingering it all morning. The weight of the pillow might have made it sore. And you probably were smothering under that pillow. Don't sleep with a pillow any more," he said anxiously.

She laughed a little unsteadily. She said, "I don't want to believe that someone was trying to kill me. And God knows I don't want to get neurotic."

"You're not neurotic," he said stoutly. "But you've had so much horror, which you are trying to keep from thinking about, that it is not surprising you have these dreams—and fears. Your subconscious won't let you off. There's a transference of horror to something you can be openly afraid about. I don't know how to say it—Niel could wrap it up in medical jargon—but that's the general idea. You don't dare think about the real horror, so your subconscious comes up with something else, dreams about drowning, about an octopus, about pillow pressing. Deep down inside you, you know it's all a substitute."

She was silent for quite a time. Then she said, "And the man in the woods? Was that my subconscious too?"

"It could have been. It could have been an accidental trespasser. Or it could have been the real criminal."

She said acutely, "But you don't think it's the real criminal now? You think I imagined it."

He thought about it. He said honestly, "I'm inclined to think it's nerves. But I'd have those woods searched, just to make sure."

After another silence she said, "But where is the man? If Tex didn't do it—and you're inclined to think he didn't—"

"Only inclined. And that counts for nothing."

"All right, only inclined. Call it a fifty-fifty chance. But if he didn't, someone did. Where is he now?"

"Not necessarily in the woods. He might have got straight down to Somerset and his family is covering up for him. I think there's a lot to be done about this case."

She drew a long breath. "I guess you're right. And it's a comfort."

There was a knock on the door. At Helen's "Come in," Ida appeared and said, "Miss Van Hoyt's downstairs."

"Van Hoyt— Oh, Betty!" Helen put on quick animation. "That's Betty Meade, Calvin. You remember."

He remembered Betty Meade but she was hard to recognize in the young woman who sat chatting with John Cauldron. The blonde hair that had glinted so brightly across the tennis courts had become dark blonde, and the girlish prettiness wore a sophisticated air. Her skin was a smooth honey color.

"I heard you were in town," she told Calvin. She looked at him interestedly. "I hear you're a great success in New York."

"You've been listening to Aunt Abbie."

"Mother has. I got here only last night. And I came right up—" she transferred her attention to Helen—"because I want to hear about Burk's getting married. Here I was, counting on his beauing me around this summer."

"You should have come last summer," said Helen.

"Maybe Calvin will do." She gave him a direct look again. "Now tell me about Burk's girl. I used to be madly in love with Burk."

"She's very, very pretty—and very young." Helen was animated and bright, a different Helen from the tense girl who had said, "He tried again . . . to kill me."

They had tea in the corner of the big room. "This is natural," said Betty. "Your father always had tea. It's one of the first things I remember about coming here. I was fearfully impressed."

She did most of the talking. Calvin learned that she had not been back for three years. "Mother and father like coming to see me in Chicago." She threw out to Calvin, "Ren lived in Chicago, you know."

Calvin had no notion who Ren had been—he seemed in the past tense—but he gathered he had been someone prosperous, for Betty's pearls were lustrous and the pin on her pale-gray frock was not costume jewelry.

"I'm going to make up to you," she told Calvin. "I get to New York once in a while. I'd adore to have a handsome gent take me to the Stork Club and Twenty-One."

Calvin laughed. "The waiters don't know me. Better settle for Three Little Indians. It's off the tourist beat."

Helen was called to the telephone. Betty looked after her and said, "She's wonderful, isn't she? Not giving a sign . . . but I know how it is."

"Do you?" said John Cauldron. The sudden words had a grating rasp. "Have you, too, lost a child?"

The hard, detached voice was as unfriendly as a thrust of cold steel. Startled, Calvin thought, Why, his nerves are on edge. The plain, gingerbread face was so quiet and unrevealing that harshness from it was a minor shock.

Betty Van Hoyt stared at him, her lips parted. Then she sat up a little straighter. "I never had a child," she said. "So of course I don't really know. I can only imagine."

Calvin began to like her. He said, "That's all any of us can do."

John got up. "If you'll excuse me—"

"*Well,*" said Betty expressively, "he certainly has changed from the young man who used to try to kiss me behind Burk's back!"

"He did, did he?"

"Oh, once or twice. I didn't encourage it. I expect he has never liked me since. Though that's a long time to bear a grudge."

Calvin tried to think what young John Cauldron had been like but gave it up. "I didn't know he was that much of a wolf."

"Oh, not a wolf. Definitely not a wolf. More the hungry orphan outside a bakeshop."

"Well, he *was* an orphan," said Calvin reflectively. He added, "Like me."

"Oh, not like you! You were a charmer. Even though I was in love with Burk I couldn't bear it not to have you even *see* me."

Calvin laughed out. "You're a lovely fraud. But John isn't bearing any grudge. He's on edge with all that has happened and that hit him the wrong way. Nobody can compare to Helen."

"Hello, you too!" That was Abbie Nordstrom's voice, coming across the wide room. Calvin felt mildly annoyed at the interruption. He had been amused by this new Betty. His aunt was going on: "So glad to see you, Betty. Your mother said you'd come."

Betty went to meet her, and they embraced, guarding Betty's lipstick. They said a few things back and forth, then Abbie turned to Calvin. "I wish I'd known you were coming. Then you could have brought the Sanka."

"Sanka?"

"Niel said that Helen had a quart thermos of coffee on her tray last night. I think she is drinking far too much coffee. So I brought her some Sanka."

Calvin stood still, his hand on the back of the chair from which he had risen. A quart of coffee. Helen had not said the thermos held a quart. That was a lot of coffee to drink without remembering it. Four very large cups. More of the average size. The answer, of course, was that the thermos had not been filled.

Abruptly he turned, said hastily and vaguely, "That reminds me—" and went to the back of the house.

Chapter Six

The kitchen was vast enough, as Burk Cauldron had said, for a battalion of cooks. There was a huge fireplace in which, presumably, the first Peter Cauldron had roasted half an ox at a time, until he had beggared himself of the price of an ox. Now a chimney pipe ran into it, connecting with an old black range, and another pipe served an incongruously modern white stove. At a table by the window a colored woman was sitting, peeling apples into a yellow bowl in her lap. She had a smooth, unlined face, which she lifted at Calvin's approach.

"I was looking for Ida," he told her.

"I'm Dolcey." She had a voice like her face, smooth and pleasant. "Ida's upstairs. You want I should get her, Mr. Morse?"

"I want the one who took care of Mrs. Cromer's tray last night."

"I fixed Miss Helen's tray. And I washed it up this morning when Ida brought it down."

"Then you can tell me." Calvin sat down on the edge of the table. A black-and-white cat came out from under it and rubbed against his leg. He said, making it very casual and friendly, "We've been arguing about the amount of coffee Mrs. Cromer is drinking—or should drink. My aunt thinks it's too much, so she brought out some Sanka."

"She gave it to me," said Dolcey. She smiled. "I like your aunty first rate but she got notions about eating and drinking."

Calvin smiled back. "Yes, she has. The thing is, Mrs. Cromer says she didn't drink any coffee last night. Do you remember if the thermos was full when it went up?"

"Indeed it was. I let it run over before I put the cork in so it keeps scalding hot."

Well, that disposed of the theory of emptiness. Calvin said slowly, "How much of it did she drink?"

"She drank it all."

"You're quite sure?"

"I'm sure," said Dolcey firmly. "Ida, she noticed it too, when she brought down the tray. Miss Helen hadn't eaten a bite but she drunk up both the milk and coffee."

"A quart of coffee?"

"A night's a long time."

"It's odd," said Calvin. "Mrs. Cromer says she doesn't remember taking any coffee. I had an idea the thermos hadn't been filled. . . . She said she wanted some coffee early this morning and the thermos was empty then."

"She took it in the night. That thermos was full up when it went upstairs. She took it in the night."

Calvin sat thinking about it. He had wanted facts and he had been given a fact, but his mind, unsatisfied, turned it over and over. Finally he asked, "Were there two cups on the tray?"

"They was two cups," said Dolcey patiently.

"Then there must have been traces of coffee in one?"

The woman glanced at him, a veiled scrutiny in her eyes. The knife went slower on the apple she was peeling. "It's funny you ask that," she said reflectively. "One of the cups was clean. Never used at all."

"But the other—did it have coffee in it?"

"No sign of coffee at all. Just milk stains. . . . I guess she drunk the coffee up first, then drunk the milk."

"No, it wasn't like that. She says she drank a cup of milk last night, then poured out a second cup and let it stand. This morning, she says, it was gone. So she must have taken it in the night and not remembered. . . . And she must have taken the coffee too, and not remembered."

"She got a right not to remember with all this trouble on her," said Dolcey pityingly. "And all this wedding coming." Then she said consideringly, "But she didn't use the cup for coffee. . . . Funny. . . . It isn't like Miss Helen to drink out of a bottle."

The spirals of apple peeling dropped slowly into her lap, as slowly as her words. "But I guess that's the way of it."

Calvin sat silent, intent. Then, abruptly, he got up. He said, with forced casualness, "Well—that accounts for her not sleeping well."

The mild voice told him, "No trouble accounting for her not sleeping. Her one ewe lamb set on and destroyed."

He said, "Thank you," in a preoccupied voice and went out into the back garden. He struck off along a hedge-lined path, his hands deep in his pockets.

Like Dolcey, he didn't see Helen putting a bottle of coffee to her mouth. The stuff would be too hot to drink. And he didn't see Helen pulling out the cork and waiting for an entire quart to cool when she could have poured out a cup at once.

Helen had been positive that she had poured out a cup of milk and left it on her tray. Now, suppose she drank that milk without remembering it. Suppose that at some time in the night, before midnight when the telephone definitely roused her, she had roused enough to want coffee and to pour it into the used empty cup. There would be coffee stains left in the cup.

But Dolcey had said there were no coffee stains.

Helen had said the milk jug held only two cupfuls. If there was a drop or two left, and she had poured them into the cup later, that would not be enough to obliterate coffee stains. So it could not have happened like that.

Now, suppose she didn't drink the cup of milk. Suppose it was there on her tray when she wanted coffee. Wouldn't she pour the coffee into the empty cup? It was the natural thing to do. But the second cup had not been used. So you must either believe that Helen had drunk out of the thermos—waiting an indeterminate time for a thermos of scalding coffee to cool—or that she had poured the milk in the cup back into the jug and used that cup for her coffee. For cup after cup of coffee. Then, after downing the quart, she had poured out the milk again and drunk that, thus removing the stains of coffee.

That was nonsense. Helen, in a hurry for coffee, would have used the empty cup.

He went over and over it, arranging and rearranging the possibilities in his mind. He went over Helen's story. She had believed—until he had talked her down—that the thermos had been heavy when she first lifted it. She had been right. She had believed—until he talked her down—that she had not touched the second cup of milk or taken the coffee or the pill. And he had felt she was too tense and shaken to be credited. He had prated about fear transference and substitutes.

But now—

All right, he said to himself, his hands making fists in his pockets as they did in stress of argument, now look at the other side of it. Suppose he accepted absolutely the story Helen had told in such detail. What had happened last night?

The liquids had been drugged, heavily drugged, because one glass of milk had sent her off. And someone had come into her room in the dead of night, carefully emptied the telltale stuff, and taken away the pill. Then he had put a pillow over Helen's face and tried to smother her—he would have smothered her except for the accident of the telephone.

According to Helen, it was the second time this had been tried. The first time the dog had saved her. Now the dog was dead. Died of grieving, they said, but he could have been put out of the way.

According to Helen, there had been incidents in the woods. The rock flung at her horse. The stealthy sounds following her. One such incident might be accident. But a succession . . . followed by last night's attempt.

Now, what did this mean? Who would want to kill Helen? The same person who had killed Lucy? There was no way to know, Calvin thought, balancing possibilities. Lucy's death might have been a sex crime. Or it might not have been—it might have been linked to these attempts on Helen, and last night's attempt was not made by any sex fiend. It had been deliberate, premeditated. It had been made by someone who knew very well what he was about.

Who would benefit by Helen's death? That was the cold, brutal question. Who would benefit?

Helen had money, the money her father had left her outright. What was she doing with it, now that her child was dead? She had given Niel ten thousand for the hospital, Abbie had said. She must have made a will after Lucy died—Will Bently would see to that. Probably made some division between Burk and John. That was conjecture but, it seemed to Calvin, very reasonable conjecture.

In that event Burk would benefit but not John. For money, Calvin felt, would mean nothing to John against the loss of his home here with Helen.

But the money was a small part of Helen's possessions. Cauldron's Folly. That was her great treasure, hers to enjoy but not to dispose of. The vast stone pile, the temple to implacable pride, which the first Peter Cauldron had reared and the succeeding generations had served.

Calvin swung about and stared up at it. The upper stories were flushed with late sunlight, and the square tower looked made of rosy stone, but the lower walls were black in shadow, dark as the patches of ivy on them. Calvin said softly, "Damn you!" to those hard walls.

Cauldron s Folly. If Helen had died last night, who would have title to it?

He must get hold of the will, he thought, but in the meantime his mind worked on the terms he'd heard so often quoted. To Helen for life, then to her surviving children. If she had no surviving child to take, then to the children of Burk. Burk, at the moment, had no child to take, but the courts, Calvin knew from experience, normally allowed subsequently born children to take. There had been a case similar to this, he recalled, recently cited in his office.

Burk had been bitter yesterday because his children, not himself, had been named in the will, but, Calvin reflected, as soon as Burk had a child he would be guardian for the twenty-one years before that child reached maturity. He would be in possession of the Folly. Twenty-one years is a long time. And if the child died, Burk, as its natural heir, would inherit.

Burk. He came back to Burk each time. Burk had been in the Folly last night. He was in a rage against Helen. Calvin could hear his light, hard voice, edged with threat: *But I think I shall, Helen. I think I shall someday bring home to you what it is to be hurt. Really hurt.*

As if her child's death were not enough!

Burk had been in the Folly the night after Lucy was killed. He had been there before she was killed. He and Rita had driven off about the time John left to go for the girl. He had driven Rita home and left. He might have hidden his car in the woods and come back on foot to the Folly. But that would mean premeditation. That would mean he knew Lucy would get out at the gate and he couldn't know that.

No, it was more reasonable, if you were to work on the supposition that Burk was guilty, it was more reasonable to believe that he had driven back, on impulse. Judd would not have seen him—Judd had said he had come out when the dog was howling. Burk's car might have been just behind John's car with Lucy. And Burk could have seen Lucy get out at the gate. He could have got out and run to her, just as the taillights of John's car were going off to the right.

Perhaps he meant only to talk to her, to enlist her influence. But a rush of rage might have overwhelmed him, a realization of what it would mean to him to have this girl out of the way.

And then, once he had done the dreadful thing, he was committed to go on. For Lucy's death was useless without Helen's.

But it might not have been like that. Burk might not have killed Lucy. Burk might have a perfectly good alibi for the time after he had left Rita. But Lucy's death might have started him thinking about Helen's. He might have made an immediate attempt. And then waited. Until the dog was out of the way. Until there was opportunity. And then he had acted again, alarmed at Calvin's return. Rita had said that he was "furious" because Calvin had come back, fearful that Helen might remarry.

Calvin had been tramping blindly up one path and down another, instinctively keeping away from buildings; now he found he was back in the rose garden, beside the boulder that marked the grave of the first Cauldron wife. He had a sudden feeling that someone might be watching curiously his erratic marching, and, for something natural-seeming to do, he stooped and read the name rudely lettered in the stone. Rosamund. From Fairfax, Virginia. A once-lighthearted belle in crinoline.

He straightened, still staring at the boulder, his thoughts racing. Burk was a possibility. Who else? Who else had opportunity and motive? . . . What about Rawley? Perhaps illegitimate children had legal rights in Tennessee—they could inherit, in California, if the father had acknowledged the paternity. He had no proof at all that Rawley was Burk's natural child—only the memory of a face, but that memory was one of the things indelibly engraved on a boy's mind. It had been overlaid, forgotten, but once the attention found it, there it was vivid and unique. There was the likeness and the name.

It was a strange tangle. Burk's son—if it was Burk's son—there in that house. He looked up at the Folly again.

The shadows had crept higher; only the top windows caught the light, reflecting it in blurred and desultory gleams. And there in that house was Helen, in the renewed confidence in her surroundings that he, like a blind fool, had restored to her.

He went quickly in, through the terrace door. His aunt was in the front hall, rising from the telephone. Helen had gone, she told him, to have dinner with Betty. She had been staying to do some telephoning. "We couldn't imagine what had become of you," she said. "Dolcey said you went out back. I know Betty would have asked you if you'd been here."

He said, "I'll leave Helen a note."

Abbie was fingering. "It's too bad we each have a car."

"Do you mind if I don't show up for dinner tonight? I've got my key, if I should be late."

"That sounds like old times." She smiled at him affectionately. "There's paper in the writing room."

He found the desk and wrote hurriedly: "Helen dear, you were right and I was wrong. That was no dream. Be on your guard." He stared distastefully at what he had written. It sounded theatrical as all hell. That was why murder was so easy, he thought. You felt such a fool when you had melodramatic suspicions. So murder could sneak up on you.

He could picture Helen staring at it, incredulously at first, then with rising panic, and impulsively he added: "My dear, dear girl." Then he wrote: "Tell no one what you told me till I see you again. I'll see you as soon as possible."

He addressed the envelope and sealed it carefully and gave it to Ida, whom he discovered in the dining room. "You'll see Mrs. Cromer gets this as soon as she comes in? It's important."

"I'll see to it." Ida put it in her pocket, then her hand came out with a small object she held out to Calvin. "Oh! I kept forgetting to give this to Mis' Nordstrom. It must be the doctor's. Would you give it to her?"

It was a clinical thermometer. Ida explained: "I found it in Miss Helen's bed this morning. . . . It must be the doctor's, for hers is in the bathroom."

He pocketed it. "I'll give it to him. You'll see she has the letter at once?"

"Don't you worry about it, Mr. Calvin. I'll see to it."

She smiled to him as she used to smile in the old days when he had hung about waiting for Helen Cauldron and he smiled back though there was no mirth in him.

He came back into the front hall just as Rawley was going up the stairs. Calvin glanced after him, hesitated, then the urge in him made him follow. When he opened the door into the gallery Rawley was across the room, stooping over a picture on the floor. He spun about quickly.

Calvin said, "I saw you coming in."

It seemed characteristic of the young man to make no reply. He stood, waiting. It was too dark to see his face—his back was toward the windows—but his attitude was unwelcoming.

"I want to ask you a question," said Calvin. His voice was frank and friendly. "Are you, by any chance, a relative of Robin Rawley's? I met her as a boy—and there's a remarkable likeness."

For a long moment Rawley stood looking at him, palpably taken by surprise, uncertain. Then he said, as if feeling his way, "Do you think there's a likeness?"

"A very strong one."

Rawley was silent for a moment more. Then he said softly, almost jeeringly, "You're smart. I had the feeling you were looking at me."

"Why not? Your mother was a very unusual-looking girl."

Then Rawley said truculently, "What business is it of yours?"

"No business at all." Calvin's voice was easy, though his nerves were taut. "I was just interested."

"I'm not hiding it," said Rawley, his excitement mounting. "I'll tell them when the time comes. . . . Or have you been talking about me?"

"Not at all . . . I merely wondered . . . Anyone who ever saw your mother couldn't fail to wonder."

"*He* didn't," said the young man shortly. Then with a sly triumph, "But I didn't give him much chance."

"But you must expect people to guess . . . since you use the name."

"I'm not ashamed of the name!" The young man's voice was so savage that Calvin felt he had touched off dynamite. "I could use another if I'd a mind to, and maybe I will, someday you don't expect. But my mother's name was a good name."

"Of course. I only meant—"

The other came a step closer. "You think my mother was easy got, don't you? You think Burk Cauldron only had to whistle and she came running. Well, I'll tell you one thing. She was married by a hill preacher and she had a paper to prove it. She gave it to me before she died. Words by a preacher and a paper are good enough for any court."

"Then why don't you—"

"Never you mind why I do or don't! That's purely my business." He stopped; he seemed to realize that his outburst had said more than he had intended. The anger in his voice gave place to sullenness. "I wouldn't have told you that much only you guessed, and you were looking down on my mother."

"Indeed I was not."

"My mother was a fine woman. She went to some place where no one knew her and she was always Mrs. Rawley there. She had taken money not to make them trouble— that's the way the Cauldrons did things," he said bitterly. "The high and mighty Cauldrons. But she brought me up to know I was as good as they were. That's why she never married again. She wanted that paper to be good."

It couldn't be good, Calvin thought, or old Peter Cauldron would have taken steps about it. A hill preacher marriage. The man might not have been ordained.

"My mother was wonderful. She was a singer, a natural singer. She earned money by it, in clubs and eating places. She sang hillbilly songs, mostly, all sad and sweet."

It was strange to think of the little girl on the log growing up into a singer who sang her plaintive songs in smoke-filled city rooms. What was that Bible verse—? About singing your songs in strange lands.

Calvin said sincerely, "I think she must have been very fine."

"She tried to teach me to sing. But I never wanted to do anything but paint. But you can't make money at painting. That's why I took the job at the Institute. It was an office job—in Lambert's office. That way I could study, part time."

"It is rather extraordinary," said Calvin. "The coincidence. Your being sent here."

Rawley gave him a sharp look. He said suspiciously, "They haven't told you?"

"Told me what?"

"I wasn't sent." Rawley gave a short laugh. "My job was in Lambert's office and I opened that letter and sent the answer. It was like it was meant," he said, with sudden intensity. Then, defensively, "But Lambert couldn't have come anyway. He's got more work than he can take care of. So that part was all right. . . That letter was my chance. I'd always meant to come someday, to take a look at the high and mighty Cauldrons, and this was like it was meant."

It was as curious a coincidence as any he had ever known, Calvin thought. That letter from Cauldron Hall coming into the hands of Burk Cauldron's son. He said slowly, turning it over, "But why do you ask if they've told me? They think Lambert sent you."

"They don't think it now. They've got in touch. But it's all right," Rawley said, with that trace of sly triumph again. "I told John Cauldron I came because it was my chance to show what I could do. Lambert thinks he knows it all but I've learned more than he thinks."

He looked about the walls, at the paintings on them, at the paintings stacked along the floor. "I can do this as well as Lambert," he said arrogantly. "I haven't cheated them. It isn't costing them anything but my keep, and when I'm through they needn't pay me a thing unless they're satisfied. John Cauldron thought that was all right. He thought me a smart, ambitious young man."

He laughed. Calvin didn't like his laugh, it was too cocky, too full of pride in himself. But he liked the stiff dignity with which Rawley said, "Now I've got things straightened out I'd be obliged to you not to say anything. Not till I'm ready."

"You mean to tell them yourself?"

"I'll tell them . . . when I've finished my job."

Calvin said slowly, turning over those last words, "I agree that it's purely your business, as you say. I shan't mention it. Though I think it would make no difference to Helen Cromer. You could count on her sympathy."

He had used the word deliberately. Rawley's eyes literally blazed. "I'm no charity kin," he said harshly. "Someday I'll have what I'm entitled to. With no thanks to them."

There was such hate in his voice that Calvin was startled into answering harshness. "Helen never did you any wrong . . . nor Lucy."

"They're Cauldrons."

Chapter Seven

The pure hate in that voice echoed in Calvin as he left the house. And there had been hate in Burk's voice. So now there were two, he thought, and either of them could be guilty of a part or of all of this black mystery—there was no shred of evidence, as yet, to point to one or the other. And evidence, he thought, would be hard to get. The most useful thing he could think of to do, at this moment, was to check on Burk's movements after he had left Rita, the night that Lucy was killed. Rita might know where he had gone or where he had said he had gone.

Abbie Nordstrom had said that the Rands were a good family gone to seed, and the house that Calvin Morse drove to was a run-down affair but George Rand proved a spruce individual, his reddish mustache turned up jauntily. He professed to remember Calvin as a boy. Rita was not at home, he said, but in Somerset with a girl friend. "She had a little free time—some of Burk's cronies are giving him a party at the Country Club tonight. Better tonight than the night before the wedding." He winked at Calvin.

Calvin laughed dutifully, noting that Burk would not be at the Folly that night. He drove down to Somerset the short way, direct from the club, and found Regan in the Omar House, in the Coffee Shoppe again, but this time he was not alone in his booth. Rita Rand sat across from him, her bright head tilted toward him across the table, and they had an air of being deep in talk when they looked up at him. The radio, as usual, was filling the air with sound.

"So you're the girl friend," said Calvin, sliding into the seat beside Regan. He said to Rita, "Your father said you were out with a girl friend."

"I had to tell him something. *He* telephoned me," said Rita, with a nod toward Regan.

"Message from our friend," said Regan in an undertone.

"I see."

"And I've persuaded her," said Regan, "to have a little confidence in me."

"That's fine."

Rita Rand leaned forward again. There was a low, rosy light on the table and she looked very beautiful. She said, her voice a half whisper, "And he says I don't have to tell until the trial."

Calvin looked toward Regan. "I thought your client had decided to tell the facts."

"He has—to me. But why show our hand to the prosecution?" Regan muttered defensively. "Surprise witness. Mrs. Burk Cauldron. That will win, all right."

Calvin said dryly, "You think Burk will bring her back from South America?"

"South—but we're not going—" Rita looked from one to the other.

Calvin kept his voice low. "Burk Cauldron will not care to have his wife involved in notoriety. My notion is, he will take steps." Then he said bluntly, "You made one mistake. Why make another?"

There was silence in the booth while Regan digested that. The radio went into a singing commercial. A waitress came to stand by Calvin. He said he was not staying.

She went away and Rita said angrily, "What are you trying to do?"

He said grimly, "The prosecution has got to have a fire built under it. You've held back information that might have been invaluable."

"You didn't sound like that this morning!"

"A lot has happened since this morning."

He could feel Regan looking at him at that but he did not look at Regan. He said to Rita, "And you didn't sound like that this morning. You said you wouldn't marry him without telling him. You said he'd walk out on you."

"I've changed my mind. Maybe he won't—afterward." She said it defiantly and her eyes said, Anyway, I'll be Mrs. Burk Cauldron! She appealed to Regan: "You said we could wait."

"I was under the influence," said Regan slowly. "I'm allergic to redheads." Then he said shortly, "Sorry, Beautiful. But the big courtroom scene is out. I think the counsel from New York is right."

"Oh, you—you—you're both against me!" Then she said, "Suppose I won't? Not yet?"

"You'd be in one hell of a fix," said Regan soberly, "because my client is going to talk. I know—I told you I could keep him quiet, but it's wrong to play it that way. It's too much risk. If there's a chance of having the prosecution do more looking, he's got to have that chance. And you're not the girl," he said, looking at her, "to keep him from having that chance."

"No—no—of course—" She thought about it anxiously. "But not *before* the wedding? It's only a few days—"

Regan looked at Calvin. Calvin said doggedly, "Even a day is important. I told you I wouldn't talk unless I warned you first. I'm afraid I've got to warn you now. I want Mrs. Cromer to know this. And the authorities."

"But not before I've had a chance to tell Burk?" She was imploring now. "I've got to tell him myself—not have him hear it."

"When can you tell him?"

"Not tonight. He's at a party. Tomorrow—as soon as I can—"

"Make it soon," said Calvin. "And," he said carefully, "it may not be such a surprise as you think. How do you know he didn't hang around your place that night? To see what you were up to. You said he was jealous."

"I saw him drive off," said Rita impatiently. "If he'd seen anything I'd have heard from it right away."

"But where did he go? After he left you?"

"How do I know?"

"You might know where he was when he heard of Lucy's death."

"Where—why, he was right here. In the Omar House. He was getting his key and the clerk told him."

"It took him a long time to get here."

"Oh—he said something about a flat. He had to change a tire. No, he didn't hang around. He'd have walked in on us. He doesn't know a thing."

A flat—unless he'd been seen on the road—was no alibi. Calvin's suspicions swung back and forth. Burk. Rawley. He felt as if riding simultaneously two different and distracting horses. He said, rising, "Tell Burk and get it over with."

Her look at him was full of misery and resentment. She flashed, "Burk said it was bad luck, your coming back!"

He had given Regan a brief glance of significance and Regan got up and walked a few steps with him. Calvin said quickly, "There's something I want you to do tonight. With not a word to anyone. Get the clerk of the court to open up and let you see the will of Peter Cauldron. Mrs. Cromer's father."

"Peter Caldron?"

"It was probated about fourteen years ago. Thirteen and a half."

"You said tonight?"

"Time is of the essence. Get hold of it. If there's a copy, swipe it. If not, copy it—that's a commission. I'm retaining you for that service. Make it seem it's for yourself."

"Can try. If I can find Charley Schultz. But it will cost you a bottle."

"It's worth it." Calvin handed over a bill. "Where can I reach you?"

"I have to take her home first . . . give me two or three hours. Wait for me at my boardinghouse, Mrs. Pragg's house. Two doors from the Methodist church on Lee Street." More loudly he said, "Sorry you couldn't eat with us. But I'll be seeing you."

Calvin went to the drugstore for a sandwich and a cup of coffee. The hospital was at the end of the street and as he judged it too early to drop in at the Meades he turned in to the hospital on the chance that his uncle was there.

In a few moments Niel came down to him. He was in a white coat, his hands red from recent scrubbing. He carried an unlighted cigar and said to Calvin, "Let's go outside."

They stood in the quiet of the dead-end street, and Niel began talking nervously. "Another emergency. Too late, as usual. Died on the table."

"That's tough."

"Came in too late. If we'd had him here before, we could have got it in time. But there aren't beds enough. I've tried to get them to build a new hospital but nobody cares. New gadgets for the club—yes. New office buildings. New post office. But a new hospital—no. Those with money go to Nashville or Rochester. So we make do."

This bitter, angry Niel was a man Calvin had not known before. "That young man," said Niel, "He was a GI. Had the hell of a time in the Pacific. Malaria. Bugs. Boils. Landings. Got through all that and came home and got this damned strep infection that could have been stopped if we'd had him in a bed here. And he's not the first. If I'd had my way—"

He was chewing savagely on the unlighted cigar. "That's the only thing I've ever wanted money for," he burst out. "To put it to good use. A lot of people in this town could have built that hospital. A new wing, anyway. Helen Cromer could have done it. She gave me ten thousand after Lucy died, but what's ten thousand? She'd rather wait and keep her crazy castle going. Salvages her conscience with a few lines in her will. She may change that will. And the sick can't wait—"

He broke off and looked up at the dark shadows of the mountains against the sky. His face had a strained, tight-lipped expression which transformed it. "Not soon enough. If I were insured for a hundred thousand dollars I'd make an end to myself and think nothing of it. A public benefaction."

"That would be fine for Aunt Abbie."

"What's one person?" said his uncle. "What's two, for that matter?" Then his lips began to smile though his eyes did not. "Abbie doesn't have to worry," he said in his normal tones. "I'm not insured for that much."

"I'll tell her to watch it. . . . Look—here's your thermometer. Ida said you left it last night."

"Left—where did Ida find it?"

"In Helen's room. Said it had dropped into the bed."

"Oh. . . . I must have been leaning. . . . Well, I've got to get back in there."

No matter how leisurely the Meades' dinner, it must be over now, he thought. He found he was too late. Helen had left directly after dinner; Betty was driving her back. "It's too bad," said Mrs. Meade in the sympathetic manner he remembered now. "But do come in."

He told her he'd have to hurry to the Folly with the message he had for Helen and she said, smiling, "You'll find Dr. Hilton there. He's our new clergyman. He said he wanted to talk over something about the wedding but that's just an excuse—he's terribly taken with Helen. It was because he was calling that Helen had to hurry back."

That changed his plans. He could have gone to the Folly and back before the appointment with Regan, but if Helen had a caller on her hands it wouldn't be easy to see her alone. Later on, when the man was leaving. So he sat in his car before Mrs. Pragg's house till Regan appeared.

"Here it is," said Regan, handing over a long envelope. "I suppose I'm not to ask questions?"

"I may be asking you a few tomorrow. Don't forget to bill me for this."

"That's charged off against your advice," said Regan, grinning. "But, you know," he said, "the idea of that big courtroom scene was pretty damn tempting. . . . I wish I knew what you've got up your sleeve. You've got something."

"When I know what it is myself," said Calvin, "I'll come to you."

Regan lingered a minute more at the car door. "That girl," he said a little awkwardly. "She means all right— though why she's set on marrying Burk . . . But that's her funeral."

The Country Club was lighted up and a piano was sounding and voices in chorus. The party was going strong. The filling station was lighted too, and the fat man sat there in his rocking chair on the little platform before his house. Calvin had to stop to open the Cauldron gates, then he drove through and from old habit got out to close them. Before he got out he glanced up the black lane of path where Lucy had been found and he reached into the glove compartment for the thirty-eight he habitually carried and slipped it into his pocket. Then he drove on to the high level ground.

The Folly was dark, not a light showing. Again he was too late, he thought, chagrined. Behind the Folly the moon was slipping out of a cloud, throwing the long mass of building, the tower and chimneys, into dark silhouette. It was like a picture postcard, he thought ironically. Cauldron Hall by moonlight. Her crazy castle.

His letter was not warning enough. She would think the danger from outside. She would not be on guard with Rawley. Rawley might have obtained keys to her room.

He tried to think what he could do. Someone in the kitchen might be up but a sudden distaste for driving through the dark tunnel of archway made him stop in front, intending to walk around the house to the rear. A voice spoke from the shadowed steps.

"That you, Morse?"

John Cauldron's lean figure detached itself from the darkness and came forward into moonlighted space. "Just finished a smoke. Helen has gone to bed."

"I heard the clergyman was here," Calvin said, in explanation of the hour, "so I waited." He said lamely, "I didn't realize it was so late."

"She went up early. Left the clergy to me," said John, amusement in his voice.

"Then she'd be asleep now?"

"Yes, she is. Anything I can do?"

"No, just—just plans for tomorrow." If Helen had a tomorrow, he thought bleakly. Then he knew what had to be done. He said, "Might I trouble you for a glass of milk? Something I ate."

"Come in. I'll get it."

They went into the dark house and John turned on a few lights. As they were entering the kitchen, Calvin asked, "May I use your phone?" and turned back. He went

quickly to a long window and unlatched it. Then he went
to the phone and called the Nordstrom house. His aunt
answered and he told her, "Just to say I'll be late. I won't
wake you. Good night."

She'd think him at Burk's party or out with Betty
Meade—Betty Van Hoyt. He'd find something to say in
the morning.

In the kitchen John was pouring out two glasses of
milk. There was a thud overhead and John said, "That's
Rawley. In the gallery. I told him we wanted the pictures
back on the walls for the wedding and he's hard at it."

Calvin drank his milk in silence. When John had let
him out he drove off and down the hill till he was out of
sight, then stopped his car and came back on foot. There
was a light now in the right-hand wing and he sat down
and waited till it went out, till he judged John had time
to be asleep, then he went to the house, took off his shoes
and slung them about his neck, opened the long window
with careful quietness, and went in.

Chapter Eight

"Mr. Cauldron is in his room," the clerk said, "but he can't be disturbed. He left word to that effect."

Rita Rand said, "Oh!" disappointedly into the telephone.

"That you, Rita? I didn't know your voice." The clerk had a different tone now. Fred Joram had taken Rita Rand out before Burk Cauldron came back to Somerset.

"Yes. Hello, Fred. When did Burk say—?"

"That was quite a party." The clerk chuckled. "He left word not to ring him till he called down. Said he might not go to the office till afternoon. But if it's you—"

"Oh, no," she said quickly and hung up.

She wanted Burk in a good humor. She had been crazy to call him now, she thought, but when she had a thing to do she felt a driving urge to get through with it. Calvin Morse had wrecked everything. She felt a burning resentment against Calvin and against herself for having gone to him. She had been a fool to tell him. She hadn't meant to, she had meant only to find out if Helen was doing anything about those clues, but Calvin Morse had seemed so nice—and he had said that she could trust him. And now he had gone back on her and made Regan go back on her.

But perhaps it was better this way, she thought, rallying her spirits. If the story had to come out later, Burk

would certainly believe the worst. Now she could make
him see—she hoped she could make him see—that it was
nothing. She would say she had let Tex come to keep him
from making a scene somewhere else. She could not help
it, she'd protest, that Tex was in love with her.

Tex seemed almost unreal to her now. Sometimes she
thought of him and then it seemed almost unbearable that
she would never be with him again, that she would never
feel his arms about her again, but that's the way it was,
she told herself, and she had known—some part of her had
known—that when he wasn't making love to her Tex was
not enough for her.

She was deathly tired of uncertainty and frustration.
She'd be glad when the wedding was over and there was
no looking back. She thought about the day ahead of her.
It would have been a good day if Calvin Morse had not
spoiled it. Sybil Blackburn was giving a luncheon for her
at the Country Club. Helen Cromer had brought that
about. Sybil Blackburn had always snooted her but now
she'd be in the Country Club set. She tried to feel satisfied
and happy but she was too possessed by her uneasiness.

Tonight was the best time. They'd go somewhere to dinner, somewhere far out so it would be a long drive back,
and she'd tell him when they were parked some place, his
arms about her, wanting her.

Now she would try to put it out of her head and concentrate on the luncheon. *Miss Rita Rand, the guest of honor.*

The telephone operator always listened to calls to and
from the Folly, for there was the chance of something exciting. That murder had been a terrible excitement. And
now there was the wedding.

A man's voice was saying, "Helen? This is Calvin. Did
you get my letter?"

"Your letter? Oh—the note. Yes, I did."

"You *did?*" There was a short pause. "You certainly didn't act on it." He sounded angry.

"Why, I haven't said a word."

"That wasn't all to it."

"But it was!"

"The part before that—"

"There wasn't any before that."

There was another short pause. Then the man said, "Nothing about—about the dream?"

"Why—no. That was all."

"I'll come up to see you. Now." He hung up.

That was a funny talk, thought Susan Pragg, flipping out the key. *About the dream.* Something sentimental. Her mother had said that Calvin Morse used to be in love with Helen Cromer. Susan Pragg had a great admiration for young Mrs. Cromer—she had class. She was one in a million.

Susan's mother didn't like her to say "class"; she told her to say "style," but all the girls said "class," except girls like Sybil Blackburn, who said "distinction." Whatever you called it, Helen Cromer had it—so slim and straight, with that lovely refined face and that beautiful black hair, with just a trace of wave in it. Susan knew for a fact that Helen Cromer never had a permanent.

Her brother had class too. You either had it or you didn't have it—you couldn't put it on. Now, Rita Rand had glamour but not class. And what right did Rita Rand have, Susan Pragg thought jealously, what right did she have in the Coffee Shoppe last night with Andy Regan, when she was going to marry Burk Cauldron? Susan's heart swelled. She had marked Andy Regan for her own.

Calvin Morse said, "But the first part of the letter?" He had got Helen away from the Folly, out with him in his car, and they were parked on the highway beyond the Turn while he went into this business of the letter. It had been merely a half sheet, she told him, saying not to tell anyone until he had seen her again, that he would see her soon, and the envelope had been on top of the mail in the silver tray in the hall and Ida had told her Mr. Calvin had left a letter for her.

So someone had tampered with it. Someone had torn it in two, leaving only the unimportant words. Burk could not have done it. Rawley could, or John. John might have looked at it because John was undoubtedly disturbed at his return and warily curious to know what was between them. John might have torn it in two to take out the words, "My dear, dear girl," which were in the middle of it. That didn't make much sense but it was a possibility. Rawley was a greater possibility.

Calvin came out of his considering silence to tell her, "Someone tore off the first part. I told you it was no dream. I told you to be on your guard."

"You told me it was no dream?" She looked bewildered. "But you said it *was* a dream! You said—"

Yes, he had said that, and now he had to unsay it. He had to undo the reassurance he had so mistakenly built up. He told her slowly, in careful detail. The thermos had been filled. There was no trace of coffee in the cups. One cup was unused. He said, "It isn't thinkable that you drank that scalding stuff out of a bottle. Or sat waiting for a quart of it to cool when there was a cup there."

"Certainly I didn't drink out of a bottle," said Helen a little indignantly. "Someone poured it out." She looked off to the Cauldron land on the right of the highway where they were parked. "He's hiding in there."

She didn't understand and he had to make her understand. He had to make her appreciate that the man who wanted her out of the world—the man who had, presumably, taken her child's life—was not lurking in hiding. He was no sex

killer, ranging the woods. It was someone with free access
to the house, someone with motive and opportunity.

He told her so, and she listened intently. He said, "I
asked myself, 'What motive?' The answer isn't pleasant,
Helen." She waited, her eyes on him. "Your father's will,"
he said. "There is no logical reason for an attempt on you
unless it is motivated by that will. I've been reading that
will. There are two people in your house who believe that
they would benefit if you died—childless."

She looked at him blankly. "What two people?"

He said bluntly, "There's Burk—"

"Burk?" She repeated it incredulously. She stared at
him in open disbelief that he was serious. She said, "My
brother!" as if that settled it.

He told her, "The courts are full of men who have killed
sisters, wives, mothers, even their own children. Being a
brother doesn't mean a thing. Remember what he said to
you—how he threatened—"

"He was just angry."

"'Just angry!' That was a bitter anger, Helen. It had
been brewing for a long time. Remember, he had been
away from you for twelve years. Over twelve years. All the
bonds you have are early ones—and you weren't very close
then. Can't you see that he might care more about the
Folly than about you, that you might seem the obstacle—"

"But he wouldn't have the Folly! If I died, it would go
to his child and Burk has no child."

"He will have. The law gives him time to fulfill that
contingency. And it's all the better for him if the child is
an infant. In that case he would be guardian for all the
years until the child reached maturity. Twenty-one years
is a long time. And if it died," the lawyer in Calvin felt
obliged to point out, "he would inherit from it."

"And I suppose you think he's capable of killing it!" she
said hotly. "Calvin, you're horrible."

"All right. I'm horrible. But please appreciate that I don't say that Burk has done any of this. I say only that there is a possibility that he has. That he had motive and opportunity."

She was silent, staring at him as if appalled. He was amazed at the feeling in her. Once more, he thought wryly, he was up against that family feeling of hers. Then she looked down, thinking deeply. She said in a flat, abrupt voice, "I don't believe it for a minute. But is it in your mind that he could have killed Lucy too?"

"He could have come back. Rita had sent him away. He could have reached the gate just as Lucy went in. He would have seen Lucy getting out, starting off alone, and it could have rushed over him what it would mean if she were out of the way. It might have happened like that."

She stared at him stonily. "I can never forgive you for even thinking that."

"You asked me. I give you the truth as I see it. I don't say it was that way. I say it might have been that way. Or it might have been that Lucy was killed by some prowler—perhaps Tex Miller—and it was then that Burk began to plan. He has been talking to Rita about the Folly—worrying for fear you will marry again now."

"Why now?" she asked coolly.

He said as coolly, "Because I am back. Because we used to be in love."

"He can put that out of his head."

"I didn't put it there. I didn't ask to come back."

"I know." She was suddenly penitent. "I'm being hateful. I know you're only saying what you think you must say." Then indignation swept her again. "But you sit there, detached, and cold as a stone, telling me that my brother—"

"I am not cold as a stone," he gave back irately. "And I am not detached. I am horribly worried over all this.

What do you think made me sit out in the hall opposite your room all last night? I sneaked into the Folly like a burglar and sat in that passage off your hall till morning, hoping to catch him in an attempt and find out the truth. I was furious you hadn't locked your door. I tried it when I came to make sure. That's why I thought you hadn't got my letter."

He had done more than try her door. He had opened it in a panic when he found it unlocked, and had stood there till he made sure she was in bed and breathing. He had felt tender and protective.

Now he felt disgusted. He said, "If you think I relish having to tell you unpleasant things—having to sit out there in the dark because someone might creep in on you—"

"Don't glare at me," she said, in a soft, funny voice. "I didn't know."

He muttered, "You make me so mad—"

"I'm sorry. I always did, didn't I?" Then, getting away from that quickly, "When did you get your sleep?"

"Oh, I slept my head off after I got back."

"But how did you get in?"

He told her, a little impatiently. He said, "But now you must have police protection."

She looked instantly alarmed. "You mean you'd tell this to the police?"

"There has been an attempt, several attempts, made on you. You believe that, don't you?"

"Yes, I believe it. I'm sure of it now I know the thermos was filled. And the cup not used. I think we ought to tell the police that much. But if you're thinking of mentioning Burk to them—"

"He has got to be mentioned—as one of the possibilities."

"He is not a possibility," she said stubbornly.

"All right. Then look at the other possibility. Burk's son. His natural son, Rawley."

He was nettled enough to enjoy her dumfounded look. He said, "Did you ever hear of the Rawley girl—long ago?"

"Something—afterward. I never really knew. You mean this is her boy?"

Calvin told her the story. He told of the ride back to the hills with Burk, when they were boys, and of Burk and the little hillbilly girl. He told how, when he had seen Rawley, he had been struck by some resemblance he could not place, but the remembrance had come back to him, and how he had taken Rawley by surprise with his direct question and Rawley had told his story.

Calvin said, "He says he came only to look you over. That's understandable. It could be merely a queer coincidence. But it's thinkable that having come and seen the place, and believing that his paper gave him rights—"

"Yes," she said breathlessly. "I felt there was something strange."

"He has no love for you, Helen. He's bitter—naturally. And he's unstable and sly."

"Of course. It's Rawley!" Her voice was almost glad in the escape from the things he had made her consider about Burk.

"But there's no proof."

"Isn't the letter proof?" she asked quickly. "Burk couldn't have torn that letter in two. Rawley didn't want me to get the warning."

"John could have torn it in two. To take out the emotional words I wrote in the middle. I got emotional writing that grisly warning. I don't know what he'd make of that part about the dream and being on guard."

"I'll fix that," she said. "Yes, John might—though it's hard to believe of him. He's so detached."

"He's not detached about you. But this is all sheer conjecture, Helen. We have to remember that there isn't a scrap of evidence against anyone."

After a moment she said hesitantly, "Don't you suppose that Sutton might find out by questioning Rawley?"

"Third degree?"

"No, no! I meant that if he's so unstable he'd get confused."

"He's shrewd enough not to incriminate himself. I have a notion that he was ready to be recognized, ready to make a bid for a place in the family. He wasn't wearing any eyeshade at that tea with Burk. He's had his look-see. Now he's got some plan in that foxy head of his."

She sat thinking about it. Then she asked, "You think he will try again soon?"

"If it's Rawley, he'll have to. He won't be staying much longer. And he may feel that he'll be thrown out at any moment. And if it's Burk," Calvin said deliberately, "he hasn't much time either. That's why you have to be guarded."

"And if I talked of going away—" She was following some thought of her own. "If I talked of going off to travel, to visit, wouldn't that hurry things up?"

He said grimly, "I should think so."

"Then it's perfectly clear what to do," she said in a calm, reasonable voice. "If we go to the police, without any proof in our hands, and they start questioning Rawley, there never will be any proof. You said yourself he wouldn't incriminate himself. And he wouldn't make any more attempts. That's true, isn't it?"

He looked at her warily. "What are you leading up to?" he asked.

"That it would be stupid to go to the police now. That we must keep things as they are, not let anyone know that we suspect a thing. I'll take care of that warning from you. Then he will make some move that will give him away."

"And you'll get hit on the head. Not for a moment."

"Calvin, forget protectiveness! I'll be on my guard. I won't eat anything that the others don't eat. I'll only pretend to. And I won't be alone with anyone you think is suspect. I'll be careful."

"You wouldn't know what to watch out for. It's too risky."

"Please think a moment. It isn't risky if he thinks I'm drugged in my room and I'm not—I'll be locked in Lucy's room. It's the only intelligent way to find out."

"To use yourself as bait?"

"I'm not afraid. I'm somehow not afraid now when I know what to look out for. It was that feeling of being in the dark, of not knowing whether I was imagining it all. Trying to decide whether I was crazy or not. And I've a right to do it," she urged. "I have a right to find out the truth."

"Better never to know than—"

"And have Tex Miller convicted for something I felt he did not do? Do you think I could bear to live with the memory of that? And never to know whether the man who killed Lucy was someone near and dear to me? Calvin, you know this is the only possible way to find out the truth. You have to admit it."

Yes, he had to admit that cold logic was on her side, but he went on arguing. And he had to admit that she had him on every count. But it went against the grain, he said, to have her risk herself.

"I'll be careful," she declared. "I'll have my revolver, remember. Lee's old thirty-eight. Oh, I'll be careful."

"I don't trust your carefulness. I'd have to be there."

"Of course. I'll need you. This is what I thought: I'll have a sort of house party. Before Burk's wedding. I'll ask Burk and Rita and Betty—and Abbie and Niel too, because Abbie will feel it if she doesn't see more of you. Then I'll

talk of going off for a change, going right after the wedding. How's that for a plan?"

"It's crazy. But it has possibilities. Nasty ones," he said
glumly.

"It's risky for you, Calvin. You may be suspected of
guessing—"

"It's going to be a lovely house party," he said, with a
sudden laugh. "I look forward to it—in a gruesome sort
of way."

Driving back slowly, they discussed plans. Suddenly he
said, "There's one other possible motive, Helen. Your own
will. In whose favor is it?"

"I've divided the money. One half goes for a hospital in
Lucy's name. The other half to Burk and John, fifty-fifty.
You don't see any motive there, do you?" she said, faintly
mocking again.

"How much is it?"

"About two hundred thousand."

Calvin said slowly, "Why leave so much for a hospital?"

"I don't know. I wasn't thinking very clearly and Niel
was urgent about it. But I don't think it is fair. If Burk had
this place he couldn't possibly keep it up on the income
from fifty thousand. Not with taxes. I've thought I ought
to change it and I will, right away. I'll have to tell Niel,
though. He won't like it."

No, he wouldn't like it, Calvin thought absently. He
could hear his uncle's voice, bitter, discouraged, *The sick
can't wait*. But Calvin's chief thought was of the fifty
thousand to Burk. Inadequate as its income might be, that
income would be no deterrent to Burk.

He said, "Don't tell Burk you are going to change it.
He might decide to wait for that."

She gave him that stony look again. "I suppose you
can't help thinking like that. No, I won't tell him."

Calvin's aunt and uncle were at lunch when he returned to the Nordstrom house. Abbie had been gone when he got up that morning and he expected questions on his night out but she was preoccupied with the telephone call Helen Cromer had just made. To Calvin's surprise Abbie was not receptive to the idea of the house party.

"Were too old for a young crowd," she said. "I was Helen's mother's friend, and though I've grown very close to Helen that doesn't make me young. And I don't think Niel will care to be moved up there for a few days."

But Niel said amiably, "It doesn't matter what bed I sleep in—I get very few hours in bed anyway, the way things are now. This influenza. Clarissa can relay my calls. Or the operator can. When does Helen want us?"

"Tonight, after dinner," said Calvin. "She said to come early and have some bridge."

"We ought to encourage her in this," said Niel. "She's been very far down the ladder from what John tells me. By the way, Calvin, I ran into the sheriff today and he said you went to the jail to see Tex Miller. Will you tell me why?"

"Helen asked me to. She was worried because of a letter he had written her—and by anonymous letters she's received. She wanted my impression of him. It was a crazy idea, but I thought I ought to go."

"And what impression did you get?" asked Niel dryly.

Calvin said, "About as accurate as you get of a man's health by looking at him in his clothes. He seems harmless."

"You would have a more accurate impression if you had seen him when they brought him in that night. With his shirt covered with lipstick."

After a silence Calvin said, "You think he's guilty, don't you?"

"The evidence is against him."

"But if he should have an alibi? Those letters have given Helen the belief that he has."

"John told me about those letters. Some hysterical girl who wants to get Tex off. John was very disturbed at the impression they made on Helen. She wanted him to see the fellow but he refused. It's a matter for the courts. Not for amateur meddling."

Abbie said defensively, "Naturally Calvin couldn't refuse to go—but Helen shouldn't have asked him. She's been very tense these weeks. She's had so many shocks. And she takes them so hard. I think Betty Van Hoyt will be very good for her. Now, Betty felt badly about losing Renfew—they were very happy together—and I think she felt badly about not having children, though that wasn't her fault, his brother never had children either, her mother tells me, but Betty always gives the impression of being a happy person. Didn't you think she'd grown very attractive, Calvin?"

Calvin laughed out. "Dear Abbie! Why switch my affections to Betty?"

"I didn't know your affections were involved—after all these years." Then Abbie gave up pretense. "I think it's nice to be friendly again with Helen but it would be foolish to be anything more. Her life is here."

In Cauldron's Folly. Her crazy castle. He said lightly, "Yes, I expect it is. Don't worry, Abigail—it's only a beautiful friendship. As for Betty, she's already propositioned me for a tour of New York's sin spots. I feel we have an expensive future."

"Ren left her very well off."

"Shall I let her reach for the check? No, Abigail, don't feel you have to do anything about my love life. There are quite a few glamour gals in New York."

"Too many," said Abbie. "You get in the habit of procrastinating."

"So I do," said Calvin. "So I do."

And when you have had a very young, very strong feeling and it had blown up on you, you were careful not to let feeling get the upper hand again. And then you drifted, with one attraction and another, none of them strong enough to pull you very far. You never plunged right in— you waited for something that could not be resisted. And that did not happen again. And why did he want it to happen? Why did he want a woman who could break his heart again? Why not a woman who would warm his heart?

But this was no time to be bothering about love. He went to Somerset to find Regan, for he wanted that young man's knowledge of Tennessee law on a couple of points, but Regan was out of town. He went to the hardware store and bought some barbed wire. Doors could be locked but windows were a hazard. Helen had asked him to get some picture wire at the same time and he told the clerk it must be strong enough for some of the heavy pictures at the Folly.

"If you're going to the Folly," said the clerk, "would you take this package along? I've got those blanks Burk Cauldron wanted. They just came in. I had to send for them."

"Blanks?"

"That's what he wanted. Thirty-eights. I could leave them at the Omar House but I guess he wants them at the Folly. We don't have any call for blanks, so I had to order them."

Lee Cromer's revolver was a thirty-eight. Calvin Morse had an instant vision of Helen firing at some assailant, firing a blank. Then he had another thought. His own revolver was a thirty-eight. How did he know Burk hadn't looked in his car? He said, "I'll take some real thirty-eights."

When out of town he stopped and replaced the cartridges in his gun with the new. Burk might have had some old blanks. Back at the Nordstroms' he stretched out and slept, provisioning for the night's vigil. After dinner his uncle and aunt drove off. "I'll be along," he said. He made another effort to reach Regan but he was still away, so Calvin went over the will again by himself.

"I, Peter Cauldron, being of sound and disposing mind—" Calvin hurried through the familiar legal words to the significant provisions. "To my son Burk the sum of one hundred dollars and no more."

That was Cauldron implacability for you! Small wonder that Burk had been bitter.

"To my daughter Helen all my other personal property, including moneys, securities, credits, and the contents of my family residence, Cauldron Hall, commonly termed Cauldron's Folly, to be hers absolutely."

Calvin put down the will and lighted a cigarette. And that was only a part of it. Only chip diamonds. Now for the Kohinoor.

"I devise to my daughter Helen during her natural life my ancestral home, Cauldron Hall, lying and situate in—" He raced through the details of location—"At the death of my daughter Helen I devise the said real property to the heirs of my son Burk; provided, however, that if my said daughter Helen should die leaving a child or children her surviving the said property shall go to such child or children in fee."

Contingent interest, thought Calvin. To Helen, to her surviving child or children, if any; if none, then to the heirs of Burk. To his children or grandchildren, never to Burk. Did Rawley know the contents of this will? His mother, through her relatives, could have got hold of a copy when it was probated.

He thought about that "paper" of Rawley's and why he had not put it to the test. Lack of funds, probably, and lack of years—Rawley was only twenty-one now—and the lack, perhaps, of anything to gain but the name, as long as Helen was alive and had a child.

The business of the blank cartridges had tipped the scales a trifle toward Burk but his mind was trying to keep Rawley and Burk in balance.

"I devise to my nephew John Cauldron in fee my house and lot in the town of Somerset situate on the corner of Lee Street and Park Lane, together with all my other property, real or personal, of whatsoever name or nature not otherwise disposed of by this will."

The ordinary residuary clause, the catchall. There had been nothing but the house for John to get; everything else had been disposed of, but Peter Cauldron had taken no chance of having his son Burk come into anything but that contemptuous one hundred dollars. A will made in unforgiving anger.

Calvin put it carefully in a small brief case which he locked and packed in one suitcase. The package of barbed wire he put with the picture wire in a small case.

There were seven people in the big room. Abbie Nordstrom, Betty Van Hoyt, John and Burk Cauldron were playing bridge, Niel was looking through some papers, Helen was doing woolwork, and a little apart from them all Rawley sat in one of the big oak chairs bending over the colored pages of a magazine. To look at them, Calvin thought, you would think them any group of nice, pleasant people.

He dropped his bags in the hall, and walked over to the table where Abbie was adding scores.

"Here's a gimmick the hardware man said you ordered," he said casually, handing over the small heavy package to Burk, and as casually Burk said, "Thanks," and pocketed it.

"We were beginning to be afraid you weren't coming," said Helen, smiling very brightly at him.

"Homework," he said lightly. "Oh—I've got your picture wire. I'll give it to you later." He looked about the room. "Where's Miss Rand?"

Burk, not looking up from checking Abbie's score, said briefly, "Not here."

Helen explained, "Burk said she wasn't feeling too well and wouldn't be over till tomorrow."

Burk grinned at her over his shoulder. "Let's not gloss it over. We had a fight and she went off in a huff. So I went and got Betty."

"But she'll be over tomorrow?" asked Helen.

Burk shrugged. "I wouldn't know." Then he bent over Betty and said something inaudible.

Betty laughed out. "You're a typical bridegroom," she said aloud.

"What?"

"They always make last-minute passes at the nearest girl."

Burk said, "Especially the girl he always made passes at?"

"Burk, it's your deal," said Abbie briskly.

"You come over here, Calvin, and tell me about New York." Helen had bright eagerness in her voice. She threw out to the world at large, "Calvin's got me all excited about going to New York. I think I'll go right after the wedding."

Burk, dealing cards, hesitated a moment, then went on without looking up. Calvin glanced from him to Rawley, saw that Rawley was looking at Helen, and that he glanced down quickly when he saw he was observed. But what did that prove? For the matter of that, Niel was regarding her very interestedly.

"I need a change," said Helen. "A complete change. Calvin tells me I ought to be on my guard against getting into a rut here. I've been having morbid dreams and he says they aren't dreams but forebodings of my dull life in the country."

So that was what she had thought up for explanation. Not bad, Calvin approved, sitting down beside her on the couch.

Niel asked, "What sort of dreams?"

"Oh—drowning mostly," Helen said indifferently. "I never remember them clearly."

"I want you to try that Sanka," said Abbie, studying her hand.

Burk raised his voice. "I said One Spade."

The play went on. Helen moved nearer to Calvin and they began to talk in low tones. Their voices were inaudible enough so that he could tell her the barbed wire was in the small case in the hall, and she nodded understandingly. He murmured, "And when I'm not around—catching up sleep in the morning—you'll stay with Abbie or someone safe?"

"Indeed, I will. Whatever you plan," she said quite clearly, her voice positively fond. He looked at her, startled, and a flash of mischief laughed at him from her gray eyes. "What plays are you going to take me to see?"

He started to say *Edward, My Son,* but thought of Lucy in time, and he couldn't say *Death of a Salesman* either, and *The Madwoman of Chaillot* sounded wrong, and *Anne of a Thousand Days* had death in it, so he said, "*Kiss Me, Kate,*" and was conscious of sudden silence at the bridge table. He said hastily, "And *South Pacific,* of course."

"You're sweet to be planning all this."

That was her fond voice again. And her face—just in case anyone turned to look, he supposed—was modeling a dovelike tenderness. Then she said under her breath, her voice anything but dovelike, "Play *up!* What do they think I'm going to New York for? An *icicle?*"

He began to laugh helplessly. She was funny. Obediently he edged nearer, examined her woolwork. Their heads close together they talked inaudibly, going over the plan for the night. He caught Abbie looking around from her cards at them. He murmured, "Never, in our most infatuated days, did we put on such an exhibition."

"Oh, didn't we! What about that time—" She caught herself. "Well, never mind about that time."

The bridge ended. Burk came over to them. "This sounds like quite a jaunt you're planning. But don't play bridge with your aunt before you go, Calvin, or she'll clean you out. She plays a cutthroat game. How's for some drinks, Helen? Will you ring?"

"Henry's gone to bed. I'll get them."

"No, no, Betty and I will serve you. What will you have, ladies and gentlemen? It's on the house."

"Scotch and soda," said Niel.

"Tut, tut! Ladies first. Abbie?"

"Sherry for me."

Helen said, "Sherry." John shook his head. Rawley said, "Nothing for me," without looking up from his magazine. Calvin said, "Scotch and soda."

"Two Scotches, two sherries. Come on, Betty, and I'll mix you a Samson and Delilah. Guaranteed to bring down the house."

They were gone quite a time. "Smooth your hair," Burk said to her in loud mock warning as they entered. Betty looked across at Calvin. "Don't believe a word of it."

But she had the air of enjoying herself. He was glad somebody was enjoying the evening. Burk's spirits seemed forced, John Cauldron looked mildly bored, Rawley as stiff as a poor actor. Helen was artificially keyed up by putting on her act.

When the drinks were over she said suddenly, "I think I'll go up. Night, Abbie." She kissed her quickly, then put her cheek against Betty's. "It's fun to have you, Betty." She crossed to Burk, who was sitting down, and bent and kissed him. That was to show me, Calvin thought. Her hand rested a moment on John's shoulder. "Good night, John." She looked toward Rawley and her voice rang almost true. "Good night, Mr. Rawley." And then, "Good night, Niel."

She was out the door swiftly—to get the small case in the hall, Calvin understood. From the stairs her voice floated down to them. "Oh—will somebody bring me some milk? Just leave it on the small table outside my door."

That was the trap they had planned. The milk, waiting conveniently. She was to be slow in taking it in, to give opportunity. She was to leave her door unlocked, to barricade herself in Lucy's room. Calvin was to watch from the passage. Operation Sleepless, he had said lightly.

There were four bedrooms along the front of the house on that side: first a room which Niel occupied, opening into the master bedroom that had been given to Abbie, with its dressing room and bath, and then the room which had been Lucy's and then Helen's room and her dressing room and bath. Opposite the first three rooms, the other side of the hall was an unbroken wall that was the back of the gallery. The gallery was terminated by an oddly narrow passage running from the back of the house into the front hall; one end of the gallery opened into the passage, but the main door to the gallery was at the other end, from the open space about the head of the stairs.

The passage joined the hall almost opposite the door to Helen's room. One angle of the junction was formed by the gallery, the other by an enclosed service stairs, with a door into the passage. Calvin's room was back of the stairs, its windows toward the back gardens. It had no bath, so if he was discovered in the passage he could be presumed on his way to a general bathroom that was beyond the service stairs, opening into the hall—a room built before Helen's grandfather had reconverted the dressing rooms.

Calvin went up to his room, hurried into pajamas and bathrobe and made a trip out to the bath for a quick cold shower to wake him up. A dim light burned in the hall. Helen would put that out when she took in the milk. The hall was dark when he came back, so he lighted a cigarette for a last smoke, dropped his flashlight into one pocket, then turned to the table where he had left his revolver when he had taken out his pajamas. The revolver was gone.

He was sure he had left it on the table, but he searched the room. No doubt about it, it was gone. Anyone could have slipped into his room while he was out. He thought, I'm the hell of a detective. The most disturbing thing about it was that he was being suspected, his room entered. He was not operating in the obscurity that he had hoped.

A knock sounded on his door; he heard his aunt's voice saying "Calvin?" Surprised, he opened the door and Abbie Nordstrom came in. She was in a dark-blue, tightly belted robe, her hair plastered against her head in what Calvin appreciated must be a "set," and covered with a dark net. "I knew you'd be up," she said. "You're such a night owl. And I wanted a chance to see you. Have you a cigarette to spare?"

He lighted it for her, wondering what this was all about.

Abbie sat down and came directly to the point. "Calvin, I wish you wouldn't urge Helen to go to New York."

"But why?" he said guardedly. "Don't you think a change—"

"She can have plenty of change in Chicago with Betty."

He wasn't going to argue, he wanted to hurry her out. So he smiled down at her as he stood, leaning against the fireplace, and said casually, "Well, she can work that out later."

Abbie was not to be deflected. "She's taken with the idea now because she's restless. But it wouldn't bring you any happiness, Calvin. That's what I'm concerned about. Helen is never going to live any life but her own."

He said lightly, "Let's not worry about that now."

"I do worry," said his aunt. "I didn't bring you back here to have you fall in love with Helen all over again."

He kept his voice bantering. "My dear, you began taking me to the Folly the moment I arrived."

"I didn't expect you to be anything but friends."

"Well, that's all we are."

"You've been rushing to her every moment. And if she goes to New York—" Abbie looked anxiously at him through a cloud of cigarette smoke. She said bluntly, "You've got charm, Calvin, but it wouldn't do you any good." She met his quizzical glance and told him, "Because she's going to marry John Cauldron."

The quizzical look stayed on guard on his face. "Now how do you know that?"

"Because John Cauldron told me so. He told me tonight. Before you came. It's been understood between them for quite a time."

"That's interesting," he said in a neutral voice.

"I expect she turned to him after Lucy died."

"I expect."

"She doesn't want anyone to know because John is still staying here."

After a moment Calvin said, "Then why did John tell you?"

"He told me in confidence," said Abbie.

"Knowing you'd tell me and warn me off?"

"N-no, I don't think he thought I'd *tell* you," said Abbie reflectively. "Not exactly. I expect he did think I'd warn you off. Of course, I'm telling you in confidence."

Calvin gave a dry laugh. "The same sort of confidence you keep with John?"

"No," said Abbie. "Men are different about confidences. I ask you not to give me away to Helen and I don't think you will. She'd be fearfully annoyed at John and at me. But women don't keep confidences when it's a matter of someone they are very fond of. And I'm very fond of you, Calvin. You were like my own son to me when you were a little boy. I used to look forward to those vacations of yours more than you know. I was sorry when you stopped coming, but I understood. Now I don't want anything to happen that would hurt you again."

He said, "Don't worry, Abbie dear." He held out an ash tray to her. "That cigarette's all gone."

She ground out the stub but she wasn't ready to go yet. She said, "Helen would rush around New York with you, but in the end—" she made a little gesture—"it would be John. Because her life is here and John belongs to that life. And I expect she wants to get married now to have another child. There would be a sort of justice," said Abbie consideringly, "in having it his child. It was hard on John, being left out of everything."

"Oh, hell!" Calvin exploded. "I'm sick of this Cauldron inheriting and disinheriting!"

So she was going to marry John. And she had never told him a word about that. He remembered her hand on John's shoulder tonight—John's upturned look at her. Then, why in the name of all that was reasonable hadn't she told John about these attacks on her? What was it she had said? *John is utterly convinced it is Tex Miller. John thinks I'm all worked up, anyway.* Well, he could see why John had been skeptical. He, himself, had been skeptical. But not to tell him about John!

But why should she tell him? He had not come in any spirit except friendship. All the talk about New York, all the eager, interested voice, the dovelike eyes—he had known that was all an act. Part of their game. But why wouldn't it have done as well to come out and say she was going to marry John? *That* would hurry things up as well as New York and an infatuation for Calvin Morse.

But that would risk John. Calvin Morse did not matter.

He had no idea what Abbie had been saying. He cut in, "When are they going to be married?"

"John said some time this fall. Now, you won't let Helen know that he has told me?"

"I won't let her know. Why should I? I don't give a damn whom she marries. If John's her notion of a bridegroom—"

"He'd make a very good husband."

Another Prince Consort. An older, less beautiful, but docile Lee Cromer. Then Calvin shut his mind sharply from examining the fact. This did not change the plan for tonight. He had to get Abbie out of here. Deliberately he yawned.

But Abbie was slow to leave. She talked along, shifting to her worry about Niel and the way he was trying to make money through stocks when he did not know anything about stocks. "It's for that hospital," she said. "I wish you'd give him some advice."

"I will. Now, Abbie—" he put his hands lightly on her shoulders and turned her about—"I've got to get some sleep. Last night was a big night. I don't know how Niel manages without sleep, but I know I can't."

She stepped out into the passage, then turned back. "Have you a flashlight?"

"It's not working."

She disappeared and he picked up a big brass candlestick and dropped that into his pocket. When he judged Abbie had regained her room he went out to where he could see through the darkness the darker oblong of Helen's door. He was uneasy at the time that had elapsed before he had come on watch, though it was not likely, he thought, that an attack would come so soon, and he had a sour, disagreeable feeling at Abbie's news.

Not that he cared personally, he told himself. Not that he minded being used—he had come in simple friendship. But that talk of another child—how women could talk of things like that!—set his teeth on edge.

But Abbie had a confoundedly realistic way of knowing what she was talking about.

Chapter Nine

Helen left the milk out for some time, to give plenty of opportunity in case it had not already been dosed. Slowly she made ready for bed, wondering if the trap had been too obvious. She went out into the hall and turned off the light and took in the milk, looking at its innocent air with wry curiosity. She poured it into a bottle and hid the bottle carefully.

Then she did something she had not done for a long time; she sat down at her desk and took out her diary. It was an intermittent record. She used to jot down happenings of any importance, and sometimes interesting stories that she wanted to remember exactly, but she had made only two entries in it since the night that Lucy died. One line gave the date of Lucy's death. Another line was the date of her burial.

Now she turned the pages to find the first blank page, intending to write in such cryptic milestones for memory as *House party beginning. Plans for New York*. She came to the page opposite the two brief entries about Lucy; the page should have been blank, but it was not blank. Scrawled raggedly across it was a line of writing.

Helen sat staring at it. It was not her writing but it was enough like it to pass for hers. Big and black and sloped. But she had never written those words. Never in her life—

131

unless she was losing her mind and memory—never had
she written those words.

Too hard to go on—to pretend to care for anything.

Her heart began to hammer in her as she realized what
they meant there. They were the confession of despair, the
last words of a woman too despondent to go on living.
Whoever had written them—and it could have been done
during any of the long time she had been downstairs before dinner—whoever had written them had already a plan
for this night. He had not known that she would ask for
milk. He had not depended upon that. He had a plan. She
was to die, and die apparently by her own hand. The diary
would be found, open, on her desk.

How had he dared write that beforehand? Because
he knew she never touched the book now. Because there
would be no time later. To make its effect the diary must
be found at once. Mechanically she reached farther into
the drawer. It was no surprise that the revolver was gone.

She thrust in the book and shut the drawer quickly as
if that would shut away the horror. She felt an impulse to
rush out into the hall and tell Calvin—but that was too
rash. *He* might be already watching—from a distance. She
must do nothing suspicious.

Perhaps the milk had changed his plan. It would be
simpler to have her sleep her life away than to overpower
her, and have a shot ring out. Perhaps he had made the
milk wholly lethal. Perhaps he would not be coming at all
now. No, he would come—he would come to make sure.
He would not run the risk of having her brought back to
life next morning.

She jumped up and heaped the bedclothes to simulate
a body. She placed a pillow obscuringly. If he saw at once
that the bed was empty he might slip away before Calvin
could be on him. She was not quite clear what Calvin
Morse had in mind to do—whatever the opportunity

offered, she supposed—but it was clear that there must be time to make the recognition positive.

She caught up the small case and took it into Lucy's room and shut and bolted both doors. The old bolts were strong; the first Peter Cauldron had not depended upon keys. She put on a low desk light and spread the barbed wire beneath her window. Calvin had told her to wear gloves but she had forgotten to bring them into the room, and though she tried to be careful her hands shook and got badly pricked.

It was hard to make herself get into Lucy's bed but she got in. She lay waiting for something to happen. If she had taken the milk she would be very soon asleep. He would come.

She thought about it very carefully for what seemed a long time, then she held up her wrist and stared at the luminous dial. Only a few minutes had passed. She lay still again, every faculty absorbed in the faculty of listening. Then she reasoned that he would not be coming at once, that he would give the stuff ample time to work on her. This time, he was telling himself, there was no dog in the next room to give the alarm. This time, by no fortuitous chance, would the telephone ring and wake the house. This time there would be no failure.

She asked herself why the dose had not been lethal before. Well, the last time, she thought quite detachedly, there had been too much fluid and one could not be sure how much she would take. The first time? There had been only one cup of milk that first time, and she could have been killed quite easily, but *he* had evidently preferred to have it seem an accident. The pillow over her face. Everyone knew she had taken a sleeping pill that night. Now *he* was tired of half measures.

But it was not Burk. She told herself that resolutely. She had few illusions about Burk but she clung to the belief in his family feeling. Then the word took on irony. Family. That boy he had fathered, had never known, never thought about, was his family. That bitter boy. Did Rawley know about her diary? Yes, of course he did—when he had told some stories about painting, John had told her to write them down in her commonplace book and Rawley had been naively offended at the word "commonplace" until she had explained. Rawley, an artist, would be good at imitating.

She looked at her watch again. The hands had scarcely moved. She wondered if it seemed as long to Calvin out there, for he must be there now. It was strange that it should be Calvin who was standing guard. Well, he owed her that much, she thought, not bitterly now, but remembering the old bitterness. Calvin had been cruel once.

Her thoughts drifted and for a few moments she ceased to be aware of listening. And then a sound broke in on her, a soft, muffled sound, coming from within the room, and her heart stood still with shock. She listened, her head stiffly lifted from the pillow, her body rigid, unstirring, and she heard it distinctly. A creak, a rustling. It came from a huge wardrobe against the wall. With sudden, awful clarity she understood. *He* had hidden there, was moving from behind the clothes to come out.

He had slipped in, after they had all come upstairs, to avoid too many appearances in the hall, meaning to enter her room through the connecting door. He must have heard her come in, have wondered. But he had felt sure she had taken the milk. He was coming out. . . . In a moment that wardrobe door would open.

There was an instant when she felt as if paralyzed, unable to move, then she flung off the numbing terror and heard herself saying in loud, normal tones, 'That you, Ida? Wait—I'll let you in."

She sprang out of bed, rushed to the door, wrench-ing at the old-fashioned locks and talking in a clear, high voice. "What's the matter? Someone sick? I didn't hear any phone. I came here to get away from that phone if it should ring."

To be out in the hall was to be in another darkness, but Calvin was there in the darkness and she plunged into the passage. Calvin was not there. She fumbled for the door to the service stairs, and fled through it, closing it behind her, and ran up the stairs to the third floor.

It was important, she was thinking frantically, it would be important tomorrow to have *him* believe that she had really thought that Ida was at her door. So she went to the room where Henry and Ida slept and knocked and called softly, "Ida, Ida!" There were sounds from within the room, the creaking of springs and a sleepy, interrogative murmur. "Ida!" she called more clearly.

Then Ida's voice answered, wakened to alarm. "You calling, Miss Helen?"

"Yes. I thought you were at my door just now. I thought I didn't wake in time and you went away. Did you want me for anything?"

"Me—at your door?"

"I thought so. Were you calling me?"

She heard feet thudding on the floor and then the door opened. Ida stood there, a small shape in a voluminous nightgown outlined against the window behind her. Ida said, "Miss Helen, I never called you. I been right here in bed. You been having a dream."

"I guess I have." Helen gave a shaky laugh. "I thought you were wanting me—maybe you were ill—and I hadn't heard you in time, so you went away."

"I'll go back with you to your bed."

"Oh, no—I'm perfectly all right. Just a dream. But I wanted to make sure you were all right." Helen's voice had gained assurance and authority. "I'm sorry I disturbed you. I hope you get to sleep again."

She turned quickly away, standing at the head of the stairs till she heard Ida's door close. She hurried along the upper hall, past empty rooms, to the room waiting for Rita Rand. She went in, flashed on the light, bolted the door. She could say she had slept here because there was no reminder here, nothing to make her dream.

Had she deceived him with her feigned talk to Ida? Not if he saw that barbed wire beneath the window. But he might not see it—the wardrobe was not near the window. And he could not have watched her through the wardrobe.

But where was Calvin? Why wasn't he there when she needed him? She felt betrayed.

Calvin shifted, in forced patience, from one foot to the other. There are surprisingly few positions to be assumed when keeping in readiness to leap forward or backward. He had tried them all. He thought about the direction from which a man might come. Rawley's room was in the back of the central part of the house, so he could come down the hall or he could step into the gallery and emerge into the passage. At a sound from the gallery Calvin meant to vanish within the service stairs.

Burk's room was on the other side of the house, just beyond the enclosed entrance to the tower, and he could come down the hall or go up the service stairs on his side of the house, cross over, and come down these stairs.

A sound from any direction was suspect and it was disconcerting how many sounds there were. Last night the house had been sepulchrally quiet but tonight a wind was rising, and it went up and down the chimneys and sent the oak branches against the windows at the end of the hall. Calvin wondered if Helen was getting any sleep or if she was sitting up in Lucy's room, waiting. Then he wondered if this was all a piece of hysteria. But his revolver had been taken. That was a giveaway, he thought. And then he thought that if Helen was shot with that revolver, who would know that she had not come into his room herself, and taken it? She had Lee Cromer's revolver but perhaps that was hidden.

He thought about Burk and about Rawley. Conjecture was useless without evidence, but it passed the time. That business in the woods, following Helen, throwing a rock at her horse, seemed more in line with Rawley than Burk. Rawley was on the place, could watch her movements. But the night attacks on her had come only on the nights when Burk was here. Well, there might be a reason for that. If she was to be found dead it would be sensible to have plenty of other people in the house. Niel and Abbie had been there each time too. Very smart to have a doctor on the place, to certify to the accident.

But why had Burk bought blank cartridges?

He thought about the relation of Burk and Rawley to each other. He wondered how well Rawley's "paper" would stand up in a court of law. Ironic, he thought, if Burk was trying to clear the way for himself, for some future child, and all the time it would be Rawley who would inherit.

He thought about Burk and Rita Rand. She had made her confession, Calvin judged, and Burk had quarreled with her. Now what? He'd see Rita as soon as possible and try to find out what Burk had said. He might have let slip something.

Then he thought about Betty Van Hoyt. His impression of her was not quite clear, for the image of the present, self-possessed young woman was blurred by old pictures of a more helter-skelter girl very much in love with Burk, but there was something distinctly provocative about the thought of Betty Van Hoyt—it would be a pity, he thought, to have her revert to her old fondness for Burk. He wasn't good enough. Calvin definitely didn't like him. He didn't like Rawley either. For the matter of that, he didn't like John Cauldron.

Actually, though, he had more sympathy for John than for the other two. And he could understand, he thought, as his first anger cooled, why Helen had not told him about John. There was that business of John's living here with her so long—she would probably move John out before she let their engagement be known. It would make talk, though Helen would hold her head high and ignore the talk. In the end people would say it was the right thing. . . . No, he could see why she had not told him.

Odd that John, the more cautious of the two, had told Abbie. John wouldn't be worrying whether Calvin Morse got his fingers burned or not—what John was worrying over, Calvin decided, flattening his tired back against the wall, was the fact that Helen seemed so interested in the returned Calvin Morse. John didn't know it was an act. John wanted Calvin to shy off.

Evidently John wasn't any too sure of his hold on her. He must know it came from long habit and association. Well, John needn't worry. He would have no rival for the position of Prince Consort. It would be rather a shame too, Calvin reflected detachedly, to do him out of the reward for his long services.

Deliberately he wrenched his mind away from John and Helen and thought of Abbie and Niel and Niels passion for making money for the hospital. He'd do what he could, get him to let a good investment man handle the money Helen had given to his care. Doctors were notoriously poor investors. Sitting ducks for sharpers.

Finally he ran out of things to think about. No use trying to concentrate on anything in New York, for New York had no relation to him now, a man in a corridor of

Cauldron's Folly, gripping a candlestick. Incredible that he had been back in Somerset only a matter of sixty-one hours.

It was an hour later that he heard sounds from down the hall, to his left. It might have been a door opening, or a creaking floor board. He drew back into the passage, listening intently. Someone was coming—coming very quietly. His nerves tightened; he edged back against the wall, prepared to make a rush when the prowler turned into Helen's room. Then, from the hall, a sudden ray of light shot out, swung about into the passage and beamed straight into his eyes.

He flung himself out of it and at that instant a hushed voice spoke, in mild surprise. "Calvin?"

Calvin said, "Niel?" excitement abruptly deflated.

"You on the same errand?" said Niel, with careful quietness. He explained, "I didn't want to wake Abbie, crossing her room—and that plumbing there sounds like Niagara."

"On my way back," Calvin murmured. "I heard you coming and—" Niel must think his spring away from the light exaggerated, so he threw out, "Your light startled me."

"So it seemed." For all its mildness there was an odd undertone in Niel's voice, a hint of dry suspicion, and Calvin wondered if Niel could possibly imagine that the proximity of Helen's door had anything to do with his excursion. A general practitioner in a small town was probably capable of imagining anything.

Hastily Calvin withdrew to his room, and was careful not to emerge till Niel had time to return. He felt chagrined because he had been so easily detected. He told himself it was natural for Niel to be using a flashlight and that a prowler would not be flashing a light about but that argument did not ring true—a prowler might very well examine the vicinity. Especially a prowler who had thoughtfully removed a revolver.

And then he thought that during the time Niel had been in the bathroom and he had been in his room Helen's door had been unwatched. A man could have come and gone. The thing to have done, he saw now, was to have hidden within Helen's room. He had not thought of that and if Helen had she had not suggested it. Probably John wouldn't have liked it, he thought sourly. Well, she had better get John into this, and let him take his turn standing guard. As far as he was concerned, the first fine careless rapture of these nights was wearing off.

For a moment, on waking, Helen did not know where she was. The window was in the wrong place, the picture on the opposite wall was unfamiliar. Then remembrance flashed through her; she sprang up and wrapping the woven bedcover over her nightgown, she slipped swiftly along the hall and down the service stairs on her side of the house. She heard people moving about the house, heard the cheerful morning noises, but she got to Lucy's room unseen.

She started to unbolt the connecting door but it was already unbolted. She flung open the door to the wardrobe where young, bright dresses were hanging—yes, a man could well hide in there. She wondered vaguely about fingerprints. She went to the barbed wire at the other end of the room, worried for fear it had been seen, and carefully gathered it into the small case again and thrust the case in the wardrobe.

In her own room she looked about. The bedclothes still lay humped into the human semblance she had made; had *he* come in and peered at them, had he realized that heaping up was purposeful? She pulled open the desk drawer and took out her diary. Her eyes widened incredulously as she saw the revolver behind it. Why had it been replaced? Did *he* think she had not missed it the night before? It was like a mad game of cross-purposes.

She opened the diary and there was no page of ragged writing; the page after the entries about Lucy was gone. It had been taken neatly out of the rings. So, now, she could not prove—

But she had seen it. She knew.

There were voices under her window, Abbie Nordstrom's voice, talking to one of the boys about plant cuttings. Such an easy, normal voice—if she told Abbie any of this Abbie would think she was crazy. She must be careful not to show any excitement, not to betray her awareness, to look well and unconcerned. The day was cool and she put on a light wool frock of pale lavender and looked at her image in the glass with critical appraisement. She was too pale, and she looked as if she had on eye shadow, but she could not do anything about that. She brightened her lips and they smiled, in light mockery, at their reflection. You'll do, she said to her image. You look very well for a girl who was to have died last night.

In the dining room Niel Nordstrom and John Cauldron sat at the long refectory table where places were set and she called out cheerful good mornings as she picked up a plate from the buffet table, against the wall. Bacon was in one dish, sausages in another, fish kedgeree in a third. There were eggs in a mound by a receptacle of boiling water, and an urn of coffee.

Niel looked over his shoulder at her. "Do you do this every morning? The perfect English country house."

"You know we don't," she said. She brought her bacon and coffee to the place by his. "We have a sit-down breakfast at the little table by the window. This is a party."

"I don't imagine many English are keeping it up now. But you are certainly carrying on the tradition. Even cold toast." His eyes flicked amusedly to the silver rack of toast before him. "How you can eat that—"

"I suppose it's the way you were brought up."

"Your mother was brought up on hot breads. And your father ought to have been—he was born in the South. Your grandfather too. But that first fellow set the pattern."

"I'm sorry—I'll get you some hot bread."

"Oh, Henry brought me hot corn bread from the kitchen. At least you've given up morning tea," he said, smiling. "Your grandfather had that."

She smiled back at him. "You think it's pretty silly, don't you? Traditional living."

"I think everything's pretty silly that doesn't make for the welfare of the human race."

John said mildly, "I might ask you to define welfare."

"No time for definitions." Niel got briskly to his feet. "All I know is that there's work to do." He stopped and looked down at Helen. "How'd you sleep?"

"All right—after I found the right room," she said lightly. "I tried Lucy's for a change and I dreamed that Ida was calling me—it was so vivid I actually went up to her. Then I went to the room next to Betty. I slept all right then. No reminders," she said impersonally.

"Yes, I think you do need a change. A complete change," said Niel slowly. Then, brisk again, "Well—I'm off. Abbie and I will be back to dinner. I'm dropping her at the house."

John said, when he had gone, "Niel's getting obsessed."

"I expect we'd be obsessed if we saw as much suffering as he does. And felt as warmly about it."

"The thing is," said John, getting up and going to the buffet table, "that Niel's ruthless about anything but the sick."

"Ruthless? I'd never have said that."

"You'd never notice it. . . . These are nice strawberries. They're from the new bed."

He brought back two plates of big, red berries yet in their hulls and put a plate by her. He said, "Niel ate his fruit first. No English ways. Are you really going to New York, Helen?"

He was so careful to make his voice expressionless that she almost said, "Not actually!" in reassurance, and then she thought suddenly that it might be fun to go to New York. She said, "Oh, I may!" very airily because John never argued when she was being airy and light. Now he only said, "How soon?" and she said absently, "Oh—soon!"

"That's the girl!" said Burk from the door. "Never let a scent get cold. . . . You should have been out this morning," he went on, a warm smell of horse and leather entering with him. "It was a great morning. . . . A gallop would do you more good than a New York jaunt."

He roved along the buffet table heaping his plate, then brought it to the place next to hers. "I hope Henry keeps these sausages coming. Are they our own? I mean your own?" His voice was gay and chaffing.

"Yes. . . . Have you phoned Rita?"

"So early? Good God, no!"

"But I want to know if she's coming to lunch at the club. Burk," she said in a lower tone, "did you two really quarrel last evening?"

"Why else did I arrive with another gal?"

"But that's so childish—at this time."

"The time for a quarrel," said Burk, "is when you feel like it."

John got up and went out. Helen persisted, "But aren't you going to telephone?"

"You telephone if you like. This isn't my house and I'm not making the plans."

"It's your wedding," she retorted. "I certainly will telephone." She got up and went out to the hall phone.

The maid at the Rands said that Miss Rita wasn't home. "She's at Cauldron's Folly," she said importantly. Helen began, "Oh, no," then said, "Thank you," and hung up.

"Burk," she reported, "she isn't home. The maid says she's here."

He said indifferently, "She said something about staying with a friend in town."

"What friend?"

"I haven't the faintest idea."

Helen looked at him impatiently. "The wedding is Wednesday. This is Saturday. This isn't any time for funny business. Where did you leave her?"

"She got out, by her request, on Main Street. Main and Lee, to be exact. . . . You seem very edgy this morning. Didn't you sleep well?"

"Sleep well?" She said it rather loudly, for she saw Rawley in the doorway. "No, I had dreams of Ida's calling me—I went up to her to make sure she hadn't wanted me. Then I slept upstairs—in the room ready for Rita. I seem to sleep better in a strange room." She was careful not to look toward the doorway again.

"Well, you've got a lot of choices in this house," said Burk. "I can't see why you didn't put Calvin in a decent room instead of tucking him into that old nursery. Unless you've gone Edwardian," he said with a broad laugh. "Where is he? Isn't he down yet?"

"I haven't seen him." No, and she hadn't seen him last night, when she had needed him.

Restively she got up. Rawley had vanished from the doorway and she heard the front door closing. She went out and saw him standing outside, looking about indecisively. Not breakfasting with his father, Helen thought bleakly. She would be sorry for this boy if there was not that dark suspicion coiled in her.

He had started to move away, as she came out, and on impulse she called, "Mr. Rawley!"

He turned, his movement reluctant. She went toward him. "Haven't you had your breakfast?"

"Not yet. I'm not hungry."

She was conscious that she was staring at him—as if she could read in a face what lay behind it!—and she said hastily, "But do eat now while the things are warm."

"You don't need to worry about me." There was something mocking in his voice—it was like Burk's mockery, she felt, though the voice was so different. He seemed to be studying her, and she thought, He wants to see if I've changed. If Calvin Morse has told me who he is.

He said, "I've got the pictures back on the walls. Like you wanted."

"Thank you, Mr. Rawley." Her voice was stiff for all her effort. She tried to make it light and impersonal. "Have you found out anything more about the pictures? Even if the Institute didn't send you," she said, very gaily now, "I think you know about pictures."

"Oh, I know what I'm doing, all right," he said confidently. He seemed reassured. Then he told her, "Yes, I've found out something. Something I'd like to show you."

"What is it?"

"It isn't a thing to be told. You have to see it. It's all ready to show you any time you can come up to the gallery. Could you come up now?" He seemed suddenly eager, his eyes on hers. She had never noticed before, she thought, how unstirring his eyelids could be.

"Now?"

"Now's as good a time as any. It's a trick picture. Something the artist had fun with. You've got to see it just a certain way—and just one person can see it at a time. Can you come now?"

She hesitated. This was what Calvin had warned her against, the risk she had promised not to run. But there was no risk with people about, when she was on her guard. And if Calvin could stay away last night, she could act on her own now. This waiting was unbearable.

"I'd love to see it," she said quickly. "Let's go."

They went up the stairs together. He opened the door to the gallery and she went through first, but talking to him as it was natural to keep looking at him. "Which picture is it? What sort of trick?"

He closed the door. She couldn't suspect that—doors were kept closed in this house. "It's the man in armor," he said, going toward the wall that faced the windows.

"Old Goeffrey Cauldron."

"That's the name on the list."

They stood before the painting. She felt utterly eager and alert. Last night she had been terrified, taken by surprise, helpless in the dark; now she felt no fear but only wild impatience to have this suspense ended. It would be dreadful to know but definitely more dreadful not to know. If he made one threatening move she would know.

He might, she thought, standing by him, looking with bright interest at the picture, he might strike suddenly at her, to knock her out. Then hurl a picture down on her, making it final. Pretending the picture had fallen. He didn't know that she was ready to run at a move.

"Take a good look at him as he is," said Rawley.

The painting was a big one, next to the small painting of the first Peter Cauldron, the man in armor a stiff fellow with a consciously noble look as if the artist had worked hard to make him impressive. It was a three-quarter portrait, the hands folded on the hilt of a sword, and everything was meticulously depicted in thick paint, the sheen of the armor, the design on it, the jewels on the fingers. Each hair of the eyebrows and the beard was an individual thing. Helen looked back at Rawley questioningly.

He asked, "Do you know that painting on the edges of books—I forget the name for it, but it's a way of painting on the edges of the leaves so that you see a picture when you look straight at it. And then sometimes it's done so there's another picture when you slide back one cover and tilt the edges. It's very fine, delicate work—kings used to have it done for them—"

"I know," said Helen. "I've seen a volume or two."

"Well, this is like that—in a way. The man looks one way when you look straight at him, up at him a little, the way he'd always be shown. The way you're seeing him now. But the painter had some fun—I've got to show you."

He hurried off to the end of the gallery and came back with a ladder, which he set as close to the wall as he could get it, beside the picture. Oh, no, Helen was saying to herself, I shan't mount that, but Rawley said, "I've got to get up there and move it out—I've got it on a long peg so I can move it out. You have to tilt the bottom back to the wall."

He went up the ladder and his long arms reached toward the cord that was on the peg above the picture. He said down to her, "You have to stand close. Close to the wall and look up. Then you'll see something."

He spoke excitedly. She looked up, watching him work the cord farther out to the end of the peg. "I fixed this on purpose," he said. "Now you'll see what the artist thought of this Goeffrey Cauldron." There was a gloating quality in his voice. "But you've got to stand close," he repeated. "And push the bottom of the frame in against the wall. Then look up—"

She was a fool to do this, she thought. But she could jump away in time. The danger—if it was danger—was so obvious.

"Like this?" she asked, stepping forward and taking hold of the frame.

"Push it harder—to the wall." She pushed and the picture tilted outward at a pronounced angle. "Now look up!" he commanded.

She looked up. He had told the truth. This was a trick painting. The pigment piled on so thickly held a secret.

No platitudes now, no noble, composed face. There were dark, griming eyes leering down at her startled look and a red, hungry mouth stood out from the shining hairs of mustache and beard. It was an evil mouth. Avarice and mean-unmasked were in this face. She stared up at it, her attention wholly caught.

And then it happened. The face seemed to swoop down at her, the whole picture came toppling down at her. She dropped her hold, springing sidewise but not quickly enough, and the frame struck her arm a glancing blow. She slipped and fell and the painting fell beside her with a thud and a splintering.

She looked up at Rawley, conviction blazing in her. He was staring down in such utter dismay that her conviction became confusion—she did not know what to think. And then there was no time to know what he would do next, for Betty Van Hoyt was calling from the doorway, "Helen— are you hurt?" and running to her to help her up.

Helen scrambled to her feet, gripping her arm. She said breathlessly, "Oh, no—only my arm—"

"Is it broken? Did that thing fall on you?"

"Yes—I was under. . . . But it didn't hit me . . . only my arm. . . . No, it's not broken." Her eyes were still on Rawley, who was coming down the ladder.

"What goes on?" That was Burk's voice behind them. The crash must have resounded, she thought. There was Calvin in a bathrobe, his hair on end, coming in the other door, from the passage. Oh, if only she knew what to think!

Betty was explaining excitedly to Burk. "It knocked her down. She was on the floor. She says it's only her arm—"

"I slipped," said Helen. "I slipped—getting away from it. I was under it, holding it in."

Rawley said, in a flat voice, "I was showing her some- thing—it got out of my hands. I had to get it out on the peg to have her see it and the peg broke. It got away from me."

"You blundering bastard!" roared Burk. "You might have killed her!"

Rawley lunged at him. His blow struck Burk's chest above the heart with a force that made Burk grunt and stagger. He rallied into a fighter's crouch and drove a right to Rawley's head and Rawley ducked and the blow passed him. Burk rushed him and landed two quick blows, both on the face, and Rawley shook his head, his nose running blood, feinted with his left, then sent a right below Burk's belt. Burk bent over with a groan.

Calvin Morse was between them, and John too—she had not known John had come. She heard Calvin's voice, sharp and edged, "Fight fair!" and she heard Rawley's voice, high and shrill: "You heard what he called me! That's a fighting word. . . . Any fighting is fair enough for *him!*" And then she heard Betty's voice, faint and uncertain against the voices of male anger: "You know he didn't mean anything."

Burk was straightening up, holding onto himself. He managed to stand upright, he managed even a twisting smile and a jeering tone. "So that's a fighting word where you came from? It must have struck close."

Oh, no, no—Helen was saying mutely. Don't say that! Don't say that to him.

Rawley wiped the blood on his face with the back of his hand. His cheek was bruised and his lip was cut and the blood on his mouth made it thick and red. He looked at Burk, hate and calculation in his eyes, and the malevolence of that look, the red, sly mouth gave Helen the shocked feeling of seeing again the secret face in the painting. Rawley said, "You'll eat that word, some of these days," and walked out of the gallery.

Burk made some joke. She did not want to hear it; she could not bear his forced lightness. John began to question her and she told him about the picture and the trick of painting in it, and how it had to be tilted outward to be seen. She was conscious that Calvin Morse looked at her scathingly. Without comment he went up the ladder and examined the peg. The tip was dangling, held by only a splinter. From his face, as he came down, she could tell nothing.

John went to the picture. The canvas was undamaged, he said, and the frame could be repaired. "But you might have been badly hurt," he said soberly. Burk, his breath still uneven, proposed setting up the painting to get the trick effect.

"I don't want to see it again," said Helen. "It's horrible."

"Not till I've had breakfast," said Betty. "I was on my way down when I heard the smash."

"I'll go with you," said Burk.

"I'd better get shaved," said Calvin. "I seem to have overslept."

"New York hours," said John Cauldron a little dryly.

"That's right. Catching up on my night life."

Chapter Ten

"So it's a blank," said Calvin. They were driving to the Country Club for luncheon, four of them in two cars, and Helen had told him about the man in the night. "You don't know who was in the wardrobe, and you don't know whether Rawley meant that picture to fall."

"Was the peg sawed?"

"It didn't feel like it. But it could have been weakened by a knife so it would splinter." And then he said, very coldly, "And you said I could trust you—to be careful."

"I was careful," she insisted. "I got away." She urged, "It was a chance to find out."

"But you didn't find out."

"N-no." She hurried into an offensive. "But if you'd been in the hall last night we could have trapped him."

"I told you how it was. Abbie came in." He added, "Incidentally, my revolver's gone. It was taken out of my room while I was having a bath."

She turned toward him, startled. "Then he suspects you?"

"Evidently. Or maybe he merely wanted a weapon."

"Mine was taken too. And this morning it was in the drawer again. But the strangest thing—" She told him about the line written in her diary, the desolate, defeated words, and the way the page had vanished today.

He looked at her so oddly that she protested, "You don't think I dreamed that all up?"

"I wish I could believe that. It would make life a lot simpler. But my gun's gone. I know you didn't dream that up."

"You can have mine. I hid it carefully before I left."

"No, you may need it. I'll give you some fresh cartridges for it. That package I gave Burk, from the hardware store, held blank cartridges. The hardware man said he'd ordered them."

She stared straight in front of her. Calvin's eyes flicked toward her. There was something touchingly innocent, exasperatingly stubborn, in that clear profile of hers. She said in a low voice, "It wasn't Burk."

"No? Then it must be Rawley." He pressed, "If you're so sure of that, why aren't you sure he let the picture fall?"

"Because he looked so—startled. So chagrined."

"He could be chagrined the plot hadn't worked."

"It could be," she admitted. "I just don't know . . . And it could be that it was Rawley in my room last night and yet this picture thing might have been an accident. I just don't know."

"Neither of us knows a damn thing about anything. This isn't a game for amateurs." His voice was hard. He didn't know when he had been in such a bad temper. It was lack of sleep perhaps, yet he'd gone to sleep again after breakfast.

"We'll know more when we find out about the milk. . . . I gave it to that cat of George's with the broken leg. He was going to have to kill it anyway."

"We'll only know about the milk. Not about who drugged it."

She said hesitantly, "I suppose it's because I find it so hard to believe—"

"You don't want to believe it of Rawley because he's a poor chap who had a bad start. I think he's a sly, cocky devil who could be mean as dirt. . . . You don't want to believe it of Burk because he's your brother. And Burk's another cocky devil with a temper that can blow him to Hades. . . . And you don't want to believe it of Tex Miller because he's another poor chap with a nice smile. Tex Miller is a chump who could get silly drunk and grab at what he wants. . . . Tex is out of these last devilments but he may be involved in the first. You'll simply have to make up your mind to believe it of somebody."

She was silent and he said in the same belligerent way, "Do you want to believe it of John?"

"Of John?"

"Of course you don't because he's near and dear to you. And I'll concede that John is out because he has no motive. And he has every motive for keeping you alive." And to himself he said, because he's in love with you and you've promised to marry him. Aloud he said, "Or do you want to believe it of Niel?"

She said, "Niel?" in the same astonished way that she had said "John?"

"You could, you know. He's been here every time that anything happened. He couldn't have hurt Lucy but he's got a motive to get rid of you. He's got his pocket full of yellow pills and he was bending over your bed that night or his thermometer wouldn't have dropped into it. He gets a hundred thousand in your will—or the hospital does, which is the same thing to him. He told me he'd kill himself, if he were insured for a hundred thousand. He said to me, 'What's one person?'"

She looked at him. "Calvin, how can you think such things?"

"How can I not think them? If I use my head. You don't imagine I like thinking them, do you? But I have to face facts. I was facing them all night in that hall."

They had been driving slower and slower, but the Country Club was before them now. She roused from the silence that had lasted since Calvin's last words and said, in a light, trying-to-be-funny voice, "Well, it's nice to know John hasn't a motive. It's nice there's someone I know who isn't trying to kill me."

Calvin stopped the car. He put his hand over hers. "I'm not trying," he said. "Yet I'm letting you risk yourself, and I don't like it. Shall we stop it, Helen? Shall we throw in the sponge and call for the cops?"

"Oh, *no!* If we sit tight, he'll make some move."

"Yes, and the next time the picture, or whatever the booby trap is, will hit your head."

"At least now, if the milk is drugged, we'll have something definite to give the police."

"Yes—if it is. We can give them a dead cat." He asked dryly, "What have you planned for tonight? You can't work the milk thing again. *He* must know now that you're suspicious, for you didn't drink it."

"I'll say I spilled it last night. I'll take some up myself and leave it about. But I don't like your sitting up all night. We might tell John and get him to take a turn only—"

Only that would risk John, he finished silently. He waited to see what she would say instead of that.

"Only John would put a stop to it."

"You couldn't prevail on him as you prevail on me?"

"You sound so cross, Calvin. I mean John's too cautious. And it would take too long to convince him. He didn't believe in those anonymous letters."

"I might not have believed in them—so completely—if I hadn't discovered, the next day, who had written them."

"You *did?*" Her eyes flashed astonishment at him. "The girl with Tex? Why, how—?"

"Very simply. She walked in the next morning and told me. She was very uneasy about it and wanted some legal advice. There was no harm in the date with Miller, really, but she hadn't told because she thought it would play hob with her plans. You see, it's Rita Rand."

He ignored Helen's startled sound. "Tex Miller had fallen for her and she'd seen something of him till Burk stopped it. She felt she had to see him a last time to make him understand she was serious about marrying Burk." Helen didn't need to know, he thought, how wildly crazy Rita had been about Tex Miller or that Tex had a wife from whom he was separated.

He went on: "I don't see any harm in the meeting, but it seems she had lied to Burk and she was sure he'd think the worst. And he would be furious to have her get up in court and tell the story. She was afraid Burk would leave her flat. But I insisted that she tell him. My idea at the time was to get all the facts to the prosecution so there would be a more comprehensive man hunt. That was before you and I had our bright idea of setting traps. I didn't see her, after we'd cooked that up, to call off the confession. I didn't think about it, really. And now I am exceedingly bothered," said Calvin deliberately, "because it is now quarter of one, and no one knows where she is, not since Burk left her last evening."

He explained: "I wanted to talk to her so I phoned and the maid said she was at the Folly. I phoned her father and he thought she was there."

"Oh, I can tell you that! Burk told me that she was going to stay with some friend in Somerset."

"I thought of that. I asked her father for her friends in town and he gave me a couple of names. No one knew anything."

"She's to be at this luncheon. I told her I was giving it for her."

"Why wasn't she home dressing for it? I don't like it," said Calvin, not looking at her, but staring ahead at the Country Club, "because I'm the one who pressured her into telling Burk at once. And it may have occurred to Burk that she was the only witness who could give Tex Miller an alibi. And it might suit Burk to have Tex Miller convicted. . . . A little item that hadn't suggested itself to me when I was talking to her."

They sat in silence. Then Helen said, very quietly, her voice carefully repressed, "You have to think of that, of course—because you think of Burk as you do. But other things could have happened. She could have picked up a ride home—she'd do that. Something could have happened. With her looks—"

"That could be."

"Or she could have gone to some friends her father didn't think of."

"She could."

"She may be at the club this minute. She may have put on the dress last night that she was going to wear today so she didn't go home to change."

"I hope you're right," said Calvin. "I hope it's just one of my unpleasant thoughts. I hadn't meant to tell you before there was need to, but if she isn't there, someone has got to start looking."

There was a big Saturday crowd at the club but Rita Rand was not there. Helen vanished from the cocktail throng to telephone and when she came back she told Calvin that Rita's father was trying to locate her. "I had to tell him that she and Burk had quarreled," said Helen, "to account for her getting out in Somerset. He tried to joke that off but he was upset. He said she might be staying away from the luncheon because she was 'miffed.'"

"Is that likely?"

"I'll find out from Burk how serious the quarrel was."

"Don't tell him you know the reason for it. Don't speak of the alibi for Tex Miller."

She said, "Very well," stiffly, and went off. He could see her speaking urgently to Burk, and Burk shrugging it off. Betty Van Hoyt, surrounded by friends who had rushed to welcome her, was introducing them to Calvin. Bill Hutchinson, with whom he used to play tennis, was pumping his hand. Then Bill called to Burk, "Boy, am I looking forward to next Wednesday! To see you get the ball and chain about your ankle." He looked about and asked, "Where's the girl?"

"I wouldn't know."

"Run out on you, eh?" said Bill, too heartily, after a moment.

And Helen said, too brightly, "We're expecting her later."

The luncheon turned into a luncheon for the returned Mrs. Van Hoyt. Betty was a star performer, Calvin thought; she kept the talk going easily. Her only mistake—and how could Betty know it was a mistake?—was to drag in the morning's excitement of the falling picture and Helen's near escape. Helen played up, describing the trick painting and the horrors of the ancestral face very, very gaily and promised to give a showing soon, with the picture on a sturdier peg.

"Where is your mysterious artist?" Bill Hutchinson asked. "Why don't you produce him?"

Burk said curtly, "He's a guttersnipe."

"Oh, no, he isn't!" said Helen in that same gay voice. "He comes from a very good family."

Calvin got away as soon as luncheon was over. Helen slipped off with him; she asked him to drive her to Somerset. "Some one of us ought to see Mr. Rand," she said. "Burk won't. He says Rita is sulking somewhere and that he's not going to pay attention to her dramatics."

"I see," said Calvin politely.

There was a glass wall between him and Helen Cromer now.

She said, elaborately polite herself, "Drop me at the bank and I'll talk to Mr. Rand. I think we ought to get the sheriff to notify the police in the next towns—to see if she's been seen there."

"I imagine Rand has already started inquiries."

"If we could only be sure that she hadn't accepted some ride!"

Calvin said to himself grimly, Go on—skate over the thin ice. Pretend while you can. For all his sympathy for her he could not shake off his antagonistic mood. He said bluntly, "Don't be afraid I'm going to mention my own peculiar suspicions now. The sheriff will look just as hard for her without knowing the knots we're tied up in. I'll wait around and take you back to the Folly. I want you to find out how that cat is."

Helen reappeared quickly. "Rand is off with the sheriff now. I'll phone from the house."

They drove to the Folly in silence. Helen said, "Drive through the arch—George's house is back of the stables."

He drove through the arch and then through the courtyard where half the stables had been turned into a garage, and then down the hedged road to George's house. George's wife met them. "Oh, the kitty?" she said. "George put her in the incinerator. She died, you know. Right after you were here, Mrs. Cromer. But it's just as well—that leg wouldn't mend right. She'd never be a good mouser again."

"But how—how did she die? I mean," said Helen, "she seemed all right except for that leg."

"Well—there must have been some infection. She just went to sleep and died."

"I see. Yes, it's probably as well. And how is George's hand?"

"It's getting along all right. You saw it this morning," said the woman, a little surprised.

"I don't want him to do too much with it."

They walked to the house in silence. Then Helen said, in an ironic voice, "So we haven't even a dead cat to show. I thought we'd get it analyzed."

Calvin said, "I was thinking about what would have happened to you if you'd taken the milk."

Earl Sutton was a mild-spoken man with a soft voice and very serious eyes. He settled into a chair with an air of comfortable occupancy, but the others, Calvin saw, kept to the edges of theirs. There was a young sandy-haired officer, there was George Rand and there was, to Calvin's surprise, A. J. Regan. Politely they declined the after-dinner coffee. They had asked for Burk Cauldron and Burk asked, with a parody of expansiveness, "Now, what can I do for you, gentlemen?"

"Well, sir," said the sheriff, "we're after a description of what Miss Rand was wearing last evening, if you can give one. Her father says he did not notice."

George Rand said, "I merely saw her a moment in the hall—as she was going out—"

"I think you are taking it very seriously," said Burk. "But if it makes you feel better to phone about—"

"Twenty-four hours is a long time for a girl to be away," said Regan.

"Yes, it is. But Miss Rand is a very unusual girl. Very capable of taking care of herself. . . . What was she wearing? Something green. Quite a bright green. Really too bright. She had a black coat lined with green. But the coat was left in my car. In back. Her bag too. Neither of us happened to think of it."

"A green dress," said Sutton. The sandy-haired young officer had produced a pad and was writing it all down. "Any hat?"

"No hat. Black sandals. Nylons. And a string of jade I'd given her. No one that she'd encounter, casually, could possibly know the beads had any value," said Burk as if reassuring them.

"Just where did you leave her, Mr. Cauldron?"

"On Main Street Main and Lee."

"Can you place the time?"

"Only vaguely. It was early in the evening. We'd had dinner on the other side of town, at the Dixie Inn, and were driving here."

"Well, would you say it was seven or eight or nine?"

"Not seven. I know we'd dined early, about six-thirty, I'd say. But we took quite a little time to it. And the Dixie is several miles out. I dare say it was about eight. Does it matter?"

"We'd like to fix the time, if we can," said the sheriff mildly.

Burk turned and addressed Betty Van Hoyt, who had retired to the background with the Nordstroms. "What time would you say I came for you, Betty?"

"It was after nine—quite a little after. I'd meant to start earlier, but I was slow getting packed—"

The sheriff nodded. He asked Burk, "Had you planned to call for Mrs. Van Hoyt?"

"No. That was impulse." Burk smiled. "But what difference does that make?"

"Just getting it straight in my head," said the sheriff. "Let's see—if it was after nine when you called for this lady, and about eight when you left Miss Rand—"

"It might have been later. I don't know. And I didn't go directly to Mrs. Van Hoyt's. I dropped in at a tavern and had a drink."

George Rand said sharply, "Just why did you leave my daughter like that?"

"She asked me to." Burk looked at him with not too veiled derision. "We'd had an extremely vigorous disagreement, if you're interested in knowing why. What you might call the very devil of a row. And if you want to know what it was about," said Burk, in the same detached, sardonic way, "it was about that young killer that Sutton's got locked up. Tex Miller. Miss Rand chooses to believe he isn't guilty but a victim of circumstantial evidence. And I think he's guilty as hell. Naturally, our difference was pronounced."

The sheriff's eyes went involuntarily to Helen, then quickly away. "Naturally," he said in an embarrassed voice. He added musingly, "She doesn't think him guilty?"

"He's too good-looking to be guilty," said Burk lightly. "I understand several girls in town hold that view. But I lost my temper."

Rand said, "And left her to get home alone?"

"She wasn't going home. Or to the Folly. She spoke of staying with a friend in town. I didn't ask what friend."

"Lee and Main," said the sheriff slowly. "That's in the center of town. . . . Then why would you say, Mr. Cauldron, that you and she were driving past Laurel Avenue a little after eight o'clock? That's on the edge of town on the way here, you know."

Burk stared. "You seem to be checking up on me, sheriff."

Sutton said patiently, "We're trying to find where she was last. Some people in a car saw you crossing Laurel Avenue. That kinda puzzled me because you say you left her at Lee and Main."

"Well, I didn't drop her at Lee and Main going through town. Our quarrel lasted halfway to the Country Club. The woods there were no place to leave her, so I turned back. Now, does that answer your question?"

"It answers that one," said the sheriff amiably.

"But I've got one," said Regan. He leaned forward, his squared jaw bluntly hostile. "If you drove her back, why wasn't she with you in the car? I saw you driving back alone. You were alone in the car, coming into town. It was after eight-thirty then."

Calvin tightened in attention. There was suspicion in Regan's voice. Regan didn't know what Calvin Morse knew, but he knew that Burk's temper wasn't to be trusted.

"Oh, hell!" said Burk, but still sounding ironically amused. "I'll have to tell you the whole thing. We had our fight, as I said. She didn't like something I said, so we parted, just like that, out in the country. And I drove back, thinking I'd get Mrs. Van Hoyt. But before I got into town I cooled down. I knew I couldn't leave her like that, to walk home, as she'd said she wanted to. I turned around and went back. She said then she wanted to stay in Somerset so I took her to the exact place she wanted, Main and Lee, and left her there. Under the bright street lights. And now will you kindly tell me what difference our comings and goings make?"

The sheriff said gently, "Were just trying to get this straight, Mr. Cauldron. To know at what time she might have picked up a ride. We know now it couldn't have been till after eight-thirty."

"All right. After eight-thirty." Burk's temper was showing. "I don't see the time makes a damn bit of difference."

Calvin was thinking, Half an hour. A little less than half an hour. . . . With Lucy it had been a matter of minutes. But Lucy had been left lying in the woods. There were woods beyond Laurel Avenue. Nothing but woods and fields till the Country Club.

"Any further questions?" Burk was smiling at them scoffingly.

"Anything you want to ask, Mr. Rand?"

"Yes." George Rand was not a too genial little man with jaunty mustaches now; he was a worried, uncertain man, irate and snappish. "I want to ask Burk Cauldron if he thinks he's behaved like a gentleman! Leaving a young lady like that. If anything has happened to that girl of mine I'll hold you directly responsible," he said, turning toward Burk.

"I don't see why. I left her on Main and Lee, under the bright lights."

George Rand got up. "I think you're a cold-blooded proposition, Burk Cauldron! Here you and Rita were to be married on Wednesday and you sit there now as if you didn't give a goddamn—I beg your pardon, Mrs. Cromer— what has happened to her."

"Nothing's happened to her," said Burk. "She's working up a little excitement to get me worried—and I'm not getting worried."

"Well, we hope it's like that," said the sheriff, getting to his feet. He turned to Helen Cromer. She had risen and was facing him, her face ashen white, a shadow perceptible about her mouth. "I'll let you know if we hear anything, Mrs. Cromer," he said kindly. "In the meantime we'll have to do some looking."

"Let's get going on that," said Regan, jumping up.

Calvin said, "I'll go along with you."

"All right, all right," said Burk, "if you think it's necessary." He got up with a slowness that reminded Calvin of that blow below his belt. "Come on, John—let's never have it said the Cauldrons failed in a woman hunt."

From the back of the room Niel said, "I'll go, too."

The sheriff turned back. "That isn't necessary, doctor. You save your strength. There's a lot of young fellows I can rout out by phone and we'll spread out by twos and start to comb the country."

The young sandy-haired officer stuffed his notebook in his pocket and buttoned his jacket over it. "We'll start close to the road first. If she got a pickup ride, they wouldn't be carrying her very far in."

The sheriff gave a warning glance toward George Rand's back. "You button your lip, son. Do your thinking inside your head."

A night search was slow, though after the moon came out the visibility was better. The men worked in twos and Calvin Morse was paired with the young sandy-haired officer who had been in the search for Lucy Cromer and talked incessantly about it. "I think we ought to get the hounds on this," he said. After a few fields and a wood had been thrashed through, the search was abandoned till morning. "Be seeing you at sunup," said the young officer cheerfully.

Calvin drove back to the Folly to find that Burk and John were already there.

"Silly business, wasn't it?" said Burk. "Have a nightcap?"

"Thanks. I'll pour it."

Burk had hot toddies on a tray. Calvin hunted up a bottle and poured out a drink. Helen appeared suddenly behind him. "I'll change my mind," she said in a casual, carrying voice. "Pour me one, Calvin. Straight." In a lower voice she said, her voice remote and indifferent, "I'm sleeping with Betty. Worrying about Rita is the explanation. So get your sleep."

"Thanks," he said briefly.

The phone rang. John answered it and said to Calvin, "It's for you, Morse."

It was Regan. He said, "I found her."

There was a quality in his voice that fed Calvin's forebodings.

"In a ditch," said Regan. "By the road. The bushes hid her."

"Is she—can she say what happened?"

There was a pause. "She won't be saying," said Regan harshly.

Shock held Calvin silent. Then he said, "She's dead?"

"Next thing to it. Concussion. In a coma. It seems to have been a hit and run—"

He went on talking in jerky sentences, giving the details, and Calvin listened in silence. At the end he said, "I'll tell them. I'll see you tomorrow." He hung up and turned around to the half circle of listeners. A hard anger was grinding in him. He spoke directly to Burk. "She isn't dead. But she's unconscious. Hit by a car, apparently. She was found near a highway, outside town. Why was she there if you left her in town?"

"I wouldn't know," said Burk levelly.

Abbie demanded, "How badly is she hurt?" and Calvin repeated what Regan had said. "Concussion. Nothing broken."

"And she was lying there all the time?" said Betty. "All last night and today?"

"All the time," said Calvin. He could see Rita Rand, a limp bundle in a ditch, her bright hair hidden by the bushes. Cars had gone past. . . .

"It's sickening!" said Betty. "While we were at the club." She looked at Burk. "You should never have left her like that!"

"Why not?" said Burk defiantly. "I left her at Lee and Main. If she chose to walk out of town, that's not my affair."

"But why would she do that?"

Burk shrugged. Calvin said grimly, "She'll tell us when she comes to."

Chapter Eleven

Regan's office was a one-room affair over a corner drug-store. There was a transom above the door which Calvin Morse thoughtfully closed when he came in. Regan sat down in a swivel chair before an old-fashioned roll-top desk, nodded toward it, and said, "Inspires rural confidence in low fees," then swung around to face Calvin. Tersely he told the story of the night before. He had kept on searching, after the others stopped, and it was he who had found Rita Rand.

"She was close to the road," he said. "All of our cars had been going back and forth but the ditch was deep there and the bushes hung over her. The green of her dress didn't show up. Anything can have happened. She might have jumped to get out of the way of a car and slipped and struck her head and rolled into the ditch, or she might have been knocked down and got up and staggered into it—we won't know till she comes to."

"Is there any change?"

Regan shook his head. "She's just lying there as if asleep. Brennan says she'll be all right," he said, a little insistently. "It may go on for days or she may snap out at any moment." He added, "There are no cracks or breaks, that's one good thing for sure. And her face isn't hurt." He said soberly, "That kid would have felt badly to come to and find that face of hers was hurt."

Calvin nodded. He was still charged with relief that Rita Rand was living.

Regan went on: "Either Burk Cauldron is lying about where he left her or she changed her mind about staying in town and started to walk home. . . . You heard him say her bag was in the car. . . . There's one thing that makes me think he left her off in town, as he said. My office here is on Main Street and I live on Lee. I was out that evening and there wasn't a light in either place. Susie Pragg—that's my landlady's daughter—told me she thought that Rita Rand walked by our place sometime after dusk. Susie has eyes like a cat. She wasn't sure enough to make a statement to the police but she ribbed me about it. Because I took Rita to dinner. I think that maybe Rita wanted to get in touch with me, wanted me to drive her home. I wish I'd been home."

"I wish you had."

"Of course that could be only Susie's idea. As I said, she wasn't sure enough to tell the sheriff."

"All we can do then is wait."

"That's all."

"In the meantime—" Calvin Morse got a big envelope out of his pocket. "I've been wanting to ask you two or three questions about Tennessee law," he said, "but now I'm going to do more. I'm going to retain you as counsel and put this thing on the table. Here's the story."

Quickly, concisely, he told of Helen Cromer's uneasiness at what seemed attempts on her life and of her appeal to him to come. He told of the renewed attempts at smothering, from which the phone had saved her. "Her idea," he said, "was that there was some criminal, some madman, lurking in the woods—the one who had attacked her daughter. That is one of the things that made her feel that Tex Miller was not guilty. But to me," said Calvin, "it wasn't like that. Only someone inside the house could have drugged those drinks and had access to her room."

Regan's eyes went quickly to the envelope in Calvin's hands, then back to his face.

"That's it," said Calvin. "Motive. That's what I was looking for. Why I asked for this copy. . . . That suggestion hit her hard—at least the suspicion against one of my suspects hit her hard. We hadn't anything but conjecture to bring to the police, and she was determined to find something positive. She reasoned that if her assailant did not know he was suspected he would try again. The idea was that I'd be on watch to catch him. A lot of use I was!"

He told of the glass of milk left out, and how Helen had heard the sounds from the wardrobe and saved herself by pretending Ida was at the door. He said grimly, "Of course that had to happen before I got on guard—my aunt came to my room and delayed me a bit. By then it was all over. . . . That stuff was quick-acting. The cat Helen fed it to died right away."

He set down item after item. Regan listened without comment, his forehead knotted. Finally he asked bluntly, "Whom do you suspect?"

Calvin spread out the will. "Under this will there are two people who—but, first, there's something you should know."

Quickly he sketched Rawley's story. Regan said, "Burk's woods baby, eh? And Burk doesn't know?"

"I don't suppose Burk ever knew he existed."

"Queer he didn't spot him, if you did, using his own name."

"I don't think Burk ever took a good look at him. It happens I've an uncanny memory for faces and that girl had an unusual face. I asked Rawley straight out—oh, very pleasantly—and he was taken off base and said a lot more than he'd intended. That's how I know Burk went through a hill preacher ceremony with the girl and that Rawley has this paper of his that he seems to think will prove him legitimate."

Regan's eyes narrowed to slits of calculation. "It's a funny thing his being in the office of the man that Mrs. Cromer wrote to—to ask to come here."

"It is a funny thing. But funny things happen."

"That's for sure. Does Burk know yet?"

"No. Rawley asked me not to say who he was, not till he was ready or something like that, and I more or less agreed. But I told Helen Cromer. . . . I've a notion that if this chance through Lambert hadn't happened, Rawley would have found his way here, on some pretext or other. He's probably been waiting till he was of age. With his belief in his paper, he's a suspect that sticks out like a sore thumb."

"But—"

"But he's taking chances, not getting his legitimacy established? Why, if he'd gone to court first he'd have had no opportunity to get into the Folly unsuspected, to get at Lucy and Helen. Another thing—he may have certain rights as an illegitimate child. I don't know the Tennessee law and I wanted to ask you about that. But my notion is he thinks he can prove he is legitimate. So he's got motive. Yet we haven't a definite thing on him except he let a picture fall on Helen Cromer yesterday—but Helen isn't certain it wasn't accidental. Much as she'd rather suspect him."

Regan asked, "Rather than whom else?"

"Than her brother. Burk is obvious—except to his sister. The Folly would go to his child."

"He hasn't a child to take."

"He'll produce one, undoubtedly. The ultimate title doesn't have to vest instantly now, you know. In New York

if he ever had a child that child would take. There's been
a statute there for about a hundred years doing away with
the common-law rule that a contingent remainder must
vest at or before the terminating of the preceding estate.
Burk would be guardian of the infant for twenty-one years.
He'd have the Folly for twenty-one years and if the child
died he'd inherit from it."

"You're going too fast for me, counselor. Let's look at
that will again."

Regan came and looked over Calvin's shoulder, his
blunt-tipped fingers moving slowly beneath the lines.
Calvin said, "One of the things I wanted to ask was how
Tennessee takes care of—"

"That's what I thought." Regan's finger had come to
rest beneath the words "to the heirs of my son Burk." He
said, "This isn't New York, counselor. Did you ever hear
of *Ryan* versus *Monaghan?*"

After a moment Calvin said, "I don't recall—"

"A Tennessee case. You wouldn't run across it in a hundred years unless you practiced here."

"But what—?"

"That's a case that turned on the old common-law doctrine that no one is the heir of a living person. And in that
case," said Regan, "'Heir' was held to mean 'heir,' and not
construed to mean child."

Calvin exploded, "Good God, you mean—?" He said
sharply, "Have you got that case?"

Regan went to his shelves, searched about and laid a
volume before Calvin. "Here you are, counselor. *Ryan* versus *Monaghan*. Ninety-nine Tennessee, three three eight."

Calvin read it carefully. He said slowly, "Then—unless
Burk's dead—unless he predeceased Helen—his child can't
take."

"Not in Tennessee," said Regan. "That case is still
apparently Tennessee law."

Calvin found himself arguing. "But that decision defeats the intent of the testator—"

"It probably did in the Monaghan case. In the Cauldron will, I wouldn't know. Maybe old Peter Cauldron was saving a wallop for the future. He had it in for Burk and he could be taking it out on Burk's children."

That fitted in with his own idea of Peter Cauldron, Calvin thought. He said, his voice chagrined, "A New York court would have no difficulty in construing the word 'heirs' to mean children. I could put my hands on several cases to that effect. That's what misled me."

"You had it thrown at you cold, counselor."

Calvin was reading the will again, checking it against the printed page, and Regan leaned over his shoulder again, reading with him. "This Cauldron will," he said, "for some reason—your guess is as good as mine—follows as nearly as possible the phraseology of the will in the Monaghan case. Will Bently—he drew this instrument, didn't he?—must have known what he was doing."

Calvin said, thinking it out, "Cauldron might have instructed Bentley not to interpret this. I wouldn't know. He might have wanted it this way, so Burk, if alive, could never see a child of his in the Folly. But it seems clear to me that Bently has never explained this will. Because Helen Cromer does not know the meaning of it. Helen believes the will to mean exactly what it says—what it seems to say."

"Bently might not have thought it important. Helen Cromer was young and had one child already. I expect Bently never thought it would get out of her line."

"And Burk does not know. I've seen and heard enough myself to be sure of that. Burk was away when the will was probated. He undoubtedly took his copy to mean what a layman would think it meant. What I thought it meant," he said, in frank disgust.

"You're from New York," Regan repeated. "You had it thrown at you cold."

Calvin followed out his reasoning. "So Burk could perfectly well be acting under the belief—"

"He could. He wouldn't see any reason to get a Tennessee opinion on it. Bently wouldn't open up—not if I know Bently. He's a tight-mouthed little clam. . . . Yep," said Regan thoughtfully, "it looks like Burk hasn't stumbled over Ryan and Monaghan yet."

"Nor Rawley. . . . I imagine that Rawley's mother got hold of a copy of the will when it was probated. To Rawley it would look like plain sailing. If he could prove he was legitimate."

"So you've still got your two suspects."

"I think so. Very definitely."

"Plus the third."

"The third? Yes, there is a third possibility," said Calvin reluctantly. "Not one I like to think about." Then he stopped short and looked quickly at Regan. "What third did you mean? Who gets the Folly if Burk's child cannot take?"

Regan did not answer till he had read the will, again. Then he said, "John Cauldron gets it."

"John Cauldron?"

Regan said didactically, "Under the doctrine that no one is the heir of a living person Burk's children are out, so the remainder fails. And since there is a residuary clause that devises to John Cauldron all real property of whatsoever name and nature not otherwise disposed of by the will, John Cauldron takes."

"I see . . . I wasn't sure . . . John Cauldron must know this."

"He may. He may not. He's bookish, I understand, but that doesn't mean he knows law," Regan argued. "And Bently may have seen no reason to tell him."

"John Cauldron has a very exact mind," said Calvin. He thought about the secrecy of John's smile. "I can imagine his knowing it and keeping the knowledge to himself."

"Maybe out of delicacy," said Regan. "At any rate, he's the fair-haired boy who gets the Folly. If Helen Cromer dies as of this moment. So, for my money, you've got three suspects."

"The trouble with that—" said Calvin. He stopped, then went on crisply: "He's going to marry Mrs. Cromer. They are to be married in the fall. This is strictly off the record, Regan."

Regan eyed him interestedly. "You sure of that?"

"He told my aunt. He told her yesterday. They don't want it known yet, while he is living there."

"Well, that let's him out," Regan said. "He's sitting pretty."

John Cauldron had told Abbie. The words kept twisting back and forth in Calvin's mind. But Helen had not told her. Helen had not told him. And Helen had not turned to John Cauldron when she felt menaced.

John Cauldron had been sitting pretty, as Regan said, as long as Helen was unmarried, as long as he could watch her movements. There was no need for violence. Not then. But Lucy had been growing up. She was going away to school in the fall.

It seemed unbelievable that John could live in such intimacy and could plan such horror. But when you live long enough with a thought it loses its strangeness, it becomes so firmly embedded in intention that John himself might not know when it had ceased to be a fearfully debated thing and become a fixed resolve.

Calvin got up and said abruptly, "I've got to go. Thanks for everything."

Regan was looking at him curiously. He said, "There was some third fellow you had in mind—"

"That can wait."

Helen had to know this. And he had to know if John had told the truth about himself and Helen. Then he said to himself that John Cauldron would never risk such a false statement to Abbie. But he had to know.

He was getting into his car when a "Calvin!" in a clear feminine voice made him turn. Betty Van Hoyt was coming out of the drugstore. "I saw your car," she said, gaily. "I bought six different kinds of bath salts to keep at that counter, not to miss you."

"Any news?"

"News? No, I haven't heard a thing. I left right after you did this morning. I took one half the list of guests and your aunt took the other, and between us we've been keeping the wires busy. But it's done, thank Heaven! Every guest has been notified not to show up. You know," said Betty, "it was a little quaint—my telephoning people not to come to Burk's wedding."

"You and Abbie both left?" said Calvin, ignoring the quaintness. "You mean Helen's alone?"

"Alone?" Betty echoed. "Well, hardly! Everybody was bustling about—she was up to her neck in telephones to people to come take the extra chairs away, and to ice cream people not to deliver."

"Yes," said Calvin vaguely. "Yes. . . . May I take you back?"

"I'm not going back till night, thank you. And I've got my own car. But you could run me out to the White Poodle and buy me a cold drink." She said persuasively, "I could do with a spot of quiet with you."

"I'd like to," said Calvin. "I'd like to very much." And that was the truth, he thought. A quiet corner at the White Poodle, a cold drink and a relaxing girl. He said, "But I can't just now. Give me a rain check."

"That's the kiss of death," said Betty.

They looked at each other a moment. "Oh, well . . ." she said resignedly, then, "What's the word about Rita Rand?"

"Just the same," Regan said. "No change since I was there this morning."

He was getting in his car, a hand on the door to pull it shut, but Betty came closer, and he had to hold it open. She said, "Don't think too badly of Burk. He's behaving badly—not showing he's sorry. But you know how Burk is. If you try to force him into an attitude, that's the one he won't take."

"It's no hunt of mine what attitude he takes," said Calvin curtly. "Well—be seeing you."

He drove off quickly. He had a feeling of having been too long away. He had gone with Niel to the hospital to see Rita Rand, and he had gone to the Nordstroms to look over his mail, because, after all, he had an office in New York that wanted instructions about a certain case, and he had waited about for Regan, who had been in court, on an assault case. Heaven only knew what Helen had been up to, during that time. The picture Betty had given ought to have been reassuring but he wasn't reassured. She was probably standing under another picture with Rawley, he thought, or sitting on the edge of the tower with Burk. The mood of cold exasperation was forming in him again. Then he thought that she was probably in the library holding hands with John. Oh, the devil with that!

She wasn't going to like what he had to say about John. And he wasn't going to like what she'd say. She'd tell him she was going to marry John. John wasn't good enough for her. Good old faithful, good old dog in the manger didn't make him good enough. But if that was what she wanted—

A car from the Folly was coming across the level ground toward him, stopping just in front of him. John Cauldron was in it, leaning toward his left-hand window, and Calvin drew abreast and stopped.

"Going to Somerset," said John. "Helen wants some things. Anything I can get you?"

"Just came from there." He was staring too hard at that plain brown face and turned his eyes away. The face told nothing. The voice told nothing. "See you at dinner," said John politely. "Good day."

Calvin said, "Good day," and drove on. He went through the archway to the garage court, left his car there, and stepped into the kitchen. Ida looked up with some astonishment from the dough she was kneading on a floured board.

"Where's Miss Helen?" he asked.

"Why, she's gone to meet you."

"I didn't meet her on the road."

"She didn't go out the road. She went out the fields."

"To meet me?"

Ida looked down on the dough and began to flop it about vigorously. "I got that idea," she said, vaguely.

"Did she say to you she was going to meet me?"

"I don't rightly remember. I just got that idea."

"Ida, please! This is important. I've got to know where she is," Calvin said quickly. "It isn't safe to have her out alone. We're not sure that young man they've locked up is the right one. Somebody in the woods has been following Miss Helen when she was alone."

Ida looked sharply at him and her small, inflexible-looking face altered as his words went home. Without speaking she dusted off her hands and went up the back stairs. When she came back she handed him a small piece of paper. "This was in her room," she said. "I found it when I was picking up after her."

There was a pencil scrawl on the paper. "Meet me as soon as you can at our old Hideaway. Important. C."

The scrawl was not unlike his writing. The Hideaway. Their old meeting place. The rock cave by Cairn's pool.

Even as he stared at it something in him was thinking, This is Burk. Rawley could not know about the Hideaway. There was open fear in his voice when he asked, "When did she go?"

"Not so long ago—just so long it take me to run up and straighten her room. She'd got on her riding clothes. Then I took down my bread—"

"All right, Ida. Thank you. I'll catch up with her."

He ran out to the back. Before the stables a boy was polishing a bridle in slow motion.

"I want a horse," said Calvin. "Will you get me one, at once?"

The boy's hands paused. His eyes roamed over Calvin's tweeds. "You mean right now?"

"Right now. Is there a horse?"

"Not a right good horse," said the boy slowly. "Mr. Burk, he out on Hunter and Miss Helen's on Dandy—and Mr. Burk had Dolly out this morning and brought her in lame."

"Any horse," said Calvin desperately. "Any horse that can move."

The boy chuckled. "Castor can move allrighty. But he's right ornery when he takes a notion."

"Castor then. I'll help you saddle."

Luckily the horse was in his stall. Calvin was wild with an impatience that communicated itself instantly to the big bay. The boy said soothingly, "Whoa, now, whoa."

"Which way did Miss Helen go?"

The boy's hand stopped as he answered. "Way down the fields. Into the woods. I dunno whichaway she went then."

"And Mr. Burk? Did he go out before Miss Helen?"

"Quite some time before. A little after Mr. Rawley went out."

Rawley out, too? But Rawley could not know of the Hideaway. Wait—Burk could have told the Rawley girl in the old days. The girl might even have stolen there to meet him.

He asked, "Was Rawley walking?"

"Yes, sirree. He walking as if the devil was after him and catching up."

The big bay was saddled at last, blowing through widened nostrils as the boy held him for Calvin to mount. "He don't like to go through no gates," said the boy. "That's where he does tricks. He'd rather jump."

That was fine, Calvin thought grimly. That was just fine. He never could stay on a jumping horse. He'd get pitched off just when Helen was needing him. Whoever had sent her that note was waiting for her in the Hideaway.

He headed Castor across the fields and the bay stretched out in a long gallop. Calvin's trousers worked up about his calves. The stirrups were too long for the Italian seat he had acquired and he slid back into something like an old cavalryman's form. He took the pasture fields and, luckily, the gates in them were open, except the final one at the woods. He felt the horse gathering under him and he leaned forward, gripping the saddle without shame. Somewhat to his surprise he was still in his seat when the horse landed and streaked on.

He pulled him in; he saw where recent tracks led ahead. In a short distance the road forked and he took the trail to the left. The marks of the other horse were there. It would not be long, at this speed, to Cairn's pool. Helen could be only a few minutes ahead of him. The hoofmarks showed her horse was going slowly.

It was a curving way with no long perspectives and he heard the horse coming before he saw it. It came galloping, racing as if in panic, the saddle turned. The fear in Calvin tightened. He had to swing into the bushes, and as the horse plunged past, its eyes white rimmed, Castor reared and tried to follow and Calvin had to fight him before he could force him on. He galloped warily, his eyes searching the way ahead, his hands ready to meet the instant need for pulling up. But there was no sign of Helen. There were two lines of tracks now, the one going, the one coming in wild haste.

The pool was just ahead. There was a thicket, he remembered, shutting off all view of it; now the thicket was taller, a high hedge of green, the opening through it overgrown. He slid from his sweating horse and tied him to the nearest tree. Another horse had been there. The ground was pawed, as if he had been tied. The hoofmarks, going away, were deep at the tips, and wide spaced, as if the horse had sprung off in panic. Quickly Calvin pushed through the branches of the thicket that were lacing the old opening.

Before him was the mass of jumbled rock that stretched to the water's edge. Cairn's pool was a dramatic-looking spot, rimmed, except in this one place, by a steep-faced cliff. There was no way up the cliff at the right, for there the edge was sharply cut as if by a giant cleaver, but to the left a rubble of rocks formed a slope on which you could climb to the narrow shelf that ran for a few feet along the face of the cliff. The Hideaway opened on that shelf. It was not an impressive cave; it was a narrow, dark affair, leading back and down into the cliff, and he could not remember whether they had ever carried out their childhood dream of completely exploring it.

Helen was not on the rocks around him, she was not on the shelf before the cave, she was not anywhere that he could see. Terror for her was tightening like a hand on his heart. He began to climb the slope of broken rock, his eyes searching every crevice. He reached the shelf and stopped before the entrance to the cave.

The light fell only a little way on the rock floor, then there was darkness. He said, "Helen!" out of a parched throat. There was no answer. He stepped back, not to offer the back of his head toward that darkness, and turned to find a rock on the shelf, to have a weapon in his hand as he entered. Some remote place in his mind was remembering the hours that he and Helen had spent on this rock platform, looking off to the dead tree across the way that jutted out from a mass of rock at the cliff's base. The fish-hawks used to plummet from that tree.

From the edge of the shelf where he was the cliff went straight down to the water. He looked down to it. And there he saw her. She lay still and quiet, her face a queer green-white in the green depths.

Chapter Twelve

He had no consciousness of coming down from the cliff. There was a moment when he was standing, looking down to the drowned girl in the water, and there was another moment when he was down from the shelf, on the edge of the jumbled rocks, tearing off his coat, trousers, shoes. Then he was in the water, swimming down, down, down, till his hands clutched at her.

It seemed an eternity that he struggled and lifted, his lungs bursting, before her dead weight was on his shoulder and he was clawing his way up to air. He fought his way back to the rocks, bearing that weight, clambering with her across the boulders. He took her through the thicket to where there was earth on which to lay her.

He put her face down, her head turned, one arm stretched out from the shoulder, the other bent at the elbow. He crouched, straddling her slender thighs, his palms on the small of her back, his fingers on her ribs, hoping desperately that he was remembering the right positions he had been taught. He went forward, pressing gently, his arms straightening, then he snapped back. Then forward again.

You must never stop. You must never give up. A doctor had told him that he had worked over a man for two hours before he had shown a sign of life. The Red Cross book said that people had been brought back after four hours of unconsciousness—even after eight hours.

Helen could not have been in the water long. He had been close behind her. That horse had passed him only a few minutes ago. But she must have been in the water before that. She must have tied her horse, climbed to the shelf and been flung off. She had been in long enough to give up the struggle, to sink.

But Helen was a good swimmer. She must have been unconscious before she reached the water. She had been struck in the back of her head—he could see blood seeping through the wet black hair. He could not stop his rhythmic motion to touch it but he told himself insistently that it was not a deep cut.

She was only stunned. And if she had been unconscious when she fell she could not have taken in much water.

What time was it now? He would not move his hand to look at his watch. Probably it had stopped. Time did not matter. He would go on forever. Eight hours. He had thought that improbable at the time but now his hope clung to it.

His eyes were on her blood-drained cheek, and suddenly it seemed to him not so pale, but he told himself that was the sun tricking him. And then the fingers of her bent arm began to curve, to make little clutching motions, and there was a sound in her throat. His hands stopped, ready to resume instantly if the tenuous attempt at breathing failed. But slowly, slowly, she breathed in deep-drawn sighs. The wet black lashes stirred.

He felt an emotion so intense that it was like agony. He lay down beside her and put his head close to hers. "Can you hear me?"

"Of course," she said in a perfectly natural but faintly wondering voice. She made a sudden attempt to sit up and he sat up quickly and eased her back. "Lie still—you have to lie still."

She said distinctly, "I'm all right," and sat up, struggling against his arms, and then bent over a little. "I'm all right," she said again, and then wonderingly, "I'm all wet."

"You must keep still." The book had said there must be no strain on the heart. But Helen had not been half drowned, she had been stunned. . . . But there must be no chill.

"Keep very quiet. I'll be right back."

He hated to leave her even for a moment. He looked searchingly about; Castor was standing peacefully, his ears unmoving. They would have been pricked, Calvin thought, if anyone were near. He parted the branches of the thicket and looked through. Nothing to be seen but the stretch of churned-up looking rocks and the blue water and the steep face of the opposite cliff. He crossed the rocks quickly, his feet wincing now, and snatched up his clothes and shoes from the water s edge. He looked up at the ledge in front of the Hideaway. It was empty. He raced back through the thicket.

She was sitting up, smoothing back her wet hair. He knelt, taking off her wet coat and putting on his dry one. He said worriedly, "We ought to get your wet things off."

"Did I fall in?"

"Don't you remember?" He was hurrying on his trousers, kneeling again to put on his shoes. "Don't you know what happened?"

"I was just standing there. Up on the shelf. Waiting for you."

"Oh, my darling!" he said, his throat tight. "Don't you remember anything more?"

Her gray eyes, looking at him, were clear with consciousness with no memory of fear in them. "Not a thing. Just standing there, looking out at the pool—"

That could happen. Memory stopped at the moment before. It had happened to him once with a horse. He demanded, "Your head—does it hurt?"

She said surprisedly, "It feels all right—just a little funny." She put a hand to the back of it and said surprisedly, "It's cut—that hurts a little."

Shock was anesthesia. He must get her back before the numbness wore off.

"But what happened?" she was asking now. "What happened?"

"I didn't write that note," he told her. "But never mind that now—we've got to get going. Can you stay on a horse?"

"Of course."

"Take it easy," he warned. He was facing her, drawing her gently to her feet. "Take it easy."

"I'm all right." Then he saw her eyes go past him and fill with surprise. She said, "Why, John!"

Calvin whirled. John Cauldron's lean figure was behind them, just emerging from the thicket. He was staring at them with a singular astonishment on that usually shuttered face of his.

"Why, how did you get here?" asked Helen, in that same welcoming surprise.

"On foot. From the outer road." John spoke as if giving himself time to take his bearings. The astonishment was gone and his face held only thoughtful speculation. "It doesn't take long—motoring along the road."

"But how did you know? Did Calvin—"

"I suppose I could carry it off," said John Cauldron, his voice empty of everything but a quiet considering finality, "But it is too much trouble to do all over again."

He added, "And Calvin Morse has some brains. Don't move," he said to Calvin, in the same measured, unexcited tone, "the gun in my pocket is trained on you." Calvin had been looking at that bulging pocket in which John's hand was hidden. "I shoot rather well. I take no chances. Though I admit to some astonishment," he said dryly, "at this—revival."

As if to exonerate that astonishment, John said, "In the Hideaway I could have no notion what was happening. When I'd sent off your horse I went to see if I could get you closer to these rocks—I wanted it to look as if your horse had thrown you there, when you were trying to make him drink—and I heard a horse coming so I went back to the cave. You were very careful, I saw, Morse, not to turn your back to it," he said with dry amusement.

Calvin was silent, his eyes never leaving John. He could feel Helen's fingers tightening on his arm.

"From the way you disappeared, I imagined you were rushing to the rescue and I thought it all waste motion. I waited to give time for you to get her out, to get her on the horse—I could not hear from the cave whether the horse had started or not. But I certainly thought you on the way back. Then, when I was crossing the rocks, I heard sounds—but you were at such an angle—"

His voice changed to sudden savageness. "You had to come blundering to the rescue, didn't you? Dragging her back to life. And now I've got to put a bullet through your head and make it look like suicide at discovery of her drowned body. But you've done me one service, dragging her back. Now I can put her just at the edge of the rocks where her horse might have thrown her."

The distance was too great for a rush, Calvin judged. But if he could get his body between John and Helen. . . .

John's head was cocked, listening. "No one coming yet. But time's short. Her horse will give the alarm. I must get back to the highway—" He ordered, "Walk down to the rocks. Single file. Morse ahead." He moved along, farther from the opening, to keep the distance between them. "No tricks. If you try any tricks, Morse, I'll make her suffer before she dies."

Calvin heard Helen say "John!" in a strained, muted voice.

"Yes, 'John!'" John mimicked. "What did you think John was? The tame cat? The harmless, necessary cat? The ever-grateful orphan? I am more a Cauldron than you! And I have had to take as charity what should have been my own. But not forever. Not forever. I always knew—oh, for a long time I've known that there would be an end. *This* end. Walk on!"

"But, John, why?" Helen's voice was stronger now. "Why?"

"You don't know your father's will, do you? You'll have to die unknowing—but know this much. The Folly comes to me. *Not* to the children of Burk. To me. To *me*. But I had to clear the way."

Helen said, "Not—Lucy?"

There was horror in her voice. She had, Calvin thought, she had desperately to know.

"That was not pleasant," said John. "This is not pleasant." Then his mouth thinned to a grimace of mockery. "But you wanted a complete change."

He brought the revolver out of his pocket. He said to Calvin, "It ought to be close, for suicide, but cigarette burns will do. And it's your gun too."

There was no sound in the silent woods behind them, no sound of a hurrying horse. Hadn't Helen's horse gone straight home? Had he refused the closed gate and veered off into another trail? Or had he quieted, crossing the fields, and stopped to graze? But some one might come at any moment. At any moment. If only he could delay, could gain a moment more of time.

He said mockingly, "You think you're foolproof, don't you?"

"I always have been."

"Always?"

John Cauldron looked at him with that old air of suck-
ing on secret amusement. He listened again, then, reassured, said mildly, "They always thought Lee Cromer's
death was an accident, didn't they?"

"Lee?" came from Helen.

"You never doubted but that his gun went off acciden-
tally, did you, Helen? Clambering over rocks. These very
rocks you will die on. I met him here. He thought it by
chance. It was not difficult to get behind him, with a rock.
Then I set off his gun." The amused, gloating voice turned
savage again. "You didn't think I'd let you have more children, did you? Now—on with you. Morse ahead!"

Calvin said, "Run! Run to the horse!" and hurled himself on John. He could not make it, he knew; the gun was
on him, point blank, aimed at his guts, the bastard, so
ducking was no good, but in his death struggle he might
bring John down, give Helen time. He saw the finger move
on the trigger and in the same split second heard the roar
of the shot.

But he was not falling. He felt nothing. And in the moment that he was lunging forward he saw John Cauldron's
face changing, like a face in slow motion, from ferocity
to stupefaction, and then he was on John and they were
rolling over and over on the ground, and he was twisting
John's wrist behind him and John shrieked and kicked and
got away, crashing through the thicket, and Calvin, not
stopping for the dropped gun, took after him.

John fled across the rocks and up the slope of tumbled
rocks. He stooped, then ran again, and Calvin slipped in
his untied shoes and when he gained on John, John whirled
and sent a rock back that he dodged and then another that
caught him in the middle and knocked the wind out of
him. John made the shelf, but Calvin was right behind

him now, and John ran past the entrance to the cave, on to the limit of the shelf, then scuttled, like a frantic crab, up the face of the cliff to the top. He raced on about the edge of the cliff, circling the pool.

He came to the spot above the point of rocks and with a scream that the cliff walls re-echoed he flung himself down, his body splintering through the branches of the dead tree from which the fish hawks used to plummet. From the first boulder that it struck the body fell like a sack onto a lower rock.

Calvin came slowly down the slope. Helen was standing on the rocks, staring across the water, her face a mask of horror. Calvin put his hands gently on her shoulder and turned her about. "It's all over."

She was in a big chair in the main room, her head resting against the pillow behind it. It did not hurt, unless she jarred it, and the room was steady unless she moved her head, and then it moved from left to right, dizzyingly but only for a moment. Niel said she would be all right in a few days.

Niel was there now with Abbie, and Burk and Betty Van Hoyt, and Sutton was there with the sandy-haired officer with the notebook, and A. J. Regan was there. Calvin had been talking. She was very proud of the way he told them; he did not say anything that was not true but he left everything unsaid that was irrelevant now, and hurtful.

"And that's the story," he said. "We were very much in the dark until Mr. Regan gave me the important facts in Tennessee law." He added, "And here's the gun. It's my gun all right. He took it night before last."

"Oh, no, he didn't," said Burk. "I did." He said, smiling broadly, "And you can thank me for it. The cartridge that didn't hit you wasn't a dud—it was a blank."

He explained, "I dropped in your room to get some cigarettes off you. You weren't there but the gun was and I borrowed it. You see, I'd promised to let Joe and Carl have mine and I'd forgotten to bring it along, so this would do just as well. I wasn't sure what they were going to do—shoot some game Helen didn't want shot, I supposed—so just for the hell of it I'd ordered some blanks. So I put in the blanks."

The sheriff asked, "How did John Cauldron get it?"

"Oh, he saw it in my room next morning—he was in there when I was getting out early to go riding. He asked what I was doing with a gun and I said it was Calvin's and I'd taken it to give the boys. I didn't say anything about the blanks. I wasn't going to spoil the joke. I expect he pocketed it after I was gone. I never thought about it again. Not with that fracas in the gallery and then the excitement over Rita Rand."

Rita Rand. How casually he said it. And that casualness wasn't assumed. He had been very cheerful when he had told her that everything was over, had been over since the night of the quarrel, between him and Rita. "It wasn't a good idea," he had said. "Not one of my best."

Burk would never know what Calvin had feared, with Rita Rand. And there had been a moment when she too—but, no, she never really had believed.

It hadn't been a good idea for Rita either, Helen thought. She was too young.

Regan was talking about Rita now, asking the sheriff if he had any line on the car that had sideswiped her. Rita had recovered consciousness that afternoon and made a statement.

"She never saw it," said Sutton. "She said she was walking along, and it came up behind her. That's something we'll never know. But she's coming along fine now." He gave Regan a quizzical look. "Your visit cheered her up a lot."

Regan would be good for Rita, Helen thought. He was young and vigorous, a coming lawyer.

Regan was changing the subject. "There's no question now, is there, but what my client is in the clear?"

"No question at all, son. Not after the statement made to Mrs. Cromer and Mr. Morse. Just a few formalities."

Sutton was getting up, and the sandy-haired officer put away his notebook and rose too. Sutton came over to Helen, and she sat up quickly to shake hands, and for a moment the kind, sober face whirled before her, then it steadied. "I guess you don't need to have me tell you how sorry we are, ma'am, nor how grateful it didn't turn out worse. I expect he wasn't right in his head, that's the kindest thing one can think of him."

"Yes." She must make herself smile, she thought. No use explaining that never, never while there was the breath of life in her would she think one kind thing of John Cauldron.

The sheriff held her hand a moment longer before he let it drop. "A lucky thing for you that Mr. Morse was around."

Now she could really smile. "Yes. Yes, it was."

"I'll be going along, too," said Regan.

"Now we can really talk," said Helen. She had not leaned back. She wasn't going to be a wan invalid when she said this, she thought. She wasn't going to say it all tonight; she and Burk could talk later about Rawley, and what could be done for him. But the part about the Folly had to be said.

"I want to tell you what I'd like to do," she said. She wasn't sounding excited or emotional, she thought approvingly, but quiet and controlled. "Niel is right—this place

is too much for me. I want to get away from it. The memories are too dreadful. I can't give it away, but I can let half
of it be used as a hospital or a convalescent home— Niel
will know. And if Burk wants to live in it—"

"In the other half of it?" said Burk scornfully.

"You'll find half of it is big enough to care for."

Betty Van Hoyt said quickly, "Why, yes, Burk. You
could throw the front hall into your side—and run a wall
out from the archway."

Burk gave a sudden laugh. "Not too high a wall if there
are pretty nurses! But what are you going to do, Helen?
Move into the tower?"

"I never want to see the place again!" she said, her
feeling breaking out. "Too much has happened. Oh, I'll
change, I know, and come back for visits, but I want something else. Another life. A life of my own. Away from
Cauldron's Folly."

She couldn't say it any plainer than that, she thought
desperately, and if he had meant anything by that *Oh, my
darling*—if the long years of love and longing had meant
anything . . .

"You know," said Calvin Morse, into the sudden silence,
"that in China, when you save someone from drowning—"
He was speaking to them all, but his eyes were looking at
her and she would never, she thought, never forget the
look in them, never, any more than she would forget the
moment when he had thrown himself at John Cauldron
facing that gun.

"So," she heard him saying, his voice still light, and
now very gay, "I am taking Helen to New York."

NICE PEOPLE
MURDER

Part I: Chapter One

I came home early that summer evening just as Jeff Ryder—we share the walk-up—was saying some last words to a caller I'd never met before. His name was Hazlitt and he was a very prosperous-looking citizen, somewhere over forty, in dark gray tweeds I'd have liked to afford, and from the way Jeff introduced us I could see that he was somebody important to Jeff.

Jeff told him that we were old college friends and he asked if I was an attorney, too, and I said, "Engineering." I had finished college after the war. He asked what firm I was with and I told him and he said they were good people. He said it in an abstracted way, as if turning something over in his mind, then he said, "Since you two live together why don't you both come? My brother, I know, would be glad to have you, Mr. Kent."

Jeff elucidated, "Mr. Hazlitt has asked me for a weekend at his brother's place in Maine."

Well, I didn't know his brother, and I didn't know this Hazlitt—he was just a nice-seeming, older guy to me—and it didn't look like a lot of fun, so I said, "That's very kind of you, sir, but—"

"It would be doing us a favor," he said, before I could get out an excuse I'd have to stick to. He said it in a very serious way. "I'd like to take you both up by plane.

Your traveling expenses, naturally, would be part of the arrangements."

He turned to Jeff. "It would make your coming seem much more casual. I would be bringing two young men, two friends, and it would not be obvious that I was bringing an attorney. As I told you, my brother would rather not have it known that any legal work is involved."

So this was business, not jaunting. I was glad for Jeff, for it was hard work starting to practice law all over again. He'd been in with his father before the army took him, and his father had died while Jeff was overseas. Some of the old clients were coming back but a good many had made other connections.

Jeff said bluntly, "His brother is T. D. Hazlitt, Cal."

I knew the name then. It was a fairly big name. The Hazlitt Steel Corporation was a good company. I knew something about it, as an engineer, and from way back, ten years back, I knew something about T. D. Hazlitt.

"I know the name," I said. "And I used to know Mrs. Hazlitt."

Hazlitt gave me a look that made me feel something was wrong. It occurred to me that ten years is a long time and maybe there had been a switch. I hadn't heard of any divorce when I was home, in upstate New York, and my people would have been likely to mention it, for they knew Helen's people, who lived near there.

"You know Mrs. Hazlitt?" You couldn't say his voice was disturbed but it had a cautious sound that went with his look at me.

"I knew Helen Hill," I said. "Before she was married. I haven't seen her since." I added, "I never knew her very well."

In a way I hadn't but in a way I had. Helen had been one of the stars in our young world, but there had been times when she came down to earth a little.

"I see. . . . I think that would make it seem even more natural," Hazlitt said thoughtfully. Then he told me, "But I would appreciate it, Mr. Kent, if you would not let Mrs. Hazlitt become aware that Mr. Ryder is there in a legal capacity."

"Certainly . . . but suppose she asks me what Jeff does? Perhaps it would be better if I didn't come."

"No, it would be better if you came. She'd be as likely to ask Mr. Ryder himself, and if he were alone his profession would have more significance. If you come he can seem to be there because I had invited you. The fact that he is an attorney isn't necessarily significant—it is the fact that he is acting as attorney for my brother that is to be regarded as confidential."

"It will be," I said. "And I'll be glad to come if you think my coming will be more use than detriment to Jeff."

"I think it will be. And we'll try to give you a good time. Both of you. This won't be all business, you know, Mr. Ryder."

He went over the arrangements he had made with Jeff about the plane for Thursday afternoon, shook hands briskly, as if satisfied that everything was under control, and took himself off.

Jeff and I got out the Scotch we'd saved for something special. Going up to Maine to do a piece of business for T. D. Hazlitt was a big thing to Jeff.

"Not that anything more will come from it," he said. "This is just a job, period. Something his brother had scruples about handling."

"Scruples—?"

Jeff explained, "He's making a will—a new will. Stanley's a lawyer and does all the legal work for the company but he doesn't want to draw the instrument—the will—because he benefits under it. He could perfectly well draft it but he'd rather not. Keeping clear of undue influence. So T. D. told him to go get an attorney."

"That's an important will," I said. "He must have scads of money."

Jeff nodded. "It will be the biggest will I ever drew."

"How come you know this Stanley Hazlitt? You've never spoken of him."

"I don't know him well. I've run into him at several places now and then and he was very pleasant—said he used to know Dad. He told me tonight he'd picked me partly for that and partly—" Jeff grinned, cocking those peaked black eyebrows of his—"because of my 'youth and inexperience.' His brother told him not to bring anyone from a firm that Mrs. Hazlitt would know, and Stanley thought I'd seem too young and unimportant—that's what it boils down to— for her to suspect I'd be employed by T. D. Hazlitt."

"They're making quite a point of keeping Helen in the dark," I said. "Looks like they're putting something over on her."

"What's she like?"

"Helen—she's quite a girl. Or was."

I thought back. Ten years is a long time. The picture I had was of a girl in her teens with shoulder-length blonde hair. Slim and restless.

"Strictly from impulse," I said. "Used to talk a lot off the top of her mind. Maybe that's why they don't want her to know about changes in the will. Maybe that's all there is to it."

"Could be. Or could be he's cutting her out of a chunk. . . . Any children?"

I said I didn't know, that I'd never seen her since she married Hazlitt ten years ago. She was eighteen then, two years younger than I was, and I was away at M.I.T. when she was married. That was about the time I had met Jeff, when he was at Harvard Law. Before Pearl Harbor.

"He must be plenty older," said Jeff, getting out the *Who's Who*. He turned the pages. "Yeah—he's forty-five."

Then he had been thirty-five when he had married. That didn't seem so old to me now, but it had seemed so to Helen's crowd then. There had been lots of excitement and headlines about that wedding.

"He's a smart cookie," I said. "He built that company up from nothing."

"No children," said Jeff. "Unless there's a recent Blessed Event. I thought he might be making a trust for a child— but why keep it so hush-hush from her? . . . Stanley isn't here," he said. "Doesn't rate. He told me he wasn't any part of the company."

"Must make a nice living from its legal business, though."

"Very nice. Notice how he spoke of 'my brother' as if he were God? I got plenty of that before you came."

"You'd feel the same if you got your living off him and were being nicely remembered in his will."

"I don't know what the hell to charge," said Jeff, tilting back his chair and ramming his hands in his pockets. "Whether to make it commensurate with T. D.'s stature or modest like my youth and inexperience."

I said that maybe they'd charge off my keep against his bill and we kidded back and forth. Jeff felt this business was really going to town and I was pleased as punch for him. I liked Jeff Ryder a lot and I'd always got on well with him, though he didn't always get along with people. Sometimes he rubbed them the wrong way. He was a lean, lanky chap with stubble-brush black hair and sharp-pointed brows and a quirked mouth that gave him the look of laughing at you. He had high cheekbones and a stubborn jaw and his face was a homely one but interesting. He had fewer prejudices than any human being I ever knew. His mind was as wide open as a prairie.

We both looked forward to that weekend. I was curious about all the mysteries and now that I'd been reminded of Helen I liked the idea of seeing her again and in this setup. I knew something of Maine but nothing of the sort of Maine that I fancied T. D. Hazlitt might provide and I imagined it would be worth seeing.

It was. The harbor was a wide sweep of beach and rock between great promontories and the Hazlitt place had the southern promontory. The point of it was really an island, for a chasm cut sharply across it, but a steel and stone bridge took care of that. The tide was roaring under the bridge as we drove in. I took in the drawbridge effect, and then the road curved about a ledge of rock, and there was the house, seeming part of the long gray ledges on which it was built.

The car stopped in a covered entrance and Jeff and I followed Stanley Hazlitt inside. From the hall I got the impact of a big, baronial room beyond, with a fire burning in a stone fireplace. The place was empty as a Hollywood set except for the man who opened the door and a younger man who popped out behind him to help the chauffeur carry up our bags.

We went into the big room and up a wide staircase into a hall that ran like an open gallery along one side of the big room below. Hazlitt, leading the way, stopped before a door on our left. "This must be yours," he said, but the houseman said, no, the gentlemen had the two single rooms farther on. He said, "Beyond your room, sir."

"This is pleasanter," said Hazlitt. His voice had a stubborn sound, as if he didn't like to be wrong in even a small thing. "I think they'd like to be together." He threw the door open. "It's ready, of course?"

The houseman said, "Certainly, sir," with wounded pride, and nipped inside and turned on the lights. It was a fine big room with two single beds and long chairs and tables and a chaise longue.

"You'll like this," said Hazlitt genially. "More fun to be together. Mine's next. We're on the cliff side."

I went over to the windows and looked out. It was like looking out from a small mountaintop. Across the bay I saw the other promontory dark against a sky stained with sunset color, and off to the left was the sweep of harbor and the shapes of houses back of the beach and piers running into the water, and boats anchored at buoys. Then I looked down and I was looking straight into the ocean. "Cliff side" was right. This side of the house was built on the edge of a sheer precipice with the sea crashing away below.

I gave an exclamation that made Hazlitt laugh. He said, "Don't walk in your sleep!" then, reassuringly, "No danger—the casements are too small for a man to go through. T. D. saw to that."

Jeff Ryder came and looked with me. He said, interestedly, "I'll bet I could get through."

"I doubt it," Hazlitt said. "Though you're unusually thin. . . . The gulls are rather noisy this side, I'm afraid." I said, "After New York, gulls won't mean a thing."

"Good. Dinner at eight. Informal, as I said. Be down about twenty before eight. My brother is always punctual."

He went out and the chauffeur went out and we told the houseman, who had been lighting the laid fire, that we wouldn't need him to unpack, so he went out. Jeff and I grinned at each other.

"Nice billet," he said.

"C and G billet," I agreed.

He glanced at his wrist watch and went over to his case on the stand at the foot of one bed. "Informal," he muttered. "Tweeds or the gray suit? I've got no country clothes."

"Tweeds," I said. I began to zip open my old flight bag.

There was a knock and the houseman was back with a bowl of flowers, from one of the prearranged rooms, for he asked, "Shall I bring the other flowers?" Jeff said no, that one bowl was enough, and after the man had gone I shook my head at him.

"Rugged!" I said. "Making do with one bowl of flowers."

We got downstairs at twenty to eight and both the Hazlitt men were there. The two were alike, yet not alike. You would know them for brothers but Stanley was like an expurgated edition. T. D. had the vitality, the authoritative lines, the darker hair and eyes. There was a scattering of gray in his dark hair and he was beginning to get a little heavy but in a hard, solid way that made you feel he paid attention to keeping fit. I never saw better tweeds nor better-cut tweeds. He evidently paid attention to every little thing. And you paid attention to him. No doubt about it, T. D. was quite a person.

He looked us over sharply, then said he hoped the flight hadn't been rough. Then he said, "My brother tells me you know Mrs. Hazlitt."

"I knew her when she was a girl. We lived in the same place . . . I missed the wedding, though. I was away at college."

His eyes switched to Jeff. "Are you from Malone, too?" he asked.

"No. Kent and I met at college. When I was at Harvard Law."

"I see. . . . My brother has a high opinion of your discretion, Mr. Ryder. I'll be seeing you—on business—the first thing in the morning."

Everything T. D. said was short and sharp. He moved quickly, too. His turning was the first I knew that Helen was coming toward us. She had come out of some door under the gallery behind us.

Hazlitt said, "My wife—Mr. Ryder. Mr. Kent."

I would have known Helen anywhere. Her hair was scooped up, instead of floating about her shoulders, but it was the same shimmering fairness. She had big pearls in her ears and a string of them about her neck and the gown she wore might have been an informal hostess gown, but it had a regal touch—a medieval-looking thing with long loose sleeves. Its soft green-blue color was just right for her.

She didn't know me for a minute. When I said, "Helen—?" those sea-green eyes of hers were vague before they brightened.

"Calvin Kent! How bizarre!" she cried then. "I'm so glad!"

She sounded glad. She said, "It's been years—" and I said, "Ten of them."

"The last I heard you were in the war."

"That's a long time ago. I've been out five years."

"I haven't been back to Malone since the war." Then she asked, her voice sharpening, "What do you do now?"

"Engineering."

"Oh!" She turned to Jeff. "Then you, Mr. Ryder, must be the attorney?"

Her voice was light and brittle, the way women's voices are when they say devilish things. In the same airy way she tossed out, "My husband said that Stanley was bringing one," and I felt—and Jeff must have felt—that a small booby trap had gone off among our careful plans for secrecy.

Jeff said with a stiffness I knew he was trying not to show, "That's my profession."

"Interrupted by the Army," said Stanley Hazlitt. If he was disconcerted he didn't show it. He'd been a lawyer a longer time than Jeff. He went on, "He was in the Judge Advocate General's office overseas."

"You must have had a lot of excitement, Mr. Ryder," said Helen. "I'm afraid you'll find making wills very dull after that."

It was the way she said it that gave you the feeling of inner fireworks. She didn't say it as if it were a piece of business that she and her husband were agreed upon; she

said it as if she wanted you to know that she knew what
was going on, as if she enjoyed shying verbal rocks around
on the thin ice of appearances.

"Have a martini, Helen?" said Stanley Hazlitt, gently,
and handed her one from the tray the butler was presenting.

She said, "Oh, thank you, Stanley!" in an exaggeratedly
sweet and mocking way.

I hadn't looked at T. D. before, not wanting, somehow,
to have him catch me spying on domestic tension, but I
looked now and T. D. seemed unconcerned. He was occupied in selecting his particular old-fashioned, one without
fruit, and the hors d'oeuvre that he liked.

He advised us, in his short, quick way, "Try the salmon.
Not bad."

Then he looked up and something tightened in his face.
A girl in black was coming across the hall. She was as spectacular, in her dark way, as Helen was in her fairness. She
had sleekly smooth dark hair and great dark eyes that gave
her a Spanish look, but her face was not the narrow Spanish type. She had a strong-angled jaw and a short chin.

She came up to us without a word or a smile and she
merely repeated our names, when we were presented, in a
stiff, detached way as if this was something that she was
compelled to do but that she'd be damned if she pretended
to like it. If ever I saw a woman in a black, stifled rage it
was this Miss Gaynor. Judy Gaynor, her name was.

Helen greeted her with a "Well, Judy—?" with a hint of
mockery too obvious to mistake.

The girl gave her a level look.

"A martini?" said Stanley Hazlitt.

"Thank you."

Her voice was as taut as her bearing. It was a beautiful
voice, low and vibrant, but with a hard edge to it.

I had a feeling—I didn't need to be very bright to have
it—that she and Helen were at swords' points. I wondered

where this Judy Gaynor came into the scheme of things. She could be family—she could be having something to do with this new will that Helen hadn't been supposed to know about. Or the antagonism might have nothing to do with the will. It might be over bridge or clothes or any feminine thing.

Anyway, there they were, giving off electricity like cat's fur, and there was T. D. with his hard, handsome face, his air of "I am Gibraltar, and to hell with you waves down there," and there was Stanley Hazlitt trying staunchly to pretend this was a pleasant gathering, and there were Jeff and I, the outsiders, being very careful not to look at each other for fear we'd give away our awareness of the tension we felt about us.

At dinner I was on Helen's left with Miss Gaynor on my other side. Jeff sat across from me, between Helen and Stanley Hazlitt. As we sat down, Helen began to ask me about people we used to know, but we didn't get very far with that for neither of us had kept up with the old teen-age crowd. We were all pretty well scattered. I talked a little about Malone, for I had just been back, but she hadn't been there for some years. She said her people usually visited her in New York.

Everything she said was perfunctory. The flicker of interest that had sprung up when she recognized me had died out and she was in some world of her own. Sometimes her eyes fixed and grew bright as pinpoints and sometimes they slid restively around the table. She was in a state of tense, inner excitement. There was no mistaking that. I had the feeling—perhaps because I had known Helen when she was a little girl and knew her reactions—that there was something defensive in her tensity.

Our talk shifted to New York, but it didn't do well there, either, for we weren't living in the same echelons, though we'd seen some of the same shows, and, anyway, she was only attending to me out of the top of her mind. After a while she turned to Jeff, going through the motions of a hostess, and I turned to my left.

Judy Gaynor was sitting there as if insulated. I don't know how better to describe her air of having no part in anything happening about her. She did not show the slightest awareness of my attention, so I made the opening gambit. I used the weather. Colder up here, wasn't it?

She looked at me then briefly. She said, "Yes, it's a good place for gulls."

Around my shoulder came Helen's voice, switching from something she was saying to Jeff. It was very bright and merry.

"What did you say about being gullible, Judy? Not you, surely!" The mockery was fairly blistering.

The dark girl merely looked at her, then turned to the platter the butler was offering at her left. I waited until he had come to me, then leaned toward her again.

"How's the swimming?"

She said, "Bracing," as a minimum of response.

T. D. was at her left, at the end of the table opposite Helen. I saw him looking toward us, toward the girl, rather, and among several things I couldn't interpret I thought I caught a sardonic amusement.

"We'll have some good swimming for you before you go," said Stanley Hazlitt across the table.

I said that would be fine. But, having a streak of perversity in me and just for the heck of it, I kept on at the girl.

"Are you staying at the house, Miss Gaynor?"

She gave me another of those brief looks of frantic exasperation at having something teasing and futile to attend to, something outside the periphery of the storm that was within her. I could not exaggerate the impression her big black eyes gave of stark, raging fury.

She said in a clear, cold voice, "Yes, I am staying at the house. I am Mr. Hazlitt's secretary."

Helen's voice whipped across me again. "And a very dear friend to all of us."

Judy Gaynor smiled. It was a grimace of a smile, seen from the side, with a tensing of muscles about the sharp-angled jaw.

Helen ran on, inconsequentially, "Oh, Judy—I borrowed your binoculars—you don't mind? They were on your window seat. . . . Remind me to give them back to you, tomorrow."

"One really doesn't need binoculars," said Judy Gaynor.

No one said anything, for a moment. It was one of those silences.

Then Stanley Hazlitt said, his tone determinedly casual, "The air up here alternates between fog and clarity."

"Yes, doesn't it?" said Helen, and laughed.

Even Stanley gave it up as a bad job. Helen went on talking to Jeff, her voice elaborately light and gracious. Presently T. D. began to ask us questions about our ideas of the condition of the country and the chances of recovery. They were intelligent questions, the kind you might expect, and the rest of the dinner passed like any other dinner.

Directly afterward, a man and his wife, the Willard Bronsons, came in for bridge. They seldom dined out, it was revealed, because he was on a diet for ulcers and she on another diet. Stanley explained that T. D. was keen on bridge as relaxation. So T. D. and Helen and the Bronsons played. Judy Gaynor sat reading for a while, then disappeared and we three men played canasta for low stakes. Jeff won. Then the bridge broke up and there was milk and fruit juice for the Bronsons and highballs for the rest of us and the Bronsons asked us to cocktails the next day. They were giving a party for somebody who was something very important in the U.N. setup and the Hazlitts had already accepted.

Up in our room Jeff and I talked over the situation in carefully lowered tones since we weren't sure of the sound-proofing between us and Stanley. He thought Helen was "unstable" but said Judy Gaynor was terrific and he wanted to know what made her tick.

I said she ticked like a time bomb and I didn't want to be there when it went off. We agreed it had been a pretty moment when Helen chatted about the will. Jeff said he was looking forward to getting the answers the next day. "Which professional secrecy will prevent my revealing," he said, grinning like a gremlin. "You know, Cal, this is going to be very, very interesting."

"What do I do with myself?" I said grumpily. "Show my battle scars to that proud beauty who spits in my eye?"

We were ready for bed then and I drew the curtains back and opened the casement and found I was looking into fog. The cries of the gulls came out of it like cries of distress.

I muttered, "A long weekend." Then I said, "I'll bet I know why T. D. made these casements too small to get through—so his guests won't just jump out and end it all."

"I could get out," said Jeff, pulling up his blankets.

I said, "The hell you could!"

"She's got nice eyes, though."

"Nice? They're gorgeous. And they're all yours, brother. Not my type."

"I'm scared to death of women," said Jeff.

That was the truth, too. It had been, in college, and it still was, as far as I could see since I came back. He'd got engaged to a girl at college, through no fault of his own—one of those things where you think it's for fun and find it's for keeps—and he'd had the devil of a time getting loose. Now he was wary. And he liked logic, reason, fact. Girls were like booby traps to him.

But he wasn't indifferent to them. That was why he was scared.

Chapter Two

In the morning the fog was gone and I felt cheery again.

The air was crystal clear with that salt tang that Maine air has and the lines of the harbor were sharp and beautiful. The sea below us was green-blue mottled with white foam from the waves that crashed against the rock.

I wanted to get into that sea but there wasn't time. At Stone Ledge there were breakfast trays for the feminines but the men breakfasted downstairs at eight and Stanley had mentioned again that his brother was always punctual.

Nobody talked much at table. There was a paper apiece—T. D. took all kinds—and we read comfortably while we ate. After we got back to our room, the interroom phone buzzed and T. D. said he was ready for business, so Jeff went down the hall to where they were to work. Then the phone rang again and it was Helen calling me. She asked, "How's for a walk—to show you our rocks?"

I said that would be fine and she said she'd be downstairs in the hall at ten. Unless Helen had changed a lot, she wouldn't be ready by ten or near it, but at ten I crossed the gallery and looked down and she was sitting there, smoking. T. D. had had his influence. She waved up at me and I waved and ran down the stairs.

She wore a yellow sports frock and her hair was down on her shoulders again and with that floating hair and her slim bare legs and sandaled feet she looked more like the Helen I remembered. When I told her so, she laughed with a pleased ring.

We went out, not by the front entrance but through a side door into a garden that was blazing with bloom, and I stopped to look at it.

"T. D. had all the dirt brought in," she said. "It really is something, isn't it?"

Her tone was queerly dispassionate, with no pride of possession. I said it certainly was something. Then she said, "Come on—it will be here when we get back," and that was the voice of the girl Helen, always hurrying somewhere, driven by swift urgencies.

The garden sloped down to a pool of water that was turquoise from the tiles. There were small cabanas about it and beyond were stone steps leading to a small beach that slid into the ocean. This was on the southern side of the promontory and the morning sun was bright on it.

"How's for a swim?" I asked, but Helen said the tide wasn't right and hurried me along, not out toward the point, but toward the mainland. There were starfishes in the sand, left by the last tide, and I felt the compulsion I'd always had as a kid, to throw them back into the water. We came to a rock, slippery with seaweed. I picked up some of the rubbery stuff just for the fun of popping it with my fingers.

We climbed more rocks and came down into a sandy cove. Here was where the promontory was cut across. I'd been wondering where that cut was and now I saw it angled across the promontory, much closer to the mainland on this outer side. On the harbor side it had been a chasm between high-piled rocks but here it was like a stream of fairly shallow water. T. D. would have had a lot less expense with his engineering if he'd made his road on this side, but he wouldn't have had that dramatic approach.

Helen was looking across the cut toward the mainland.
The rocks were piled up on the other side, shutting off
the view so all you could see of the shore was a retreating
curve to the left, so far away the houses on it looked like
doll houses.

"That's where the resorters live," she told me. "Along
there and up to this point. The village is farther inland,
though in the old days, when it was just a fishing village,
it ran down to the shore. The nice places are all in the
harbor. You'll see, this afternoon."

The "nice places" and the resorts were two different
communities, I gathered. I asked, "Anybody else on this
promontory?"

"No. Just us and the gulls."

She turned and looked back at the distant house. Only
the top of it showed from here and you could hardly have
told it from the gray stone on which it rested except that
the windows gave off brightness in the sun like tiny mirrors in the stone. I looked at it estimatingly, reflecting
that the architect and the engineer must have had fun
coping with the problems of that place.

"Let's get out of sight of it," she said abruptly.

She picked a place back against some rocks and we sat
down. The sand was white and dry and the sun beat warmly on us but Helen didn't relax; she sat bending forward as
if waiting for something.

"This is nice, isn't it?" she said, after a time, as if conscious she ought to be saying something.

I said it was fine. I waited for her to say more—I had
a notion she had brought me there to talk to me—but she
said nothing, just looked out at the ocean, and I looked
out at it, too, lazily, through half-shut lids. There were
some white sails out there but too far away to touch the
lonely quiet of this place, and the gulls wheeling and crying about us seemed part of the loneliness.

Suddenly she was on her feet, her head turned, and I turned, too, to see what she was looking at. A young man was splashing across the shallow waters of the opening. He was in bathing trunks and his body, in the sun, was a rich mahogany. It was a fine body, and he handled it finely, with balanced ease.

I scrambled to my feet and he came up to us and Helen said, "Hello." Her voice was a give-away. She said, "Nick— this is Calvin Kent. He's an old friend, from my home town. Cal, this is Nicholas Murray. He was a captain, too. With the Marines. In the Pacific. Then Korea."

We shook hands—his was wet with salt water—and his eyes slid quickly over me, then turned back to Helen. There was something urgent and asking in his look.

Helen said breathlessly, "I've got a message for you, Nick . . . you won't mind, will you?" she said to me. "I'll be right back."

She walked off with the young man among the rocks and disappeared. I stretched out and lit a cigarette. I had time for a good many of them. Sometimes, when their voices were louder than usual, the sound of them came to me but not the words. Then I heard nothing at all and thought they had gone farther away. Finally they came back.

They came walking together silently and Helen looked as if she had been crying. Her eyes were red. The young man looked furious. He had a vigorous, arresting face— deep-set eyes under level brows—and when he had looked at Helen, at meeting, there had been something eager and happy in him. Now he looked in as black a rage as Judy Gaynor had been bottling up in her the night before.

They walked almost up to me, then stopped to say some last, low-toned words to each other. I looked away, staring at the sailboats, and did not glance around till Helen said, "Cal—"

She was close beside me but still looking after him. She watched till he crossed the opening and disappeared behind the boulders on the other side. Then she murmured, "I'm sorry to have been away so long—"

I said, "So it's like that, is it?"

Her eyes flashed to me and she smiled faintly. "Was I so obvious?"

"Good God, yes."

"Well, I wasn't trying to cover up with you, Cal."

She spoke as she might have spoken back in high-school days, and she looked young and unhappy and defiant as she went on, "Yes, it's like that. It's the real thing, Cal."

I didn't say anything—what was there to say?—and she asked, "How did you like him?"

That was funny, I laughed. I said, "I liked his analysis of the Japanese very much but I thought he was way off the beam about the next election."

"You dope! You know what I mean. Isn't he—quite a man?"

"He looked like a swell guy."

"He really is. He has a terrific record. He was in all the landings."

"Nobody was in all the landings."

"Well, as many as anyone could be in. He's got all the decorations anyone could get."

"That's fine," I said. "Now sit down and make sense. You haven't fallen for his decorations, have you?"

We sat down on the sand and I lit a cigarette for her and one for me and she began to talk breathlessly. She had met this Nicholas Murray at a cocktail party in New York in the winter. He was from California, had been on a paper out west before the war, and meant to try journalism in the East. But, first, he wanted to write. He was writing now. He was brilliant and vivid and terribly in earnest.

They had fallen for each other at that first cocktail party. They'd gone off by themselves to some café and talked and talked. They'd seen each other as often as they could and he had followed her up here.

She said, "I want to marry him, Cal. I want to, terribly. He is the only one I ever felt like this about."

"All right," I said. "Then why don't you?"

"Tod won't give me a divorce."

"You've asked him?"

"I asked him yesterday."

"Yesterday?"

"Yes. Just before you came."

"Judas!" I said. I didn't wonder the place had crackled with electricity. I thought of T. D. standing there in the hall like Gibraltar. I couldn't help but feel a little sorry for the guy.

I asked, "Does he think you'll snap out of it?"

"He doesn't care what I feel. He doesn't mean to let me go."

I said cautiously, "Well, you can hardly blame him. If he cares for you a lot—"

"Cares?" she said bitterly. "All he cares about is position. Prestige. Avoiding scandal. He says he won't have a divorce. That he intends to keep the status quo. He really hates me, I think, but I'm to stay right with him."

"Well, it isn't easy for a man to let the world in on his losses. . . . But maybe he'll change his mind. When he gets used to the idea."

"Not Tod."

"You never can tell. He may think this is just a flash in the pan—"

"He knows better. He knows. . . . But he won't change. It isn't what I want, it's what he wants. . . . Like having children. He didn't want to be bored with them. . . . No, he won't change."

I repeated, "You never can tell. You sprung this on him—"

"He knew already. Judy told him."

"Let me get this straight. Judy Gaynor told him you wanted a divorce?"

"Of course not—she didn't know I wanted one. She thought I was just playing around." Helen spoke impatiently, as if it was a bother to make all this clear. "But she found out about Nick. I'd had him at the house once or twice—with people—I guess she suspected. So she spied on us and told T. D. She thought that would make him so mad he'd divorce me."

I said slowly, "Just because she doesn't like you or because—?"

"She's crazy about T. D. Poor Judy! She thought this was her chance."

The pieces were fitting together in my mind. After a few moments I asked, "When was all this? When did she tell him?"

"I don't know exactly—sometime last week, I guess. That's when he began to make it hard for me to go out alone. . . . But he didn't say a thing. Not then. But that's when he decided to change his will."

"You knew about that?"

"Not then. He wasn't going to let me know. He was just going to make sure that if he dropped dead I wouldn't have his money to spend on some other man."

I couldn't blame him for that, either.

"I knew he was acting sort of funny," Helen said. "I was afraid he'd heard something—I'd been out in the car with Nick and we'd had lunch—" she nodded toward the distant shore—"and he might have heard something. I could see he wasn't letting me have any time to myself. I was getting frantic. Nick had been urging me to ask for a divorce but I'd been afraid to. I knew it would mean trouble and

I wanted to go on seeing Nick in peace as long as I could. But if I couldn't see him. . . . Well, we made a date over the phone for yesterday, after lunch, and when I was starting out in my car Tod told me I couldn't go alone, and then we had it out."

Her voice, that had been dry and hurried, took on emotion. "I told him I was terribly sorry, but I couldn't help it—I couldn't go on the way we were any longer; I begged him to let me go. He wouldn't. He said I had to stay his wife and he proposed to make me behave like a wife. And then he told me about his will. He said he had been told about me and Nick and that he was going to change his will so we'd never benefit from it—no other man would spend his money. That would be the first thing he'd think of! . . . But I don't care about his hateful will. That doesn't mean anything now. And I don't care about his money. I'd go to Nick without a cent if I could only go."

She meant it, or thought she meant it. She looked forlorn and desperate sitting there in the sand beside me, her hands gripped about her knees.

I said, "Couldn't you get the divorce?"

"In New York State—? That's our residence."

"Well, you spoke of Judy Gaynor as if—"

"I haven't got anything on them—I don't honestly know whether Judy's slept with him or whether she's been playing hard to get. All I know is, she's crazy about him and plays up to his ego till it prances. And he loves it. It's one of those things. . . ."

"You could go to Reno."

"What's the use? He told me he'd contest and see I didn't get a judgment. He said if he had to he'd use the evidence against me so I'd be shown not to be coming into court with clean hands. I said there wasn't any evidence, that I hadn't done a thing wrong, and he said that sitting in the sands in a man's arms was all the evidence the court

would need. That told me where he'd found out about
us! Judy and her binoculars . . . I was a fool not to have
thought of that before."

"He didn't tell you it was Judy?"

"He didn't have to. I knew. . . . And you heard her last
night."

I remembered. I thought of Helen's light, reckless voice
and of Judy Gaynor's fury. I probed, "Was she in a rage last
night because he'd given her away to you or because—?"

"Because he won't divorce me and marry her, of course!"
For all its dolorousness, Helen's tone held an odd feminine satisfaction. She went on, "She was lying in wait for
him, in the hall yesterday—when he went out my door she
pounced on him and they went off to the study. Then he
came back to me and said I needn't hope to accomplish
anything for myself by planning for him—he thought I
was backing her. He said that he made his own decisions
and they would stand unchanged."

I thought, "Afternoon of a tycoon."

First the showdown with Helen, then with Judy Gaynor. Then he had marched downstairs and stood beside
his stone fireplace with the logs burning behind the steel
mesh curtain and played the host. "Try the salmon. Not
bad." I remembered how his face had tightened when he
saw Judy Gaynor coming toward us. Even his assurance
must have been secretly afraid of her temper, in the raw-
ness of her disappointment over whatever hopes he had
raised during the years.

"It's a situation," was all I could say.

"Yes," said Helen bleakly.

She began to pick up the sand and let it run through
her fingers. She had beautiful fingers, slim and tapering.
They were strong fingers, too. I remembered that she had
played the harp as a little girl. I had vague recollections
of a Historical Pageant, by the Women's Club, it seemed

to me, with Helen, in an Elizabethan dress, sitting at her harp.

"That was what I had to tell Nick," she said, after a silence. "He's crazy. He wants to see Tod but I talked him out of it. It would only make trouble."

Remembering the anger in the young man's face, I agreed.

"Nick says he could choke him to death with his bare hands."

"That wouldn't do either of you any good," I pointed out. "It seems to me the only thing to do is to wait and let everything cool off. Maybe Judy can get in some work for herself."

"Not a hope. She's had her big chance and lost out. Now she'll just go on, the way she was."

I wondered. After a time, I said, "And you and Murray—?" Helen made a little gesture of despair.

"Oh, he'll meet someone else, I suppose." She said nothing for a while, then she said, "If there was only something I could *do!*"

I couldn't think of anything so I said nothing and we sat there in silence. I was terribly sorry for her, she looked so lost and forlorn. It made me think of the time I'd sat with her long ago—it was the evening she'd failed to get the part, Rosamund, in the graduation play.

That sounds like a small thing but she had set her heart on that part and worked hard for it. And she deserved it— she could act and she gave the best performance of any girl before the trial committee. But she'd been turned down. I guess the committee thought that Helen had too much as it was, too much glamour, too many easy things, so they wouldn't give her the thing she had worked for and merited.

It wasn't only the disappointment that hurt her, though that went deep. It was the realization that she had enemies, people who wanted to cut her down. She knew she ought to have had that part. The girl they gave it to was a dud. And Helen felt bewildered and bitter and unsure.

I knew how she felt and so we two went off together and sat up on a hill, saying nothing. That was the one time I felt close to her. Helen had always been like a star out of reach and I'd never tried to reach—at dances I'd been careful not to cut in so often that I'd be a bother, but just often enough to heighten the whirl she always was having.

It was queer that here I was again, at this crisis, sitting in the same sort of silence beside her.

After a while, I said, "How come you married him?"

"I don't know." She said that absently, coming back from wherever her thoughts had been. "I just thought it a good idea, I suppose."

She added, with a flash of that honesty I remembered, "You know I always was a show-off." Then she said, defensively, "But I liked him—I truly did. And it was all so terribly exciting—sort of moving out into a big world. You know what a crazy kid I was."

I gave her a faint grin. "You don't seem to have got over it."

"It's the first time I've been crazy over a man," she said. Then she burst out, "Cal, I'm desperate! So desperate that I—that I—well, I lay in bed this morning staring at those casements and thinking what a pity they were so small I couldn't push him through them. That's how crazy I am!"

"Don't, Helen. Don't say things like that."

"I could do it, I tell you! You don't know what it's like to have someone near you who makes your flesh creep!"

Her voice rose hysterically. Then she jumped to her feet. "Come on—we have to go back. And after lunch we'll have a nice swim with dear Judy and perhaps with dear Stanley—"

I asked her about Stanley on the way back. She said that Stanley would be against the divorce because then T. D. would marry Judy. She said, 'I've always thought

Stanley had a hankering, himself—no, I don't know that. You never know about Stanley. Except that his one idea is to stay close to Tod and the main chance."

"He's not married—?"

She shook her head. We didn't say much of anything more.

When we came down the rocks onto the bathing beach Judy Gaynor was there, just out of the ocean. She had on a black bathing suit, a two-piecer, and her black hair was loose over her shoulders. I hadn't realized how long it was.

"Hello!" said Helen very amiably. "How's the water?"

"Wonderful," said Judy.

They stood a moment, looking at each other.

"I thought you'd be too busy to go in," said Helen.

"Oh, no," said Judy easily. Then she spoke to me. "I thought you liked swimming."

"I was being shown the rocks," I said.

Helen said, "I always take young men to my cove, you know. I've discovered some fascinating caves in it."

Her bravado seemed both silly and pitiful. I cut in, "I would like to have a swim. Think there's time now?"

Judy looked toward the cabanas. "You might find a suit there."

I didn't like to borrow a suit. I said, "I'll wait."

She turned toward a cabana, then called back, "You could try the cavern for a quick dip."

"What's the cavern?" I asked as we went on through the garden, and Helen said hastily, "Oh, it's a hole under the house. An old cave. You don't want to go there."

"You swim in it?"

"Yes. It was one of Tod's spectacular ideas." Then she seemed to change her mind about it and said, "For a quick dip it's all right. If you want to go down, just take the elevator in the hall—it's between Tod's room and his study. I'll show you."

"I'll find it," I said.

But I didn't look for it because Jeff was in our room
and we got to talking. I told him I'd been out with Helen
all morning and he cocked his black eyebrows at that. He
told me he was working in a study next to T. D.'s room,
just around the corner of the hall. I asked him how he
liked T. D. and he said T. D. had a good brain and knew
what he wanted.

I said, "I understand that what he wants is to cut his
wife out of everything."

"So she told you that, did she?" said Jeff.

"Why not? Everyone else seems to know it."

"It's his money."

"Can he do it? Hasn't she dower rights?"

"Dower was abolished in the State of New York after September, 1930. The Hazlitts are domiciled in New
York." Then he added, "By Section 18 of the Decedent
Estate Law the right of the surviving spouse to take his or
her intestate share is in lieu of dower."

"Then she *has* got some rights by New York law—?"

"Not if she—" He stopped. "It's a nice question," was
all he said.

"You mean he's got something that makes him think he
can cut her off and make it stick?"

"You put it like a layman. But that's the idea. I'd say
its arguable."

And Hazlitt had the money to argue it. Or, rather,
whoever inherited would have the money. I thought about
it a moment, then came out with, "What about this Maine
property?"

"Maine has abolished dower but established right of
at least one third in absolute ownership. Only T.D. was
thoughtful enough, some months back, to get a big mort-
gage on the property."

"How come she signed? Didn't she have to sign the papers?"

"I imagine she thought it was some device to ease taxes."

I said disgustedly, "He's a sharpshooter."

"It's his money," Jeff repeated.

After a moment I asked, "Did he say why he told her about the will? After all his requests to us for secrecy?"

"He did not. It wasn't any of my business."

"Yours but to draw the instrument."

"That's it."

"Well, I can tell you," I said. "Strictly between ourselves—though everyone else seems to know it, too."

So I told him about Helen and Nicholas Murray. I didn't mention the meeting with Murray, for that was Helen's affair, but I told him what Helen had told me about Murray and that she wanted a divorce and T. D. wouldn't give her one. And—I don't quite know why—I didn't mention the part Helen thought Judy Gaynor played. I just said that T. D. had found out.

Jeff listened with an unsympathetic air. "She's a fool," he pronounced.

"Sitting in judgment, are you?"

"I don't like people who flop around. I'm tired of those babes who take all the stuff some earnest guy gives them and then fall for a glamour boy."

"That's a slick way to put it She made a marriage that was a mistake and wants out. What's so lousy about that?"

"Plenty," said Jeff. "T. D.'s a regular fellow and if she wasn't crazy about him when she married him she certainly had him fooled. He was sold on her. Do you know how his first will reads? He gave it to me so I could use the descriptions of the property involved. It's a honey of a will. Stanley made it."

"I thought he wouldn't make his brother's will."

"He could make this one all right, because he didn't get a cent under it. Not a cent. Everything T. D. had—every damn thing—he left to his wife. 'I give, devise, and bequeath to my wife, Helen. . . .'"

Those were haunting words. I give, devise, and bequeath. . . . they made me think of "To have and to hold" and "With all my unworldly goods." . . . And now all the words were being unsaid. I said, "I suppose Stanley gets it all."

"He benefits—yes."

Jeff's voice was guarded, and I asked, "Anybody else?"

"That's T. D.'s business, Cal."

"Okay," I said. "Family retainer department." But I was curious. I wondered if leaving Judy Gaynor a lot of money was T. D.'s idea of a solution. I thought about it while I got out a clean shirt

I told him, "I still think Helen is getting gypped."

"A will doesn't mean a thing," said Jeff. He was running a comb through his short, crisp hair. "He can make another tomorrow."

I asked—I don't know why—"That first will still in the study?"

Jeff looked at me. "It will be destroyed after the second is executed."

"Hang onto it," I said lightly, "and let me slip it to Helen. Then she can burn the second."

Jeff grinned. "I call your attention to Section 41 of the New York Decedent Estate Law. It says—I quote—if, after making of any will, the testator shall duly make and execute a second will, the destruction, canceling or revocation of such will, shall not revive the first will, unless it appear by the terms of such revocation, that it was his intention to revive and give effect to his first will; or unless after such destruction, canceling or revocation, he shall duly republish his first will.'"

I turned that over. I said, "I thought a will was good as long as there wasn't any other."

"Most people think so," said Jeff. "But that's neither here nor there. There won't be any first will after I get my work done."

Chapter Three

Luncheon was very quiet. Everyone was polite and there were no verbal daggers from the arras, but the feeling of tension was there. Last night, I thought, had been like sitting at a play where you didn't know the first act. Now I felt I was behind the scenes.

I remember that T. D. spoke only once to his wife. He said, "We are going to the Bronsons this afternoon, you know."

"Are we?" said Helen.

"We are."

Helen said, "That's nice."

After lunch Judy Gaynor asked me if I'd like to have a swim. She asked me before everybody and then said stiffly, turning her head toward T. D. but not her eyes, "If you don't need me, Mr. Hazlitt."

T. D. said he didn't need her, but he gave her and then me a sharp look and so did Helen. There was quick mistrust in her eyes.

We had a good swim. We got beyond the surf and swam out against the tide. Judy Gaynor had a powerful crawl. We raced and got tired and then came in.

I asked her where she'd learned to swim and she said, "In Maine. I'm a native."

"You live near here?"

229

"No, farther south. Near the New Meadows River."

"I'll bet your grandfather was a sea captain."

"Yes, he was."

"And brought home a Spanish bride."

"That was my great-grandfather."

"It didn't do you any harm."

"It didn't do me any good, either."

She said that, not gaily, but with the hard, painful smile I had seen the night before when Helen was mocking her. I hadn't been thinking about her relation to Hazlitt—it had gone clean out of my head watching her swim—but now it came back with a thud. It gave me a disagreeable feeling, but as we walked back toward the cabanas I began to make allowances for her.

She must have been young and inexperienced when she went to work for Hazlitt, a small-town girl with Spanish eyes, and she might have fallen for him before she knew it. And fallen hard. Could be. Or it could be she had fallen for his money.

Outside the cabana where I'd left my clothes I stopped, and she stopped, too. She didn't say anything for a moment, then she said, as if she were nerving herself to say it, "You're a friend of Helen Hazlitt's, aren't you?"

"Why, yes."

"Then perhaps she'll listen to you."

She had been looking down, but now she turned her big, black eyes on me and they were full of wild urgency. She said in that low, really lovely voice of hers, vibrant now with the same urgency as her eyes, "You tell her to do what she wants to do. Tell her to run away. Tell her to force his hand. She can do it."

After a moment I said, cautiously, "You want me to give her this as a message from you?"

"Oh, no, no! She would suspect everything I said. You don't understand. . . . but perhaps you do. Perhaps she's

told you. If she hasn't, you can get her to. Get her to
explain. Then say to her what I've said. That's her only
way out. She'll have to make that way for herself."

"I'll remember what you say." I was picking my words
slowly. "But—whatever she tells me—I can't promise to
give her that advice. I'll have to say what I think."

Her eyes blazed at me. "How can you form a judgment?
. . . You tell her to go. Tell her to have the courage to go.
It's what she wants. She can do things on the spur of the
moment. If she acts quickly enough. . . . You'll be doing
her a kindness if you get her to act. And *now.*"

She brought her voice down on that hard.

I didn't say, "And doing you a kindness," because that
would give away the fact that Helen had told me about
her. But I had a queer feeling that I would like to hurt her,
to get through to her the hard way.

She stood there a moment, looking as if she wanted to
say more. She was holding her bathing cap in her hand,
her hair streaming down her neck, and I suppose to the
Portuguese gardener who was pottering about we looked
like any young couple that finds it hard to part. Then she
turned with an abruptness in which she managed to infuse
a suggestion of despair, and went to her cabana.

The army had taught me to dress quickly and I didn't
wait for her, when I was ready, for a note in my cabana
said a gentleman was waiting to see me in the garden. I
must have had a hunch, for I wasn't particularly surprised
when I recognized the figure. It was in gray flannels now,
but it showed strong and muscular, though every line of
it expressed dejection and doggedness. He sat leaning forward, elbows on his knees, a cigarette in his fingers. He
jumped up quickly and came toward me.

"You remember me? Nicholas Murray."

"Of course," I said. I shifted my wet trunks to my left
hand and we shook hands.

"I asked for you because they can't refuse your callers. When I ask for Helen she's not at home. And Helen told me you were a friend."

This weekend seemed to have turned into a play where I was playing the unrehearsed role of "Helen's friend."

I said, "Right. Let's go," and walked him off among some bushes that I hoped would hide us from Judy Gaynor when she came along.

Murray said hurriedly, "I want you to give Helen this. I can't phone. She thinks they listen. Be sure to hand it to her yourself."

With a quick motion, he thrust a folded letter into my hand.

"I'll give it to her," I said.

"Thanks a lot. . . . I expect she told you—?"

"Yes, she did."

He gave me a look of bitter unhappiness. "Hell of a note, isn't it?"

I said it was. We walked up and down, smoking. He said, in a low, angry voice, "If he thinks he can keep his dirty hands on her—"

"Look—this isn't any affair of mine," I said, "but I think you're all pressing too hard. Give it time. He'll see that it doesn't make sense to go on with a marriage that Helen doesn't want. He'll change his mind then."

"Helen doesn't think so."

"Well, I wouldn't know. But I still think you're pressing too hard. You have to give him time."

"He's pressing, isn't he? Sitting up there—" his dark head jerked toward the house behind us—"making a will that cuts her out."

"I can't see that means much now." I was surprised he brought the will into it. "If she wants a divorce, she must know he'd cut her out of his will—"

"Oh, sure. But don't you see why he's doing it now? He's hanging onto her and making her realize that if she looks at me again he'll keep her from ever having anything. She's not only got to stay with him, she's got to give me up. If she does, then, someday, he'll make another will again, in her favor. It can't help but influence her—"

He stopped short. Then he flung out, "I don't care about his lousy money. But he ought to have made a settlement. After these ten years . . . if there was any decency in him. . . . *I* can't give her what she ought to have."

There was raw despair in his voice. He said, as if talking to himself, "How will she ever break away when—"

He brought himself up short again. "I'm going bats," he said.

I thought, You ought never to have gone to that cocktail party, brother. It had been his bad luck to meet the glamorous Mrs. Hazlitt. But there was nothing I could do about it and nothing I could say that made sense to him. We walked up and down a little more, then I went into the house to change for the Bronson cocktail party.

Helen tucked the letter in her handbag with a breathless "Thank you, Cal!" We were off in a corner of the Bronson drawing room on a small sofa and she turned toward me, excluding the roomful of chattering people, and begged me to tell her everything that Murray had said.

I did a little editing. I didn't mention T. D.'s "dirty hands" or the settlement, but I did say that Murray was bothered about how they'd make out if she managed to get free to marry him.

Helen said softly, "Poor darling—he's always worrying about how he'll take care of me."

"I don't wonder," I said, looking at her thoughtfully.

Her hair was swooped up under one of those French hats that are all filmy feathers, and she wore a frock you

couldn't mistake for price. I looked at her diamond brace-
lets and her pearls and I said, "You could sell your jewelry.
That ought to last you quite a while."

"It isn't mine." Her fingers went up to the string of
pearls and twisted it nervously. "Tod made that clear yesterday. Title hasn't passed." She had a bitter smile for that.
"He told me if I ran away with them he'd have me arrested."

"For God's sake, don't run away till you've thought
things over," I besought.

She made an impatient movement. "Of course not," she
said, as if she never did an impulsive thing.

I thought of what Judy Gaynor had told me to tell her
and put that in the discard. Running away wasn't the answer. I didn't know what was the answer, but I knew Helen
ought to give herself time. I thought of mentioning that
she'd have a third of the equity in the house in case she
didn't know it, but that didn't seem an asset but a liability
with someone like Stanley owning the other two thirds. I
said, feeling a heel toward Jeff, "You know, you do have
rights, under the New York law. Have you any idea why he
thinks he can get around that?"

"He said he could. He's got something." Then she
caught sight of a girl coming toward us and cried very
brightly, "Claire Beveridge! Where did you drop from?"

As soon as I could get away from Helen and the Beveridge girl I went over to join Stanley Hazlitt. It occurred
to me that the butler would probably report about my
caller and that I'd better mention him myself. Stanley began looking about for the Bronson nephew for me to meet,
but I said I'd already met him, and we'd arranged some
tennis for the next day. Then I said, as casually as I could,
that it had been a social day, that a former Marine I'd met
in New York had heard I was here and looked me up. "He's
doing some writing here," I said.

"Indeed?" said Stanley. His voice was noncommittal. I thought he looked at me suspiciously and I didn't blame him. Then he said, "If it was a Mr. Murray, I trust you will not encourage him to return. . . . You know, Mr. Kent, I was very glad you could come up here because I felt that Mrs. Hazlitt—" his voice grew colder, or I thought it did, when he spoke of her—"would benefit from seeing someone from her past life. Someone with—"

He hesitated, then said, "With perspective."

I turned the word over in my mind as some dowager claimed his attention. It was a good word. Perspective. It was what Helen needed. She never took the long view.

Stanley Hazlitt, I imagined, was in something of a dilemma. He didn't want anything to happen that would reflect on his brother's prestige—that was the way I reasoned it—or leave his brother free to marry Judy Gaynor, but at the same time, if what Helen said of him was true, he certainly wasn't sorry that his brother's wife was behaving badly enough to incite T. D. to change a will that left everything to her. He must have felt very bitter, ten years ago, drawing up that will for his brother.

I felt in something of a dilemma myself. Helen had rushed me into sympathy but now I wasn't sure that a moneyless marriage was the thing for her. I didn't think she could take it. Nicholas Murray, as much in love as he was, had glimmerings of apprehension about the future. Apprehension, too, that there wouldn't be a future, because of the influence of Hazlitt's money.

Neither Helen nor Jeff Ryder came to dinner that night. Helen had a headache, T. D. reported, and Jeff was dining on a tray in the study where he was working. After dinner Stanley offered to take me to a play given by a summer theater in the Harbor, but I said I was going to write some letters on their elegant paper and went up to my room.

What I wanted was a spot of quiet and a book that wasn't about emotions. What I got was the foghorn blowing and the buoy bell tolling and a book about shipwrecks.

Jeff came in, finally. When I asked if the will was finished, he shook his head. "Hell of a lot of work to it," he said.

"When do you think you'll get through? I'm just sweating this out."

"Sunday for sure. Maybe tomorrow night."

The fog hadn't gone the next morning. It blanketed us. You looked out into gray nothingness. It came in the open windows and everything you touched was moist with it. The house was lighted but when I went out into the garden after breakfast it was eerie to see how quickly the lights were blotted out. My tennis was off, of course. There was nothing to do but stay inside.

Stanley Hazlitt showed me the library, a big room on the corner of the house, part toward the point, part over the cliff, and told me to make myself at home. Helen did not show up nor did Judy Gaynor. I figured that Judy might be copying for Jeff. Everyone, except Jeff, came to luncheon but there wasn't any talk, except about the fog.

Coming out of the dining room Helen walked close to me. She said under her breath, "When is he going to get it done?"

"Tomorrow, for sure. Maybe tonight."

She nodded. Her face was tense. Knowing the thing was going on in that room upstairs was a strain. It would be better, I thought, when it was over. Like having a tooth out.

Yet I couldn't see why it mattered so much. She must have known he'd change his will when he found she wanted to leave him. It was his refusing the divorce yet shutting her out of the reward of staying with him that worked her up, I thought. Nobody is quite rational about money.

Perhaps, too, she felt he was doing something handsome for Judy Gaynor.

Upstairs, a little later, I met Stanley Hazlitt in the hall and asked if it was all right to swim in the fog if I kept close to shore. He was horrified. He told me to go down in the cavern. It was an old pirates' cave, he said, in the rock on which the house was built. They had sunk a shaft through the roof of the cave and put in an elevator, and he showed me where the elevator was, around the turn in the hall, just between T. D.'s room and the study. He cautioned me not to go out the cave entrance in the fog.

It sounded gloomy but interesting and at least it was something to do. I meant to go down then, but Jeff came into the room to get something and said he'd go, too, if I'd wait till the end of the afternoon, so I read magazines and waited. I got impatient, at last, and changed to my swimming trunks, and just then he came in and hustled into his swim things and we went together.

It seemed queer and incongruous slipping down in a modern elevator into that old cave. The light from the elevator cage helped us find the cave lights and we turned on every switch, but the fog filled the place. We could scarcely make out the opening. It was just an arch of thinner darkness in the rock wall.

Jeff looked about with interest "I thought most of the Maine coast was granite."

"Not all. This," I said with the smugness with which he had quoted law to me, "is metamorphosed sedimentary rock. Plenty of undercut caves in it. Some were really pirates' hideouts. This could have been, all right."

It was a long, narrow cave with its opening toward the harbor. It was all filled with water except for the shelf on which we stood. There were low benches on that shelf and there were bath towels hanging on racks fitted into the rock wall behind us and more racks on which to hang our bathrobes. We stepped down off the shelf into the water and found that the rocky bottom sloped toward the entrance. The old longboats could have come in here. I wondered if T. D. had ever hunted about for treasure.

The water was icy cold and the air was dank with the peculiar dankness of a place where the sun never shines, and it wasn't much fun swimming around like a gold fish in a foggy globe. I swam to the entrance and back, then climbed out and reached for a towel.

I dropped it and picked it up. That's how I happened to catch the glint of the thing the towel had fallen on. I picked it up and looked at it. If Jeff had been with me I'd have shown it to him, but Jeff was still splashing, so I took another look, closer to the light, and saw the initials. N.R.M. After that I slipped it into the pocket of my bathrobe.

Jeff had an appointment with T. D. before dinner, so we hurried back up, and he dressed in a rush. After he left the room I transferred my find into the pocket of my jacket. It was ten minutes of eight then and I went out into the hall with a guilty look over the rail to see if I was late, but only Stanley Hazlitt and Judy Gaynor were down there, one on each side of the fireplace.

I ran downstairs and came up to the fire. The place was full of silence and my voice sounded loud when I said I'd just been in the cavern. Stanley told me again it had been a pirates' cave and Judy said, her voice scornful, that every cave in Maine was called a pirates' cave.

They were both looking up, toward the gallery, and I stood, back to the fire, and looked, too, infected by their feeling of unease. I heard steps, and then I saw Helen, walking quickly, not looking down at us. It struck me that the stairway was not conveniently placed for the master bedrooms—Helen had to go down a long hall, past four other rooms, to reach those stairs. But she didn't have to use the stairs. The elevator was next T. D.'s room, a few steps diagonally across the hall from her door. It had a stop on this floor between the library and the butler's pantry. Being an engineer, I'm always figuring how people get in and out of places.

Helen came down the stairs and across to us and I conceded the stairs made a dramatic approach. She was wearing the same medieval-looking gown she had worn the night before, with the long hanging sleeves. Long lines became her. Her hair was down now, on her shoulders, and she looked like something out of a tapestry.

She glanced about with an air of exaggerated astonishment. She said, "Not here—?" and Stanley countered with, "Where's T.D.?"

"But I thought he was down . . . He must be with Mr. Ryder. It seems to take a lot of time to disinherit me. Or isn't disinherit the word?"

No one said anything to that. Helen moved about restively. "We may as well have our drinks." She pressed a bell.

It was five after eight then. I found myself glancing at the time like the rest of them. It seemed an extraordinary thing to them, to have T. D. late. Even the butler, passing the trays, had a perturbed air. I asked if it was Kant or Schopenhauer that people had set their watches by and Judy said, "Kant, I think. Look out, Helen—you're spilling."

Helen set down her glass and dabbed at her dress. "It's that foghorn—I never get used to it. It always makes me jump!" Then she burst out, "Think of being wrecked in this fog! How can people keep from being wrecked when they can't see?"

"Instruments," I said.

"The little fishing boats haven't instruments."

I knew she wasn't thinking about the little fishing boats. I was as sure as you can be of something that you haven't seen with your own eyes, that Nicholas Murray had brought a boat in and out of that cavern, some time before Jeff and I went down.

Stanley made a diversion, speaking of news he'd got over the radio. Then he said, "It's quarter past eight, Helen. Nearly twenty past. Is T. D. dining with us or with Mr. Ryder? Perhaps you had better find out."

Helen looked about for the butler. "Did Mr. Hazlitt notify you of any change of plan, Caldwell?"

"No, madam."

"Then we'd better sit down," she said. "He'll come when he's ready."

But Stanley wasn't going to dinner in T. D.'s house without T. D. He told the butler, "You had better ring my brother's room and see if there's been any change in his arrangements."

Caldwell went off and we stood about, waiting. A man's being late to dinner seemed a small thing to create such uneasy tension, but everyone seemed tense. I know I was thinking that probably T. D. was signing the will—Jeff said he expected him in the study before dinner, and the will might have been so nearly finished that they had decided to polish it off right then. I wondered who was witnessing it. Perhaps the chauffeur and the houseman. Theirs seemed lowly signatures to be on a will of such magnitude.

Helen must have been thinking of the will, too, for when Caldwell came back and reported that Mr. Hazlitt's phone did not answer, she asked, "Did you ring the study?"

Caldwell said, "No, madam," and his tone said he had not been instructed to ring the study.

Just then steps sounded along the gallery. We all looked up. It was not Hazlitt. Jeff Ryder was looking down at us; then he came on quickly and ran down the stairs. I thought the will was surely finished and that T. D. would appear next.

But Jeff asked, "Where's Mr. Hazlitt?" Then to Stanley, "I was waiting for your brother—"

"We're all waiting for him," said Helen.

Jeff glanced back toward the gallery. "He said he'd be in before dinner. I thought I'd missed him. Then I heard the bell in his room ring and he didn't answer, so I thought he'd be down here—that perhaps I might catch him before you went in."

"He may have gone out," said Judy Gaynor. It was the first thing she had said.

"In this fog?" said Stanley.

"He may have overslept," said Jeff. "He told me he was going to take a nap."

"I have never known him to oversleep." Stanley's voice was actually taut. Then he said, "But he may have been washing his hands when the phone rang, and didn't hear it. You had better ring again, Caldwell. No, go up and see."

"I'll go," said Jeff. "I'm coming back, anyway."

"Yes, you go," said Helen. 'Then you can have your conference." She gave a nervous laugh. "But won't you have a drink, first?"

"Thanks, no. I'll go." Jeff started for the stairs.

Someone screamed. It was a woman's voice, in a single scream of sheer terror. It came from the upper hall, and our heads jerked toward it and we stood like frozen pointers for just the moment it took for that scream to die away. Then we started for the stairs, Jeff in the lead.

But it was Caldwell who made the quickest time. He disappeared and took the back stairs, evidently, for he was outside the open door of T. D.'s room when we came running down the hall. Behind him, backing down the hall that ran at right angles to ours, along the east side of the house, was a maid with an apron over her head, one arm stuck out stiffly pointing in front of her. I remember thinking idiotically that she'd back into something and hurt herself.

Caldwell made a gesture that stopped us. He had been standing in the room but now he turned and faced us. He addressed Stanley Hazlitt. "There's been an accident, sir." Then his manner broke. His jaw shook as he stammered, "He—he's been shot dead."

Part II: Chapter Four

For a moment, after Caldwell had blurted those words, we stood there like fixtures. No one spoke or moved. Then Helen cried, "Oh, Caldwell, no! Oh, no, no, no!" with such utter repudiation in her voice that the thought went through me that perhaps she had been fonder of him than she knew. No matter how much she had wanted freedom, she hadn't wanted it like this.

Stanley Hazlitt, sounding strange with shock, breathing heavily from the run up the stairs, demanded, "What do you mean? Where is he—?"

The butler, pasty-white, looked toward the open door. Stanley brushed by him and entered. Then he said, his voice now sharp and sounding so like T. D.'s in that sharpness that it was startling, "Mr. Ryder! Will you come here?"

Jeff Ryder went in. We all followed, hesitantly. There were soft lights on in the room, one light by the bed, which was turned down for the night. It was a big corner room with windows on two sides, toward the harbor and toward the point. Stanley was standing by the windows on the harbor side looking down on his brother.

T. D. was slumped on the floor, face down. He was in trousers and shirt, a white shirt, and a dark stain was spreading through the whiteness from the back of T. D.'s head. The curtains were pulled back as if T. D. had gone to look out on the fog. One of the casements was half open.

There seemed no need for Stanley to kneel down by his brother to make sure that he was dead, but Stanley knelt. He made himself look closely. He reached out and touched one of the sprawled hands. Then he rose slowly.

He said, in that sharp, hard voice so like T. D.'s except for the inner trembling in it now, "We mustn't touch him. You didn't touch him, did you, Caldwell?"

"Oh, no, sir. I just stepped into the room when Hannah pointed." The butler was craning forward fearfully. He went on, voluble with excitement, "Hannah was backing out the room when I came upstairs—I'd gone up the service stairs when I heard her scream. She was backing out the door, not making another sound. She just pointed her arm. You see, sir, she'd gone in to make the room ready for the night, thinking Mr. Hazlitt was downstairs—"

I looked again at the turned-down bed. There was a bowl of fruit on the table beside it, beneath the reading light. On the floor, in the middle of the room, was a pair of crimson silk pajamas and a crimson-and-black patterned dressing gown where Hannah had evidently dropped them on her way from the dressing room. Caldwell made an uncertain motion toward them, then stopped.

"Oh, God! It's too awful! It's too awful!" Judy Gaynor was sobbing out loud, her hands tight against her face. "Oh, God, oh, God!"

"Be quiet!" said Stanley savagely. He seemed trying to collect himself, to take command rationally. "What time— when did—didn't anyone hear a shot?" he demanded.

He looked at Helen. She was standing in the middle of the room, by the dropped pajamas, staring at the dead body of her husband, her face so white that the red on her lips was garish. She gave no sign of having heard the words until Stanley repeated them. Then she moved her head in slow negation.

"But you must have!" he insisted. "In the next room."

"I was—out of my room—for a while."

Her voice was almost lost beneath the blare of the foghorn, unmercifully loud through the open casement. Stanley looked toward the window as if he wanted to close it, but he did not. He raised his voice as he demanded of us, "Didn't any of you hear anything? You, Mr. Ryder—you were in the study. Was there any sound, anything unusual—?"

"I heard nothing," said Jeff. He spoke slowly, consideringly, but positively. "I was out, too, for a time. Just before dinner." Then he asked, "Are you sure he was shot, not slugged?"

The blunt practical words made Stanley flinch. He stammered, taken aback, "No—why, no—I took for granted—Caldwell—"

"I just said what came into my head," said Caldwell anxiously. "It's what you think of—"

"We'd better make sure," said Jeff.

Stanley looked down irresolutely and Jeff said, "Turn the lights on, will you?" to Caldwell, and when the full lights went on he knelt beside Hazlitt's body, parting the dark hair carefully beneath the thickened blood. I wouldn't have cared to do that but Jeff Ryder has a way of doing what has to be done. He got up, wiping his fingers on his handkerchief. He told Stanley, "Yes, he's been shot."

"Have you got the gun?" Helen suddenly cried out.

Jeff turned and looked at her. "There isn't any gun."

"But there must be!" Her voice rose higher. "He couldn't shoot himself without a gun."

Jeff said quietly, "He didn't shoot himself, Mrs. Hazlitt."

"But he did—of course he did! It's all part of it—don't you see? He made the new will and then—and then—"

"The will isn't finished, Helen." Stanley Hazlitt spoke with remote distinctness. "It wasn't to be finished till to-night . . . You knew that."

"But—but—" She looked toward Jeff again. "It must be under him," she insisted.

Jeff told her, "A man doesn't shoot himself in the back of his head—in that particular spot. At that angle. But if you wish me to look—"

He knelt again and groped beneath the dead man. He said, getting up, "There's nothing there."

"Then he threw it out the window. The window's open. It could have dropped out."

"He was dead, Mrs. Hazlitt, the second after the shot was fired. If he had been holding the gun—which he was not—he would not have had time to throw it out the window. And it could not have fallen out. His right side is away from the window."

"There's nothing to be gained, Helen, by all this," said Stanley Hazlitt

Judy Gaynor cried wildly, "Oh, God, you're all standing there wrangling about a gun! Someone broke in and killed him and you're letting him get away—"

"Nobody could break in. You're hysterical—both of you," said Stanley sharply. He turned to Jeff. "Will you stay here and see that nothing is disturbed? I must telephone—"

"Wait, Stanley!"

Helen ran between him and the door to the study. She urged, distractedly, "Wait, before you call people in. We've got to think what to say. If it wasn't suicide it was an accident. He was cleaning his gun. He was always cleaning his gun; you know he was. He loved guns. That was what he was doing and the gun is somewhere here—or Hannah carried it away—"

"Helen, I beg of you—"

"Don't you see what it will mean? All the notoriety, the sensation? People prying, asking question . . . the news-papers—"

"I don't like this any better than you do, but—"

"It's got to be an accident! We've got to say that. That's bad enough, but—"

"Please go to your room, Helen. You had better pull yourself together before you talk to anyone."

"Talk!" She put a hand to her throat. Even in her disor-der it was an unconsciously lovely gesture, the slim hand lifting from the long, loose sleeve.

She burst out again, "That's what I mean. To have to talk, to explain. . . . It's so much better to have it an acci-dent. We could put one of his guns beside him—"

"You don't know what you're saying." Stanley glanced uneasily at Caldwell, who was lapping this up. "I advise you to go to your room."

"I'm going to look for that gun. It may have rolled."

"I'm leaving you in charge, Mr. Ryder; nothing must be touched," Stanley warned. "You were attorney for my brother. Please carry on."

He went toward the study door and I stepped ahead of him. I said, "In case anyone is lurking—" and went through the door in front of him.

The door didn't open into the study but into a short hall between the rooms, that ran between T. D.'s dressing room and the enclosure about the elevator shaft, and there was another door at the other end. I didn't think anyone was in the room ahead, for a man who had killed T. D. would not be inclined to linger, but there was the chance that he might be trying to get hold of a will that he be-lieved had been signed, a will he wanted to destroy.

I said to Stanley, "There's plenty of space between these two rooms. Jeff might not have been able to hear a shot."

I said it loudly, for even with the picture of T. D.'s body before me I was full of angry pity for the poor devil I believed had done him in. Murray had been half crazy with love and hate and he had fired too many shots at other heads to feel that one more mattered very much. I know all about the difference between war and murder, but when you get to feel that your private enemy is as mean a guy as the public enemy. . . .

Anyway, that's how I reacted, and if Nicholas Murray had been in the study I'd have waved him to the other door—hoping he wouldn't plug me before he got the idea—before I let Stanley Hazlitt see him. But no one was in the room. It was quiet and empty, a room of book-lined walls and soft carpeting. The light on a table desk shone on some papers that Jeff must have been working on.

Stanley walked to the desk and looked down at the papers, then pushed them aside. Jeff's old briefcase was beside them and he moved that a little away. It was locked, and he noticed it, too, for he said, "I expect Mr. Ryder put the will here before he came down."

There was nothing in his voice to tell you what he was thinking, but he couldn't help but be thinking even in that moment what a difference that will would have made to him. Only a few more hours and he would have been a rich man. Now everything would go to Helen.

The briefcase gave me a flash of relief, for I thought Murray couldn't have been here or he would have taken it, suspecting what it held. Then I thought again and realized that Murray must have known from Helen that the will was not signed. That was why he had worked fast.

Stanley picked up the telephone and I made a circuit of the room. There were three doors, one to the outer hall, one to the small passage to T. D.'s room, and opposite that a third into whatever room was next. I didn't ask where that led, for Stanley was talking on the phone. The man he wanted wasn't at home, but at a neighbor's, and Stanley had to get another connection. It made me realize how small this Maine community was and what a stir this death would make.

I pulled aside the curtain at the window and looked out into the fog. I wondered why the window in T. D.'s room had been half open. It didn't make sense to be dressing for dinner with the window open in that damp weather, but the curtains had apparently been drawn across it and maybe that amount of air was what T. D. liked. Or maybe he had just opened it, himself. The killer must have crept up behind him.

It wasn't a pretty picture. But creeping up on mean guys had been all in the day's work to Murray.

Stanley was talking now. He said what he had to say in the fewest words and hung up. He stood looking down at the telephone as if he couldn't quite believe, himself, in the things he had just said. Then he looked at me. He said, in a tight voice, "This is going to be difficult, Mr. Kent."

It certainly was. I said so and then I said, "I expect your brother had a lot of valuables in his room?"

"You are thinking of a thief?" He sounded surprised.

I said, "The window was open—"

He said positively, "A man couldn't have got in—or out—by the window. My brother gave those instructions to the architect."

"A second-story man can make a fool out of the best architect."

I had jeered at Jeff for that opinion, but now I argued, "If he had the right build—knew how to handle himself—"

Stanley looked toward the windows, then shook his head. "Impossible. And the open window was on the cliff side."

"A man could crawl up this side, then edge around the corner."

"Fantastic," he said, more curtly than ever. He added, "However, we will see if anything has been taken."

He was going to be a hard man to fool, I thought. Now that T. D. was not there to overshadow him you could see he was keen in his own right. I thought, "Accessory after the fact," and then, "No, damn it all, I'm not being an accessory. Because I picked up something and didn't hand it over—"

But I knew that I was covering up. I knew what would happen if I pulled out that cigarette case with N.R.M. on it and said, "Look—here's something I picked up in the cavern just before dinner."

It wouldn't take long, then. The evidence would look as big as sky writing. A hardy man, a Marine, could pilot a boat along the coast in the fog and nose into the old cave. Pirates had done it. The case couldn't have been there very long, for the Hazlitt staff must see to the clean towels and things down there every morning, at least.

Helen had said she had been out of her room. She hadn't said when but she must have meant about the time the shot was fired, and that was when T. D. was dressing for dinner. Helen might have gone down to the cavern, met Murray, then brought him up and hidden him in her room, only a few steps from the elevator door. That could have happened before Jeff and I went down to the cavern.

No; what did that make Helen? She wouldn't connive at murder. Or would she? She had sounded proud of Murray when she told me he was so angry that he could choke T. D. to death with his bare hands, but there's a big difference between admiring a man's hot spirit and sending that man out, deliberately, to shoot down your husband.

No, Helen could not have known what Murray was intending. She might have met him in the cavern—their desperation might have fixed on that for a meeting place. The letter from him I had given her could have arranged

it. But she had not known what he was going to do. She
had come up alone from the cave, thinking he was going,
and then, when she had left the elevator, he had signaled
for it and gone up and slipped into T. D.'s room.

But Helen knew now. Her frantic insistence on suicide,
on accident, proved that she knew.

But there was no evidence against Murray. Not yet.
There was only the cigarette case in my pocket. I wanted
to put my hand on it to make sure it was there, but under
Stanley's eyes I didn't make a move to it. I thought his
eyes were distrustful already. He knew Murray had been to
see me, the day before, and I'd said I'd known him in New
York and he must have been adding that up to my prompt
mention of a second-story man.

I asked if there was anything I could do and he said I'd
better go down and eat something and he'd send Jeff down.
Mrs. Hazlitt and Miss Gaynor—he named them with equal
remoteness—would, he hoped, have some coffee in their
rooms before the local police arrived.

"We don't want any more hysterics," he said drily, and
I felt he was thinking not only of Helen's desperate insistence but of Judy Gaynor's wild sobbing. It wouldn't be
pleasant to have her grief exhibited to the local authorities. Probably there were already stories about her.

I kept thinking about Judy Gaynor as I went downstairs
in that hushed, uneasy house. She had cried as if her heart
were broken. She must really have cared for T. D. and it
wasn't very comforting for her to have to remember that
their last times together had been a furious clash of wills.
She'd learned the hard way that he didn't mean to marry
her. I thought about the black rage she'd been in, two
nights ago, when she walked stiffly into that room, hating
us all with her eyes.

But she hadn't given up hope of the divorce. She had
urged me to encourage Helen to cut and run, to force the

issue. Once the scandal was out in the open, she seemed to feel she could have had her way with T. D. . . . How much, I wondered, did Stanley know about all this? And how much truth was there in Helen's guess that Stanley had a feeling for Judy? She was a luscious gal if you looked only at the spectacular eyes and hair and skin and didn't consider the cut of her jaw. It wouldn't be long, I thought, before that girl told of Helen's meetings with Nicholas Murray in the cove, the meetings she had spied on with her binoculars.

I kept thinking about her while Jeff and I ate hurriedly. We did not talk much, for the houseman who waited on us was all ears. The kitchen must be seething with excitement. A murder in the house. A real-life mystery story.

It was a perfect setup for a mystery story, I thought grimly, but it wouldn't be much of a mystery. In fiction the first suspect is never the criminal—the killer is somebody pulled out of a hat in the last chapter. But in this case there couldn't be much preliminary fumbling. It wouldn't take long to focus on Murray.

Stanley had not mentioned the elevator when he brushed off my suggestion about an entrance through the window, but that didn't mean he wasn't thinking about the possibilities of the cavern. I wished that I could get away before they got their hands on Murray.

I wondered how Jeff would feel. Jeff had never been a chap who let sentiment stand in the way of justice. He had very clear-cut ideas about the value of law. He wouldn't like a killer any the better for being an ex-Marine.

Well, Jeff didn't know about the cigarette case. He'd been splashing in the pool when I found it, and I hadn't shown it to him, for I'd seen the initials in time. And Jeff didn't know that I'd met Murray in the cove with Helen yesterday morning. But he would find out that Murray had

come to see me yesterday afternoon, because the household knew. I was glad I'd had wits enough to mention that
to Stanley, knowing he'd find out.

If they began questioning me about that, was I going to
stick to the story I'd told Stanley about meeting Murray in
New York? Murray didn't know I'd told that lie and he'd
give me away without meaning to. And was I going to own
that he'd handed me a letter to Helen?

Suppose I kept still about that and Murray came out
with it—? Suppose I told about it after Murray had kept
still—?

I ought to get in touch with Murray, but that was just
the thing I couldn't do. There wasn't anything I could do
but sit tight and wonder how much evidence it took to
charge a man with murder.

Chapter Five

The police came as we left the dining room. A little file of men, hats in hand, followed Stanley Hazlitt up the stairs, on their grisly errand of viewing the body. The last man had a bag in his hand and I guessed he was the doctor.

Jeff and I went to our room to wait till we were sent for. Jeff said there would be general inquiries and a check on doors and entrances, all routine stuff to city officials, but out of the ordinary to these local men. I asked about fingerprints and Jeff said if they hadn't a good man they'd send for one. I reflected that even the Hazlitt money couldn't get anyone here quickly in this fog and I hoped Helen would remember to wipe off the doorknobs.

I'd imagined we'd be questioned separately but when we were summoned to the study, Helen Hazlitt was coming out of her room, just on this side of T. D.'s, and Judy Gaynor was coming out of a room on the other side of the study. She could have used the connecting door, I thought wryly, but evidently she wasn't stressing her private access to T. D.'s rooms.

Then I remembered something Helen had said. She'd said that after the scene with T. D., when he'd refused her the divorce, Judy had been lying in wait for him in the hall and had gone in the study and had it out with him. Why

had she waited in the hall? Had T. D. locked the connecting doors against her?

Helen had put on black and her lipstick was pale, and
with her fair hair swept tightly up against her head she
had a wan, fragile look. She was quiet but tense. Judy
Gaynor was in black, too, and her big Spanish eyes looked
enormous. Their lids showed she'd been crying, but they
were dry now and watchful. Her lipstick was as brilliant
as ever.

We filed in, and a lean, sandy-haired man behind the
desk, in T. D.'s big chair, stood up and looked with grave
sympathy toward Helen, who bowed and sat down. A stout
gray-haired man jumped to put a chair beside her for Judy
Gaynor. The two women did not look at each other.

The sandy-haired man was Sheriff Saunders. He had a
noncommittal face and sober, slate-blue eyes, and I judged
he took his policing seriously. This must have been the
biggest thing that had come his way, but, being a Maine
man, he was careful to show he wasn't impressed. The stout
gray-haired fellow was Dancy, of the state police. He had
alert eyes and a cheerful smile that he was keeping under
control now. Rowe, the County Medical Examiner, came
in and sat beside him.

Stanley introduced us and sat down at one side, between the desk and the half circle of our chairs. He said it
would expedite matters if we pooled our facts, and I had
a feeling he wanted to be on hand when Helen and Judy
talked. He looked worried. Everyone looked worried, except Jeff Ryder. Jeff looked interested, keen as a hawk.

Nothing had been taken, Stanley went on to say, so
theft did not enter into this. Suicide was an impossible
theory. The County Attorney had been sent for, but there
would be delays, and he, himself, said Stanley, very formally, had every confidence that the authorities on the
spot would see no time was lost.

"You can be sure of that, Mr. Hazlitt," said Saunders. He had a flat, uninflected Maine voice that could be heard across a room without his raising its key. He looked toward Helen, then down at some papers before him. "We want you to know we regret this, Mrs. Hazlitt," he said soberly. "All I can say is, we'll do our best to see justice is done."

Helen said "Thank you," faintly, her eyes on him like a child's on the teacher.

His tone grew businesslike. "We want to fix the time, as nearly as we can. Mr. Hazlitt was dressing for dinner. Now what time do you folks have dinner?"

He looked toward Helen as the lady of the house and she said, "Eight o'clock."

Stanley Hazlitt added to that. "My brother was downstairs, invariably, by twenty before eight. Or a little before. For cocktails."

Saunders put down the figures carefully. "Regular in his habits, then?"

Stanley said, "My brother is—was—always punctual," and it was the first time I had heard that without amusement.

"Now he was all ready except for putting on his necktie and coat," proceeded Saunders. "How long would you say, Mrs. Hazlitt, it would take him to put them on?"

She hesitated and he prompted, "Ten minutes?"

"Why, yes—he could—"

"That would make it about seven-thirty, then? Or a mite before?"

"No!" said Helen sharply. "You can't be sure of that. Sometimes he got ready—almost ready—quite early and then—then sat about. Doing things," she said vaguely.

I had a horrible feeling she was going to say, "Cleaning his guns," but she seemed to have come to her senses about the uselessness of pretending accident. She went on, "It could be he was ready—almost ready—quite a long time before seven-thirty."

Stanley gave her a quick look. It had open surprise in it, but a wife should know more than a brother about her husband's habits, so he said nothing.

The chief of police asked, "You don't know what time he had his shirt on, tonight?" and the plain, homely words were queer in that formal room.

"No, I don't," said Helen. "I wasn't in his room—not while he was dressing."

"What was the last time you saw him?"

"I couldn't say exactly. I was in his room a little while before we started to change. I think I left about six."

"I'd say it was later," said Jeff Ryder.

Helen looked at him in a startled way—the first time she had looked at any of us—and the officials looked at him inquiringly.

"Mr. Hazlitt was in to see me at six-thirty," Jeff explained. "I was working in this room, on some business of his. I'd been expecting him for some time and he said he'd been detained, been talking with Mrs. Hazlitt. I had the impression he came to me directly she'd left."

"Well, six—six-fifteen—six-thirty—I couldn't say," said Helen defensively.

"We appreciate that, Mrs. Hazlitt," said the chief. There was sympathy in his sober voice but he turned to Jeff with a hint of relief at dealing with an unemotional man. "How long did he stay, Mr. Ryder?"

"Fifteen minutes," said Jeff. "He said he'd be in to see me again before dinner, that he wanted to think over a few last things. He went back to his room at quarter to seven. He said he always took a short nap before he dressed for dinner."

"You sure of your time?"

"Dead sure. I was working against time. He wanted his business finished this evening."

Saunders had a chart of the rooms before him, drawn in big, bold outlines. I could see the squares. There was our room, then Stanley's, then the two empty guest rooms where the houseman had intended to put us, then Helen's room and then T. D.'s room on the corner. All these rooms opened on that long hall which ran like an open gallery over the big room below. T. D.'s room looked east and north and next to it, on the east side of the house, was this study and Judy's room. The hall there was an ordinary inside hall. Across from the study was an enclosed service staircase, and strung along after that were closets and small service rooms.

Saunders' pencil was on the square that represented Helen's room, on the connecting door between her room and her husband's. Only a wall divided them; there were no dressing rooms or bathrooms between them. Saunders asked, "Mrs. Hazlitt, when you were in your room did you hear any unusual noise or disturbance?"

"Nothing," said Helen. "But, you see, I wasn't in my room all the time. When I started to dress for dinner I was feeling so bored with all this fog that I slipped away for a plunge to freshen up."

"You went swimming?" The sheriff was frankly astonished. "In the fog?"

"Oh, I didn't go out in the fog. We have an inside pool."

Judy Gaynor turned her head. "You went down to the cavern?"

"Yes. Yes, I did."

"I thought you hated the place."

"I do. But I wanted a plunge."

It was a quick, queer interchange with strain in both voices. Judy seemed to be saying, *"You hated the place—so I never thought to watch it,"* and Helen was taunting, *"I counted on that!"*

Helen went on, "I was away quite a time. That was when it must have happened. For I certainly would have heard a shot."

If she could make it seem to have happened while she was away, and if she swore that Murray was down with her, all the time she was away, maybe that would be an alibi for him.

"You'd probably have heard it," said the chief. "Unless someone used a silencer."

"But that makes some sort of sound, doesn't it? A muffled one. And I'd have heard that."

"What time were you away, Mrs. Hazlitt?"

"I can't be exact—you see, I had no reason to watch the time. If Mr. Ryder says my husband came in to him at six-thirty, then I was back in my room at six-thirty. But I didn't go down directly after I'd come into my room," she said slowly, consideringly. "I think I went down about seven. And I stayed later than I meant to. I know I was late to dinner."

She was deliberately stretching out her time in the cavern to extend her alibi for Murray, I thought. I didn't know how much credence would be given that alibi but I did know she was making a mistake to try to fool Jeff.

He looked at her searchingly as if to discover whether her error was accidental or not. He said flatly, "You could have been down to dinner much earlier. We were in the cavern after you were."

Her face showed she had not known that. Then she said with a nervous lightness which grated on the seriousness about her, "But it takes me longer to dress! I had a stupid time with a zipper."

"You were in the cavern before seven," said Jeff, "because you were out of it before ten past seven. Kent and I went down then."

"Really!" She gave a vexed, uncertain laugh. "I seem to be all wrong about my times. But I said I wasn't sure. And I had a stupid time, as I said, with a zipper."

"I was in this room till seven," said Jeff. "We went down at ten past seven. At twenty to eight we were back in our room. At ten to eight I was here in the study." He looked at the chief of police, who was writing down these times. "Just before I left here at seven o'clock I heard the elevator come up to this floor. Mrs. Hazlitt must have been coming up then. If you think that Mrs. Hazlitt would have heard the shot in her room, even though the gun had a silencer, and that the shot was fired in her absence, then that shot was fired before seven o'clock."

I was struck by the queer precision of his words. *If you think that the shot was fired in her absence. . . .* What the devil did he mean by that? Or was it only the careful, legal, way of putting it?

Saunders said slowly, "You were in this room up to seven?"

"Yes."

"Did you hear anything like a shot?"

"Not a thing."

"He couldn't have heard," Helen broke in. "Not with all the space between the rooms. There's a dressing room, and the elevator with a passage between them and the passage has a door on each end. And the gun might have had a silencer. A man breaking in would certainly bring a silencer."

"With a silencer I might not have heard it," said Jeff. "Without a silencer I would."

"Don't forget the foghorn," said the sheriff. It was sounding as he spoke.

"I'd have heard it even if it synchronized with the foghorn."

That positive manner of Jeff's often rubbed people the wrong way. The sheriff asked drily, "You familiar with the sound of gunfire?"

Stanley Hazlitt had been leaning forward, following each word. He said, before Jeff could answer, "Mr. Ryder was an officer overseas."

"Not combat. Judge Advocate General's office," said Jeff. "But I know gunfire."

The sheriff was quick to make amends. "Maybe I can swear you in then as deputy. I certainly could use more men."

"That would suit me," said Jeff. "I'd like to work with you."

Saunders looked thoughtfully at his plain, sharp-angled face. "We could use you," he agreed. "Now about the time of the shot—"

"Does the exact time matter?"

Judy Gaynor flung the words at him with a breathless impatience, an anger that could no longer be restrained. Her hands were clenched in her lap and her big black eyes were blazing. She rushed on, "You sit here talking about these details, piecing these silly bits together, and all the while you're letting the man who fired that shot escape!"

"Nobody's escaping," said Dancy calmly. "Not out of this house. We've got men downstairs."

"He isn't in the house! He—"

"And the exact time is important," said Dancy in a nettled tone. "You remember, Ben—" he turned toward the sheriff—"it was a matter of five minutes that settled whether it was Bolaski or Ryan the night that fellow was shot in the juke joint."

I saw Stanley Hazlitt stiffen at the analogy.

Judy Gaynor swept it aside. She said urgently, "I tell you—" but the flat voice of the sheriff dominated hers.

"Just a moment, please. We have to get these things straight. Now, this cavern you were talking about—what's that?"

"A cave under the house," said Stanley. "My brother had it converted into an inside pool."

"That must be the old pirate cave," said Dancy with instant interest. "The one we used to play in, as kids. I remember hearing you had it all fixed up."

Saunders asked, "How do you get down to it from the house?"

I thought, "Here it comes."

"Elevator," said Stanley. His tone showed impatience, and that seemed odd, for I'd imagined he would see the possibilities of that cave at once.

Saunders saw them. "That's another way into the house."

"Hardly that. The cave has an opening into the harbor, yes, but scarcely navigable in a fog. I really wouldn't call it a way into the house."

"It is a way." Judy Gaynor was speaking again, with determination. "A man could get in that way. And go up in the elevator. Or he could get in any door, if it were opened to him."

We all looked at her. The room filled with the muffled blare of the foghorn, then emptied of sound. Saunders' voice sounded very mild after the horn as he asked, "Who would open the door?"

Dancy spoke up indignantly, spoke to Helen as if this were a suspicion that both women had concocted.

"Your help wouldn't, Mrs. Hazlitt. We've looked into that You've got two kinds of people here—either people that have been with you a long time, that Mr. Hazlitt here vouches for, or girls like Hannah and Elsie Tyler that live here and work for you summers—girls we all know are reliable."

"Of course, of course," said Stanley in quick appeasement. "No one suspects them of any treachery." He looked at Judy in sharp questioning and she stared back defiantly and said, "I wasn't speaking of them."

The words fell with hard distinctness. Stanley said nothing, watching her with puzzled wariness. I thought I knew what she was going to say next—I thought she was going to accuse Helen. What she did say set me back on my heels.

"Calvin Kent could have done it. He was very friendly with that man yesterday. Hiding in the bushes with him."

I stared at her. I could feel myself getting angry. You bitch! I thought. You black-eyed bitch! Do you actually believe that I'd open a door to a man bent on murder—?

"That's a crazy speech," I said curtly.

"What man do you mean?" asked Saunders, looking from her to me.

I said, as off-handedly as I could, "She means Murray, I suppose—he came to see me yesterday. We were walking in the garden. I don't know what she means by hiding in the bushes. We were walking up and down."

"Trying not to be seen!" said Judy hotly.

She was right about that, but I said stolidly, "Why shouldn't we have been seen? He had a right to come to see me."

"He had no business to. You knew he wasn't allowed in this house. You knew he hated T. D."

"Let's get this straight," said Saunders. "Who is this Murray?"

"An ex-Captain of Marines," I said. "I believe he is doing some writing here. Living in the village. He dropped in to see me for a few minutes."

Judy looked straight at me. "Why did he come to see you? Tell them that."

"That's absurd, Judy."

For once, Stanley forgot his careful "Miss Gaynor," but he picked his other words cautiously as he said to Saunders, "I don't feel there is any mystery about this call. Calvin Kent had met Murray in New York and when Murray heard he was here he called on him. Kent mentioned it to me. A perfectly casual thing on his part . . . But it is true my brother disliked the man, and had forbidden him the house. He had—his reasons. But Kent was not aware of that."

"Oh, wasn't he? Don't you think Helen confided in him? Don't you know Calvin Kent spent all yesterday morning in the cove with Helen and Murray?"

Oh, Judas, those binoculars! Helen had kept back against the rocks when Murray was there but he could have been seen splashing across the water, coming to us. I felt as if a depth charge had exploded under me.

They were all looking at me now. I could feel Jeff thinking, "You didn't tell me about Murray's being in the cove. Nor about the time in the garden. What goes on?"

Stanley actually stammered. "Why, no—I was not aware—" He gave me a look of sharp mistrust.

I said, "We ran into Murray at the cove. That was how he knew I was here and came to see me in the afternoon. We exchanged, perhaps, two dozen sentences. I haven't seen him since and I haven't opened any doors to him," I finished shortly. "And I don't see that this has anything to do with what you were discussing."

"It has everything to do with it," said Judy vehemently. "That man hated T. D. because T. D. wouldn't give Helen a divorce so she could marry him. He was the one person who hated T. D. enough to want to kill him . . . I don't mean that you knew he wanted to kill him," she flung in an aside to me. "You might have thought he only wanted to see Helen . . . but he was dangerous. He hated T. D. And he had no money and Helen had no money and T. D. was making a will that took everything away from Helen. But that will wasn't signed and until it was signed the old one was good, the one that left everything to Helen. T. D. was shot only a few hours before the new will was to be finished."

She looked straight at Saunders. "That's the story and you ought to know it, Sheriff Saunders. T. D.'s dead, and you can't bring him back, but you can see the man who killed him doesn't get away with it. And if you don't punish him," she said in a voice that started to choke, "I will. I swear to God I will."

I didn't dare look at Helen. Neither of the Maine men looked at her. They glanced briefly at each other, their faces embarrassed. I could feel them thinking, "So this is what goes on in these big houses." They sat there, turning the words over in their minds, and the foghorn had time to sound twice before anyone spoke.

Then Saunders turned toward Stanley Hazlitt. "This does look as if we had hold of a motive, Mr. Hazlitt," he said consideringly, his voice flatter than ever in its effort not to show constraint. "What do you think?"

Helen said in a trembling voice, "My personal affairs have nothing to do with this! Nothing!"

Then Saunders did look at her. He looked so long and steadily that he seemed to be examining every line of that white, defiant face.

"That's what we've got to find out, Mrs. Hazlitt," he said.

"Yes," said Stanley. "Yes, you might as well know the facts." His voice held distaste and repugnance for what he was laying bare but he went doggedly on. "My brother and Mrs. Hazlitt—were alienated. That was why he was making this new will. Mr. Ryder was here to make it." He hesitated a moment, then explained, "I preferred not to make it myself. I—well, I was the beneficiary."

"He was making a will to leave his money to you?"

"That was his intent."

"Not all of his money," said Jeff.

Stanley looked around at him. "Naturally there were a few bequests—"

Jeff said bluntly, "I don't know what your brother's first intentions were. He didn't tell me. I know only the instructions he gave me. You were to receive a share of his estate but not the bulk of it."

Stanley's face showed utter astonishment. He said, his voice rising, "I had understood—"

"I expect your brother changed his mind."

It took Stanley a moment to hide that chagrined astonishment. Then he said stiffly, "Share or all, it does not matter. Whatever my brother did—it was more than generous. . . . I was only surprised because I had so clearly understood—before I came to New York to get him an attorney."

The chief had been looking from one to the other. Now he asked thoughtfully, "Who was to get the money, Mr. Ryder?"

I hoped, nastily, that it was Judy Gaynor. The publicity would serve her right for shooting the works.

Jeff said, reluctantly, for it went against the grain to reveal professional secrets, "Mr. Hazlitt was creating a trust fund to endow a foundation for scientific research. It was to bear his name." He said to Stanley, as if to soften the blow, "He said he wanted something to carry on his name."

Helen gave a gasp of mockery. I remembered she had said that T. D. had refused to be bored with children.

"It was the detail of establishing such a trust that took so much time," Jeff explained.

"In any case I benefited by the will," said Stanley, "so I preferred not to make it . . . and I wish to make it clear," he went on, looking about at us, "that from the first, when my brother first spoke of his intention, I did not regard this disposition of the estate as final. I believed—I hoped—that in time he would convince Mrs. Hazlitt of the unworthiness of the course she wished to take and that there would be a reconciliation. In which event he would, naturally, make a will similar to his first."

The chief listened carefully to the stiffly spoken words. I had the notion—though his Maine face did not betray him—that he did not believe that Stanley would be exactly praying for that reconciliation.

"Well, however the will split things up," he said, "it left the money away from Mrs. Hazlitt?"

"It did," said Jeff. "As much as could be done."

"How could he do that?" said the sheriff. "A widow has her rights. This house now . . . that would come under Maine law, wouldn't it?"

"It would. Rights with regard to land are always settled by the law of the place where the land is situated. She'd get a third. But the place is heavily mortgaged. I expect he did that purposefully. As to the rest . . . his Steel Company . . . the real money. . . ."

He hesitated and Stanley Hazlitt spoke up. "I know what was in my brother's mind. In New York, by Section 18 of the Decedent Estate Law, neither spouse can be disinherited by the other except under certain conditions. Abandonment is one of them. That is to say, a wife can be disinherited if she has abandoned her husband."

I didn't see it. How could Helen have abandoned T. D. when she had been in his house? The Maine men were looking puzzled, too.

Stanley explained, "My brother was advised, not by me but by a firm experienced in such matters, that Mrs. Hazlitt's conduct could be construed as abandonment. For some time," he said, his voice dry and detached, "she had denied him marital rights. She has stated that this attitude on her part is a final one. He felt that constituted abandonment, that he had a case, an arguable case."

One that would be argued for years, I thought, looking carefully away from Helen. The sheriff was staring down in an embarrassment that showed, too, in his voice. "But that will wasn't signed?"

"It was not finished. It would have been finished this evening."

"And there's a first will still in effect?"

Jeff looked toward the locked briefcase on the table. "It should be in that case. It was given me to use in describing the property."

"Maybe we'd better see if it's here now," said Saunders. "You got the keys?"

Jeff unlocked the case and drew out the long legal papers. He put a single sheet before the sheriff. "It isn't long," he said.

Saunders looked down at it attentively. His lips moved as he read. I knew, from Jeff, what he was reading. "I give, devise, and bequeath, to my wife Helen. . . ."

He looked up finally, at Helen, his eyes expressionless beneath his sandy eyebrows, then he put the paper back in the case and put his hands on it. "We'll take this into custody," he said drily. Then he glanced toward Dancy. "Hadn't you better get your hands on that young man, Will?"

Alertly Dancy stood up. "Know where I can find him?" Saunders asked, "Where does he live, Mrs. Hazlitt?"

Helen said defiantly, "I don't remember."

"He boards in the village," said Judy Gaynor. "His name is Nicholas Murray."

"I'll find him," said Dancy. "Excuse me," he said politely, passing before Helen and Judy, heading for the door into the hall.

Stanley got up and stood in front of him. "Just a minute before you go. You will want to question the man, of course. He may be able to tell you something. But he was not in this house at the time my brother was killed."

Chapter Six

The words were said with such conviction that we waited for the next as for a revelation. When he said nothing more, the sheriff questioned, "Why, what do you mean, Mr. Hazlitt? You mean, you know he was somewhere else?"

"I know nothing of his whereabouts," said Stanley. "But you will find he was not here. I know—my reason tells me—it was impossible for him to have been here at the time my brother was shot."

"I don't see how you figure that—"

"Look at the circumstances," said Stanley. He stood, as if in a courtroom, facing Dancy and Saunders at the desk. Stanley said, very slowly and precisely, "My brother was shot at the stage of dressing he reached about seven-thirty. Mrs. Hazlitt would have you believe that he sometimes reached that stage much earlier than that and then—sat about." His voice was heavily sarcastic. "I am not acquainted with any such habit of his."

He waited for the foghorn to die away, then said, with harsh distinctness, "If I had no other proof than my knowledge of him, I would know that his death did not happen until seven-thirty. But I have other proof."

The room was very quiet. Then came Saunders' flat voice. "What other proof?"

"I have the certain knowledge that my brother was alive at seven-twenty-five."

"You saw him alive then?"

"Saw him, no. I heard his voice . . . I had come here, to this room, to speak to Mr. Ryder. The door was ajar and Mr. Ryder was not here. At the moment I heard Miss Gaynor speaking. Her voice came from the passage between this room and my brother's bedroom and I judged she was standing in the passage, outside his door. She wanted to see him about some matter and he refused. I heard his voice distinctly."

The sheriff swung around and looked at the door to the inner hall and I looked, too, then looked at Judy. She was gazing at Stanley in consternation. She must have been begging T. D. to see her, I thought, and it was sickening to her to know that Stanley had overheard.

Then Saunders asked what I wanted to ask. "Why didn't you say so before, Mr. Hazlitt?"

"Because I was interested to hear what the others would say," said Stanley grimly. "You were interrogating Mrs. Hazlitt and I wished to hear her account."

And that account had been misleading about time, I thought.

"And you, Miss Gaynor?" asked Saunders. "Why didn't you tell us? Since you thought we were wasting time."

"I said the exact time didn't matter—and I don't see that it does."

Judy had pulled herself together from the shock of knowing that Stanley had overheard whatever he had overheard and her voice was more spirited as she flung out, "It's the motives that matter."

"I agree with Miss Gaynor on that," said Stanley. "And I consider that Murray had motive. But I cannot see, anxious as I am not to believe—" He broke off, then said doggedly, "I cannot see that he had opportunity. Not at seven-thirty."

"Why not, Mr. Hazlitt?" The sheriff reflected a moment, then brought out, "He could have got in earlier, before the men went down—before Mrs. Hazlitt went down," he said hurriedly, ignoring the possibility of Helen's complicity. "Then he could have hidden in one of the guest rooms till he got his chance."

Stanley looked at him in silence for a moment. Then he asked, "How did he get out? After seven-thirty?"

"Wouldn't you say the elevator?" asked the sheriff, with Maine caution about statements.

"I would not. I was in my room, the door open, waiting for my brother from seven-twenty-five, twenty-six, to be exact, until ten minutes of eight. I would have heard the elevator. I did hear it when it came up with Kent and Mr. Ryder. That was the only time it was used. About ten to eight Mr. Ryder went back to the study just as I was coming out into the hall. You remember that?" he said to Jeff, and Jeff nodded, following every word with that hawklike attention of his.

Stanley resumed, "Then I went downstairs. I kept looking up at the gallery for my brother and listening. It was unusual for him not to be punctual. . . . I would have heard the elevator. Sounds carry along the gallery."

"Well, now, you can't be sure," said Dancy uncertainly. "There's the foghorn to consider . . . no, sir, you can't be sure he didn't slip out then."

Stanley turned to Jeff. "You were in this room, Mr. Ryder, after ten minutes of eight. While I was downstairs. There is only a wall between you and the elevator. Did you hear any sound from it?"

"Not a sound."

The sheriff said, "But you might have been absorbed in your work—"

"I wasn't working. I was waiting. And I notice things."

"Mr. Ryder was here," said Stanley, "until he came downstairs just a few moments before we heard the scream. You see, Sheriff, you will have to rule out the elevator."

"Well . . . but there's the back stairs."

"They come out into the butler's room where Caldwell was waiting with the drinks. That room is in open view from the kitchen. But if, by some miracle, a man got through the butler's room, and out into the corridor—how did he get out of the house? Every exit was locked and barred on the inside."

The sheriff pulled thoughtfully at his ear lobe. "That's a fact. But—"

"It is a fact. My experience as an attorney makes me take facts into careful consideration. I do not deny this young man had reason to wish my brother out of the way. And out of the way before the second will was signed. When I saw my brother dead—"

Stanley stopped, then went bn in a controlled, expressionless voice, "Naturally I thought of him. But I am confronted by these facts. The elevator was not used. The doors of the house were barred on the inside."

The sheriff worried his ear a moment more, then said stubbornly, "I know you and Mr. Ryder feel sure about that elevator. But with the foghorn—"

"Another fact, Sheriff. If the elevator had been used, it would have been left at the cavern level. Instead, it was on the same floor as my brother's room. I looked, when I had finished telephoning you gentlemen."

"I don't get this. You mean—"

"The elevator stays on the floor where it's left. It only moves when you operate it from within or when you signal for it. What I mean is, you can signal *for* it but you cannot signal it away. It stays where it is left."

"I get you. It stays at the floor where it's left. Until it's signaled for. Or until someone gets in."

"Precisely. It's a very usual arrangement."

"And you're sure it was up when you found the body?"

"It was up. I looked to see, after I had telephoned you. Caldwell did not come up in it. I asked him. He came up the back stairs."

No one seemed to know quite what to say for a moment, then Jeff spoke up. "There's the window."

"Down that cliff?" said Stanley skeptically. "It would be suicide."

"It would break my neck," Jeff conceded, "but a Marine might make it."

"He couldn't get out the window, in the first place. They were made too small for that. Then there is a drop of over a hundred feet. I think we may dismiss that conjecture, Mr. Ryder . . . much as I should like to believe that a man did get out."

Much as I should like to believe that a man did get out. Thirteen hard, precise little bullets of words.

Helen got to her feet with a gasping sound. "That is an abominable suspicion," she said in a trembling voice.

I thought she meant the suspicion of herself that every word of Stanley's, every fact he brought out so relentlessly, was deepening, but she flashed out, "It is abominable to suspect Nicholas Murray of murder because he was planning to marry me. It is an insulting, degrading, sordid suspicion. . . . This killing was done by someone else—someone Tod had hurt in business. He used to tell me about men who hated his guts, he said. He didn't care. He used to laugh about it. It was someone like that who killed him. I don't know how he got in or how he got away but I know he did and it's cruel and shameful to throw suspicion on an innocent man."

After a moment Saunders said quietly, "If he's innocent, Mrs. Hazlitt, he has nothing to fear."

"But it's dreadful to go asking questions—dragging out
all our private affairs—"

"Murder is dreadful, Mrs. Hazlitt."

He had a different manner with her now, the manner of
authority. I could see her shrinking under it, realizing that
she was suspect with Murray, that she had lost the deference and sympathy that had been hers when she came into
this room. She had been a grief-stricken widow to them
then. Now she was a woman who had a boy friend. Who
had reasons for not wanting her husband to live.

"And I should like to say—" Stanley was speaking a
little excitedly now—"that I am not aware that my brother
ever injured anyone—I handled his affairs and I am in a
position to know. He is not here to defend himself and I
propose to defend him. I propose to do all that a brother
can do to bring his murderer to justice. There is no consideration that can stop me."

That means you, Helen, I thought. This is going to be
bad, very bad, for you.

The Sheriff was looking down at the briefcase, his face
troubled and serious. "You can count on the law, Mr. Hazlitt," he said soberly. Then he shot a glance at Dancy.
"Will, you'd better go get that Murray. We want to know
what he has to say, anyway." He added, consideringly,
'This gives us something to go on."

It certainly did. They had the love affair, the refusal
of divorce, and the new will. They had the cavern and the
elevator. Within twenty-five minutes they had all the
secrets of the house.

Not all of them. They didn't know that Judy Gaynor
had wanted to marry T. D.—but Helen would bring that
out, I thought, before this thing was through. Though
that was immaterial—immaterial and irrelevant. It could

have no bearing on this murder. The material evidence was
that cigarette case in my pocket.

But finding that case in the cavern did not prove that
Murray had killed Hazlitt. Murray could have come to the
cavern, seen Helen, and gone away. Queerer things have
happened. It could be that Helen had gone to her room
and brooded and grown desperate—

No, I wouldn't let myself believe that. Not of Helen.

"You go get him," said the sheriff. "But first come over
here, Mr. Ryder, and I'll swear you in as deputy. I need
some extras."

Saunders stood up, the briefcase under his left arm.
I noticed he had a very businesslike automatic on his hip.
I had the idea that he would be an excellent shot.

"I think that's all," he said slowly. But for the gun
he might have been a country schoolteacher dismissing a
class, and Judy and I rose obediently. "I'll have to ask you
to keep to the house, of course, during the investigation."

After an uncertain moment, Helen walked out, without
a word. Judy Gaynor waited, then went toward the door
and turned toward her room. We could hear the two pairs
of heels clicking in their different directions. I started to
leave but Saunders called me back. He said, "There's a few
more things I'd like to ask you, Mr. Kent."

It could have been worse. He wanted to know about
Murray, of course, how long I'd known him and how well,
and I had to own I hadn't known him, that I'd lied to
Stanley to give a reason for Murray's call on me, to avoid
explaining about the meeting in the cove. I didn't blame
Stanley for the way he looked at me. Saunders asked a few
more things, about what Murray had said and how he had
acted, but he didn't ask whether Murray had given me a
letter to Helen and I didn't mention it. Then I went back
to my room and waited for Jeff to come in.

Chapter Seven

"The trouble with you," said Jeff—this was hours later, back in our room, talking it over—"is that you don't look at things impersonally. You see them through a blur of cockeyed sentiment."

"The heck I do!"

"Sure you do." He had been walking up and down the room, his hands deep in his pockets. Now he stopped in front of me, as I sat on the arm of a chair, and fixed his black eyes mockingly on me. "Take this ex-Marine, for instance. He was nothing in your life. He might be the worst sort of heel, for all you knew. But you felt so soft toward him you stuck your neck out and lied to Stanley to cover up that meeting in the cove. Then you had to own up you lied."

"Okay, I lied," I said. "But I had to give some reason for his barging in on me that afternoon."

"Just why did he come? You slid away from that with the police."

"I said he wanted to talk about the spot he was in and he did."

"I'll bet he was in more of a lather than you admitted. You made him out just downhearted."

"See here," I said, "you're a deputy sheriff now and if I've got to have a deputy in my bedroom, okay, but I'm damned if I'm going to have you practicing your sleuthing under the guise of honest talk."

Jeff laughed, then grew serious. "That's what I mean, Cal. You're covering up instead of helping. Because a man was a hero on a beach, you're so dead sure he couldn't be a killer in private life that you won't give a straight account of him for fear he'll be suspected."

I wasn't sure at all that Nicholas Murray wasn't a killer. In spite of all the facts about the doors and the elevator I thought he could have got out. The elevator might not have been heard—the sheriff had something about the fog-horn. And Helen could have signaled it up again.

Jeff went on. "And you hate to have Helen Hazlitt suspected—"

I said quickly, "Helen couldn't have done it. I know Helen."

"There you go! What do you know about Helen Haz-litt? Donkey's years ago you knew a little girl with blonde curls—but what do you know about Helen Hazlitt?"

"Well, when you've known someone as a girl—"

"What did you know about her as a girl? Rash and im-pulsive, wasn't she? Didn't you say 'strictly from impulse' when I asked what she was like? You know she liked to make a splurge. You know she married a man years older because that made headlines and gave her a lot of dough. After this, you don't know a damn thing about her except that she went to a cocktail party this winter and met an ex-Marine she fell for."

Those sharp-angled brows of his shot up derisively. "You see that sympathetically because of the little girl you used to dream about—but what are the facts? Not so pret-ty. She didn't tell her husband straight out. She let the boy friend follow her here, hoping to see a lot of him under cover. Isn't that so?"

It was about what Helen had told me but put less appealingly. I said, "She could be giving herself time to be sure."

"My guess is—I could be wrong—that she'd have gone on like that indefinitely, trying to eat her cake and have it, too, if her husband hadn't caught on and slammed down the brakes. There's no doubt she was crazy about this Murray and what she wants she wants but quick. So then she wants Murray and she's furious at her husband."

He admonished, "Now, mind you, I don't think that, in itself, would have been enough to drive her to kill her husband—supposing, for the sake of argument, that she did kill him—but the fact that he immediately started to change his will led to thoughts of his death and of how much better off she would be if he died before the new will was signed . . . you can't deny that she had motive. Motive, and opportunity."

"Okay. I don't deny it. But I say Helen isn't the sort—"

"Why isn't she?" Jeff argued. "She's high strung, unstable, reckless. She's also blonde, beautiful, and beguiling, and because you used to know her you think she couldn't kill a man. . . . Seventy-five per cent of murder is done by nice people—ever know that? That's where murder differs from every other crime."

"Are you arguing that she went in his room and shot him five minutes after he stopped talking to Judy Gaynor through the door? Then came down and joined us?"

"She didn't come down right away. She took time to pull herself together . . . no, I'm not arguing—yet—that she did it. I'm saying it's perfectly possible that she did it."

"You've let Stanley Hazlitt prejudice you."

"Not a bit. I'm keeping an open mind. I admit Stanley is prejudiced. It was his brother who was shot. And he was shot just when it did Stanley out of money. Not as much as he'd expected but a lot. If you were Stanley you'd leap at conclusions."

"Why does he leap at Helen? Why not Murray? It would be a lot nicer for the family name to have it Murray."

"He's a lawyer and governed by evidence. And all the evidence he sees is that Murray could not get away."

I said stubbornly, "I don't see Helen standing behind her husband with a gun—"

"Somebody stood behind him with a gun. Stanley said Helen was a good bird shot. She's used to guns. She could have hidden it in that long sleeve of hers till she got him to look out at the fog."

"You think of everything, don't you?"

Jeff grinned. He shook the last cigarette out of his pack, and flung the pack into the embers of the fire. Lighting his cigarette, he said, "She could have flung the gun out the window."

"What about your theory that the murderer went out the window?"

"Not a theory—a possibility. Can't build theories till we get more facts."

"I thought you were going to do it by brain work. Playing at being Poirot and using the little gray cells."

He met my jeer seriously. "That would get me nowhere. I can't project myself into people's minds and figure out their angles. I have to spread out the facts and see what they tell me about the people. I can look at facts without prejudice. You can't."

He was right about me. I'd got into a nostalgic mood with Helen the other day on the sands, feeling sentimental because it brought back that boy-and-girl time on the hill. If I hadn't had that old feeling for Helen I might not even have liked the woman I was with—I might easily have thought her spoiled and shallow. When I thought about it, in a hard-boiled, down-to-earth way, I could appreciate

that this sudden shooting was just the crazy sort of thing
she was capable of.

I asked, "How deep is the water under the window?"

"Twenty to thirty feet in low tide. They are going to
look for the gun but there isn't a chance in a carload they'll
find it."

But if I threw out the cigarette case it would be just my
luck to have it found. And that would prove Murray had
been there. I'd better hang onto it, anyway, I thought, in
case it was needed to help Helen. But it wouldn't help her
much. They'd think she was in on it.

I asked if any gun in the house was missing and Jeff
said they couldn't tell. T. D. had quite a collection. Those
in the cases were all there but nobody knew how many
others he kept about the place. I asked about the bullet,
but they hadn't found that, either. It had gone through
T. D.'s head and out the window, apparently, which seemed
to show the window was already open.

That was lucky for Murray, I thought. Now they couldn't
prove what gun it came from. A Marine wouldn't be likely
to part with his gun.

I asked if they'd taken T. D. away and Jeff said, "No,
he's there—on the bed."

I thought about the bed, so neatly turned down for the
night, with fruit and books beside it. I stood up and went
over to the dresser and took off my tie, and that made me
think of the tie he had put out to wear. I'd seen it in his
room. Dark red. He must have liked red. The pajamas and
dressing gown were red. . . . The poor guy. . . .

Jeff was pacing slowly up and down again. "Taken as a
problem, this is a honey," he said. "A regular who-dunit.
On the face of it, there are three people who could have
done it. Helen Hazlitt, single-handed or as an accomplice
to Murray, or Murray, either alone or in cahoots with
Helen, or Judy Gaynor. The first two had motive. Did

Judy Gaynor? She was mad as hell at T. D. and everybody else, when we got here. What went on? And now she is certainly carrying a torch for T. D. Stanley looks scared to death every time she opens her mouth. He took pains to tell Saunders very carefully how close to the family Miss Gaynor was. It looks to me as if she was close to T. D."

"Bright boy!" I said, taking off my tie. "Deputy sheriff scents situation. Rising New York lawyer stumbles over affair."

In the glass I could see his quick look at me. "Oh, it was like that, was it? . . . Helen tell you?"

"Helen told me Judy was crazy about T. D., that she wanted to marry him. It was Judy who told T. D. about Helen and Murray, hoping he'd get a divorce. But he fooled her. He settled for changing his will and that's when Stanley came posting to New York for an attorney."

I stopped at a sudden thought. "Wonder when T. D. changed his mind about leaving the works to Stanley. Wonder if he had it in the back of his head all along and pulled a fast one on Stanley about having someone else make it—so he could keep Stanley in the dark?"

"He was keeping him in the dark, all right," said Jeff. "He was damn firm with me about not mentioning the trust to his brother. And to Judy Gaynor, when she started copying."

"So he trusted her to keep her mouth shut even when she was mad," I said. "Well—he must have known she wouldn't want to do herself out of her job."

"What was she mad about? His not getting the divorce?"

"Just that." I turned around. "Helen came out and asked him for it—that was the afternoon we came. He refused it—said he'd fight any attempt she made. Then he told her what he was doing about the will. Just to let her see what she was losing, if she didn't behave."

"I know. But Judy—?"

"Judy was waiting for him, Helen said. He seems to have walked out into the hall instead of into his room. And he and Judy went off to the study for a talk. After that he came back to Helen and told her to stop her planning for him. He had the idea that Helen was backing Judy's hopes."

"H'm. . . . Bit of a shock for Judy."

"Department of understatement," I said, thinking of the blazing-eyed girl and her air of visibly holding herself in check. "But she didn't give up," I said, and told him what Judy had said to me, the day we'd gone swimming, how she'd urged me to advise Helen to run off, to force the issue with T. D. "Thus leaving the field to her," I mentioned.

Jeff listened intently. He demanded, "Why the devil didn't you tell me?"

"And spoil a beautiful friendship—? I thought you were taken by Judy."

"Not I—you. This was more of your tender covering up. What else do you know?"

I told him what Helen had said about Judy, that she hadn't known whether Judy and T. D. were sleeping together or not, and that she thought Stanley had a craving for the girl, too, but he was all for brother and the main chance. I said, "Deputy, that's all the dirt."

"Well, there's our motive," said Jeff. "Hell hath no fury like a woman scorned."

"You think she blazed up, when he wouldn't talk to her—?"

"She could have got a gun—or maybe she had it with her. She could have got to him through the hall door. He wouldn't have that locked. Or maybe he opened the other. Then she slipped back through the connecting doors and came downstairs."

"You make it so real." I could see Judy standing in stony silence by the fireplace when I came down to dinner. I said, "Maybe they all did it."

"Any one of them could have done it."

I thought of the way Judy had accused Murray. Was that self-defense, running to get suspicion focused—? Was she such a rat—? Perhaps she thought nothing could be proved against him, since he was innocent. But it wasn't a pretty action. . . .

"Look," I said, "there are more possibilities than these three. Aren't you taking the staff too much for granted? Suppose a man has been with Hazlitt for years—that doesn't prove he couldn't hate his guts, does it?"

"No, Watson, I am not taking the staff for granted. I am too smart for that," said Jeff, "I am giving thought to Caldwell."

"Caldwell—?"

"Ah, that surprises you. The last one you'd suspect. The perfect butler. Years in service. But what about Caldwell? You'd imagine he's a worldly minded snob. Fact is, he's a crank on some sort of religious belief. Belongs to a queer sect. Won't wear jewelry—no cuff links. Buttons. Thinks the rich are all going to be damned. Now how do we know he didn't believe he was singled out to hurry T. D. to his damnation? T. D. couldn't have been an endearing person to serve."

"Is this a gag?"

"Not at all. I had it from Jimmie the houseman. Jimmie and I grew pally when he brought me my trays. He was smarting under some rebuke from Caldwell, nothing about his work, but about his personal life. Jimmie thought that was carrying things a bit too far. 'Always hearing about fire and brimstone,' he told me. And he said, 'If you ask me, I think he's a bit out of his head.'"

"Well, I'll be damned—"

"Doubtless Caldwell concurs. I am going to cultivate Jimmie. He is not called by his last name because his last name is Buddy and employers do not like to say, 'Buddy, another Scotch.' He wanted legal advice about changing his name and I am going to give him more dope and then work on to Caldwell."

"He could have sneaked up the service stairs," I said hopefully.

"On the other hand, he seemed completely shocked."

"He had reason to be shocked if he'd done it."

"Right. It's an angle."

"Caldwell's my candidate," I said firmly.

"What, no sentimental emotion against sending a poor old gray head to the chair?"

"He wouldn't go to the chair. Just to an insane asylum."

"How cozy. Well, I'll look into Caldwell, I promise you." He felt in his pockets. "Got a cigarette?"

I pulled out the silver case. It was in the pocket where I usually carried my own and my hand was out before I knew what I was doing. It was too late to put it back. I snapped it open and held it out. "Here you are."

It's queer about voices. They give you away. The forced unconcern in mine rang false as Judas and I wondered Jeff didn't look at me. But he was looking at the cigarette he had taken. He asked, "How come you smoking these?"

They were a kind with paper tips. I said, "Oh, I like them for a change," and put the case away quickly.

He asked, "That new?" with frank curiosity.

"Lend-lease for the trip." My voice was still overcasual. And why had I told him that? Why hadn't I said Murray had handed it to me in the garden and I'd forgotten to give it back? I was a rotten liar.

I said quickly, "Another thing you ought not to forget is what Helen said about a business enemy. Stanley to the contrary, I bet T. D. had plenty. A man who felt he'd been gypped might turn killer."

"He might."

"He might have slipped up early, the way the sheriff said. And slipped down the stairs, when Caldwell wasn't looking. It's all a matter of luck and timing."

I thought about the locked doors. "He could have hidden himself somewhere. There are miles of strung-out rooms."

"If he did, he won't get out tonight," said Jeff, yawning. "That's for sure. They have men posted and there's an alarm system on the doors—that goes for the doors to the elevator, too. I'll get a posse, and go the rounds come dawn."

Neither of us said much more. We started to undress. When he was in the bathroom I shifted the cigarette case into a bureau drawer, into a fold of underwear, planning to shift it back in the morning. I remember that as we got into bed I said, "That foghorn's stopped," and he told me, "It stopped when you were taking off your tie. . . . You know, that butler's room isn't in such plain view of the kitchen as Stanley said. Not when the swing serving doors are shut. And the door to the corridor is right beside the stairs. A smart cookie could duck through."

I wondered if I had hit on the truth. Maybe there was an unknown killer lurking in some recess of the house. Maybe they'd find him in the morning and all this balancing of suspicion would be over. My mind was churning so with the possibilities that I couldn't get to sleep for quite a while. When I did, I slept heavily.

I came out of it with a jump. A woman was shrieking—I heard one shriek after the other, far away but penetrating the room, high-pitched and sharp. A woman had shrieked like that on a night in Italy when the Krauts came over and she'd been pinned down by rubble, and for a moment I thought I was back in that night and I jumped for the corner of the room because I'd found that corners held up better in bombing. Then, when I fell over the chaise longue, I came fully awake and knew where I was.

Jeff had flashed on his bed lamp and was streaking to the door, a gun in his hand, and I went after him. The shrieks seemed to be coming in the open window, but when we opened the door we could tell they were coming from the end of the hall. Another scream sounded, then broke off suddenly, and we raced down the hall, through the darkness that was so dark we didn't see Stanley by his door till we ran into him. He staggered, then ran along with us, and behind us we heard heavy feet pounding along and a Maine voice calling something we didn't wait to catch. We ran past the guest rooms and came to Helen's room. The door was open and there was a figure sprawled on the floor in the doorway.

Part III: Chapter Eight

It was Helen. I could see her vaguely in the pale light from the open window across the room. She lay unstirring, a whitish heap in the darkness, and I thought she was dead until the Maine man, who had come up behind us, flashed his light on her and I saw her eyes were closed as if she had fainted. There was no sign of blood.

I dropped down beside her and Jeff said quickly, "Don't lift her! If she's hurt—"

Then her eyes opened. They were blank for an instant and bewildered, staring into the light, then they filled with terror and she started to struggle up. Jeff and I helped her and she got to her feet, clutching at our arms and shivering in the wind that blew her nightgown about her.

We began to ask questions, but all she could choke out for a moment was "A man—a man—"

Then she gasped, "He stood over me—he tried to kill me—"

Someone—I think it was Stanley—turned on the lights and we saw the room was empty, the sheets trailing from the bed, and the casement behind it wide open. The door into T. D.'s room was open, too, and we could see the big bed with the sheeted figure on it. Helen saw it and she shrank against me with a gasp.

"In there—he went in there—"

The Maine deputy—I hadn't seen this one before—
dropped his torch into his pocket, held his gun ahead of
him, and went gingerly toward the open door, Jeff went
with him. They were gone a few moments, then came back.
Jeff reported, "No one there."

I was asking Helen if she was hurt. She said shakily, "I
don't know—I'm all right, I guess—only frightened—"

Her lips were trembling so she could hardly frame the
words. "I woke up—I don't know what waked me—but I
felt afraid. And I looked right up at him. He was just a
dark shape between me and the window. I couldn't speak
or move. I felt I was dying."

A fit of shuddering seized her. I said, "You're all right
now, Helen," and Jeff said, "Go on, Mrs. Hazlitt. Go on."

"Then he moved—and I came to life. I flung myself
out of bed just as something came down on it. I screamed
and ran and he lunged across and caught at my gown, but
I got free—"

Her gown was torn at the shoulder. Judy Gaynor, who
had come silently into the group, her dark hair streaming
over a long yellow robe, picked up a dressing gown from a
chair and placed it about Helen.

"I got to the door," Helen went on, her voice higher,
with a hysterical note in it, "and I was screaming all the
time. Then—then he must have struck at me. I went down.
But I didn't quite pass out," she insisted. "I'd have known
if he had run out over me. I kept waiting for him to kill
me. But he didn't come. He went out the window—he
must have gone out the window."

"Did you see him, Mrs. Hazlitt?" asked the Maine man.
"Did you get a look at him at all?"

"No—no, he was just a shape. A man's shape. A big
man—I mean, tall, terribly tall. And thin. He was horrible." Her eyes closed a moment.

"You said he went into T. D.'s room," said Stanley.

"Did I? . . . because I saw the door was open, I suppose. I just thought so . . . I expect he came from there. He must have been hiding in there."

"We searched—" said Stanley, but he said it in an inconclusive voice that made me wonder how thorough the early search had been.

Undoubtedly they had opened doors and poked at garment bags, but I didn't imagine they had explored high shelves or peered under the bed. The dead man's room was the last place where they would have expected the killer to hide.

There was a bruise on Helen's forehead, a faint mark over her eye, and she put a hand to it and said, "He must have struck me here. It hurts."

"That wouldn't strike you down, Helen. It's only a skin bruise."

Stanley's voice was dry and skeptical. He went on, each word extinguishing the excitement as a caretaker might go about turning off the lights in a garish room, "You're hysterical, Helen, and overwrought. Better get back to bed."

He turned to the deputy. "Stebbins, you and Mr. Ryder had better see to the doors. But I expect you'll find them untouched. I imagine that Mrs. Hazlitt has had a nightmare."

"Nightmare!" Her voice rose. "I saw him! I saw him, I tell you. And of course he didn't go out the doors. He went out the window."

Stanley went to the window and looked out. His shoulders could not go through the opening but he thrust his head forward and stared down. Then he withdrew his head without a comment. The deputy went over to him and they exchanged silent glances, then the deputy said he would phone the sheriff and get him here, and hadn't he better bring the doctor with him?

"I expect so." Stanley gave a sigh that sounded both exasperated and resigned. "I'll get dressed. Mrs. Hazlitt had better go back to bed." Two frightened maids had appeared on the edge of the group and he said, "Elsie—you and Hannah stay with Mrs. Hazlitt."

"Yes, stay—stay," said Helen, hysterically. "That man means to kill me."

Jeff said practically, "If he went out the window, Mrs. Hazlitt, he won't be coming back."

"Perhaps he didn't go. Perhaps he only wanted us to think he went. He may have gone out the door from Tod's room."

That made some sense. A man could dart out from there and come down the service stairs. I had known too many impossible things to happen overseas to be as skeptical as Stanley. You couldn't ask a better place to hide in than this great house. And if a man hated T. D. enough to kill him, that hatred might well include T. D.'s wife.

"Is there anything that I might do, sir?"

The voice of Caldwell was smooth as oil and only a trifle smug at the perfection of its performance. Caldwell was redeeming himself for his panic when he had found T. D. He had put on trousers and shirt and coat but no tie—to wear a tie, to be in complete garb, would be out of key with the scene. Fanatic or not, he enjoyed his role of perfect butler.

As no one spoke, he cued us suavely. "Perhaps something hot to drink? Some tea for madam?"

"Yes, tea," said Helen. She was leaning weakly on the maids, being escorted back to bed. "Very hot. With brandy."

"Yes, madam."

"I'll have coffee downstairs. As soon as I get my clothes on." Stanley sounded tired and exasperated. "Do you gentlemen—?"

"I'll join you," said Jeff. "Then I'll make the rounds with Stebbins."

I felt Stanley didn't trust me to make a search so I said I'd go back to my room and get some sleep. Judy Gaynor followed me into the hall and touched my arm. "Come back to the study," she said, under her breath, then moved away.

Back in our room, Jeff jumped into his clothes and after he'd gone I brushed my hair, wrapped my big maroon bathrobe about me, stuck my feet into slippers, and went down the hall again. I could hear Stanley moving in his room as I passed—he wasn't as quick a dresser as Jeff—and I hoped he wouldn't come out and think I was going to see Helen. Not that I cared what he thought of my actions, but it wouldn't do Helen's cause any good to be thought conniving with me.

The doors of the two empty guest rooms were open, their lights blazing, as if the Maine deputy had been there, and Helen's door was closed. I turned the corner past T. D.'s room and opened the door into the study.

Judy was there, and that yellow robe and her big dark eyes and dark hair suddenly reminded me of a painting I'd seen years ago in Italy. It was of another Judith, a dark, gorgeous beauty, in a robe that shade of yellow, holding the head of Holofernes and holding it as indifferently and unconcernedly as if it were a bowl of cherries. The artist—I forget his name—had painted his mistress as Judith and his own head as Holofernes.

The likeness was all in the yellow robe and the dark beauty of the girl. The painted Judith had stared out at you with lazy, heavy-lidded indifference, with the arrogance of a full-blooded beauty, but this living Judith looked tormented, both defiant and miserable, and she was pacing the room like a tiger in a cage.

She was smoking and I got a cigarette from the box on a table and lighted it, waiting for her to do the talking.

"You hate me, don't you?" she shot at me, suddenly.

I perched myself on the edge of the table. "Not exactly," I said. "I don't exactly love you, either. You didn't endear yourself to me when you said I might have let Murray in."

"I didn't mean you knew what he was up to. You'd have thought he only wanted to see Helen."

"However you slice it, I don't like it. But what you were really a bitch about," I said, "was Helen. You certainly knifed her, spilling it out about her divorce. Yet you were glad enough she wanted that divorce."

Her eyes flashed about to me with a defiant "So you know that?" look.

"In fact," I said, "it was your spying and telling that fixed it so she had to own up and ask for a divorce. You wanted Helen's husband and Helen—do her that justice— would have been glad to give him to you. I don't say she was glad from the beginning. There must have been quite a while when Helen wasn't happy about you. But after she met Murray, she didn't care."

She looked at me bitterly. "That's her story, is it?"

"She hasn't gone into details. But I got the general idea. . . . You were making a play for T. D. before Murray came on the scene. She could have said a lot about you tonight and she didn't."

The girl said in a low voice, "I could have said a lot about the men she flirted with before Nick Murray. About the empty life T. D. had."

"And which you were damn glad about so you could compensate him for it," I said, "and feel justified. . . . But that isn't what gripes me. It's the way you tried to use her, then threw her to the wolves."

"I told the truth," she said in a shaking voice. "I had to tell them the story to make them see it was Nick Murray.

And it's not true I was making a play—but that doesn't matter now. It doesn't matter what you say about me. Nothing matters but getting that killer."

A perfectly wild look swept across her face and she stared at the wall ahead as if she were looking right through it and into the room beyond and at the sheeted figure on the bed. I never saw a creature look so utterly despairing. Then she made a helpless gesture and began to walk up and down the room again.

"I didn't accuse Helen," she said after a few minutes, as if she had remembered what we were talking about. "I never believed she did it. She isn't like that. There's no iron in her. Only sparks. Helen wasn't in any danger from the police. She would have been all right. But now—"

She made that distraught gesture again and looked at me from across the room with eyes that seemed utterly sincere in their despair and desperation.

"Now she's deep in it—the fool! She was hiding him."

That was what I'd been afraid of, myself. I hoped my face didn't give me away.

Judy's voice went on, "Either he came right to her—after he shot him—and she hid him then, or he got to her room tonight." She was walking again. She pushed a chair out of her way obliviously to extend her space. "She could have let him out the window. There are belts and cords on her clothes that could lower him. He could find a foothold."

The heavy yellow robe rustled as she walked. It was a padded-satin Chinese robe, very straight up and down. Her hair wasn't streaming now. It was smoothed into a sleek tight knot at the back of her head.

I watched her curiously. Finally I said, in a carefully detached voice, "You think that scene was an act?"

"But of course!" Her eyes flashed toward me with contempt that anyone should think anything else. "She wants to create belief in some outside killer. That bruise on her head wasn't anything. She hadn't the nerve to gash herself. And the way her gown was torn—she'd jerked it open at the front."

I thought it over. She could be right. Not about Helen's letting Murray out the window—my own idea was that Murray had found a way out before. In the elevator. Stanley and Jeff, no matter how sure they were of themselves, might not have heard it above the foghorn. Helen could have signaled it back. But Judy could be right about Helen's staging an act.

Lying awake, thinking of Judy's accusations against Murray and of Stanley's cold hostility, Helen might have worked herself up to faking that assault to throw them off the track. She might have opened the window, yanked the sheets off the bed, hit herself on the head, and begun screaming. Now that I reviewed them cold-bloodedly, there had been something methodical about those screams. True, the woman in Italy had screamed methodically like that, but she had been pinned down. She hadn't been dodging an assailant, racing across a room.

Judy flung at me, "You don't mean she took you in?"

"Why are you telling me all this?" I really wondered about that. "Why not Stanley? He'd agree with you."

"Oh, Stanley—!" Her voice was scornful. "He wouldn't agree she was hiding Murray. He doesn't believe Murray was here because he doesn't see how he could get away. Stanley sees facts—he never sees *through* them."

She went on, "Because it's a fact the windows are small, he won't believe a man could wriggle through. Because it's a fact that doors were locked and the servants reliable, he's convinced no one could have got out. So it has to be Helen. He's never trusted Helen. . . . But Helen wasn't in any danger. The police couldn't have proved her guilty when she wasn't."

She seemed to be speaking what she thought was truth. She seemed utterly convinced that Helen wasn't guilty.

"But now she's really got herself into it," she said despairingly. "Oh, I don't know what to do!"

She stopped in front of me, looking at me as if she weren't seeing me at all. "I don't know what to do," she repeated.

"Do you have to do anything?" I said, but she went on, thinking out loud, "If those police swallow this—if they're thrown off the track and waste time—oh, God, he could get away while they're milling round! But if I tell them— that's showing Helen up for an accomplice. Accomplice after the fact." Her staring eyes suddenly focused on me. "That's bad, isn't it?"

"She won't go to the chair," I said. "I expect they'd let her off with life. Maybe only twenty years for complicity."

She continued to stare at me a moment more, then turned away with a suggestion of actual despair. It was the way she had turned from me on that day on the beach, before the cabana, when she had tried to make me believe that I ought to tell Helen to run away.

"She's such a fool!" she said, under her breath.

"For helping him out—if she did help him out?" I asked her. "Isn't that what you'd do in her place?"

That spun her around. She said, "That's why—"

She looked distracted. She looked sick with grief and anger and worry . . . I wondered why she was saying all this to me. She must have known I'd take Helen's side. Perhaps she wanted me to; perhaps she wanted something to help her fight the compulsion to revelation that was driving her.

I pointed out, "If the police get to think she sheltered him *afterward,* you can be sure they'll think she was in it *before.*"

"That's what I'm afraid of." Her cigarette had scattered ashes over her robe and she brushed them off and ground out the stub in a small jade bowl. Then, suddenly, she picked up the bowl and sent it flying into the fireplace. So violent was her gesture that I expected more from it than the small breaking sound that ensued.

"But what am I going to *do?*" she burst out. "Let her put over this fake about an unknown killer? I won't have that. Murray killed him. He came into this house and shot him down. So Helen would be free and rich. . . . He can't get away with that—I won't let him get away with it . . . I can tell them . . . I—"

"Why do you have to tell them?" I was on my feet, standing in front of her then. I said, "It seems to me you've said enough. The police can go on from there and do their own thinking. . . . And you could be wrong about tonight, you know. Maybe it wasn't an act. She was wrought up enough to have a nightmare."

"Nightmare—?" she mocked.

"It could have been one," I insisted. "I'd go slow about more accusations. You may find that Murray wasn't here at all. Dancy may have picked him up hours ago."

"No, he hasn't. Stanley told me he hasn't been found. He left his house the end of the afternoon and hasn't been back."

Well, that was bad, I thought.

She said, "He was here, all right," and her jaw set obstinately. I'd been struck before, not pleasantly, by the firm angle of that jaw. She was a strange combination, that girl—extravagant beauty, and temperament, and the hard reasoning of a man. Perhaps that was why, in the show-down, she hadn't been able to get T. D. over the last stile. Instead of charming him on, she had probably gone at him hammer and tongs.

There was something in her obstinacy that made me want to hit back at her. "You haven't always been right in your guesses," I reminded her. "You could be wrong in this. It doesn't mean a thing that Murray isn't back. There must be plenty of taverns along the shore—or whatever Maine has for taverns."

She said mistrustfully, "Do you mean that? Or are you trying to gain time for him?" Then she shot at me sharply, "Don't you know he did it?"

"Well, how do I know?" I was angry to be so badgered. "I'm no crystal-gazer."

There was something supercilious in her eyes, as if she understood I was trying to deny my own conviction, and it stung me to say, coldly and levelly, "For all I know, you did it yourself in one of those fits of insanity that get girls off with juries. Then you picked on Murray as a red herring."

Her eyes widened and her lips parted in what seemed to be sheer horror. I couldn't tell what was in her mind. I couldn't tell whether her voice was choked with horror or just using a stage effect when she whispered, "You think that—?"

"No, I don't think it," I snapped. "I don't know enough to think a damned thing about it."

That wasn't quite the truth and because it wasn't I got angrier. "I'm only saying it could be anybody. And the more you go accusing Murray—without any evidence against him—the more it looks as if you had a reason to frame him."

I wished I hadn't said that the moment it was out, but I couldn't stop myself from going on.

"You guessed wrong once about what T. D. would do, if he would get a divorce. Now you might be guessing wrong about Murray. I'd let the police do their own guessing."

I was braced for fireworks, but she went to pieces. She began to cry. She cried the way she had in T. D.'s room, when she had seen him lying there. She sobbed as if she'd tear her throat out. She hid her face in her hands, as she had in his room, and turned away from me.

"Go away—go away!" she said, in a shaking voice. "I can't take anything more—"

She flung herself in T. D.'s big chair and twisted around to burrow her face into its back. Her shoulders were shaking. I stood looking down at her uncertainly. I felt a heel.

I said, "I'm sorry—" but she kept on sobbing and after another "Go away!" I turned and went.

Chapter Nine

That was about four o'clock. I tried to sleep but couldn't and when Jeff came in, a little after five, for a shower and shave, I got up and dressed. He reported that they had made a grand tour of the premises and had found everything as tight as a drum.

"Nobody could have got out unless the help are lying their heads off," he said, "and they are all decent people. . . . And if anybody's hiding in this joint he's in a bottle. We've looked into everything else. We even opened the cook's wardrobe trunk."

I asked if they'd heard from Dancy and he said that the sheriff had just phoned that there was no trace of Murray yet.

"Murray," said Jeff, "rooms with a Mrs. Peterkin, known locally as a widow woman, and a widow woman of good character. He left the house in the late afternoon, and has not come back. But that, Mrs. Peterkin reports, has happened a time or two before. Nobody knows where he went. The only clue—I am being frank with you, my friend, hoping for equal frankness in return—is that Murray was seen around one of the wharves. The fisherman who saw him is sure it was Murray, in spite of the fog. The closest he can come to placing the time is the end of the afternoon."

Just the time to take off to meet Helen in the cavern, I reflected.

Jeff went on, "The wharf was where a Portuguese keeps some boats and Murray had rented a boat from him. Whether he took out a boat then or not the fisherman couldn't say. He says he didn't hear the sound of oars, but then he wasn't there long."

"Are the boats all there now?"

"All present and accounted for."

"Then if he went out, he's back."

"Elementary, my dear Watson. But when did he get back? That is the sixty-four-dollar question. He could have been out all night. Dancy only turned up the fisherman an hour ago, so if Murray took out a boat he could have been gone till, say, well, four o'clock. All it proves is that, if Murray took a boat out, he is now back on the mainland."

"Do they leave their oars in the boat?"

"No, but Dancy said there was a broken paddle in the boat. And until the wind came up last night it was still as a pond."

"Was the paddle wet?"

"Saunders asked that. Everything was dripping with fog."

"Saunders here?"

"He's been here since the alarm. And the doctor has come and gone."

"To see Helen? What did he say about her?"

"Nothing—except that he'd given her something to make her sleep. His visit," said Jeff, turning to look at me, "was while you were closeted in the study with Judy Gaynor."

"Oh, they know about that, do they?"

"Naturally. This place is lousy with watchers. And now—speaking as I was of equal frankness—" Jeff's eyebrows went up clownishly—"what goes on between you and Judy?"

"Judy had the jitters," I said. "She wanted somebody to talk to. When we were going out of Helen's room she asked me to come back to the study. So I went."

Then I thought I might as well tell him, for Judy would probably blurt it out herself. "She was all worked up," I said. "She thinks Helen put on an act tonight. She thinks Helen helped Murray out the window, and then pretended she was assaulted to make it seem a stranger."

I told him more about it, though I didn't tell what I'd said to Judy at the last, partly because I was ashamed of it and partly because I felt I'd been a fool to let her know she might be suspected. I hadn't been very bright, I thought. I told him that Judy seemed to be sure that Helen had had no part in the murder, but that she had got herself involved now, helping Murray to escape.

I said, "Judy's going round in circles—she's hell-bent on accusing Murray but she really hates to accuse Helen. She's got a sneaking sympathy for Helen's loyalty to Murray."

"Involved," murmured Jeff. "Female psychology department."

"Anyway, she's all broken up. She was hard hit by T. D.'s death."

I was thinking of the way she'd gone to pieces after my nasty speech to her and some of my compunction must have shown, for Jeff looked at me mockingly.

"So now you don't think she could have shot T. D.?"

"I don't know what to think . . . yes, she could have shot him and be sunk about it now. . . . No, I—"

I gave it up. "Look," I said, "this is just clawing at the air. So even if you are a deputy you don't have to tell this, do you? That Judy thinks Helen was putting on an act? Judy will probably say so herself, soon enough, but until she does—"

"Good Lord, don't you think I've thought of it?" said Jeff. "What sort of lunkhead do you think I am? I told

the sheriff to look through Mrs. Hazlitt's stuff to see if
anything had been twisted or knotted, but he wasn't for
it. He's as sure as Stanley that a man can't get through
those casements. I'm going to try it myself, to see what the
answer is."

"Try it downstairs," I said. "Maybe you'll only break
half your neck."

"I've got a plan."

It would be just like him, I thought, to get through.

I said sourly, "And what a policeman you're turning out
to be!"

He swung around on me. "Get this, Cal. This is murder. A man had his brains blown out last night. Maybe it
was for his money, maybe for his wife, maybe for revenge.
Whatever the motive, it was a nasty job. And my business
is the law."

He began walking up and down the room, not pacing
like a tiger in the cage, the way Judy had, but in slow,
easy strides. Jeff always liked to think on his feet. He said,
"My job is to find the killer. It makes no difference to me
whether it's an ex-Marine, a wife, a girl friend, or a butler
who's dotty in the head. Whoever stood behind a man and
fired a gun into his head is the one I want."

Something remote and impersonal had come into his
face. All the clowning had gone out of it.

"Here it is," he said, "right in this house, and there
isn't one real clue. Everything is nebulous, hypothetical.
It could be this one—it could be that one. I want to get
hold of something definite. Something concrete. Some bit
of evidence. It's here. It has to be. There isn't any perfect
crime. There's always a mistake. Something overlooked.
Something forgotten. The trick is to grope around till you
get your hands on something—and then see it for what it
is. That's the hard thing. I haven't a doubt that I've seen

something significant already and not known it for what it was. That I've heard something. . . ."

His black brows drew together. "Actually, we've one clue on one of the suspects. Murray was near a boat. But what does that prove? Even if we can show he was out in a boat, that doesn't prove he was here. Not without evidence."

"And if he was here that doesn't prove he shot T. D.," I said.

"It would help prove it."

I kept busy putting on my necktie. After a moment I said, in an offhand voice, "Look—you're all set. You go get your chow, and I'll be along."

When he'd gone I went to the dresser drawer to get the cigarette case I'd hidden last night. It wasn't there. I took everything out of the drawer and I looked in all the other drawers. Then I went through my pockets in case I'd walked in my sleep and put it in a pocket as I'd planned. It wasn't anywhere.

I wasn't exactly upset, but I didn't like it. It gave me a queer feeling. I'd been out of the room two times. Once when we were all in Helen's room, once when I'd gone to the study. Somebody could have taken it either of those times. But why would anybody rummage in my drawer?

My money wasn't taken. I looked to see. Of course, a man—even a Maine man—might pick up a gadget when he wouldn't take money, but how had he happened to look for it inside a fold of underwear? My own case, just as good a one, was in the pocket of my coat which had been hanging on a chair all night.

Could Jeff have taken it? I felt a heel to think that of Jeff, but if he felt it in the line of duty—? There was something remorseless in Jeff when he got going. I half made up my mind to ask him but when I got down to that early morning breakfast he was nearly through, hurrying to go to the mainland with Stebbins, our deputy friend of the night, to help scout about for Murray, so I didn't speak of it.

I went back to our room. I kept thinking about what Jeff had said, about clues lying about unnoticed, and when the maid came in I got her to talking. It wasn't hard, for she was keyed up by the excitement. She was Elsie Tyler, Hannah's sister—they were the Tyler girls that Dancy had spoken of so warmly—and she was voluble about Hannah's part in the tragedy.

"It was a dreadful thing to have happen to Hannah," she said, and I said it certainly was. I had a vivid memory of Hannah's rigidly pointing arm and apron-covered head as she backed blindly away from that room.

"She'll never get over it, never!"

Elsie had such serious blue eyes that I didn't say that Mr. Hazlitt would never get over it, either.

She went on, "She said to me, 'Elsie, I'm never going to feel the same, going in a room after this. When I think of how I turned down that bed and him there all the time—'"

I asked where she had been when Hannah went upstairs. She had been finishing her dinner, I found, in the small dining room off the kitchen. Jimmie the houseman was with her. "Mrs. Benton likes to get some of us out of the way early," she explained. "That way it's easier with the dishes, too."

Mrs. Benton, the cook, had been in the kitchen with Opal, her helper. Opal was the daughter of the Clements, who lived on the place the year around as caretakers. Clement was head gardener and Mrs. Clement did the laundry and some cleaning. The Clements had been in their cottage all the time. The chauffeur, Mrs. Benton's husband, had been in the garage.

"You're a big household," I said, checking on them, but Elsie said, "Not for the work, we aren't. And we're short-handed right now. By rights Pauline should be here."

Pauline, I discovered, was a New York maid who usually took care of the Hazlitt rooms. She was sick in New York and not expected for another week or so.

Well, there was the cook, cook's helper, the houseman, two maids, chauffeur, gardener, and laundress all accounted for. Only the butler was left, and he was the one I really wanted to know about.

"It was a shock to Caldwell, too," I said. "When he looked in that room."

Elsie merely nodded, stepping briskly about a bed, smoothing blankets with great exactness.

"He must have been devoted to Mr. Hazlitt," I said. "Hadn't they been together for years?"

"Quite a time."

Her voice was cool and I asked, with a little smile, "Or isn't Caldwell the devoted type?"

"I don't know, I'm sure."

"I'm sorry," I said. "I was curious about him because he seems, somehow, a little unreal—as if he were playing at butler. As if being a butler were just a character he puts on. I got the impression, somehow, that it's a sort of act—that he has a very different character of his own behind all that manner."

She stopped and looked at me. "It's queer you say that," she remarked, her eyes according me more intelligence than she had supposed.

She said thoughtfully, "Yes, he's like that—an odd fish. Preaching to us already on the wages of sin and how it's harder for a camel to pass through a needle's eye than for a rich man to enter the Kingdom of Heaven. With Mr. Hazlitt lying dead in his bed! He might wait till the poor man's in his grave."

Her voice colored with indignation. "There's no human feeling in him, and that's a fact. That's what I told Hannah. I don't call that being religious. My church has more religion in its little finger than he has in his whole body."

"I should think so, if that's how he feels."

"Not that he didn't do everything right for Mr. Hazlitt while he was alive," she added, as if anxious not to do injustice. "He was always on the dot. Last night I thought he'd jump out of his skin, he was so uneasy because Mr. Hazlitt wasn't down on time. He kept putting his head into the kitchen and saying, 'What can be keeping him?' And Mrs. Benton was in a stew because dinner was held back and she'd planned a custard soufflé for dessert."

"When you say he put his head into the kitchen—you mean through the swing doors?"

"Why, yes—"

"That means they were closed. And if they were closed nobody in the kitchen could see into the butler's room?"

"Why, no—"

"Then if a man came down the stairs the only one that could see him was Caldwell. And if Caldwell was looking into the kitchen—or coming out to serve drinks—"

"Of course, a man could get out of that room without Caldwell's seeing him," said Elsie. "It's exactly what happened. He could get out the door into the hall—it's right beside the stairs. That man was right in this house all evening," she said, with intense conviction. "A murderer . . . it's a wonder he didn't kill Mrs. Hazlitt."

Part of her conviction came from her refusal to lose a single element of thrill, but it was conviction. She had the escape all worked out. The man, she said, had gone down the stairs and then along the hall to the library, and hidden there. "It was the first room he'd come to," she said, "and he'd nip in there, quick. And there he stayed, flattened behind the curtains," she said, her eyes round with drama. "Waiting for night to come to sneak up and finish his work."

"That sounds okay to me," I said. "Have you told the police?"

"Indeed I have. I told Ben Saunders it was a sin and a shame he didn't make a better search the first time. Men just give a look and a glance."

"You've got something there."

"Mrs. Hazlitt thinks I'm right," she said, triumphantly. "She thought that was the very way of it."

"But Mr. Hazlitt—Mr. Stanley," I said slowly, "doesn't seem to think that a man was in the house at all. He doesn't think there was anyone in Mrs. Hazlitt's room. He thinks she had a nightmare."

"Oh, men always think a woman is imagining things," said Elsie easily. "My mother heard a noise in the night once that my father wouldn't get up for and it was a thief who took all our smoked hams. . . . She never let him hear the last of it."

She gathered up the soiled linen, glanced at her wrist watch and said, "Eight o'clock! It's a queer feeling, isn't it, to have it eight o'clock and Mr. Hazlitt not sitting down at his breakfast?"

There was a queer feeling to every hour of that day. The house was a hive of hushed activity. People slipped in and out, police and undertakers, all looking self-conscious and curiously furtive. The morning papers were full of the story and the New York papers carried it on the front page—Stanley called up and had them read to him.

I saw the accounts when they were flown in. Planes were flying again now the fog had lifted. MYSTERY KILLING IN MAINE MANSION. *Unknown Shoots Steel King, Attacks Wife.* None of the papers made anything but a mystery out of it. All the suspicion was pointed toward someone outside the house. Those Maine police kept their own counsel.

Telegrams poured in, and notes and messages of shocked sympathy from the Hazlitt friends—I could imagine the excitement in the colony at the Harbor. The big room began to be banked with flowers as if in preparation for the funeral.

Judy Gaynor, in a plain black dress, was doing her secretary's job, listing offerings and names and taking down messages. I heard her say, "Yes, Mrs. Van Cleve, I'll tell her when she wakes. She's sleeping now. . . . Yes, a great shock. . . . No, not hurt. . . . Thank you, I'll tell her."

Nothing in her controlled voice, nothing in her self-contained manner had the remotest connection with the frantic, grief-maddened creature of the night. This was part of the unreality of the day, the bleak, efficient performance over the fury and the desolation. Nothing was what it seemed. The air of sympathy for Helen, the routine of respectful service was all part of the illusion. Everyone was acting, pretending there was nothing more than the sadness of death in the house. Pretending there was no suspicion, no scandal.

Reporters were ringing up, trying to get in, and a guard was established at the bridge and at the doors to repel intruders. The county attorney arrived about the middle of the morning and was closeted with Stanley. After that, he looked me up for a few words. He was a wiry, vigorous fellow, with a small black moustache that seemed to be trying to make him look like Dewey. He didn't ask me anything Saunders had not asked; he merely wanted, I felt, to see what I was like.

There seemed no end to that morning. I spent most of it in the library. It was a nice day, with an offshore wind that whipped the top of the waves to foam, and the sun shone as if there never had been any fog. I would have liked to go out, but it seemed out of place, somehow, and then, too, those Maine police might have thought I was trying to reach Murray. So I sat in the library, a big corner room, just under T. D.'s room and over the cavern, and read *Field and Stream*.

About noon Stanley Hazlitt came in. He looked harassed and strained from coping with the emergencies of sudden death and police inquiries and social amenities, and his face, until he rearranged it, showed he had forgotten all about me and wasn't particularly pleased to be reminded.

I came over and asked if there was anything I could do. He said there wasn't. I felt a title embarrassed because I was holding *Field and Stream,* which seemed out of key with the atmosphere, and I started to leave the room because I felt the man wanted to be alone. But he said, "Don't go, Kent. There was something I wanted to say—"

He had to hunt about for it in his mind. "Oh, yes—I am sorry you were the target of those accusations of Miss Gaynor's last night. I hope you realize that I appreciate the suspicion was unjustified."

"That's all right," I said. "It was all very confused."

"Miss Gaynor—" his stiff manner grew more constricted—"is unduly—emotional." That was putting it mildly, I thought. He went on, "And in the shock . . . she is so close to the family that she feels my brother's death keenly."

"That's all right," I said again. "She told me afterward that she didn't mean I'd let the man in knowingly."

"Yes. Yes, she told me she had taken occasion to make that clear."

"She did. She asked me to the study last night and explained it."

I didn't want any misunderstanding of why Judy and I were in the study. "She also told me," I went on, "that she was sure that Mrs. Hazlitt was innocent of any complicity. It is only Murray that she suspects."

Stanley looked at me, then down at a book he was holding. But he didn't look down quickly enough. I'd seen the glint of opposition in his eyes.

"Her opinions are dictated by her emotions," he said very drily. "That was apparent in her speech against you.

. . . You can judge by that how much credence can be given her statements."

He had me there. I didn't know what to say. I finally said lamely, "I think you have to get hold of a lot more facts before you can suspect anybody."

He let that gem fade away in the silent setting it deserved. Then he looked up and gave me a singular look, sharp and searching, charged with a somber bitterness.

"Mr. Kent—I am in an unfortunate position," he said abruptly.

He broke off. He had seen Jeff coming in the room before I heard him, and turned.

Jeff was hatless, his light topcoat swinging open, and he looked brisk and purposeful beside Stanley's strained solemnity. He gave me a casual nod, then turned to Stanley. "Just back," he reported. "No trace of Murray yet."

"Not back at his house—?"

"No. No one has seen him since that fisherman saw him at the wharf."

"That's—peculiar."

I thought Stanley seemed more bothered than he wanted to show. For an instant his face had an uncertain look as if he were questioning the validity of his convictions—a soul-searching job for a guy as set in his ways as this one. Then his face got back its composure and he said with an air of forced casualness, "Probably sampling some of the vino so prevalent along this shore."

"Dancy's making the rounds. But he's beginning to think that Murray has high-tailed it. There were some cars passing, even in the fog, and he may have got a lift."

"But why?" Stanley's voice was edged with exasperation. "He had no reason—"

"He may have had reason," said Jeff. "It looks as if he was out in a boat yesterday. I found this in a boat at the wharf where he was."

He took a small gadget out of his pocket and held it out. "I went over those boats myself and found this under a floor board. It's a Navy compass."

If he expected cheers, he didn't get them. Stanley looked at the compass without any great interest. He commented, "I imagine that type is quite general now."

"The Portuguese says it isn't his. And no one has rented his boat but Murray."

"But he has rented it before. The compass could have been lost earlier."

"It could. But it wouldn't be needed except in a fog."

"There have been other fogs."

"None so thick, they tell me."

"Quite as dense, I would say. I can't see that this has any special significance, Mr. Ryder. . . . It is perfectly possible that Murray was out in a boat, but what of it? My brother was not killed until seven-thirty and after that time Murray could not have left this house."

"That's the question," said Jeff. "Oh, about that window—"

"Still harping on the window, Mr. Ryder?" Stanley smiled thinly. "Are you suggesting that Murray got through in the night and that his body is washing about on the rocks?"

"I thought of that," said Jeff.

So had I and I wanted to know what he had to say about it.

"I measured the casement and had the carpenter nail me a frame that size," Jeff told him. "I wanted to see if I could get through."

"I hope you are satisfied—?"

"I am." Jeff grinned cheerfully. "I got through."

Stanley didn't say a word for a moment. When he did, you could almost smell the smoking rubber of his brakes.

"Indeed! You are an ingenious young man, Mr. Ryder. . . . You are also an exceptionally thin build. . . . Our architect, evidently, did not allow for such proportions."

"You're right, there." Jeff was just as cheerful about that as about his own triumph. "It was a tight squeeze, even for me. I had to take off my shirt, or I'd have torn it off. A man heavier in the shoulders and hips couldn't have done it. That's what I wanted to find out. I saw Murray's clothes at his boarding house and he's two sizes wider. Murray couldn't have got through."

"That was my contention." Stanley looked happier now. "Perhaps it was well, however, that you demonstrated it." Then he added, in a burst of painful honesty, "I wouldn't have believed that *you* could have done it. My brother always said it was impossible."

"I wouldn't want to try it over the cliff. Not even with a rope to clutch at. A very thin man who was going to try that drop would have to wriggle through and hang by his hands."

Helen had said the man who attacked her had been tall and thin, terribly thin. I had an ironic feeling that the man was going to get thinner and thinner as Helen gave her testimony and by that feeling I knew I wasn't believing in that man, much as I wanted to.

"Well, you have settled the question about Murray and the window," said Stanley with a sort of grim satisfaction. He stood a moment looking thoughtfully at Jeff. "You are a very ingenious young man," he repeated.

His eyes dropped to the book in his hands and as if reminded he moved toward the shelves, and put it in place. He went out telling us that a buffet luncheon was being served.

It was like Jeff's curiosity to go over to the shelves and take down the book Stanley had put there. It fell open in his hands and he stood reading with instant absorption. I put my *Field and Stream* back on the table and went over to him and asked, "What you got there?"

"Page on Wills," he said, absently.

I looked at the shelves and from the number of law books there I judged Stanley did a lot of work here in summertime. Then the title sank in and I said, "Boning up on testamentary law, was he? Ready to help with the will-making?"

I remembered the raw astonishment on Stanley's face when he heard the new will would not have given him the works. But Stanley's dead-and-gone hopes were pretty far behind us now, so I said, "Come on to lunch."

"Well, I'll be damned!" said Jeff, softly and interestedly. "I'd forgotten this. I need a refresher course."

"Not now you don't. You're through with wills here. You need some chow."

But Jeff stood reading—he could stand like that reading law for an hour at a time when something struck him as interesting—so I started for the door. Just then the buzzer rang on the phone and I went to the desk and picked up the instrument.

A maid's voice said, "Mr. Kent?" and I said, "Speaking," and the voice said, "Here you are—" and then the operator's voice, a woman's voice, said, "Mr. Kent?" and I said, "Speaking," again.

The operator's voice said, "Go ahead, Littlebeach," and I heard coins dropping into a box and then a man's voice, curt and sharp, "Calvin Kent?"

"Speaking," I said for the third time.

"I hope you know who I am. Don't say the name."

"I think I do," I said. I inched about till I could give Jeff a glance. He looked lost to the world in that book of his and I tried to make my voice casual. "I'm not sure, though."

"Coves. Beaches. Get it?"

"Right."

"I hear Hazlitt's shot."

"That's right."

"Who do they think did it?"

"I wouldn't know . . . not right now, anyway."

"I get you. Now what's this about Helen? Is she hurt?"

"No." I was damning "Page on Wills" as I glanced again at Jeff.

"It said she was attacked."

"She thinks so."

"The same time?"

"No."

There was dead silence and I thought the connection was broken. Then the voice said desperately, "I've got to see you."

"Where are you?"

"That's no good. I'm pulling out. How about a swim?"

"Where?"

Jeff was listening, of course. I'd have to cook up some explanation.

"Not the cove. Ask Helen," Murray was saying. "Where it's private. I'll drop in for cocktails." He gave a ghastly laugh that wouldn't have deceived a wire-tapper if he had meant it to. "I tried to phone her but couldn't get her. You'll have to do," he said brusquely, and then—this through the voice of the operator saying "Deposit another dime and nickel, please"—"or get her to come."

He hung up and after a moment I heard another click and felt sure someone had been listening. But I didn't see how it could mean much. I wouldn't have known where he wanted me to swim if it hadn't been for that cigarette case found in the cavern and his "Ask Helen." I lit a cigarette, giving myself time, and saw that Jeff had put his book up at last and was eyeing me.

"Reporter guy who says he used to know me," I said. "They try all the angles."

For a wonder he didn't follow it up. In a moment I saw why. His *amour propre* was licking a bruise.

"Look, Cal—did it seem to you that Stanley rather gave the compass the brush-off?"

"Well—yes. But the compass didn't mean so much. What really griped him," I said, talking fast to keep him from remembering the reporter, "was your getting through the window frame. If you cherish hope of any more business from Stanley Hazlitt, you'd better stop showing him where he's wrong. It doesn't endear you, that's for sure."

Let him worry about that, I thought. And it's a fact he did look worried. All through lunch he shoveled in his meal, army style, without a word. That gave me a nice quiet time for my own worries.

Chapter Ten

The inquest was at three o'clock, so I got in some sleep beforehand. What Jeff was doing I wouldn't know. He'd bolted out after lunch and I wouldn't have been surprised if he'd had the Portuguese gardener's kids diving for Murray's body.

He was downstairs with Saunders when I went down for the inquest. The county attorney had said the inquest would be a formality and that's what it was. The medical examiner and jury sat around the long table in the dining room and one by one the witnesses took the oath, answered questions, and went out.

A few of us stayed in all the time—Kramer, Saunders, Stanley Hazlitt, Jeff, and I. The reporters were there, too, for an inquest is public; they were mostly local boys, but a couple of them were from New York. Saunders and Stanley kept their eyes on them to see they didn't stray away and get some headlines from the help.

The witnesses went in and out the serving door from the butler's room so the newsmen couldn't get at them. Helen gave her testimony in a low, almost inaudible tone except when it came to the story of the night attack, when her voice stiffened. A light bulb flashed then and cameras clicked and I could guess the headlines. *Steel King's Widow Tells of Attack.* She sounded to me as if she were reciting

a set piece but that was natural enough, she had told it so
many times before.

Nothing exciting happened, not even when Judy Gaynor testified. She seemed to have decided this wasn't the
time and place for accusation and she simply answered what
was asked. When did you last speak to Mr. Hazlitt? What
did you do then? Did you hear any sound like a gun? Did
you hear the elevator after seven-thirty? Things like that.

Murray's name was never mentioned. The will-making
was brought in, for Jeff was asked the reason for his being
at Stone Ledge, but he was not questioned about the contents of the new will. The Maine police were not trying
the case in the newspapers.

Stanley's testimony was bleak, colorless, exact. He
made it clear that the doors were locked, both at the time
of the murder and after the night alarm, but he offered no
opinion about the alarm.

Hannah Tyler was the only one who went in for details.
This was her big moment. She was something like Elsie,
only older and thinner; she had the same round, serious
eyes, though hers were dark, and the same air of intense
conviction. Her recital was so familiar to her now that its
horror had turned to drama and she positively declaimed
it. "And then I looked to the window, noticing the curtain
was pulled back, and there was Mr. Hazlitt stretched out,
dead as a stone."

The jury trooped out and presently came back with
the verdict. Death at the hands of a person or persons
unknown.

Jeff got out of the room quickly. I thought he wanted
to get away from a reporter who was asking if the will
wasn't an angle—the others were buzzing about the night
attack—but when we were out in the main room he looked
over the little knots of people standing about as if he were
looking for someone. Some of the jurors were hanging

about, eyeing the room and the flowers curiously—this would be something to tell about when they got home. Benton, the chauffeur, was guarding the door into the butler's room, and a young policeman was sitting on the stairs. The houseman was shepherding some of the local citizens to the door. "It's all over now. This way, gentlemen."

I saw Caldwell standing under the gallery with the two Tyler girls. They were outside the door into the long inner hall you had to cross to get to the library, guarding the doors from intruders and talking it all over. Jeff headed for them and I trailed along. As we came up I heard Caldwell say something like "forget it" or "regret it"; then he broke off and moved a little away.

Jeff turned toward the girls. He said to Hannah, "There was something I wanted to ask you. How did you happen to go upstairs last night when you did?"

Hannah looked confused at his brusqueness. "Why— why, I always go up at that time."

"Yes, but how did you happen to go into Mr. Hazlitt's room? You knew he wasn't down."

Why, indeed? I wondered. And why hadn't I been smart enough to think of that?

Jeff prompted, "Did you go in to see what was keeping him?"

"Oh, no—he wouldn't have liked that at all. I thought he was down." She added, in matter-of-fact explaining, "When I heard the elevator go down."

"You heard the elevator? When was that?" Jeff's voice was very quietly keyed.

"Why—when I was in the hall. I'd come out of Mrs. Hazlitt's room, thinking Mr. Hazlitt was still in his room, and then I heard the elevator, so I took it for granted he'd gone down."

"I see. I just wondered. You're sure you heard that elevator?"

"Of course. Why else would I go in?" said Hannah, reasonably.

"But the elevator was upstairs when Mr. Hazlitt was found. So you must have been mistaken in thinking you heard it go down."

"I heard it." Hannah began to look flustered and stubborn. "Why else would I go in his room?" she repeated. "I know I heard it."

This was important. Jeff had got something at last, I thought. Something that fitted in. The elevator had gone down after Jeff had come downstairs, when he was talking with us, when it would have been hard for anyone of us to have heard it

And Helen must have signaled it back later. She could have done it in the confusion outside T. D.'s door, and we wouldn't have heard it come up, for we were inside the room, staring at the dead man, with the foghorn blaring in the open window.

The chain of circumstantial evidence fairly clanked at me. I wished I could dispose of it the way Elsie did. She said, "It was the man—sneaking down to hide. Waiting to pounce on Mrs. Hazlitt in the night!"

Jeff disregarded that. He said to Hannah, "Are you prepared to swear to that? That you heard the elevator?"

Her dark eyes lighted up. "I'd take my Bible oath!"

I left then. Murray had said, "I'll drop in at cocktails," and it was five o'clock now. As I changed into my swim suit I wondered what I'd do if Jeff barged in and decided to have a dip with me. He didn't come. No one was in the hall as I headed for the elevator. I kept close to the wall and didn't look over the rail, so I didn't know whether anyone was in the room below or not, but if anyone looked up and saw me going along the gallery in my bathrobe, what harm in that? Why shouldn't I take a plunge?

The cave was black as a hole except for the gray arch of entrance. I switched on the lights and they brightened the shelf I was on, but the rest of the place was shadowed and spooky. The air was beginning to fog up again, not thick, blanketing fog like yesterday, but thin wraiths of cloud stealing in the entrance.

I wrapped my bathrobe about me and sat down on a bench and lighted a cigarette. The water wasn't quiet like last night. The tide seemed to be going out, but a wind was blowing in from the west and little waves slapped against the shelf, throwing spray up on it, so I drew back my legs and thought what a God-awful place this was to have fun in.

Maybe it was all right on a bright day when the arch framed blue sky and the coolness of the place was a pleasant change from the sun's heat, but it took plenty of imagination to picture it. And it didn't help the general atmosphere of depression to reflect that two stories above me the man who had restyled this cave for his use was lying dead and that the man who was suspected of killing him was coming to talk to me.

I didn't see the boat come in, I was lighting another cigarette and when I looked up it was there, oars shipped, gliding across the pool. I stood up and Murray jumped out and drew the bow up on the shelf. There was no waste motion; he knew the place all right.

We looked at each other without speaking for a moment. He looked haggard and he hadn't shaved and his clothes looked as though they had been slept in, but he had the sort of rakish good looks that disorder didn't hurt.

He said, in a let-down voice, "Helen couldn't come?"

"I haven't been able to talk with her."

"Is she hurt?" he asked quickly. "What about it?"

I told him what had happened and he listened intently. He didn't make a comment and I couldn't tell how much

he knew already or how much he guessed. He asked me for
a smoke and pulled on the cigarette ravenously.

"Where have you been?" I asked.

"Drunk. Sleeping it off."

"How did you hear?"

"Saw a paper. How did it happen—the shooting?"

I told him that. I told him how they had gathered us
in for questioning and I said bluntly, "Judy Gaynor has
accused you directly," and gave an account of that. His
face showed nothing but strained attention till I said,
"But Stanley Hazlitt suspects Helen," then it grew tighter
and harder.

"What has he got on her?" he asked harshly.

"Motive. Opportunity."

"That isn't proof."

"No, but it counts. It was a lot of motive."

"Anyone could have done it. I'll bet plenty of people
wanted to bump him off."

I didn't say anything to that. In a moment he said urgently, "Tell her not to talk. Tell her to keep her mouth
shut, for God's sake. Tell her she's all right if she doesn't
get to talking."

"The only talking she's done—as far as I know—is to
defend you."

"Tell her to lay off that. They can't get anything on
me."

"I'm not so sure," I said slowly. I debated whether to
tell him about the cigarette case or not and decided not to.
I said, "Hannah Tyler, one of the maids, heard the elevator
go down after eight o'clock."

I put significance into that, looking squarely at him.
Our eyes met, but I couldn't see an inch into his.

"To hell with that!" he said.

"You can't brush it off like that. It's damned important."

"Why?" He sounded derisive. "Am I supposed to have been in it?"

"That's the idea the police are going to get."

"To hell with the police! . . . Tell Helen not to talk," he repeated. He was frowning worriedly now. "See here, why should Stanley suspect Helen? Doesn't he want to pin it on me?"

"He doesn't think you could have got out. He doesn't know yet that Hannah heard the elevator. And Helen made him suspicious from the start. She wanted him to fake an accident when we found T. D. He figures that if you couldn't do it Helen did. Who else wanted T. D. killed before the new will was signed?"

Murray said softly, vindictively, "That bastard! Somebody ought to shoot that bastard."

"That would fix everything up nicely."

"She wanted to fake an accident—?" He sounded anxious now, and worried.

"She wanted to put a gun beside him."

"Maybe it was an accident. Maybe somebody took the gun."

"Maybe somebody didn't think quick enough to leave one."

He gave me an unreadable look. "So what? . . . What do you think I ought to do?"

"Go back to your boarding house and show yourself. Fight it in the open."

"Like hell. They won't get their hands on me. I'm pulling out."

"Don't be a fool. They'll pick you up."

"They won't."

"It's a mistake to run. It looks—"

"I know what it looks like. But it takes the heat off Helen."

"They'll think her an accomplice."

He was silent a moment, then he said, his voice desperate-sounding, "Tell her not to talk. Not a word. She hasn't seen me. I've never been here. She didn't do anything. . . . Oh, Christ, if I could only see her!"

Then he said, "You dirty, double-crossing—" and his fist shot out and caught my chin. I toppled backward. I was out before he rolled me in the water because I didn't remember going in. The next thing I knew Jeff was working over me and I was gagging up salt water. I must have gone in with my mouth open and filled up like a dunnage bag.

I sat up and felt of my chin, and Jeff said, "You all right, Cal?"

I fingered my chin and the back of my neck that felt snapped in two. "What happened?"

He told me. He'd come in the entrance and was swinging his boat to block it when Murray saw him and knocked me out. Then he rolled me into the pool and jumped into his boat. I didn't come up so Jeff sent his boat straight across to me and the two boats had slid past each other in the pool. Murray had an oar ready, Jeff said, but Jeff didn't try to stop him.

"Now he's gone, damn him," said Jeff, staring at the entrance.

"Damn you!" I said sourly. "Why the hell did you come in?"

"Well, the reporter thing didn't go down with me," said Jeff. "And we had a man at the switchboard in the butler's room taking down every conversation—we figured Helen or Murray might try to communicate. He didn't make any sense of your talk but I did."

"And what were you going to do? Arrest him?"

"I wanted to talk with him."

"You should have carried a white flag."

"Don't be sore, Cal. How much did he tell you?"

"Not a thing. He was asking."

I got up and took off my bathrobe and began to wring the water out of it. Jeff's trousers and sleeves were wet from lugging me out and he squeezed water out of them and took off his wrist watch and held it to his ear. Then he strapped it back. "I want to get to him," he said.

"All right. Get to him."

"The Coast Guard can find him. That will have to be the way of it now," Jeff said regretfully. "But I wanted to talk to him first." He squeezed some more water out of his pants legs and then emptied his shoes. He explained, "You see, I thought if I came along when you were here and blocked that entrance till I had a chance to explain something, maybe he'd listen. And you could tell him who I was and maybe he'd talk."

"So now he thinks I turned him in."

"Sorry I bitched it up," he owned. "I wish now I'd told you what I wanted to find out. I thought of it, but—"

"But you had to play the Lone Ranger. Superman at the oars."

He grinned. "Why I pulled you out I wouldn't know."

"Don't think I owe you anything for it."

We both grinned then and I asked, "What did you want to ask him? Aside from whether he bumped off T. D. or not?"

"I wanted to ask who was the girl he was with Friday afternoon."

"Friday—?" I reached for a towel and began to dry my head gingerly. "That was the day he came to see me."

"Afterward, when you were at the Bronsons, he was at Scarlotti's place along the shore buying drinks for a girl with big black eyes. Dancy picked that up and phoned it in to me before the inquest."

"Big black eyes—? Plenty of Portuguese and Italians along the shore."

But I was thinking of Judy Gaynor and so was he, for he said, "The chauffeur says Judy Gaynor took a car out just before you went to Bronsons . . . and Scarlotti's place is several miles out."

I thought about it a moment. "So what? Even if it was Judy? She'd just been urging me to tell Helen to run off with him and I wouldn't wonder if she tried working on him. To get him to rush Helen into running away. She was crazy enough to try anything. If they ran off she'd have a chance . . . I don't see you've got so much there."

Jeff looked at me a considering moment before he spoke. Then he said, "Scarlotti told Dancy he saw Murray slipping her a gun."

That really took me. "He gave her a gun?"

"So Scarlotti says. He didn't think anything of it at the time, he told Dancy, for vets are always handing out souvenirs and he knew Murray was an ex-Marine. But when Dancy got to asking round for Murray, he came out with this."

"That's a queer do," I said. "Didn't Scarlotti know the girl?"

"Said he never saw her before."

"Wouldn't he have known Judy?"

"Dancy asked him that. Asked if he knew Mr. Hazlitt's secretary and he said, no, he didn't know anyone from here. They didn't come into his place."

"That's a queer do," I said again.

In a house full of guns, why would Judy want one from Murray? She must know it could be traced. . . . Was she rat enough—? Premeditation didn't seem her line. I'd thought of her as acting in sudden fury, in a blaze of anger? the way she'd sent that jade bowl crashing, but because she was sudden and violent didn't mean she couldn't be cold and calculating, too. I thought about that hard-angled jaw.

I said, "Maybe she used his gun on T. D. and Helen found it and pitched it out the window."

Jeff said glumly, "We've got so many damned solutions. In our minds. But what's the *truth?*" Then he got brisk and purposeful again. "We've got to pick him up now. The Coast Guard can get him if he's heading back to Littlebeach—that's a long way down. If he heads directly in, he'll be found anyway. Look, Cal, don't pass this on. About the girl and the gun. Dancy's working on that and I'm supposed to be helping him out."

"I'll keep my mouth shut," I said.

"Take the boat back for me, will you?" He had put the bow of the boat up on the shelf, the way that Murray had, where it was grinding away as the water pulled at it, and now he stooped and put it down into the pool. "Take it around to the beach, to the boathouse there. I've got to go up and phone the Coast Guard."

Part IV: Chapter Eleven

Jeff went up in the elevator and I rowed out into the harbor, glad of the warming exercise, and glad to be out in the open. It felt good to see the big harbor with boats at their moorings or coming along with sails wide before the wind, and hear the cheerful putt-putt of speed boats racing for the shore. It gave you a feeling of being near nice normal people you didn't have to look at suspiciously, wondering if this was the murderer or not.

Out here the fog was thin and silvery and somehow at a distance; it was like a silk curtain drawn across the houses on the shore, making them look far away like houses in a stage set. Little dots of children were running on the sands and I could hear a dog barking.

I rounded the point where the cliff broke down into jumbled rock and rowed along the southern side toward the beach. A young Portuguese ran out on the dock to take the boat, looking surprised to see who was in it now, and I told him, "The deputy asked me to bring this back for him." I walked up the beach carrying my wet bathrobe, and ahead of me I saw a girl sitting on the sand, wrapped in a dark cloak. In a moment I saw it was Helen.

She got up and walked to meet me. "What are you doing patrolling the shore?" she asked in a bitter tone.

She looked like a ghost and I told her, "You shouldn't be here alone, Helen."

"I'm not alone," she said, in that same bitter, brittle voice. "There's a policeman trailing me—tailing is the word, isn't it? He's behind one of the cabanas. He thinks I'm going to lead him to Nicholas Murray." She gave a faint, mirthless laugh.

I looked about but no policeman was in sight. "Probably a guard," I said. "To cope with reporters."

"No, he came out of the house after me. A few minutes ago."

"Just a guard," I repeated. Then I made my voice low. "Don't show any excitement . . . I've seen Murray."

Her face turned toward me quickly, her eyes widening. "He's all right," I said, to the apprehension in them. "He was out in a boat. He phoned me and made a date." I felt a heel, thinking of the Coast Guard, but she didn't have to know that yet.

"Where is he—? Where's he been?"

"He's got a hideout down the shore. He wanted to see me because he's worried about you. He said for you not to talk, not to admit anything. Not to own you had seen him or that he had been here. He said for you to keep your mouth shut about everything."

She said faintly, "Did he tell you—?"

"Nothing. He told me nothing. He said for you to say nothing."

She walked beside me up the steps and around the pool. We paced slowly along the garden walk. Finally she said, her head bent, "I'll have to say I wanted to marry Nick. They all know that."

"Of course. But don't say any more. Don't say you cared about the money. Say you expected to lose the money. Say what you said to me that morning—that you didn't care about the money."

She drew a deep breath. "You think I did it, don't you, Cal?"

"Of course not."

"But he thinks so."

I thought she meant Stanley till she said, "That's why he's worried, isn't it?"

I couldn't make out whether she was giving something away or trying to put something over. She sounded artless, but she was too desperate to be artless.

"I don't know what he thinks," I said. "But I told him that Stanley was suspicious of you."

"Stanley!" She gave a faint dismissing laugh as if Stanley were of no account. "Stanley always disliked me." She stood still a moment, looking toward the house. The light shone out the windows where some of the curtains were not drawn, and you could see the streamers of fog moving in the light like ballerinas' scarves.

She said, almost inaudibly, "Sometimes I think I really did it. I hated him so much."

"Don't say that!"

"Of course not. It was a stranger, wasn't it? Someone who came in and tried to kill me, too."

She laughed in a half hysterical, half mocking way. I said roughly, "Don't lose your nerve," and then, "Go to bed and get a good sleep, Helen. You're shot to pieces."

I wished I hadn't said "shot." I had hold of her arm and I felt it twitch.

"I've rested all day," she said. "Except for that inquest. They gave me some dope to make me sleep. I'm not going to take anything more. How do I know what they'll give me? One of those truth serums. . . . No, I'm coming to dinner tonight. It's still my own house. Stanley and Judy haven't put me out of it yet."

"Helen, please—"

"He thinks he can marry her now Tod is gone. But he hasn't got the money. I've got that. He wasn't quick enough with that will . . . and Judy loves money. Did you know Tod gave her a sable coat? She thought I wouldn't know but I heard she had a new coat and she said it was sable-dyed."

"That doesn't matter. Look—you go to bed—"

"No, I'm coming to dinner. It's still my house. And the police are still my guests, aren't they? You know they rummaged in my things when I was at the inquest, or when I was asleep. Hannah thinks she put them back all right but she didn't. She's always rushing through her work. In a hurry to get downstairs to Caldwell."

The light, inconsequential words had been sliding through my mind like sand through fingers, but I gripped hard on that one.

"Caldwell?"

She looked over her shoulder. "Is that man following—?"

"No—he was just guarding you. Why would Hannah Tyler want to get to Caldwell? I thought the Tyler girls didn't like him." But it was only Elsie who had criticized him, I remembered.

"Hannah—?" said Helen, as if she had forgotten all about Hannah. Then, as if the name had been a nickel in a juke box, the stream of words started again.

"Hannah's silly about him. And so jealous of Pauline."

"Pauline—?" Then I remembered. Pauline was the New York maid who hadn't come because she was sick.

"Yes. My personal maid. She told me all about it last summer. How jealous Hannah was. Caldwell's sly. He probably encouraged her. And now that Pauline's not here he's had time for Hannah. He has to have his feminine audience."

"Do you trust him, Helen?"

"He's perfectly honest, if that's what you mean. Everybody's sly about women. . . . But I don't like him, really." Then she said resentfully, "I expect he'll go now when he gets his legacy."

"Legacy?"

My hand tightened on her arm and I held her back. I said, more quietly, "I thought you got everything under the old will."

"Oh, I do. It isn't a legacy, really. Nothing to do with the will. It's sort of a trust fund Tod fixed for him. More for every year in service. Something like that."

"Has he got any other money, do you know?"

"He's saved a lot. Tod used to invest it for him. He told Pauline if she'd marry him he'd start a catering business. That would have been nice, wouldn't it, taking my pet maid away from me? But Pauline would be a fool to marry him. He's too old for her."

Well, that was a dead end, I thought. For a moment I'd had a vision of a Caldwell desperate for money. . . .

Helen asked suddenly, "What's the matter with your face?"

"Is it bad?" I felt of it cautiously. It was swelling. I said, "I slipped and hit it. On the rocks."

She looked at me a moment, then in a rush of eagerness she breathed out, "Oh, Cal, couldn't you have been attacked? Couldn't it be a prowling maniac?"

It was utterly childish and revealing. It was like her frantic attempt to make T. D.'s death seem suicide or accident.

"I'm sorry," I said. "Jeff Ryder was with me. He saw it."

"Oh."

Then she said sharply, "I don't like him. You don't tell him things, do you, Cal?"

"No, I don't tell him things. But Jeff's all right," I said slowly. "It's his job to find out the truth."

"What's the use of that? Now that it's done? You can't put things back."

That's your way of looking at it, I thought. T. D.'s dead—you can't bring him to life. Now stop bothering and let the widow marry again and the money be enjoyed. No questions asked.

"It isn't quite as simple as that," I said.

"No, it isn't simple." Then she gave me an oblique look. "I can't find a revolver that used to be in my room. A small, pearl-handled one. I don't remember when I saw it last."

I looked at her sharply. "It's gone—? Since—?"

"I just looked for it today. It ought to have been in my dresser—but I haven't looked for it for days."

Then she gave a funny, artificial shrug and started ahead into the house. Indoors she suddenly became Mrs. Hazlitt again, going from one mass of funeral flowers to another, putting on a wan, proprietary interest. I slipped decorously into my wet bathrobe and went up in the elevator so as not to drip on too many rugs.

Jeff had been there and changed, I saw, for his wet things were in the bathroom. For quite a time I held soaked towels, hot and cold, to my chin. It didn't look too bad—just dark and swelled. My head had begun to ache and I swallowed a couple of aspirins, then put on dry clothes and went down to dinner.

It was a ghastly meal. Helen sat there like a presiding ghost going through the motions of eating, of being a hostess, occasionally saying something stiffly polite to the county attorney on her right. Judy Gaynor scarcely spoke at all. She visibly hated every moment of this dinner and she was as tense and wrought up as she had been the night we came.

Kramer kept glancing covertly at her, sensing this was something else again than the controlled, efficient secretary he had met that day. For all his brisk assurance of manner Kramer was ill at ease, with an air of wariness toward Helen. I expect he felt out of his depth, with only Stanley for a reliable buoy.

Stanley was set and stiff, himself. He was scrupulously polite to Helen but I had the feeling that he genuinely detested her. What he felt for Judy I couldn't tell, except that she made him nervous.

I felt moody, myself. I had bungled the whole business with Murray. I had been simply the obliging reporter, "Helen's friend," telling him what he wanted to know. I should have taken a definite line, have made him see that clearing out, that "taking the heat off Helen," was not enough. I wished that I had dodged that blow, for more reasons than one, and that Jeff had got in there and had a chance to ask his questions. Or, better yet, that Jeff had told me about the girl and the gun.

If it was Judy we might have something. But it might not be Judy. After all, dark eyes, or big black eyes or whatever Scarlotti had said, belonged to more girls than Judy Gaynor.

Jeff was not at dinner. He had phoned from the mainland that he would not be back.

The telephone kept breaking in on that silent meal. Twice, Kramer was called to it, and the second time he was away, Stanley jumped up and said he had to telephone. There was a private wire, I'd learned, from the study. After a short while the two men came in together, talking in low voices that broke off as they entered the room. Stanley said, "May we have coffee here? Mr. Kramer wants to get away."

I didn't need to be clairvoyant to feel that Murray had been picked up.

Kramer hurried off and Helen said formally, to no one in particular, "Shall we go into the library?" and led the way. At the door Judy turned without a word and took the elevator upstairs. We heard it going up and Stanley looked significantly at me as if saying, "You hear it?"

I wished Helen would go to her room so I could get away. Somehow I didn't like to leave her alone with Stanley, and Stanley seemed determined not to leave us together. He sat watching us somberly out of his dark, accusing eyes like the ghost of her husband.

There was a big portrait of T. D. over the desk and while the painter had exaggerated the deep-set eyes and powerful lines, the likeness was strong, and it might have been a portrait of Stanley, I thought, noting how Stanley's face had firmed and sharpened.

Helen was looking through a silver bowl of cards and letters, occasionally reading the description of the floral offerings that Judy had methodically put down. I picked up a magazine. The buzzer on the extension telephone sounded and Stanley took the call. He said, "Yes. Hello?" and I stiffened, expecting something would come, now, about Murray.

Then I relaxed, for he said, "Mr. Alben?" and Mr. Alben seemed to be the clergyman, for he began checking carefully on arrangements. "Utterly private—utterly private," he said several times. Then, "Only the Van Cleves and the Bronsons." And then, "No, no music at all. I prefer not. . . . Yes, I have considered, but I prefer not to have music."

Helen had risen and stood watching him resentfully as he talked. When he replaced the phone she said sarcastically, "How kind of you to take so much on yourself! After all, this is my husband's funeral. Perhaps I would prefer music."

"What do you want played?" said Stanley in a voice in which for once all his bitterness lashed out. "'How happy could I be with either, were t'other dear charmer away?'"

Helen said, "Stanley!" almost fearfully.

He paid her no more attention but sat down at the desk and began making lists and notes. Helen picked up the bowl of messages again. I sank my head in my magazine.

Then came another instance of the tension in that house. Judy Gaynor opened the door and stood looking in angrily.

She addressed Helen directly. "If you want me to leave, I'll go. You don't have to resort to tricks to make me realize I'm not wanted."

Helen looked at her with eyes that held what seemed exaggerated astonishment. "I don't know what you mean."

"Oh, yes, you do." The beautiful low voice was vibrant with feeling. "You've given orders to have me disregarded. My room has not been touched—Hannah hasn't been near it. No one came when I rang just now. You've told them not to do anything for me."

"Hannah?" said Helen in remote inquiry. "Is she taking care of your room?"

"Yes. Since—" Spasmodically Judy swallowed. She changed the sentence. "Since Elsie has two other rooms."

"You mean she didn't make your bed this morning?"

"Oh, yes, she made it. But she hasn't opened it tonight, or filled the carafe. And no one answered my ring. It isn't that I can't wait on myself—you reminded me once that I was used to doing it. I simply want to know if that's what you expect me to do. Or do you want me to go?"

"Why, no," said Helen in a very innocent voice. "I am sorry the maids were forgetful. I expect they are exhausted after all the confusion and the extra work and being up with me all night. . . . Of course I don't want you to leave. You have been so *very* close to us that it would seem strange without you."

Stanley had turned and looked on rather helplessly at this exchange. Now he said, sounding sharp and anxious and unutterably exasperated all at once, "There is no thought of your going, Judy. You are needed here. Indeed, you are required to stay here—as a witness. This—this household thing—it's simply an oversight. A trivial thing."

He pressed a button on the desk and said into the house phone, "Jimmie? Have someone take care of Miss Gaynor's room, please. The maids have overlooked it."

He listened, his face registering a faint surprise. "Well—as soon as she comes in." He put down the phone and said to Judy, "Both the girls are outside, he says. Hannah seems to have stepped out and her sister went after her. That's why your bell was unanswered. Now, please, no more nerves," he said, half in irritation, half in appeal.

"Well—" said Judy uncertainly.

Our eyes met and I grinned—I couldn't help it, the thing was so ridiculous. I said, "You know, that Spanish great-grandmother must have had a terrific temper."

She didn't blaze out. To my surprise, a grimace of an answering smile twitched her lips. "I'm afraid she had," she acknowledged. She looked at Helen less belligerently but said stubbornly, "But you know, Helen, this *is* one of your pinpricks," and went out, closing the door softly.

"It really isn't," said Helen to me. "I didn't have a thing to do with it."

"Helen, you had better go to bed," said Stanley. "To-morrow will be difficult. The services are to be in the morning and then—"

"Then I will have to answer questions, won't I?" said Helen. "You are so considerate, Stanley. You think of everything, don't you? But I am not going to bed yet. It's quite early. I don't like being up there."

She turned to me. "Mother and father wanted to come on but I told them not to—not in this weather. If you fly you're grounded. And there isn't a thing they could do, is there?"

"Not a thing."

"But you come to the service," said Helen. "I feel as if you were family. You sit with me and Judy can sit with Stanley."

She was a fool to get Stanley so angry. A fool to be paying out pettish words when she had graver things to think about.

I said, "I'll come if tomorrow you feel you want me," and we settled down again to the haunted quiet of that room.

But it was not long before Elsie Tyler came in. She said, "Mrs. Hazlitt, we're worried. Hannah can't be found."

It wasn't an alarm, at first, except to Elsie, who was disturbed by her fear of "that man" and what he might have done to Hannah. No one seemed to know exactly when Hannah had disappeared. She had gone upstairs some time during dinner, for Helen's room was arranged for the night, but where she had gone then no one knew. She had not been upstairs when Elsie had gone up to arrange our room and Stanley's.

No one had seen her go out but she sometimes did slip out for a walk in the garden or on the beach—"which is all there is to do here," Elsie said—and she might have gone out, though it seemed odd she would go out in the mist without a coat.

There had been a good deal of going in and out, for Clement, the head gardener, had been in about the flowers and later Caldwell had been out with the chauffeur, talking over arrangements. None of them remembered seeing Hannah. No delivery cars had come, so she could not have left in that way. The guard at the bridge said she had not crossed. There was no other way off the point except by boat or by wading the stream at the cove.

I hazarded a guess that a local boy friend had come in a boat to take her out, but Elsie quashed that. "There isn't anyone who'd do that," she said. She said anxiously, "I'm worried."

They had searched the garden and beach and cabanas but how thoroughly I didn't know, so I organized another search party and headed for the point with Benton and Jimmie, feeling positive relief at having something definite to do away from the God-awful tension in the house. I didn't feel there was much need for concern, for "the man" wasn't the figure of terror to me he was to the maids. Elsie and Opal went along with us, Elsie crying out Hannah's name every few minutes.

Systematically we searched the point, where Elsie said her sister sometimes liked to go and sit—a dolorous occupation, it seemed to me, for a lively girl. There was no Hannah there now on the rocks in the darkness looking out to sea; there was nothing there but rocks and seaweed and waves. The fog was lighter now, scarcely a mist, and a determined moon was glimmering through the clouds, diffusing a faint light.

Our searchlights probed every gully between the rocks where a girl might have slipped and fallen. Elsie called, "Hannah, Hannah!" distractedly, but only the sea gulls answered.

"She wouldn't come out here alone," I said, but Elsie murmured, "She might. She was acting upset like." Opal, who was a smart young thing about eighteen, gave Jimmie a wise smile behind her back.

"What was she upset about?" I wanted to know, but Elsie did not answer.

"You'll find she's at the movies in the village or somewhere safe," I told Elsie. "She just gave you the slip,"

I took Elsie back to the house to telephone and the other men went on to the cove. There were searchlights bobbing all over the garden and along the beach now, for the Portuguese undergardener and his family had turned out in force. The boats were all in, they reported.

In the butler's room Elsie called her home, but Hannah wasn't there. She wasn't at the movies or the drugstores or at a church social that Opal remembered about. Elsie, getting more and more panic-stricken, began to call friend after friend.

The men came in from the cove, saying there was no sign of Hannah there. Jeff Ryder was back in the house now and it was Jeff who thought of the cavern. He asked, "Anybody looked down there?"

It seemed silly to me, for the elevator was up, apparently as Judy had left it, but Jeff signaled and when it came he opened the door, and a siren shrilled out that brought everybody running.

"Good God, what now?" said Stanley irritably, appearing from the library. It proved a night precaution the police were trying.

"She'd never go down there," said Mrs. Benton, the cook. "She didn't like being in the water at all."

But down we went, I feeling a fool but Jeff with his air of matter-of-fact procedure. We switched on the lights and peered about. It was colder and foggier here than outside and the place had a rank salt smell. "Scene of my late encounter," I said flippantly.

That reminded me, and I asked, "Did they get Murray?" and Jeff nodded, turning his flashlight about the empty cave.

"Did he tell you anything?"

"Won't talk. Not a word. Put up a fight with the Guard and is being held for resisting arrest."

There was no sign of Hannah on the shelf, no bathing cap, no robe. I saw a dark bunch of something just below the shelf, but it was a mass of seaweed the tide had left.

"This is asinine," I said.

"What's that?" said Jeff sharply. His light had focused on something white against the rock wall at the left of the entrance. A tide, running in and out, could leave something there. He kicked off his shoes and socks, rolled his trousers high, and waded out.

The tide was low and the water at the entrance not much over his knees when he reached the white patch. He came splashing back and held some soaked cloth up in the light. It was a fragment of something that looked like a piece of white apron.

He gave it to me, then went in again, searching the floor of the entire pool, but there was nothing more. When we got upstairs he gave it to Elsie. She turned it about, looking at the embroidery carefully. "That's Hannah's," she said, in a voice dull with shock. "She's dead."

"She's nothing of the kind," Mrs. Benton told her instantly. "She took off her apron, not wanting to be wearing it when she met somebody, and she laid it down and it blew away. That's the way of it and you'll see I'm right when Hannah comes walking in."

Over Elsie's head her eyes swept the circle that had gathered, counseling us to play up this comforting idea. "She took it off and laid it down," she insisted, with as much conviction as if she'd seen the gesture.

Elsie murmured, "It's the man—the man—"

Involuntarily I glanced at Helen. She was standing back in the hall, staring at Elsie with an unguarded astonishment in her face.

"Now, don't worry about the man," Mrs. Benton was saying. "He got away last night."

"He could come back in a boat."

"But he didn't," said Mrs. Benton indomitably. "You'll see, when Hannah comes back. . . . Now I'll fix you a nice warm drink and Opal will be up to sleep with you. You come along with me."

That must have been a bad night for Elsie Tyler, and the morning was worse. With daylight came the word

that Hannah's body had been found beneath a pier in the
harbor where the night's tide had brought it. Saunders
telephoned Stanley and he relayed the message to Jeff, who
started immediately to dress.

"He said there were some injuries on her but they might
have been done by the pier," Jeff said. "I want to get there
fast."

I didn't want to get there at all. I didn't want to see
the drowned girl, but I went downstairs with him and saw
him off in the car that was taking Elsie home. Elsie looked
dazed, now that she knew the worst. She said to Mrs. Benson, "How mother's going to feel—"

I followed Mrs. Benton back to the kitchen and she put
some coffee and toast on a tray for me. "I knew," she said,
"when we saw that piece of apron last night, we'd never see
that girl again. Not as she was. I told Elmer, 'That girl's in
the water—she'll come in with the tide.' I couldn't close
my eyes all night thinking of her battering around out
there."

"Well, you didn't let Elsie see what you felt."

"It's no use meeting sorrow half way. 'Let her hope
to the last minute,' I told Elmer. . . . Well, there's your
tray and there'll be a regular breakfast at the usual time if
my strength holds out with all the hours we're keeping.
And that Opal sulking because I wouldn't let her go off
with Elsie—just wanting to see a drowned thing on a slab
instead of helping out here. I hope that's enough coffee.
It's all I had left from Elsie's breakfast."

I took my tray to my room and stayed there till Jeff got
back.

"She'd been hit on the back of her head, before she
went into the water," he said. "The doctor found signs of
bleeding at the roots of her hair. The water hadn't washed
it all out. But she wasn't dead when she went in. Her lungs
were filled."

I said, "What the devil—"

"Her shoulder's out of place, too. But that might be the pier."

"What do they make of it?"

"They don't know. Elsie thinks she was set on in mistake for Mrs. Hazlitt because she's tall and thin, but Saunders isn't falling for the mysterious-man theory. He's keeping Murray locked up tighter than a drum."

"Murray said anything?"

"Not a thing."

"No third degree?" I said worriedly.

"No. The Guards slugged him back when he fought, but nothing since."

"You saw him?"

"I saw him. I gave him the straight of my coming to the cave, to square you with him, and he just grinned at me. He sat there smoking my cigarettes and saying, 'I don't remember, chum.'"

"He wouldn't tell you who the girl was he gave the gun to?"

"Just the 'I don't remember' routine

"They can't pin this on him, anyway," I said. "In case it turns out that Hannah was with child and he gave her the gun to shoot herself with."

"Her eyes are brown, not black," Jeff said, thoughtfully.

"Mascara can do a lot. Hannah would be a good-looking girl when she was dolled up."

"She isn't good-looking now," he said grimly.

After a while I said, "Those rocks are rugged."

But he had something besides accident on his mind, for he said, urgently, "Cal, tell me everything that happened last night, after you left me. Every little thing. Turn that total-recall memory of yours loose."

I told him. I told him about the missing revolver. I even told him what Helen had said about my chin. "Oh,

Cal, couldn't you have been attacked? Couldn't it be a prowling maniac?" I talked fast for it was nearly time for the service and Helen had phoned asking me to come.

"That's every damn thing," I said. "None of it sheds light."

"That's where you're wrong, brother."

His voice was hard and his face was hard. He said, bitterly, "If I'd had the wits that God gave the first lousy angleworm, I could have saved that girl."

"It wasn't accident—?"

"It wasn't accident."

I had to leave him then. I left him walking up and down the room in his long, easy stride, his hands deep in his pockets. I kept thinking about Hannah Tyler all through the service for T. D., but nothing I could put together made sense. It had to be accident, I thought. Jeff was wrong. He had a murder complex. The second murder. Hannah Tyler couldn't be involved with T. D. Hazlitt and the will. If it was murder, it was an unrelated murder.

I gave it up. Let Jeff worry it out, I thought. This was his mission.

"In the midst of life we are in death—"

The clergyman was putting a throb into his voice but he must have felt it heavy going against the cold resistance of those three figures beside me. They sat rigidly side by side, with never a look or gesture toward each other. Helen wore a hat and a dense black veil; she held a handkerchief, like a stage property, in her tightly clasped hands, which never relaxed.

The casket, beneath a pall of flowers, stood under the picture of T. D. There was something gruesome about that. We were at one side, and off to the left sat the Van Cleves and the Willard Bronsons, and at the back of the room were the Clements and the Bentons and Caldwell. Mrs. Benson was crying furtively but more, I felt, for the dead girl on the mainland than for the man in the casket before her. Caldwell's face was set in a mask of mourning.

"When all questions shall be resolved—"

There were too many flowers in the room. The air was heavy with them. The curtains were drawn and only a few soft lights were on.

"And all things be made clear—"

That had an ironic ring in this house of mysterious death. I looked covertly at Judy Gaynor. She had a desperately fixed look as if every faculty, every ounce of energy, was concentrated on keeping herself quiet and unrevealing. In the casket ahead of her was everything she had cared about. If, in her fury at being denied, she had been the one that did away with him, she must be going through hell.

The service was over. I got up thankfully. Stanley was leaving with the body for the crematorium on the mainland. In due course, I supposed, there would be a memorial service, for T. D. in New York, unless this murder proved a scandal that Stanley did not want to quicken.

Mrs. Bronson and Mrs. Van Cleve were standing about Helen, murmuring to her. She had thrown back her veil, revealing an ashen face. The red mark on her forehead looked very bright. Her hair had hidden it last night. Judy Gaynor had walked out of the room. I waited till I wouldn't overtake her and went to mine.

Luncheon came on a tray. Jimmie reported, "Mr. Stanley's with Kramer. They don't want to be disturbed."

I asked if Jeff was with them. Jimmie said he was on the mainland again. "He's all over the place," he said, grinning. "If he isn't upstairs, he's downstairs." He added, his voice sinking, "They've found the gun, haven't they?"

"Have they?"

He looked disappointed. "Well, there was some talk—" he said vaguely. He put on his houseman's manner again. "Just ring the bell, please, when you've finished."

The telephone rang while I was eating and Kramer asked me to come to the study at three o'clock.

Chapter Twelve

This is it, I thought, going down the stairs. The conventions have been satisfied, time has been given for burial, for social ritual, for appearances. Now the investigation begins. This is the real thing. The other night was dress rehearsal.

All the flowers had been taken from the library except a bowl of red roses on a table at one end, but the scent of lilies and tube roses was in the air. The curtains had been drawn back and sunshine came in the windows and the desk was back before the portrait of T. D. with a stack of papers upon it.

Stanley and the county attorney and Sheriff Saunders were talking together as I came in, then the sheriff sat down behind the desk, looking grave and businesslike, and Stanley and Kramer sat at one side where they could see everyone. They looked infernally pally. Helen and Judy came in one after the other and sat silently, side by side, facing Saunders. I pulled up a chair beside them. Dancy wasn't in the room. Jeff came in and leaned across the desk to Saunders. I heard him say, "He's bringing him," to which Saunders nodded in a preoccupied way. Then Jeff took a chair by me.

The other night he had been unworried, looking on from the outside, keen and interested. He was keen and interested now but he looked worried. He said to me under his breath, "Keep out of this, Cal. No matter how it goes. Take it easy."

Saunders looked at us and cleared his throat. The self-conscious quiet of the room seemed to magnify itself. It was an encased quiet, shut in by our four walls; down below the western windows the waves were splashing against the cliff and some of them, I knew, were running in the mouth of that cavern beneath us.

"I have asked you here," said the chief, in his flat, penetrating voice, "so we could check statements as quickly as possible." Also, I thought, because the antagonisms in this house explode with revelation.

He went on, "There are some questions I want to ask. You know, of course, that you are not required to answer. But these questions are pertinent to the case and if you refuse to answer—" He recited that as if it had been prepared, and waited a moment to let the implication sink in.

"I do not need to remind you," he said, "that an accusation was made, on Saturday night, against Nicholas Murray. Certain facts were brought to light. Last night Mr. Murray was taken into custody. No charges have been preferred. He was taken for questioning and held for resisting arrest."

Out of the corner of my eye I saw Helen sitting up stiffly, her eyes fixed on him. She was visibly bracing herself.

"He has refused to answer any questions," said Saunders. "He has refused to account for his whereabouts on the night of the murder. I feel this is something we must clear up. I know that some of you—" his sober face turned toward Stanley and Kramer—"have felt that Murray was not necessarily implicated. But I wish to bring out some evidence. With your permission, Mr. Kramer, I'd like to put the case as I see it."

"You go ahead, Sheriff," said Kramer. "We don't want to overlook any angle."

"Murray had motive," said Saunders flatly. "He wanted to marry Mrs. Hazlitt. You don't deny that, do you, Mrs. Hazlitt?"

"No, I don't deny it," said Helen faintly, her eyes never leaving his.

"Mr. Hazlitt refused you a divorce. That's correct, isn't it?"

Helen said, "Yes," in the same low key.

"And you told Murray this? Friday morning in the cove?"

She moistened her lips. "Yes. I told him."

"And you told him that Mr. Hazlitt was making a new will that cut you out of his money?"

She hesitated. "I—don't remember."

"Isn't it likely you told him?"

"We were talking about the divorce. Not about money."

"Think a little, Mrs. Hazlitt. That will was tied up in your mind with the divorce. Isn't it likely you'd have spoken of it?"

"I don't remember that we did." She spoke with more assertion. "I expected my husband to change his will if I left him. Naturally he wouldn't leave his money to me then. The only thing I thought unfair was that he changed it while he was insisting that I stay. But I wasn't really thinking about that. I didn't care about the money."

"How did Murray feel about it?"

"He didn't care about money at all," said Helen quickly. "Neither of us did."

Saunders' gaze dwelt on her with calm skepticism, then shifted to the girl beside her. "Have you something to say about that, Miss Gaynor?"

"I have," said Judy Gaynor defiantly. She stated with great distinctness, "Nicholas Murray knew all about the will. He talked to me about it."

Helen's head turned to her, but Judy did not meet the look; she stared straight ahead at Saunders. These two had worked this out, I thought. Judy had put her facts before him.

"Will you relate when he did that?"

"Friday afternoon—late Friday afternoon. He had been here to see Calvin Kent. I went for a drive and passed him on the road, as he was going to the mainland, and I picked him up. He said he wanted to talk to me so we drove around."

I looked at Jeff. This must mean she was the girl at Scarlotti's. Jeff didn't turn. He was hunched forward, listening.

Saunders prompted, "You say Murray talked about the will to you?"

"Yes. He was bitterly resentful. He said there should have been a settlement on Helen. That Helen should have something for all the years of marriage. He said he couldn't support her, not the way she ought to be supported, and how could he ask her to run away with him?"

Oh, the fool, the fool! I thought angrily. Blurting out his anxieties to Judy as he had done to me. Trusting her because she wanted the divorce.

"You say his state of mind was resentful?"

"Bitterly so."

"Can you quote what he said?"

"He said—" Judy's breathing quickened—"he said, 'Somebody ought to shoot that bastard.' . . . I thought, then, that was just the way that Marines talked. Afterward—"

She broke off. Then she said, in a controlled voice, "Afterward that made me suspect him."

But how about the gun? I thought. Did she say, "I'll shoot him for you"? I looked at Jeff again but Jeff was motionless.

Saunders said, "Did he ask then when the new will would be finished?"

"Yes, he did. I didn't know myself. I had been told that I wouldn't be needed to do any copying till Saturday and Sunday. I told Murray that. At the time I didn't think much about his question. I didn't dream—"

"This was on Friday afternoon?"

"Late Friday afternoon."

Saunders turned his grave eyes on me. "Mr. Kent, you described Murray as 'downhearted.' I won't ask you whether that quite covered it or whether he spoke to you about the will or not. I don't need to, after Miss Gaynor's testimony. . . . I understand how you felt. He's a veteran and you didn't want to put him in a bad light. But a man has to answer for what he's done, whether he's fought a war or not. You want to remember that."

"Right," I said. "But, if you're to have things straight, may I correct an impression?"

He nodded, and I said, "Didn't you get the impression that Murray stopped Miss Gaynor's car in order to talk to her about the will? I would like you to ask Miss Gaynor if it isn't a fact that she motored out to overtake Murray so *she* could talk to *him*. . . . She wanted him to run away with Mrs. Hazlitt, in the hope that would force a divorce. Isn't that a fact?" I said, turning to look squarely into Judy's white face.

She stared angrily back. "Yes, I went after him. Yes, I wanted to talk to him. But what difference does that make? It doesn't alter what he said to me. That is the important thing. That's the thing that damns him."

Her voice—and it was a lovely voice for all its anger—rang through the still room.

"I want to get this straight," said Saunders. "I didn't understand you wanted to talk to him, Miss Gaynor. You didn't tell me that."

He hesitated, then, in embarrassed bluntness, "What's this about wanting him to run way with Mrs. Hazlitt?"

"Does that matter?" she gave back. "But, if you must know—I did tell him there'd never be a divorce unless he forced it. And that was true. It was the only way. . . . But that has nothing to do with what he said about the money."

Kramer's attention had been caught. He leaned forward and said, interestedly, "You were in favor of the divorce? Because you were sympathetic to Mrs. Hazlitt—?"

The unconscious irony of that flavored the silence. Finally Judy said, in a low tone, "Neither of them was happy."

Stanley broke in, speaking with labored determination. "All of us, who had my brother's interests at heart, felt he would be happier without Mrs. Hazlitt. But he did not believe in divorce."

"Don't try to throw the family mantle around her, Stanley," said Helen in her thinnest voice. "You know perfectly well she wanted to marry T. D."

"I know nothing of the sort," said Stanley.

"Well, Tod did!"

"Be that as it may," said Saunders, and the quaint phraseology was without a trace of humor, was spoken with rebuking dignity, and a practical let's-get-on-with-it insistence, "the facts are that Murray was resentful of the will and said Mr. Hazlitt should be shot. Also, he asked when the new will would be done. That's evidence of motive."

He looked toward Kramer and I saw that Kramer was listening attentively while his shrewd eyes were on Judy, appraising her afresh. Saunders went on, "Murray was near a wharf Saturday afternoon. A Navy compass was found in a boat there. I needn't remind you there was a heavy fog. I think that's presumption he was out in a boat. Now *this* was found that same night, before dinner, in the cavern under this house that's used for a swimming pool."

He took the cigarette case out of his pocket and put it on the table. "Mr. Kent and Mr. Ryder found it just after Mrs. Hazlitt was down. It has Murray's initials on it. It wasn't there that morning when Jim Buddy put out the clean towels."

I didn't even bother to give Jeff a black look. I knew that lean, determined face of his would be unashamed. . . . I had been a fool to think he hadn't seen me pick it up.

Saunders said, "And I call that circumstantial evidence that Murray was in the cavern."

"But that's ridiculous!" Helen spoke out sharply. "I left it there. I was there just before the men went down. I had a cigarette down there and then I forgot the case."

Saunders turned the case over and squared it carefully with the papers before him. He said, without looking up, "When did it come into your possession, Mrs. Hazlitt?"

"When—? Why, one day we were together—I think the day we lunched together. We went to a place called The Pink Parasol or something like that." Her voice was breathless and hurrying. "I borrowed it and forgot to give it back."

"You had time for a smoke as well as for a swim?"

"Yes, yes, of course."

"You remember that?"

"Yes. Definitely."

"What bathing suit did you wear?"

"What—suit?" she repeated. You could feel her palpably wondering what the catch was. "Why, my red one, I think. I can't be sure."

"None of your bathing suits was wet that night, Mrs. Hazlitt."

"Why—I dried it, of course."

"You left it drying when you went down to dinner?"

Her face and voice were wary now. "I may have. I don't remember a thing like that."

"You left a *dry* bathing suit on your dressing-room floor. Hannah Tyler went up to do your room as soon as you went down to dinner. She said the suit hadn't been wet at all."

"Why I—I don't know how Hannah could say a thing like that." Helen was obviously talking at random. She asked, "Is that what she told you?"

"She told Mr. Ryder that. He asked about it the next morning."

Helen said haughtily, "I am deeply obliged to Mr. Ryder for his interest in the condition of my swim suit. Perhaps you will tell me why it is important?"

"It's important because it shows you weren't swimming, Mrs. Hazlitt. And that suggests you were talking with Nicholas Murray."

"And you're probably right, Sheriff," said Stanley in a hard voice, an admission I would not have expected from him. "It's entirely possible that Mrs. Hazlitt met Murray there that day. They may have been in the habit of meeting there. The place was used infrequently."

"If you go that far with us, Mr. Hazlitt, don't you agree that this was the time she told him the will was nearly done?"

"I do agree."

"But I didn't know about the will!" Helen protested. "I couldn't have told him."

I remembered her voice, quick and confidential, coming out from lunch that day. "When will it be done, Cal?" And I'd told her. . . .

"Now, Mrs. Hazlitt," said Saunders, unmoved, "I'm proceeding on the assumption that you did meet him and you told him. That's what it looks like to me. I don't think, though, you knew what he had in mind. I think he started off and you went up and he came back and signaled the car down and went up after. Now this is the way I've worked it out."

He looked toward Stanley and Kramer. "He went into the study. That was empty, for Ryder was in his bedroom. Next minute he heard Ryder and Kent coming along the hall, then going down in the elevator. He needed that elevator for his getaway. He lost a little time there, wondering whether to signal it up or wait for the men to come up. Then—"

"Wait a minute," I said. "Why didn't we find the boat in the cavern?"

"That's well put," said Kramer. "Yes, Saunders, what happened to the boat in this guessing game of yours?"

"He anchored it outside the entrance. It had an anchor tied to it. Like that, it wouldn't be found inside, as a give-away. It couldn't be seen outside, in the fog. The tide was low then, so he could wade through the pool. I figure he left his boots in the boat so he could walk quietly."

Stanley said shortly, "That's far-fetched."

"Men do these things, in a murder case," said Saunders earnestly. "They try to figure every angle. There was a man here put his horse in a man's barn before he went into the house to kill him. So the neighbors wouldn't see a horse tied outside and wonder about it. Murray would think about that boat being found, Mr. Hazlitt. He'd put it where it would be safe and handy to find."

Maybe he would at that, I thought

"That's the way I figure it," said Saunders. "That's what I'd do myself if I was taking chances like that. And I figure he was there in the study, and before he could act Miss Gaynor came out of her room into the study and walked across it to the passage to Mr. Hazlitt's room. My guess is that Murray ducked behind the curtains and hid there while she was talking to Mr. Hazlitt. She says she was talking to him quite a time before you heard her. You heard her at seven-twenty-five. Then she went back to her room. And he went in to Mr. Hazlitt."

"You needn't describe that!"

"I wasn't going to, Mr. Hazlitt," said the other, gently.

"But try to tell us how he got away," Stanley challenged. "Not through the doors—they were locked and barred. Not out of a window. They are too small for a man his size. Mr. Ryder demonstrated that yesterday. The elevator did not move. He would have used that elevator for his escape and the elevator did not go down." He said it with a sort of triumph.

But the elevator had gone down. Hannah had heard it. I looked at Jeff but Jeff did not speak.

"I think you'll find," said Stanley, "that he was drinking somewhere along the shore. I think you'll find he has an alibi."

"Then why doesn't he give it? If he was innocent he'd try to prove it. He acts like a guilty man, Mr. Hazlitt. He fought like a wildcat. He won't talk. I think he's guilty," said the sheriff, "and I want to charge him with it. That's why I've put all these facts before you."

"But how did he get out? You can't charge a man when the facts show it's impossible for him to have made an escape."

"I don't think it's impossible," said Saunders, mildly, but stubbornly. "I don't feel as satisfied about the elevator as you do."

Stanley looked at Kramer, then leaned back. "All right," he said resignedly. "Well go over the times again."

"I've got them right here. Your brother was killed about seven-thirty. From then till twenty minutes to eight, you were in your room, the door open, listening for him to come, and you know the elevator did not move."

"It did not move," said Stanley.

"That's what your butler says, too. He was listening, down in the butler's room, waiting for Mr. Hazlitt to come down. He says it didn't move. At twenty to eight you went downstairs, Mr. Hazlitt. By then, Mr. Ryder was back in the study and he didn't hear the elevator while he was there. But about twenty minutes past eight he went downstairs."

"That's right," said Jeff, leaning forward.

"You were all downstairs—just a minute!" Saunders said quickly as a door opened behind us. Then he said, "Oh, come in, Dancy. But don't bring him in yet."

Dancy came in, closing the door behind him, nodded affably to the D. A., picked a comfortable chair and placed it beside Jeff. He asked Jeff something under his breath and Jeff said something back and he nodded, in a satisfied way.

Murray was out there, I thought, waiting to be confronted with the evidence that Saunders was piling up, brick by brick, Judy's revelations, and the cursed facts that Jeff had dug out—the cigarette case, the dry swim suit, the sound of the elevator. The elevator would do for him.

Saunders resumed, "As I was saying, you were all downstairs, talking and getting the butler to phone Mr. Hazlitt's room, and that's when you wouldn't hear the elevator go down."

"I disagree," Stanley shot in. "I would have heard it. It did not go down."

"I'm sorry to contradict you, Mr. Hazlitt, but it did go down. Hannah Tyler heard it."

"What's that?" said the county attorney sharply.

Saunders said to Jeff, "Maybe you'll tell them, Mr. Ryder, what she told you."

"After the inquest," said Jeff, speaking directly toward Kramer. "I asked Hannah Tyler how she happened to go into Mr. Hazlitt's room when she didn't know he was down. It just struck me—anyway, I thought it was worth a question. She said she came out from Mrs. Hazlitt's room to the hall and there she heard the elevator. She took it for granted that he'd gone down."

"Do I understand that Hannah Tyler told you this?" said Stanley.

"She did."

"Hannah Tyler—?" said Kramer. "Is that the girl who—?"

"She was drowned," said Jeff.

"What Mr. Ryder is reporting is hearsay," said Stanley. "It would not be admissible, of course, in court. You know hearsay is not evidence, Mr. Ryder."

"I know. But this isn't court," Jeff argued. "This is an investigation to arrive at the facts. I think the statement should be considered. It answers the question of how Murray could get away."

"You are right that it should be considered—if it were true. Oh, I don't question your good faith, Mr. Ryder. I've no doubt the girl made some such statement to you, if you say so. *But she had made an utterly contrary statement to me that morning.* I asked her then if she had heard the elevator and she denied it. . . . I asked everyone in the household. Not that I distrusted my hearing but I believe in thoroughness."

There was a silence that no one seemed inclined to break. Finally Stanley said, "I think I can account for this. Hannah Tyler had a certain flair, I might say, for the dramatic. That was evident in her testimony yesterday."

For an instant a bleak irony pleated his lips. "My question to her, in the morning, must have implanted the suggestion that it was important to have heard the elevator. Unconsciously, I expect, that worked in her. She saw herself as again a witness. . . . She was a little belated about it, but by the time you spoke to her I am sure she had succeeded in convincing herself."

Jeff said, "She mentioned it in a very matter-of-fact way."

"I daresay. I daresay it had become fact to her. . . . But I consider her earlier statement to me—before her sense of self-importance had been aroused—a more reliable statement. . . . There is no question in my mind—there can be no question in any mind, I think—that the elevator did *not* go down."

He looked at Saunders. "Not that she meant, consciously, to deceive—"

"She wouldn't do that," said Saunders. He added, "But she was high-strung."

"It is very understandable. An unconscious rationalization. . . . Fortunately, I had her previous statement. . . . But, as I pointed out, neither of these statements have any relevancy. Both are hearsay."

There was a long silence. Then Jeff said, sounding more uncertain than I had ever heard him, "In that case—"

"You haven't a case," said the county attorney neatly.

His smile at the bright young New Yorker was slightly patronizing. But not to offend the sheriff, a Maine man, a voter, he said quickly, "But you did right, all of you, in bringing forward any facts that seemed pertinent. That's what we're here for—to consider every angle."

"I should be interested to know," said Stanley in a detached voice, "how you accounted for the elevator being up at the time of my brother's death. For it was up. Both Mr. Ryder and I noticed that."

"I thought Mrs. Hazlitt signaled for it," said Saunders. "When you were outside Mr. Hazlitt's room. She's a quick woman. When she found her husband was shot, she'd know it would look better for Murray if that elevator was up."

"I—see."

The sheriff's glance went to Judy Gaynor. There was chagrin in it and philosophical resignation. He said, "I guess we figured it wrong."

"No, we didn't," Judy gave back obstinately. "I know that man was here!"

"I am afraid you are too antagonistic, Miss Gaynor," said Kramer. "We can't base an opinion on anything but factual evidence."

Dancy had been stirring restively in his chair and now he broke into the discussion. "What time was this elevator supposed to move? I didn't catch it."

"About eight-twenty or -thirty," said Saunders. "Just before they found Mr. Hazlitt"

"Eight-thirty—? Well, if I'd got here a little earlier and known what you were working on, I could have saved you the trouble."

He looked about at us with his air of ready humor, gathering us into the joke. He said, "Murray couldn't have been in any elevator at eight-thirty. He was having drinks at Scarlotti's place at eight o'clock."

"You've got your nights crossed," said the sheriff. "Scarlotti said he hadn't seen him since Friday night."

"He hadn't. But his missus did. She was serving the drinks that time Saturday. Scarlotti didn't think of that till I came by for him just now."

He looked around again at our staring faces. "Isn't that just the way of it?" he demanded, in humorous disgust. "We sit up half the night with this fellow trying to get him to tell where he was and all the time Mrs. Scarlotti knows and doesn't know we want to know."

"She sure of the time?" asked Saunders cautiously.

"Yep. Just came in from church. She says Murray was there and had three, four drinks and went off with a trucker. It was the night of the fog. Saturday night."

So that was the end of the case against Nicholas Murray, I thought. The law couldn't touch him now. Judy Gaynor's hatred could not harm him. Curious—that hatred. She

was bitter against him because she believed he had killed
T. D. and now, when it was clearly shown he couldn't have
killed T. D., her conviction had so dominated her that she
couldn't believe in his innocence.

For she flashed out, "She was bribed! She's been paid
for saying that."

Dancy swung about, staring at her past Jeff and me
with quick truculence. "Maybe you'd like to say that to her
husband?" he suggested. "I'll bring him in."

Everyone seemed to speak at once, but the sheriff's
flat voice triumphed. "We'll leave that out of it, Will. . . .
That isn't a sensible thing to say, Miss Gaynor."

"Okay, okay," said Dancy. "But it goes to show—want
I should bring him in now?"

He went to the door and came back with a stout, rosy-
faced man with receding black hair. He wore a bright blue
suit and a blue and red tie with a matching handkerchief
peeping roguishly out of a pocket. He had the good-
natured, easy-going look of the fat man, but his small
dark eyes were full of shrewd, hard competence. He bowed
politely in the direction of the county attorney, then toward the ladies, then looked interestedly about the room,
finally examining the large portrait of T. D. with admiring
attention.

"Scarlotti," said the sheriff, "I want you to say whether there's anyone here but the chief and me who's been in
your place."

"Sure," said Scarlotti. "This young lady." He nodded at
Judy. "She was in with the vet on Friday afternoon."

"Certainly I was," said Judy. "What of it?"

"I wanted you to be identified," said Dancy. "I didn't
want any mistake about it."

"I've already said that I saw Murray that afternoon."

"At Scarlotti's place?"

"No, I don't think—yes, I may have mentioned, to the sheriff earlier, that I stopped there. You all knew that, anyway. You just heard him say—"

"Will you tell us what you did with the gun that Murray gave you?"

She looked completely startled. Color rushed into her face. "You can't deny it. Scarlotti saw Murray pass you a gun. You can swear to that, Scarlotti?"

"Sure," said the Italian. He looked at Judy with even more admiration than he had given the portrait. "He gave her a gun. I thought it was for a souvenir."

Dancy said, "I told you, Mr. Kramer, there was something I'd like to bring out, and this is it. It looked funny to me. I brought Scarlotti along so there'd be no slip up. If you'd like to take over—"

"I think we would like to know about that gun, Miss Gaynor," said the county attorney.

"That gun," she said, in a queer, hesitant voice. "I never thought of it again . . . not even when you—" She looked directly at me and her eyes were bitter with remembrance. "You'd think I might have thought of it, then—"

"Just answer me, Miss Gaynor. Why did he give you the gun?"

"I asked him for it."

"What did you want with it?"

"Because it was getting late—and the place was rather far out. I thought he was coming back to the village with me but he wasn't. I've been held up once and I'm nervous about being out alone. I said I wished I had a gun, and he said, 'Take this—I've got another.' I said I'd get it back to him. So I put it on the seat beside me driving back."

"And where is it now?"

"I haven't thought about it since. I left it in the car. In the compartment. I pushed it there, behind some maps, and never gave it another thought."

"I'd like to see that gun," said Dancy. "I'd like to know if it's there now. I'll just go out and look."

"I can telephone—" said Stanley coldly.

"If you don't mind, Mr. Hazlitt, I'd rather look myself. What kind of car were you out in, Miss Gaynor?"

"The Packard. A sports Packard. I haven't been near it since. I haven't been near the garage."

Stanley said quickly, a note of stiff protectiveness in his voice, "Miss Gaynor was very busy copying my brother's will on Saturday. And on Sunday—on Sunday she was—occupied. With the messages. The telephone."

Well, there would be time between telephones to slip out to the car and replace a gun. But the gun would have to be cleaned and reloaded.

Dancy went out. I don't think anyone said much of anything till he came back. I found myself wondering, oddly enough, what it was about Judy Gaynor that hadn't made her seem alluring to me. She was gorgeous looking . . . and she had a lovely voice . . . but there was something that put you off her. Maybe it was because she was so set on denouncing Nicholas Murray. All very right in its way, if she believed that Murray was the killer, but somehow—

There's no use dragging out the story of the gun. Dancy came marching back, looking ruffled and aggressive because his bright idea had failed to come off. He had the gun all right, and it was fully loaded and from the looks of the grease it hadn't been fired since Korea. And the chauffeur, he reported, said he could take oath that Miss Gaynor hadn't been near the garage since she brought the car in. "Though how he can be sure of that—" said Dancy. "Not being there all the time—"

"This checks with Miss Gaynor's story," said Kramer. "Perhaps now we can check with Murray."

Then he tried to smooth down Dancy's feelings. "Clues are like that, Dancy. You think you have something and feel along it, like a string, and there isn't a thing tied to it. But that's the only way to get something—keep feeling along all the strings."

Scarlotti spoke out suddenly. "Say! This lady's been in my place, too. With the same vet." He was eyeing Helen interestedly. "I didn't recognize her at first—she's got her hair up now and she had it down when I saw her, but it's the same young lady."

"That so?" said the D. A. "Remember when?"

"Some time back. Before all this."

"You didn't see the vet pass *her* anything, did you?" asked Kramer, and Scarlotti laughed appreciatingly at the joke.

"Not a thing," he said. "They was just—" he gave Helen a friendly smile—"having themselves a little talk."

"Okay, Scarlotti," said Dancy. "Were much obliged to you for coming. Get Joe to run you back."

"A pleasure," said Scarlotti politely. He bowed to Stanley. "Nice place—regular palazza," he said genially, and went out.

Dancy closed the door after him, then came back and sat down. He leaned across Jeff and me to say, "No hard feelings, I hope, Miss Gaynor? Duty's duty."

Judy did not answer. She was lighting a cigarette with fingers that shook so that I held out my lighter. She ignored it. I lighted a cigarette of my own.

Kramer covered her silence. "Duty is indeed duty. Miss Gaynor must realize that the circumstances were—well, unusual. I appreciate the thoroughness with which you officers have gone into all the circumstances. I want you to feel that you have had every opportunity to present your opinions, however divergent—"

His gaze swung to Saunders and Saunders said, "We're at the end of our rope, Mr. Kramer. Murray's got an alibi and he's out of it. Miss Gaynor didn't take the gun into the house with her, so the gun's got an alibi. I guess that puts her out of it, too."

"I guess it does," said Kramer, trying another smile on her. It was his last flash of amusement. His face turned businesslike, serious and aggressive. He said, "Now—Mrs. Hazlitt—"

Chapter Thirteen

The brisk voice had the crack of a whip.

"Mrs. Hazlitt, you were in your husband's room till six-thirty on Saturday afternoon?"

"Saturday afternoon—? Yes, I was."

"You had an altercation with him about the divorce?"

"Altercation—? I wouldn't say that." Helen was hesitant and wary.

"But you spoke of it?"

"Yes, we spoke of it. Of course." She seemed to have realized the foolishness of pretending anything else.

"And since you did not agree, you argued?"

"I asked him—I begged him—to let me go."

"He refused?"

"Yes, he refused."

"And what did you say?"

"What could I say?" said Helen bitterly. "Just that it was so unfair . . . I expect I reminded him that he had his—consolations."

Kramer ignored that. "He refused and you went to your room?"

"Yes."

"Then down to the cavern, as you call it?"

"Yes."

"And there met Murray? You can admit that now, you know, without prejudice to Murray."

"I—didn't meet him. He wasn't there."

"It's a good thing you're not on oath, Mrs. Hazlitt . . . but if you *had* met Murray you would have told him of your latest interview with your husband and his continued refusal. You would have gone back to your room in a tempest of resentment and frustration."

"No!"

"You wouldn't?" His tone was almost bantering.

"I mean, I didn't."

"You were in a submissive frame of mind, then? Accepting your husband's decision as the right one?"

She was silent.

"Suppose you were *not* resigned. Suppose you wondered desperately what course you could take. Your husband was in the next room. His life stood between you and enjoyment of your freedom with the young man you loved. A few hours stood between you and the possession of a fortune, if your husband should die. . . . You heard the young men pass your room going down for a swim. You knew the study was empty. You knew the time was short."

He paused—then he shot at her, "Mrs. Hazlitt, where is that pearl-handled gun you used to keep in your room?"

Helen's face was tight with terror. "I—don't know."

"You don't know? A revolver that was always in your room. . . . But you knew where it was then, Mrs. Hazlitt. You hid it under your sleeve when you went to the door of your husband's room. Then you heard his voice in that room, raised to reach Miss Gaynor talking to him from the passage. You had to wait. The sound of talking stopped. The young men came up from their swim and passed your door again. In a few moments one of them would be back in the study. You went quickly into your husband's room. You may have made some casual observation on the weather, and he turned his head, at the window, to look out. You came close and fired. You threw the gun out the window and ran back to your room. Presently you came downstairs. There you appeared very surprised that your husband was not down."

"I was surprised," said Helen in a shaking voice.

The strong, incisive voice went on. "You had not thought ahead carefully. Suddenly now, when the body was discovered, you realized the nature of the risk. You behaved hysterically, insisting on suicide or accident, claiming the gun had been dropped out the window. Then you tried to influence your brother-in-law to perpetrate a fraud. I have the testimony of a most reliable employee to that effect . . . ask him in, Dancy."

"Damn you!" I thought, as Caldwell stepped into the room. He must have been waiting outside the door for the signal. "Damn you," I thought again. "I knew you were storing this away." I looked with loathing at his composed face and smooth, combed hair, his faultless linen and pin-striped trousers. I'd never noticed before what a beak of a nose he had. Like a superior buzzard.

Kramer said to him, "You can swear, can you not, that Mrs. Hazlitt wished her brother-in-law to place a gun by the deceased's side?"

"I can take my oath on it," said Caldwell gravely.

"That's very kind and helpful of you, Caldwell," said Helen icily.

Caldwell raised his head, which had been deferentially bent. Whether it was conscious or unconscious, he was looking into the painted face of T. D., and he kept his eyes steadily upon it as he said, in a singsong recitative, "'As a faithful witness I will not lie'—Proverbs fourteen, five. 'I have chosen the way of truth; Thy judgments have I laid before me'—Psalms nineteen, thirty. 'Bread of deceit is sweet to a man but afterwards his mouth shall be filled with gravel'—Proverbs twenty, seventeen—"

Utter astonishment held the room silent. I never saw a more dumfounded expression on a man's face than on the county attorney's. It was Stanley who shut off the geyser.

"We appreciate your motive, Caldwell."

"Yes, yes," said Kramer hurriedly. "I—ah—I quite agree that truth is a sacred obligation. Very sacred indeed. . . . Which you were forgetting, Mrs. Hazlitt," he said, neatly getting back in the groove again.

Helen said coldly, "I behaved like a fool. I admit it."

Jeff leaned back of Dancy to say to Caldwell, "Get yourself a chair and sit down." I twisted about and saw him sitting down in the back of the room. He was not the butler now. He was a witness.

Kramer was saying, "And in the night, Mrs. Hazlitt, you raised an alarm, pretending that you had been attacked. Attacked by a tall, thin man, so thin he could get out the casement window and disappear. That was folly, too, wasn't it, Mrs. Hazlitt?"

Helen was silent. Then she said, her insistence sounding forced and slightly ridiculous, "There *was* someone—someone from outside—"

"Someone who mysteriously disappeared," said Kramer sardonically. "Who plunged to almost certain death from a window after obligingly freeing you, at one stroke, for a new marriage and the enjoyment of your husband's fortune. Now only an acrobat could get out that window. And no acrobat could descend that sheer precipice. . . . But you felt you had to attempt the deception, Mrs. Hazlitt. For if there was no tall, thin man, no mysterious outsider—then who was guilty? Who killed your husband?"

Helen huddled back in her chair, staring at him, wordlessly.

"Miss Gaynor? Do you bring charges against her? . . . I am aware there are charges you might allege," he said significantly, "but she had everything to lose, through your husband's death, and nothing to gain. Are you charging her with the murder?"

"No," said Helen in a wavering voice. "I—I'm not charging her. I never thought that of her."

"But an innocent person would be quick to suspect. You do not charge her because you *know*—because you cannot be so base as to charge a woman who is guiltless. Do you charge your husband's brother? Who would have been enriched by the new will?"

He waited and Helen's head moved in negation.

"Do you charge any of your faithful and devoted household? . . . Or Mr. Ryder, perhaps—?" His irony was in full flower now.

Helen made an effort to pull herself together. "I don't charge anyone. I don't know—"

"Mrs. Hazlitt, I do not mean to be harsh. I admire the spirit which does not seek to lay the blame where it does not belong. I counsel you, in all kindness—" there wasn't a shred of kindness in those bright, determined eyes—"to tell the truth, the whole truth, and nothing but the truth. I advise you to throw yourself upon the clemency of the law. It will be better for you. Much, much better."

"But I didn't—I didn't shoot him—"

She was the type that would go to pieces on the stand. Her nerves couldn't take the steady, relentless pounding. She was going to pieces now.

She faltered again, "I didn't shoot him—"

The implacable voice demanded, "Then, Mrs. Hazlitt— *who did?*"

"I'll answer that by asking you one," said Jeff. "Who killed Hannah Tyler?"

Kramer, checked in midcharge, looked at Jeff in astonishment. "Hannah Tyler? She was drowned. An accident."

"Hannah Tyler was struck on the head and pushed out a window in this house. Then she drowned."

Jeff said it quietly, with a conviction that needed no emphasis. He waited for the words to take on their meaning.

"What—what are you saying—?"

"I'm saying the one who murdered Hannah Tyler is the one who killed T. D. Hazlitt. He is sitting beside you. Stanley Hazlitt."

The room held a stunned stillness. No one spoke or moved. I remember thinking over and over, "I hope you know what you're talking about." This just didn't seem possible. Not Caldwell, then. That thought kept butting up in my mind. Snared down in my subconscious somewhere had been the hopeful expectation that Caldwell would prove responsible.

Stanley Hazlitt—

I took a quick look at him. I never saw a man look more stiffly, outrageously affronted. He sat there rigidly, staring ahead of him, his lips pressed together as if they were never going to open. It was Kramer who finally said what I expect everyone in that room was thinking.

"Are you out of your mind, Mr. Ryder? This is appalling!"

"It is appalling," said Jeff.

His voice had been quiet and factual when he spoke before; now it was hard, and his face was hard, with that remote, remorseless quality that I had seen in it before.

"Last night," he said to Stanley, "you thought you were removing the only witness whose testimony might defeat your plot. By doing that you proved what till then I had not suspected, that you had killed your brother."

Someone—Judy or Helen—gasped. Then Stanley said, hoarsely, "I—killed my brother?" His head turned to Kramer. "Am I—are we—to take this seriously?"

"I don't know when the idea came to you of killing your brother," said Jeff. "You must have hated him, consciously or subconsciously, for a long time. You were subservient to him. He had made the money, a great deal of money. Your legal work depended upon him. It must have rankled that his first will ignored you. You resented his wife. You resented, too, the preference that Miss Gaynor had for your brother. These things were all working in you."

"Ridiculous." Stanley's voice was controlled, authoritative now. "Ridiculous," he said again.

"Perhaps you never formulated the hate to yourself, but it was there. Then came the matter of the new will. . . . I expect T. D. did give you to understand at first that you were to get the whole estate. That was when you came to New York to find a suitable attorney. I don't think you had planned then to kill him," he said, consideringly. "Perhaps you began by thinking how fortunate it would be for you if he died after he'd made that new will, before he made another. You knew that, inevitably, he'd make another. In favor of Helen, if she stayed with him. Or in favor of someone else, if he divorced Helen and married again.

"That got you thinking of his dying. But you realized it would be suspicious if he died immediately after making the new will. You had a better idea . . . I think you had it when you brought us in this house. The houseman had planned to put us in guest rooms between your room and Helen's, but you changed us to the room on the other side of you. You didn't want us between your room and your brother's room. Just in case."

Stanley looked to Kramer. "Are we to listen to this? This nonsense about guest rooms—"

Kramer said sharply, "Mr. Ryder! Unless you have something pertinent—"

"This is pertinent," said Jeff. He addressed Stanley again. "You found you were not consulted in the will-making. That made you suspect changes. You came into the study, Saturday, while I was out of the room. Miss Gaynor was copying the will and she had stepped into her room, leaving the pages on the desk. I came in and heard a door into T. D.'s room closing. The papers were disarranged. I thought T. D. had been in. Later I found he had not. I had an idea, then, you had looked at the will. Saturday night, I was struck by the astonishment you permitted yourself to show when I said you were not sole legatee. You were driving in on us the impression that you had expected to receive the whole estate. . . . Your position was good, as legatee of any portion of it, but it was better if you were expecting to receive everything."

"I don't get this, Mr. Ryder," said Kramer. He had found his assured voice again. "Is it your contention that Mr. Hazlitt shot his brother—" his voice blended irony with apology to Stanley for even using the words—"at a time when he would receive nothing from the old will? Out of resentment because the new will would not have left him more?"

Under his moustache his lips twisted as if saying, "Neatly put!" His whole manner to Jeff was saying, "I am trying to treat you like a rational human being—but this is really too much!"

"My contention," said Jeff soberly, "is that Stanley Hazlitt shot his brother at a time when it would seem that only Helen Hazlitt would have motive for killing him. That was the setup. Helen Hazlitt was to be judged guilty."

"You are talking nonsense, Mr. Ryder. I assume you are attempting to create a diversion in favor of Mrs. Hazlitt—"

Stanley said coldly, "He is attempting to secure some publicity for himself. He is a notoriety seeker. But it will be the end of any career he may have contemplated."

"Helen Hazlitt was to be judged guilty, I ask you to remember that, Mr. Attorney. He planned it shrewdly, for Saturday night. I'd told him we were going for a swim before dinner. He waited till he heard Kent and me go down the hall."

He turned to Stanley again. "When we went down, you went into the study, so as not to be seen entering your brother's room. You said the study door was ajar but I didn't leave it ajar, and Judy Gaynor hadn't stopped to open it on her way across the room. You opened it, and discovered she was in the passage, talking to your brother through the door. You had to wait out in the hall, listening. Time was getting short. We might be up at any moment. The instant Judy Gaynor went back to her room you went to your brother's hall door and went in."

"You are as fanciful," said Stanley acidly, "as Sheriff Saunders, who so expertly outlined the movements of Murray in that room. This would be ludicrous if it were not so—vicious."

"It doesn't take long to shoot a man," said Jeff. "You used the pearl-handled revolver which used to be in Helen Hazlitt's room. I don't know when you took it. She doesn't know when it disappeared. I don't know whether it had a silencer or not. The foghorn was blowing. Helen Hazlitt might have been in her dressing room, the door shut. The fact is, she didn't hear it."

"She heard that shot," said Stanley. "She fired it. You have tried to create a diversion—"

"You threw the gun out the window. You would have hidden it in Helen's things if you had known then how much you were going to need circumstantial evidence against her. But you had no idea that Murray had been near the place. You took it for granted that he was on the mainland where he would be seen. So you yielded to your instinct to rid yourself of it as quickly as possible. You got back to your room and went downstairs."

Ahead of me, Saunders was looking expressionlessly down at the revolver Dancy had left on his desk, his fingers moving absently along the dark muzzle. Beside it was the silver cigarette case. Jeff gestured toward it.

"You didn't know that case would be found. That Murray had been in the cavern with Helen. That he would be suspected of being in the house. But you were taking no chances of having any outsider suspected. When you saw the elevator, for some reason, was down, you signaled it back to your brother's floor. After you telephoned the police, in the study, you went into the hall and signaled it back. I was in T. D.'s room and you came back through the hall door."

"How would I signal up an elevator that had not gone down?"

"It had gone down. Hannah Tyler was right. But Murray, as you know, wasn't in it. It went down for the simplest reason in the world. Caldwell signaled for it to come down."

I twisted about and Caldwell was sitting on the edge of his chair, his smooth head tilted attentively, absorbing every word.

"When he didn't get an answer to his ring to Mr. Hazlitt's room he stepped into the hall and pressed the button. But he didn't wait for it. He changed his mind about going up and hurried back to report on the phone call. That is why the elevator came down."

"Caldwell," said Stanley, and there was cold anger in his voice, "you told me yourself you didn't hear the elevator! What does this cock-and-bull story mean?"

Caldwell got up with calm dignity. "Your words, Mr. Hazlitt, if I recollect correctly, were, 'Did you hear the elevator during drinks?' You asked me that after the inquest. I replied that I had not. That was the truth. I had moved away too quickly, after pressing the button. It quite slipped my mind that I had signaled for it. It was not until Mr. Ryder asked me to account for my every movement. . . . If you had asked me if it had gone down, a moment's reflection would have enabled me to inform you that it must have done so. 'Let your communication be yea, yea—'"

"Let's get the hell out of the elevator," said Kramer, and I knew how he felt. "I can't see that the elevator proves a damned thing. Or that you are proving a damned thing, Mr. Ryder. You are making a lot of nasty assertions and clouding the issues with imaginary situations, and if you have anything you call proof of your scandalous statements, I'd like you to produce it."

"I've proved that the elevator went down. You grant that, don't you?"

"All right. I grant that the elevator went down. What of it?"

"Hannah Tyler wasn't a liar, then. What she told was the truth. Stanley knew that truth put his plan in jeopardy. Suspicion had focused on Murray and if Hannah got her testimony before a jury, that jury would believe that Murray escaped in the elevator—or some other assailant escaped, if Murray was found to have an alibi. Helen might be exonerated. He had risked too much already to hesitate at another risk. Hannah's testimony had to be reduced to hearsay. Hearsay is not admissible. You heard how quick he was to point that out?"

"Any lawyer would point it out."

"And how quick he was to cancel any impression made on your minds by asserting she had made a contrary statement to him? He had his rationalization of Hannah in his pocket, ready to pull out."

"More assertions, Mr. Ryder! I do not feel that I am called on to listen—"

"I think the Maine police will hear me out. I think the men who live here will want to know how Hannah Tyler died."

"Suppose you tell us that," said the sheriff in his flat, neutral voice.

"At dinner he left the table as if to telephone. You, Mr. Attorney, were using the phone in the library, so it was natural for him to go up to the study, where there was a private wire. From the study he went through his brother's room to Helen's. He knew that this was the time the girls would be arranging the bedrooms for the night. There were some book ends of bronze in the study and he picked up one of these. The dolphin figure gave him something to grip. The heavy base was a striking weapon."

I glanced covertly at Stanley. His eyelids had shut down as if shutting out everything he was forced to hear. Not a line of him moved.

"Hannah was in the room. It was not hard to get her to turn her back, to reach for something. He struck her head. Hard. It knocked her out. But it wasn't easy to thrust her out the window. He knew he could do it because I, un-luckily, had proved that a thin body could get through that casement. But it wasn't easy. He had to wrench her shoulder. Her clothes scraped on the casement, on the sill, on the stone. Threads of her dress caught there."

Jeff put a hand in his pocket. "I've got them here. I checked with the clothes she had on and the threads are the same. Some of them are still around the window. You can see plenty if you use a magnifying glass."

"More of your assertions, Mr. Ryder!" Stanley's lids had flashed up and the eyes beneath them looked out with fury in them. "Is this a plant? This 'proof' of yours?"

"Hannah went out the window," said Jeff. "You went downstairs, and met Mr. Kramer returning from his phone call in the library. You learned from him that Murray had been picked up but refused to talk. I imagine you congratulated yourself that you were not at the mercy of any lack of alibi of his."

"You imagine—you imagine!"

"You didn't think about the threads at the window. You had closed it, drawn the curtains again. No one would dream that Hannah Tyler had gone out that window."

"If there are threads, and if they are the threads from Hannah's clothes, it can only mean that the girl sought her own destruction. She was despondent."

"There are other threads. You wore a dark blue suit last night. The sleeve got badly rubbed on the rusty steel. There are dark blue threads on the window. They check."

Stanley's face went livid. "Are you trying to frame me, Ryder? Because I wouldn't give you a chance to work into our firm? Is it your scheme to create a scandal to achieve some publicity? Let me tell you, it will be a kind you don't relish. I am not a man you can affront with impunity. This preposterous trick of yours is a sordid attempt—"

He stopped. He seemed to realize that he was talking very loud and very fast and that his hands were shaking. He drew himself up and said in a tight, scornful voice, "I have remarked before that you are a very ingenious young man. You are, indeed. You have concocted a fantastic story, built of much reading of mysteries, no doubt. I am supposed to have killed an unfortunate girl because her testimony would prevent the conviction of my sister-in-law for the murder of my brother—a crime which I am supposed to have committed! Is that the plot?"

His sardonic manner mocked it. "Ridiculous! Why would I kill my brother? You impute to me unworthy resentments against him. If I were the man who harbored

Mary Hastings Bradley

such resentments, would I kill him at the very moment when I would not profit from his death?"

"No, you wouldn't," said Jeff. "That's why you killed him at the moment when you stood to profit by it."

He went to the wall back of us and took down a book. He came back with it in his hands, let it fall open, and looked down at it with grim satisfaction.

"Sunday noon, just before the inquest," he said, "Stanley Hazlitt was here with this book in his hands when I came in the room. He put it on the shelf and afterward I was interested enough to take it down. It fell open at two very unusual cases. It has fallen open at them now."

He looked down. "One is *Riggs* versus *Palmer*. That is a New York case, 115 New York, page 506 in the New York reports. The other is *Ellerson* versus *Westcott,* also a New York case—148 New York, 149."

His eyes followed the print a moment, then lifted. "The point, in both these cases, is that the court—a New York court—ruled that a legatee who had been convicted of the murder of the testator cannot take under the will. The estate passes to the heirs."

Cannot take under the will . . . that meant—

"I was not familiar with this ruling," said Jeff. "I had not had occasion to look up the decision in such cases. Few lawyers have. It roused my interest. It was significant that Stanley Hazlitt had been consulting that book, that it opened at those pages. He knew those decisions. He knew if Helen Hazlitt was convicted of murder, the estate would go to the heirs. He was the only heir."

He looked toward Kramer. "There's the motive, Mr. Attorney."

Stanley said quickly, "That is the law. I did not make the law. If you are trying to impute prejudice—"

"Prejudice!" Jeff's voice had a bitter ring in it. "That's all I thought at the time. Prejudice! I thought I understood you. Understood why, from the first, you had not welcomed any evidence against Murray, any evidence that pointed away from Helen. I thought I could cope with prejudice. If my mind had not stopped at prejudice, I could have saved that girl. It took her death—that final fact—to point the truth. You killed your brother at the moment when every suspicion would point to his wife. You killed him because suspicion would point to her. Because, under the law, if she were convicted, you would come into possession of his wealth."

He said again, "There's the motive, Mr. Attorney. And upstairs, at the window, are the identifying threads. You'll find his prints, too, I daresay. Elsie went home this morning and no one has been there to rub them off. I've a man on guard now. Oh, yes, and the book end. He wiped it off and put it back. But there's a dark stain on the felt base."

The sheriff looked toward the county attorney. His Maine voice was hard as Maine granite. "I guess this gives us enough to go on."

Stanley seemed to rear back in his chair. "Don't you dare—"

Dancy was on his feet. "I'll take care of him," he said grimly. "Maybe he can hang only once, but I'll see he hangs for Hannah Tyler."

But it was Caldwell who pronounced the final words of doom. He rose as they passed his chair and, with a solemnity that had nothing ludicrous in it now, said slowly and resonantly, "'Bloody and deceitful men shall not live out half their days; they shall be brought down into the pit of destruction.'"

And then, believe it or not, as the door closed behind them, he turned toward Helen and asked with formal deference, "Would madam like me to serve something?"

We all liked it very much indeed. We needed it badly. Nerves were shattered. Helen was crying softly, saying over and over that she was so glad that now "he" would know she hadn't done it. I remember Saunders saying gravely to her, "Just the same, Mrs. Hazlitt, I wouldn't advise you to be in a hurry to marry anyone until this case is over," and Helen's promise, given like a child's, "Oh, I won't! I truly won't!"

Judy looked dazed and desolate. When I handed her a glass from the tray Caldwell had brought, she said to me, "How could he? How could he?" I told her, "Drink to a new life for yourself."

Kramer was making up for his past performance by congratulating Jeff fulsomely. "Incredible penetration," he told him. "Not many would have dared to reason like that. Man, I thought you'd gone crazy!" His laugh invited Jeff's.

But Jeff wasn't too pleased with himself. He'd seen the light but he hadn't seen it fast enough. "Prejudice—I stopped at prejudice," he said wryly. "The motive right in front of me."

"But you had no proof," Kramer pointed out. "Without the girl, there would have been no proof."

I wandered to the window and looked down into the water. It was a long way down, and the water looked deep and dark, with the sun gone from it. You brought him down with you, Hannah, I thought. Those Maine men won't forget you.

About the Author

Mary Hastings Bradley (1882-1976) wrote numerous short stories, historical novels, mysteries, and nonfiction travelogues recounting her adventures in different countries. She married lawyer, explorer, and big-game hunter Herbert Bradley, joining him on some of his trips. They accompanied Mary's uncle, biologist Carl Akeley, on his expedition to the Belgian Congo in the early 1920s in search of specimens for the American Museum of Natural History. During WWII she was a war correspondent for *Collier's*. Her daughter, Alice, would go on to write science fiction as 'James Tiptree, Jr.'

Also Available
CoachwhipBooks.com

MURDER
IN TEXAS

Ada E. Lingo

"The story of a big-time murder in
a small town, with the atmosphere
of a hard-boiled newspaper office,
a background of 'hot oil' and
sudden gushers, and the intensity
of a Texas heat wave."

Also Available
CoachwhipBooks.com

Also Available
CoachwhipBooks.com

MURDER TAKES
THE VEIL

MURDER AT
ST. DENNIS

SISTER SIMON'S
MURDER CASE

THE MARGARET ANN HUBBARD
MYSTERY OMNIBUS

Also Available
CoachwhipBooks.com

MURDER
IN A WALLED TOWN
KATHERINE WOODS